Praise for *Sacrifice*

"She does it to me every time! LR Saul gets her hooks into you in the first few pages and you just have to keep going . . . She draws you into the mystery and you can't escape until the last page."

"This book will teach you to hope again. Read it and you will feel what the characters feel; you can't help it. A fantastic book that is different to other fantasy novels because it is brimming with humanity and our imperfections, but also with the inner strength that can drive us. LR Saul shows us just how beautiful that inner strength can be in this unforgettable and enduring tale of powerful forces and mere mortals."

"It was so easy to immerse myself in this book. The characters were so realistic; the book full of all the elements that make a great fantasy. Once I started it, I couldn't put it down. The suspense kept me going right to the last page. I found myself desperate to get to the end, to find out what was going to happen, and yet when I got there, I was sad to say goodbye to the characters. The sequel, I can assure you, is eagerly awaited."

Following a Bachelor of Arts English Literature and Diploma of Journalism, LR Saul has been involved in just about every form of writing, editing and journalism in the many years since. Her greatest writing passion has always been fantasy novels, and she has been writing fantasy for the pure love of it since she was eight years old.

She lives in Australia with her husband and son.

Fiction Titles by LR Saul:

Bloodline Series

Bloodline: Alliance

For news on the release of Bloodline: Covenant, go to www.lrsaul.com

Sacrifice Series

Sacrifice

For more information go to www.lrsaul.com

Sacrifice

LR Saul

Glass House Books
Brisbane

Glass House Books
an imprint of Interactive Publications Pty Ltd
Treetop Studio • 9 Kuhler Court
Carindale, Queensland, Australia, 4152
sales@ipoz.biz
ipoz.biz/GHB/GHB.htm

First published by Interactive Publications, 2009
Copyright © LR Saul, 2009

LR Saul asserts the moral right to be identified as the author of this work.

Cover design by N. Blythe

Printed in Book Antiqua 11 pt on Times New Roman 36 pt by Sunny Young Printing, Taiwan.

National Library of Australia
Cataloguing-in-Publication data:

Author: Saul, L. R., 1974-

Title: Sacrifice / L. R. Saul.

ISBN: 9781921479168 (pbk.)

Dewey Number: A823.4

For Jeff, my best friend.
This one is for you – the one you've
always liked the most.

I must warn that if you are easily disturbed, you should swiftly put down this document and move to other matters, for I must record with sharp detail what I saw that dark night.

I, Castus Poet-Scribe, was one of five selected to witness the terrible sacrifice of the Daughter of the Hunstons. I hereby declare it to be a true and accurate recording of the events – as I saw them – that transpired that night, 10th of Raven Month, the year 1044.

It was midnight, an hour of some importance to the Ashrone priests, when the girl was brought into the large, icy windowless chamber with its pitched-beam ceiling and unadorned stone walls. She was already bound at the hands, but her legs were free, allowing her to walk unaided into the room between two guards sworn to secrecy. She wore a long velvet dress – white for virginity, and trimmed with black for death. Her face remained calm, regal, but as I recall, fear tainted the dark blue eyes.

From the look on the guards' faces, I knew they did not want to be here, as I did not. They directed her, through a circle of Ashrones, to the central altar – a cold grey marble slab flecked with black veins.

She stood in front of the altar, her face to me and the four other scribes. The guards departed then. Speedily, I should add, although at least in a dignified manner.

The master priest, sturdy with a youth of thirty-two years not common to his position, stepped from within the circle and up to the girl. He faced her, his blue eyes watching everything in the girl's face, as seemed to be his habit. I noted, with a dark heart, that most of the thirty other priests, all in black for mourning, did not meet the girl's eyes. To be fair in my description, perhaps concentration claimed them.

The thirty priests of Ashrone linked hands in a chain, creating an unbroken ring around the young woman and the central altar. Their chants droned, and the air reeked of bitter plath root that bound the girl's hands tightly at her stomach. The plath root held some significance the Ashrones would not divulge.

Despite myself, I felt a shiver pass at the ominous monotone chanting. Right at that terrible moment in time, I wanted to be anywhere except here, in any role save this one. I wondered that the master priest could look the Hunston girl in her frightened blue eyes and still allow the priests to circle, to chant, to begin what could not be undone.

The chanting ceased abruptly; left a chill of silence in the air colder than a dark winter's night.

"Lower her," the eldest of the thirty priests said to the master priest.

The master, still standing near the girl, put hands beneath her arms, lifted her and helped her to sit on the altar. His hands supported her briefly as she kicked her bare feet free of her long velvet dress. The thirty linked priests kept their circle tight as the girl tossed her head and flung her spun gold hair over her shoulder.

The master Ashrone's young hands helped lower her to a prostrate position on the grey marble slab. He spread her hair neatly for her, for dignity.

"Daughter of Kildes, do you know why you are here?" the master asked solemnly.

"I understand," the young woman said.

"Daughter of Kildes," the lean, young master priest continued, "you will die tonight for your country. Are you willing to accept?"

The girl nodded. "I accept for my country."

"Daughter of Kildes," the master said. "I ask you once more for the sake of the witnesses here in this room: do you freely accept this fate?"

"I accept."

The scribe in the raised witness box beside me shook his head slowly, but whether disappointed or disgusted, I could not be sure.

The master nodded. "Daughter of Kildes, we have tied your hands and I now tie you to the altar so that you do not escape when the fire hits your lungs." The master's hands worked on the twined root ropes. He tied her around the immovable, grey slab suspended on carved marble legs. "Are you willing to go through the pain?"

My eyes narrowed then, and I held my breath for the longest time. The girl's seeming bravery was born of ignorance. I had been told, forewarned, what the fire did to a person. The next three minutes would remove all traces of bravery from those eyes – would even remove the eyes.

"I am willing," the girl said, her eyes still shaped by fear – and something else. I guessed that anger lay behind the gaze, but its cause escaped me. I write this because I cannot be sure that the anger wasn't silent protest at being held against her will. All words indicated the contrary – but they were, after all, just words. Despite the eyes, her voice remained composed, gentle. "For the sake of my people, I accept."

The master priest exhaled slowly, and I realised he had – as had we all – expected the girl to change her mind. His hands worked the last of the ropes – tight to restrain but not painful. "Very well, child; please open your mouth."

The girl opened her mouth, and the priests, still holding hands in their circle, started chanting again in a strange language, their eyes glazing with concentration. I was instructed that no matter what I did, I must not disturb those chants, or cause in any way for the circle to break. I was informed that no matter how much the girl screamed, or how hideous the stunning woman became, they could not afford to break the chants or it would be worse – far worse. I could not in that moment imagine what could be worse than what the girl would go through.

The master reached under the slab, to a smooth stone shelf, for the small vial. He opened it; it issued red steam. It smelled of soured milk and salty blood. He poured the crimson contents in a thin stream slowly into the girl's mouth. He allowed her to swallow before pouring more past her lips. With a padded cloth, he wiped the excess from her mouth, giving her the final dignity she deserved, then placed a hand on her brow. "May the Almighty richly bless you for your sacrifice."

I longed to call out a blessing of my own, to praise the girl for her courage. More than that, I yearned to beg her to change her mind, but my instructions were to remain silent, and to record with my mind for later scribing, every detail that transpired.

The master moved back as far as he could – stood just a pace within the outer unbroken circle. Even from my distance, I saw a bead of sweat run down the girl's cheek and onto the marble.

There was nothing for a moment, just the sound of the ominous chanting that rose, quickened. Then pain started as a distant burning, I could tell, for the girl began to grow restless, edgy. Moments passed, then the girl shook, winced. She did not scream. Not yet. But she would.

In an instant, the girl's stunning body exploded into flame. The heat shriveled the silken gold hair to the bald, blistering head. The searing started to char her dress black. She rocked

4

her head back, arched and screamed. Flame and smoke plumed from her mouth. The fire coursed down her body, consuming everything. The blood started to boil in her body, to spit and hiss like pinesap in a forest fire. Her once beautiful features distorted into a hideous, monstrous mess that shocked me like the moments of waking from a nightmare.

She screamed and screamed and screamed, and then the fire seared up so hot, it shriveled the master's white eyebrows. With the final shock of the heat, the girl's life force had mercifully gone.

The chanting and unnatural flames dissipated swiftly, leaving only silence and a smoking pile of ash on the scorched altar.

Silence filled the space for the longest time, then we one by one, left the room, our eyes paying homage to the ash pile as though to the grave of a great king.

I found myself the last the leave the room, although as I stepped beyond the solid doorframe, I knew a part of me would never leave that room for as long as the Almighty blessed or cursed me with life.

Castus Poet-Scribe II

1

Emme knelt cautiously to the soil, traced a fingertip around the fresh imprint. The unusual footprints appeared frequently now and closer to the village. Whoever circled had not yet found what he or she looked for.

He, Emme decided. The footprints were too large, too heavy, to be a woman's.

Emme stood, scanned the area, eyes narrowed. Although the forest looked recently disturbed, the source remained illusive. How could anyone carelessly leave an imprint and trail, yet be so hard to find?

Emme followed the trail onward. It led to an aged tree trunk, the roots spreading with a partial rise from the earth. There the prints stopped as though the owner had been absorbed into the tree. The cinnamon tang of bark and acorns filled the air, but no remnant of a campfire or cooking.

Emme tilted her head back, strained eyes upward. Surely the mystery man had not climbed the enormous oak and stayed there. No scuffle marks on the trunk indicated boots had clambered up the tree, and no recently displaced leaves carpeted the grass, felled from human movements within the expansive, solid branches.

Emme peered around the tree, careful to note all signs of recent movement. Only animal trails, some fresh, others long abandoned, spread from the shadowed side of the tree. Again she knelt. She selected a small piece of grassless earth from inside the footprint and raised it to her nose, sniffed once. An unknown animal-skin boot had made the print, and the tread remained unfamiliar to her. This stranger came from no village nearby.

A squirrel shot past her boots and up the trunk of the tree. Halfway it stopped, peered at her curiously, then scampered into the thick of the leaves.

Emme frowned, deeply puzzled. The trail could not possibly have just vanished, yet it always did. No matter how far she followed it, eventually it ended in a void.

Damn him. Emme scowled, kicked the trunk of the tree.

She turned to go home and flicked a glance at the sun. The end of the day neared, and Wendaya would berate Emme for their lack of supper. Not unusual; Wendaya would always find something to abuse Emme for. If not for a lack of food, it would be the first thing that came to mind, perhaps even some lie Wendaya had been fed.

Emme broke into a run and flew down the forest trail. Summer perspiration cooled on her brow as she ran. Her long, thin legs carried her with ease beyond denser woodland to the edge of the slope that fell gently to the clearing. At its base the village sat, smouldering in the summer twilight.

Emme stopped to observe the pattern of traffic. Nothing seemed untoward. The inhabitants drifted home for meals before most would leave to commune in the village drink-house. Three hunters returned from the eastern forest border, recent kills in hand, and strode to the smokehouse. Others ambled in from tending outland crops and herds.

Tiny huts, scattered throughout the clearing, lay beneath several tree huts connected by suspension bridges. The early summer foliage of the mighty oaks and hornbeams shifted slightly, sighed in the tranquil breeze. Evening light danced between the leaves before drifting down through them to speckle the soft forest floor. It was a pretty village, spoilt only by its inhabitants.

Emme jogged down the slope, through a gap in the huts and onto the main village stretch.

"Wendaya's looking for you," one of the village boys called out on his way home. "She seems pretty mad, and we all know what that means." He had the tone and sly grin of one anticipating dark retribution.

"Yeah, and let's hope she finishes the job this time," his companion answered as Emme ran past them. "Finally gets rid of Emme."

The two laughed maliciously, and all the way down the street they congratulated each other for their stupid wit.

Emme dashed past the tiny timber huts. She ran down the narrow gap between two of them. Twine fences, supported by thick timber posts, marked the boundaries of each block. Everyone seemed so reluctant to share when they did not have to.

She hurried to the cluster of outdoor chimneys that were often lit when too hot to cook indoors. She knelt at one, felt inside the sooty chimney for the hook that should contain . . . *Damn it.* Someone had stolen her hidden basket of berries. Now she *would* get a beating.

"Looking for something?" Serasayn, the young, burly son of the village chieftain, peered around one of the chimneys. His spiteful grin revealed he knew the answer to the question.

"You pig." Emme snapped to her feet, stance ready and fists curled. "You stole my berries."

"I just wanted to see what sort of bruise you would have tomorrow."

"You vile pig. I'll give you a bruise of your own right now if you don't give me back my berries."

"I'd have to vomit them. I ate them for my lunch."

Emme launched at him, but Serasayn anticipated the movement. He bolted towards his house, shrieking his father's name. Emme stopped. Serasayn's father would have her thrown in the stocks and hurtled with stones if caught harming his smug little son.

Emme let out a string of curses as her enemy ran away. She stooped, picked up a rock and threw it at the retreating figure. It struck Serasayn on the back of the head with precise aim.

"You bitch." His bulk jolted to a standstill, and his thick hand rubbed his head. He turned sideways, glowered at Emme. The thick hand gestured at her. "You'll pay for that."

"Right after you pay for eating my berries." She took a theatrical step forward, and the coward dashed down the corridor of houses and into the safety of the homebound crowd. She could see just beyond the tiny gap in the houses where his fat figure paused on the main street to turn to her.

"Find a better hiding place," Serasayn bellowed.

She briefly watched his heavy steps as he jogged from view and away to his hut. *He'll probably run straight to a mirror where he can check his stupid looks.*

Emme sat down in the dirt and ash to think. She picked up a stick and repetitively stabbed a useless hole. She could go and find more food in the forest and receive a beating for tardiness. Or she could return home empty-handed.

Or – A better idea popped into her head, and she stood swiftly. She ducked behind houses, edged her way behind trees, until she reached Serasayn's yard – a fenced area beneath his family's tree hut. She carefully climbed the fence and crouched near the chicken coop. They weren't Serasayn's chickens; they were his mother's. Regardless, it would mean no eggs for his breakfast.

Emme felt a moment of guilt flush her cheeks. She had never stolen before, despite those countless times the villagers stole from her and her mother.

The whole village hated Emme. They listened to Wendaya too often, and too often Wendaya listened to them. When she was a child, they had beaten and teased Emme as much as Wendaya did. When she learned to fight back, they found other, crueller ways to torment her – crueller even than stealing her food and belongings. They would report false stories to Wendaya, for they knew that the worst pain would always be Wendaya's rage. All Emme had ever wanted was her mother's love.

Nearly every day now, Wendaya beat Emme for something. Tonight it would at least not be because Emme had neglected to find food.

The grubby chickens squawked and fluttered when she reached in to take the eggs. She brushed off dirt and muck, then gently, almost lovingly, tucked the eggs into the animal-skin pouch around her waist. She counted them. Eight eggs – a good number for a meal. Of course, Wendaya would only eat two. For a woman so slight, Wendaya could give such a good beating.

Emme returned home, eyes steely with resolve to cope with whatever Wendaya dished out. Emme paused at the tiny timber door, inhaled deeply and entered.

Instantly a shrill voice screamed from the back of the messy cottage. "Where have you been? You're late."

Emme knew she was not late. Not yet. Wendaya's rage would be founded on another illusive matter. Emme kicked aside a stack of Wendaya's dirty clothes that blocked the hut entrance. They struck the close timber wall and crumpled to the floor.

A sharp, shrewd face appeared from the dimness of the two-room hut. Wendaya sped towards Emme, broom in hand. Wendaya's dark hair, pulled tight off her face, made her face harsh. Still young compared to other women with daughters Emme's age, Wendaya had a speed that always caught Emme off guard.

"I've been getting us some dinner." Emme opened the pouch and carefully lifted an egg.

Wendaya swiftly swung the broom handle to Emme. It smacked against Emme's wrist and sent the egg flying across the room. The egg smashed against a timber wall, oozed sticky and orange to the floor. Pain forced a cry from Emme's lips. Emme gripped her good hand onto her throbbing wrist. *What was that for?* she wanted to scream, but nothing came out. It would not matter what it was for. It never did.

Wendaya pulled the broom handle back again and smacked it across Emme's temple. It cracked like fracturing bones through Emme's head.

She fell chest down to the floor, heard the gritty crunch as the eggs crushed inside the bag. They began to seep out the lacing. She did not cry out again as Wendaya hit her over and over with the broom handle. She simply lay quietly in the foetal position; eyes squeezed shut. *It will be over soon. It will be over soon.*

Time seemed suspended. The beating, just a few minutes, felt long in the descending darkness. The stick whacked her thigh, then no more. Emme hesitated to open her eyes. She heard scuffling about the hut, then the sounds of a fire being built and lit. Emme finally opened her eyes. Darkness hovered in the spaces the light did not reach. Wendaya would be preparing a hot tea for them as if nothing had happened.

Emme rose to her knees. Every inch of her body ached from bruises. She felt her wrists swell where the bulk of the beating had occurred. She groaned once, felt with fingertips the lump on her head, then stood.

The explanation may come. It did not always come, but this time it might. Wendaya put a hot cup on the table. She went to the store cupboard and pulled out a small sack of salty crackers. She untied the laces of the hessian bag and placed the rustling sack on the table, open for hands to reach in and grab the meagre, dull fare.

"I guess we just have tea and crackers tonight do we?" Wendaya asked snidely.

Emme felt words thicken in her throat. What was it about her mother that made standing up for herself difficult? She could outfight almost any man in the village, could bawl insults with the best of them, and yet found herself childlike and vulnerable around her mother.

Emme stiffly sat down at the table. Silently she sipped her tea.

"I'm sorry I was so angry," Wendaya said softly as if an angel, not the devil. She always apologised, and somehow, Emme always forgave. "But I heard you were seen kissing that Serasayn boy."

I've never kissed a boy, Mother. Never. But you'd never believe that. Silence was always prudent.

"I've told you a thousand times, Mistake, men are dangerous," Wendaya continued. "They'll only take advantage of you. You don't want anything to do with men. Don't you see – that's why I'm so hard on you. Why I hit you. I want you to be tough so no man will ever take advantage of you like they did me."

Emme felt tears sting her eyes. Bitter pride swept them away. "Was it so bad that I resulted from that, Mother?" Emme's voice was barely a whisper.

Wendaya gave her a dark, hard look, and Emme knew the answer. Mistake. That's what she'd been named all her life – what she had been given at her compulsory birth ceremony. Mistake. When ten, Emme had taken matters into her own hands. She had shortened Mistake to M, then insisted that people spell her name E double-M E. No other spelling would do or the person would get a swift thumping. Of course, all but seven people in the village could not read or write – Emme included. But she had at least learned to spell her name, and insisted that every other illiterate person out there learn the difference too.

Wendaya still called Emme 'Mistake'. Nothing would change that, and somehow Emme felt too weak to stop her.

When would she fight back? When would she stand up to her mother? Emme was stronger than the tiny woman who had once been the town's beauty, the town's delight. People whispered that Wendaya had been a happy, charming woman, loved by all, until one night and one drink changed everything.

Wendaya always insisted she had only ever consumed one drink at the village banquet, just one. Yet the next morning, she could not remember anything that happened. Eight months and three weeks later, Emme had been born, and Wendaya had become an outcast in a village that despised immoral women. If the father had just owned up to the child and agreed to live with Wendaya, all would have been forgiven, but no man had.

Wendaya had become bitter, angry, had hated Emme from the moment Emme was born. Had told Emme all her life not to trust men; that men were vilest of creation and would always take advantage of women.

Emme believed her. After all, Emme was living proof of what men would do. And Emme went to great pains to see that men would not take advantage of her as they had her mother.

Poor Wendaya. Emme sharply pulled herself up. She always did that. Felt sorry for her mother and the suffering Emme's birth had caused the woman. Why did her mother make Emme feel like a vulnerable little child inside?

Emme slowly finished the rest of her mug of tea and hobbled over to her mat beside the hearth. The bag of crackers lay untouched. Wendaya packed the sack away, rinsed the mugs in a bucket of soapy water, and left without a goodnight. She shut the door to her bedroom. Emme listened for the soft clack of the lock, for the familiar scuffling in the bedroom. No doubt Wendaya would be brushing her hair for the next half-hour. Wendaya always did that; stared at the tarnished mirror and incessantly brushed waist-length chestnut hair as if admiring a beauty long since passed. Resentment made Wendaya unattractive. Wendaya's brown eyes were no longer large, soft, but pinched and hard. Now only Emme's eyes shadowed what Wendaya's had once been.

Stiffly Emme lowered herself to the mat. Her bruises smarted terribly as they always did in summer. Winter's ice and snow from the forest soothed her stings and swells, but summer amplified the wounds. The pervasive heat and unrelenting mosquitoes, that even now whined around her ears, made it difficult to sleep off the injuries.

Emme lay on her aching back and stared at the underside of the thatched roof. She longed to run away, to start her own life. But where would she go? And who would accept her? Every village nearby knew the story of Mistake. She would be no better off there. And every neighbouring villager would only send her straight back rather than risk angering the chieftain of Underoak Village.

More than likely they would anger the chieftain if they sent Emme back. Emme laughed in the darkness, then groaned as bruises protested the violent movements. The bruises would heal, but somehow the hurt always remained inside.

She silently cursed the day some vile male had taken advantage of her drunken mother and conceived Emme's pitiful life.

Emme shook the thoughts from her head. Tomorrow, with distance between herself and Wendaya, Emme would be fiery again with a determination to make the most of her life. Yet here, on her bedmat, in this tiny, disorganised hut, she became the child who still longed for her mother's love. Not for the acceptance of the villagers. They could go rot. But her mother – oh how Emme longed to know what it felt like to have her mother wrap an arm around her; to tell Emme she loved her; that Emme was all Wendaya ever wanted. No, not necessarily Wendaya; it didn't have to be Wendaya. Any mother. She would accept any mother.

Emme patted the dagger in her pouch once, just to feel it was there. The egg yolk had congealed on the pelt. Emme would have to clean out the pouch, but not tonight. She was too sore, too weary to do anything but lie in the only comfortable position she could find.

Slowly Emme's eyes closed, and she fell into a shallow, fitful sleep. In the morning, she woke early. Peering out the window, she quickly deduced another hot cloudless day lay ahead. She donned an angora singlet-top, her thin deerskin pants and stiff pigskin boots, and tiptoed out of the house before Wendaya woke.

Emme had a task to complete. Find this mystery man. Of course, Wendaya would be angry that Emme had not told the villagers of the tracks sooner, but Emme did not want the villagers thumping through the forest trying to find the illusive stranger. Not one of the rotten villagers had the tracking skills Emme had and would only make it obvious to a man who did not want to be seen, that he was being pursued.

After washing her pouch in the river, Emme jogged along the forest trail, eyes focused for any unusual signs. No recent strange prints marked the forest floor. She veered down a left trail, leaving the main trail to wander where it willed. If she knew anything about her mystery man, he did not take key routes. She carefully chose a few more trails, some to the right, most to the left, then stopped abruptly.

Her eyes observed where the forest floor had been heavily disturbed as if something large had pushed through the undergrowth to find a track. The disturbance seemed to begin from nowhere as if the creature or person had suddenly appeared. Her eyes ran along the forest floor and noted where the disturbance met the path.

Emme knelt at the junction and smiled grimly. Many footprints, all careless, led along the path where it inclined upward. Cautiously she followed the imprints. This trail led to the caves. Perhaps the group had gone there. Whoever they were, they were neither villagers nor neighbours.

What foreigners would be out wandering through this part of the forest overnight? For that matter, was her mystery man one of them?

Nearing the caves, she heard voices. The trees provided ample cover as she inched her way to a better viewing point. She glanced up at the caves ahead. Five men, all dressed in similar and unusual clothes, stood around a fire. They stared at it, stretched hands over it to ward off the early morning chill. The enticing smell of cooking meat hung in the air. They muttered words to each other Emme strained to hear.

Emme immediately detected the abnormality of the men. Solid knee-high black boots, brown woollen jumpers and thick pants clashed with the brilliant summer weather the forest had been enjoying. Each wore a tiny tight white cap on their crowns that made Emme want to laugh despite the danger. If they hoped those caps would shield them from the hot sun, they were gravely mistaken. She noted the hands of some who poked sticks into the fire. Dark green and brown designs coloured the backs of each right hand – a tattoo perhaps – unrecognisable from where she stood.

Emme slid the dagger from her waist pouch. The simple bronze dagger, normally intimately familiar to her palm, felt faintly foreign. Puzzled, she glanced at the bolted bone handle, then scowled with realisation. Although she had cleaned the pouch early that morning, the dagger still felt sticky from the egg that had crushed through the bag.

Stealthily Emme moved to within earshot. Sheltered by silver fir trunks, she picked her way over clusters of broken cones.

"Well, hello there." A voice behind Emme startled her. She spun, sticky dagger curled back over her shoulder ready to throw.

An older man, early fifties, and adorned with the same tattoo and cap, stood with a pile of thick sticks in his arms. Swiftly he raised hands, releasing the sticks. The clatter of wood against wood alerted his companions. The five men around the fire stopped their conversation and looked to the disturbance. Eyes noted the dishevelled, abandoned stick pile, then the face of the man above it. They tried to follow his line of sight but from their position, could only see the tree he seemingly stared at.

"We mean you no harm," the unaccompanied man said to Emme. "My friends and I are just camping here the night."

A soft-eyed man called from beside the fire, "Anderson? What is it? What have you seen?"

"A woman here with a knife." The men around the fire shifted at the response and caught their first glimpse of Emme.

Emme stared defiantly from one group to the other. "Who are you all, and what are you doing here?"

"We're just passing through," the man before her said.

"Passing through? From where? You don't look like men from around these parts."

The isolated man seemed to notice something on Emme's arm still curled back ready to throw her weapon. His eyes narrowed slightly before his expression changed to an odd friendliness that sent a sharp prickle down Emme's back. "Will you come and share some breakfast with us?" He gestured to the fire.

"No. Tell me where you're from or I'll report this to my chieftain."

"We're from . . ." The man faltered. "Very far away. You wouldn't know the place."

"What are you doing here?"

"Passing through," he replied. "Wouldn't you like some breakfast? We promise we're not going to harm you."

"No one has ever passed through. There is nothing to pass through to. I've never seen anyone who isn't from the nearby villages."

"Could you possibly put that dagger down?" the man asked. "It's making me nervous."

Emme considered briefly. "I'll put it down, but not away. I'm very quick with a dagger, you know."

"I don't doubt it. Will you come and share our fire? We'll tell you all about where we're from."

No one spoke for some time. Not even the silver fir needles stirred. "Very well then," Emme said, all caution gone. She turned and walked confidently to the tall fire, boots cracking the fir cones. She knew if she had to she could run faster than these old men. Besides, she wanted to know if her mystery man was one of them.

She walked to the fire and feigned interest in the meat roasting over the coals whilst she glanced at their feet. No, not her mystery man, but more than likely connected. In her twenty-two years, she had only ever seen one stranger. Now she had seen six with a seventh out there somewhere. The events were entirely too unusual to be anything but related.

She briefly noted them all, their strange linen and wool clothes, no animal skins, no furs. Most had dark hair – some with flecks of grey – and white skin. Only one had hair so grey it was almost white. No tans like the villagers. The youngest seemed fifty, the eldest, at a guess, late sixties. The tattoos were of nothing notable; just a swirling, twisted design, like ropes tangled into a complex, symmetrical pattern. Difficult to copy, yet each appeared identical.

"So where are you all heading to?"

"Do you know the country well?" one of the dark-haired men asked.

"No." With the forest her whole world, she only knew the surrounding villages.

"Well then, it's no use explaining is it," the man replied with a thin smile.

Emme glared at him. "Try me."

The man she had first threatened – Anderson they had called him – turned and whispered something to the white-haired man beside him. The white one's eyes lit briefly, then to the others he tapped his wrist. Although clearly intended to be covert, it did not go unnoticed by Emme. She began to wonder how these heavy-booted, incompetent men managed to catch that creature on the fire in the first place. Especially with no weapons, Emme noted for the first time. A creeping sense of dread started to empty her insides.

She pretended not to notice the reaction to the clandestine tapping of the wrist. The men clearly knew exactly what the gesture meant, and their faces reacted with thoughts Emme could only guess at. This was entirely too suspicious. She backed away a step, feigning a reaction to the heat of the fire.

"So tell us about yourself," Anderson said.

"Nothing to tell. I come from Underoak Village. That village just over there." A hand waved with more casualness than she felt. "My chieftain is the most powerful chieftain of Oakwood Forest." She placed intentional emphasis on 'powerful'. They did not need to know he was too far away to hear any cries for help.

"And your parents?" one man asked.

Emme's face closed over. "I believe I am asking the questions here. You are intruding on *my* forest. Now, why are you travelling?"

The men exchanged questioning glances, seemed reluctant to speak.

"Are you chasing someone?"

Anderson flinched faintly. "Why do you ask?"

"Because there are another man's tracks, and he's circling the forest. Are you trying to find him?"

"A man?" Anderson asked. "How do you know it's a man?"

"Pl-*ease*." Emme rolled her eyes at him. "I am quite skilled at tracking. I found all of *you* didn't I?" *Not that it was hard, you careless thugs.*

"Is he a villager?"

"No – he has unusual shoes. Like yours but not quite. A much more impressive sole."

The men turned and whispered to each other. Hands gestured strongly. Long frustrating moments passed. But for the low voices, Emme could easily have supposed they had forgotten about her. She guessed she could have just walked away and left them to their quiet arguing, but the few intriguing phrases she caught, phrases that made little sense, kept her grounded with curiosity. "But we have no time." "Not if he's here." "But then she might . . ."

They finally seemed to reach some verdict.

"Child," the grey, almost white-haired man said.

"I'm not a child; I'm twenty-two winters."

"Of course." The man smiled gently. "Madam, this is –"

"Madam is even worse. Don't call me madam."

"What may I call you, then?"

"I'm Emme. Spelt E Double-M E."

The man smiled faintly, then the smile faded. "Emme – this is going to sound rather strange, but you are in danger. We cannot say why, but we must hurry. We do not have much time before he finds you."

"Before who finds me?"

"I'm afraid we cannot tell you his name."

"Why?"

"We can protect you from him, but you must let us. You must let us take you somewhere safe."

"Safe? My village is safe. The chieftain is the most powerful of any of the villages."

"I'm afraid, child – Emme – that your chieftain is of no use here. The matter is far more complicated than that."

"Then you'd better explain it."

"We can't," the man called Anderson said. "It will only endanger you if we do. But we can take you to a place where we *can* actually explain it to you. You just have to trust us and say that you are willing to go."

Emme took another step back. Her hand tightened on the bone handle of the dagger. "Go where? Where is this place?"

"To our city."

"Your city? What's a city?"

"It's like a very big village," one of the older men said. "Like a thousand of your village in size."

Emme laughed curtly. "Places like that don't exist."

"Yes, they do." Anderson furtively looked around as though expecting dangers any moment. He turned back to Emme. "Please, madam – Emme. I know it's a big ask, but you must trust us or he will find you. And he only means you harm."

"Who? Why are you saying all of this?"

"That we cannot tell you either, but you must trust us. You are in danger."

Emme took another step backwards. "You don't even know who I am. You didn't even know my name. You didn't even know what village I was from. You must have the wrong person."

"No, we don't have the wrong person." Anderson took a step forward, hand outstretched as if to take hers. "Please, all can be explained, if you just come with us."

Fear and determination shot like a potent drug through Emme's veins. She turned and bolted down the path.

"Someone stop her," Anderson ordered.

Behind her she heard running, the crunching of sticks, fir cones and brittle bracken. Folliage of undergrowth hissed as swift legs pushed past. Many men followed. She quickened her pace. Her long legs leapt swiftly over undergrowth and into the dense heart of the forest where every tree, every tall shrub, every vine, provided perfect shelter.

She easily lost them. Her speed and knowledge of lesser-known tracks gave her a superior advantage. To be safe, she tucked the dagger in her pouch, gripped the thick low-lying branches of a pine and scrambled up the scratchy trunk. She hoisted up into the highest branches and sat, puffing.

What was that all about? Surely they had the wrong person. She pitied the person they were talking about. Those six men may have acted politely on the outside, but something sinister lay beneath the surface of their intentions. Well, she would just stay out of their way until they found whoever it was they looked for. But at a distance she would keep an eye on their comings and goings. The sooner they left Oakwood Forest, the better.

She wondered then if she should tell the chieftain. It was her duty as forest tracker to report any incidences, no matter how minor, but those village thugs would probably march in here and destroy the strangers before she had a chance to find out answers. The chieftain always opted for violence over cunning.

Emme shifted around on the spiky branch and looked out through dark green pine needles behind her. A faint ribboning rise of smoke caught her attention. It seemed too thin, too controlled, to be the beginnings of a forest fire. Most likely it belonged to a single campfire.

Emme's brows dipped, puzzled. No village lay that way. The forest was too dense, too wild, for permanent habitation. But several trails wound through there, mostly used by hunters from other villages. However, a hunter rarely risked a fire that would scare away the game. Only winter demanded fires to ward off frostbite.

She scanned the rich-green tree line flecked with yellow sunlight. No other signs of movement caught her attention. Perhaps the hunters smoked out their game. Occasionally that occurred, but mostly in winter when the baking summer sunshine had not ripened the land for a forest fire. Still, it was worth investigation.

She waited more moments until sure she was safe from the strange men, then climbed down the tree with graceless ease. Her feet thudded onto the soft needle blanket beneath the mighty pine.

She patted the trunk as though it had deliberately provided protection for her. Then she peered around and darted into shadows.

She found a thin trail, overgrown slightly with new fern fronds and lantana shoots. The tufts of grass growing under the shady shelter of the fronds had recently been disturbed. She knelt, felt the ground. Her mystery man.

Dark excitement stirred. With careful skill, she manoeuvred through the thick woods to where the smoke rose. She stopped at the edge of a small, leaf-strewn clearing and peeped around the trunk of a young elm.

A handsome man, possibly in his late thirties, squatted trying to get a fire going that poured smoke into the atmosphere. Early morning light had not yet dried the dew from the clearing that was edged by curly fronds and soft balls of yellow flowers. The fire's rock-edged bed was neither new, nor recently used. Forest gatherers in winters past must have warmed hands and feet over the sooty circle. She noted that the stranger had courage to be occupying a spot he could not have known was no longer used. Courage, perhaps, or ignorance of brutally maintained territorial rules.

So this was her mystery man. The man stopped poking at noncompliant sticks, calmly ran a hand through his dark, neat hair. A short brown beard hugged his chin and offset apple-green eyes. His all-cotton clothes, no skins or furs, confirmed her suspicions. He was somehow connected to the other strangers. He wore a cotton tunic with elaborate woven designs Emme had never seen before, tucked in by a sword belt oddly empty of a sword. His pants were thick but smooth. He looked muscular, strong, as he knelt beside the fire, poking more green sticks into it. She smiled faintly at his poor forest skills.

Still staring at the smoking sticks, the man said, "Well don't just stand there laughing at me. You could at least come and help me."

Emme stiffened. Was there another person about? Her eyes darted sideways as she scanned the shadows.

The man looked up from the fire, directly at her. "You can come out from behind that tree. I know you're there."

Emme frowned. Her skills seemed to have greatly lapsed today. No, they couldn't have. She could out-spy, even at close range, the best trackers of any village. He must have been talking to someone else.

"I would really appreciate a hand with this fire. I'm very cold from the dew that fell this morning." He was looking straight at her, despite the heavy shadows enveloping her. Emme noted warily his well-pronounced words and polite sentences, the smooth voice so different from most of the gruff male villagers. He shrugged. "Suit yourself."

Emme straightened and stepped from the trees. "All right, I'll help you with your fire. Your sticks are too green and the wrong kind of timber. You need to find darker wood that looks like . . ." She looked at the ground around her feet for a specimen. "None of this wood is any good."

The man sat back onto the ground, leant back on immaculate hands – hands that could not have done even a day of hard labour. "Is that what my problem is?" His eyes seemed to be smiling.

Emme turned behind her and swept up a few dry sticks. Thicker hornbeam branches, a dry, very hard timber, lay a few paces away. She picked them up, ears all the while alert to any sound of movement near the fire.

She stepped back into the clearing, branches in hand. She squatted on the other side of the fire, winced briefly as stretched bruises ached on her legs, then piled the sticks onto the fire. Soon a fine blaze replaced the smoke. The sweet scent of baking timber filled the tiny clearing.

"Thank you," the man said, and Emme knew he had never removed his eyes from her.

"How did you know I was there?" she asked.

The man only smiled as though hiding a pleasant surprise. "I'm Jaimis, by the way." He stretched out his hand politely.

Emme ignored the hand. "Emme. Spelt E Double-M E."

The man's brow arched neatly. "How else would you spell it?"

"So, what are you doing here in these woods? You're obviously not from around here."

"I'm running away from some very bad people who hope to harm me."

"Would that be six men?"

The man nodded. "Yes. Have you seen them?"

"Back there." She gestured broadly behind her. "Why? What did you do to them?"

"It's all very complicated, and you'll have to forgive me if I don't want to talk about it. Let's just say that I'm trying to stop some very bad things they are doing in my city, and so now they are trying to stop *me*."

City – the big village the men spoke of. "I see. They did seem a little bit sinister."

"You spoke to them?"

Emme nodded.

"Did they ask about me?"

"Why would they think I know you?"

Jaimis watched Emme briefly. "I only meant perhaps they'd asked if you had seen me around."

"I mentioned that I had. I'm sorry if that gets you into trouble, but you people have got to stop sneaking around my forest. Wherever you came from, you should take the issues home with you."

"Perhaps you're right. I am going back to my city, today hopefully."

"How far away is this city?"

"Very far."

"And they followed you all the way here? You must have really made them angry."

"Yes – I did." The man turned to his pack and began rummaging through it. Emme's hand instantly went to her pouch, ready to remove the dagger. At last the man drew out a sack of food. "Listen, I have some salted meat here. Would you like to share some? You don't look like you eat much."

"What do you mean? I eat just fine."

"Where I come from, you would be considered too skinny."

"I'm a perfectly acceptable size in my village. Maybe I don't have hips and breasts like the other girls, but who wants that?"

A smile curled half his mouth, and his eyes danced a little. "I would have thought that girls do."

"I'm not a girl – not one that a man can take advantage of anyway."

"I see. So do you want some?" He pulled the meat from the wrappings and held it up for her to see.

"What sort of meat is that? It looks strange."

"Beef."

"Beef? What's beef?"

Jaimis watched her for a moment, as though trying to guess at her question. "Beef is from cows."

"What's a cow?"

His brows shot up. "You don't know what a cow is?" The brows lowered. "No, I don't suppose you do in this forest. Do you have buffalo?"

"No."

"Oxen?"

"Yes."

"It's the same animal family."

"You eat your oxen? What pulls your ploughs?"

"Well, no, we don't eat our oxen as such. And mostly our horses pull our ploughs."

Emme laughed. "Horses? You've got wild horses pulling your ploughs? Now I know you're lying."

"Well, they're not wild where I come from. They're quite tame."

"Is that what you're wearing on your feet? Cowskin?" Emme openly studied the stiff glossy black boots that laced up to his knees over the neat brown pants.

"Yes. We don't call it cowskin; we call it leather. So do you want to try some?"

Emme nodded. He broke off a chunk and passed her some. She settled onto her bottom and chewed. "Tough. It tastes like . . . hmmm, not like deer, but close."

Emme pulled back a little against the heat of the fire.

The man stared at her arms. "You have some very nasty bruises there. Are you okay?"

"I'm fine." Emme stiffened slightly.

"You don't look fine. Did someone hurt you?"

"I said I'm fine."

"That mark on your wrist. That's not a bruise is it."

"This?" She held up her wrist to the light. "This is a birthmark." She inspected the unusual brown mark that had adorned her slender wrist since birth. Shaped like a small wobbly cauldron with its handle up, the mark made Emme's wrist look dirty, even after she had scrubbed herself clean with pumice stone and soap. She shrugged to herself and tucked her hand back in her lap. "So tell me about this city."

"I can help you with those injuries, you know. I have a salve here."

"I'll be all right. I always heal."

"Always? Does this happen to you all the time?"

"It's my mother. She does it when I make her mad."

"She shouldn't treat you like that, you know. No one should treat anyone like that."

Emme stared at him. Of course – he did not know about the circumstances of her birth. He most certainly would not be so seemingly concerned if he knew. She decided to enjoy her anonymity, however brief it was.

"So tell me, Kara, how long has your mother treated you like that?"

"My name is Emme."

"What did I say?"

"Kara."

"Ah yes – sorry, Emme. My mistake."

"The names are very different." She stared at him coldly.

"My sister's name is Kara. You look a lot like her."

"Then your sister must look very different from you."

His eyes narrowed slightly. "Yes, she does."

"Only one sister?"

"Only one."

"Brothers?"

"None." The two watched each other briefly, then Jaimis added, "Will you let me rub a salve into those wounds? I'll feel much better if you'll let me."

Emme scowled. "You can damn-well keep your hands to yourself, you pervert."

Jaimis blinked once. "Very well, if that's the way you feel." His face relaxed. "You shouldn't have to put up with that, you know."

"I wouldn't if I had anywhere else to go."

"Don't you have any towns you can travel to?"

"I only know this forest."

He seemed to be considering something. Finally he said, "Why don't you come with me to my city."

"Where is this city?"

"It's difficult to explain. It's very far away."

"Why would I want to go there?" Emme's mouth was flat, but her eyes were faintly curious.

"It's a great place. I have a lot of influence there. I could help you get some work, find you a house."

"Perhaps you should first tell me about these bad men. Whatever those six bad men are doing, it does make me wonder if your city is such a great place to live."

Jaimis surprised Emme by laughing.

"That's hardly a funny question." Her acorn-brown eyes blazed.

"No, you're right. You needn't worry about those bad men. I know how to handle them, and you won't find them a problem."

"So how long a walk is it to this city?"

"Do you want to come?"

"I'm warming up to the idea."

Jaimis slid the leftover beef into the food sack. He dropped the sack back in his half-empty bag. Not a lot of belongings for one who had travelled so far from this – this city. "Well, I'll tell you what: you say you'll come with me, and I'll tell you all about it on the way."

"And if I don't like the sound of this city after you've told me about it? I can't exactly go home once I've run away. The beatings will be even worse." She popped the last of the strange meat into her mouth and swallowed.

"I can assure you that my city and what awaits you there, is far better than those beatings you receive all the time. Far better. Emme, do you have any other family other than your mother?"

"No."

"No one in nearby villages?"

She shook her head.

"Do you have friends in the village?"

Emme's stony silence spoke volumes.

"No? Then what have you got to lose? You have nothing back there."

Emme stuck her chin out. "I have my forest."

"Is it worth going through beatings just to live in this forest?"

Emme faltered. "No – well, I guess not."

"So do you want to come with me?"

Emme felt a flush of courage. How long had she yearned to run away? Now here was her chance. And if he turned out to be a rotten travelling companion, she could always find out where this city was and go on her own. He couldn't possibly treat her any worse than her mother did, unless he took advantage of her; but he would have one hell of a fight on his hands if he tried anything. She was well able to hold her own against a man like Jaimis.

"Well?" Jaimis asked.

"All right then. I'll go with you."

Jaimis grinned, and his eyes gleamed as though she had just handed him a nugget of gold. He stood swiftly.

"We're not going now are we?" she asked.

Jaimis ignored her and took a step to her. She snapped to her feet, fingers at the mouth of the pouch. Jaimis began to murmur something.

"Speak up, I can't hear you."

Again he ignored her. The mumbling continued. A hand traced a pattern in the air, and she felt something unnatural stir behind her. She turned fully to see a swirling, tumbling black image appear, like a large oval mirror that reflected a bleak night sky. It sounded like a rushing, howling wind, and it pulled at her as though she were water and it was a black cavernous mouth sucking her in. She steeled back against the pull, dug her foot into the dewy soil, stretched her muscles to take a step back against the current. "What the –"

Without warning, Jaimis stepped to Emme's back and pushed at her, dislodged her balance of locked posture. She felt the pull grow stronger, felt herself fall; fall forward and towards the black space. Something caught her before she fell to her face – a violent up-current. Soon she was rushing into the void, like a body trapped within a fiercely flooding river. Then the void swelled to become a confined, choking universe within a universe. Within terrifying seconds her forest, her whole world, had completely disappeared.

2

Emme felt everywhere and yet nowhere all at once. Pulled as though through time itself, the alien sensations made her ill. She stared, stunned, as blackness, the emptiness that had displaced her forest, grew to a long, pulsing tunnel. She felt herself rush through the tunnel, a mere leaf caught on a raging torrent of air. The speed, that almost sucked her insides right from her body, shocked all screams from her mouth. Then dazzling light appeared at the other end. The light swelled. Did it grow, or did she approach it? Something hidden, yet as real as the wind, flung her rapidly out of the tunnel, through the light, and into the strangest room she had ever seen.

Too stunned to be frightened, Emme could only stare openly at the plush room. A four-post bed, each post opulently carved and draped with heavy, red fabrics, rested against a tapestried wall. Solid stone formed the floor of the room and carpet, plump, red, copied the floor's shape. A hearth of polished grey rock, marked with black veins, sat on the opposite wall. The void still pulsed and yawned beside the hearth, but it no longer pulled at her. An enormous fire curled inside the hearth, indifferent to the void beside it, and warmed the entire room but for a draft from the left window near the head of the bed.

Alien tables and chairs filled remaining spaces. Patterned fabrics, with threads of red to match the bedspread, hugged contours of obese chairs. Timbers of tables, ornate, smooth, and glassy on top, reflected dull light from the window. Used to rough, knotted, and hammered furniture, to Emme the heavily carved legs, posts and corners seemed ridiculous, as though pattern and form mattered in the place of stability and function.

Unnecessary paintings, tapestries, needle-worked cushions, gold candlesticks, and silver goblets on thin sculpted legs, decorated the room. Even the wash jug beneath the gilded mirror, one of the few practical objects in the room, boasted an excessive floral design.

Emme felt and heard air rush behind her, a shot of wind against her bared arms. She spun on heels to see Jaimis materialise in the room from the vortex, then the void behind him shrank itself out of existence.

Emme flung at him, punched him on the chin. It made a thick, thudding sound. He staggered back, eyes wide.

"You bastard. You tricked me." She swung at him again. He dodged her fist. It missed his face and hit his shoulder.

"Now hang on." He threw up hands to protect himself. "I can explain."

"You'd better." Eyes blazing at him, she put knuckles on hips.

"This is the way we travel from place to place here. I thought you might be frightened if you heard how we had to go."

"How far did we come?" she demanded loudly.

Jaimis felt his chin for damage, tested the jaw for movement. "Very far. Across the sea even. We're in a totally different country."

"What the hell were you doing in my forest in the first place?"

Jaimis' fingers still played with his sore chin. He winced slightly as he tried to get proper movement in it. "It's a long story, but it was the best place to hide."

"And why did you bring me here?" Her hand cut the air; indicated the lavish space. "Is this your bedroom?"

"It's my quarters, yes. It's where I left. I didn't expect to have you with me when I returned."

"So can I leave now? I don't like being in a man's bedroom." Her tone left no room for refusal.

"Yes. You are not a prisoner here. But there is something I have to do first."

"What's that?" Her eyes narrowed.

"Let's see. Do you know what a prince is?"

"Yes." The wariness did not leave her face.

"Well – you see, I'm a prince here in this country, and this is my castle." With the hand not testing his chin, he gestured to the walls. "And if you go running around in here, especially dressed like that –"

"What's wrong with the way I'm dressed?"

"Nothing as such. It's just that we don't dress that way here, and if you go running around looking like that, the guards are likely to think you are here to harm me."

"You should have thought about that before you brought me here. I want to go back."

"Before you've had a look around?" Jaimis finally stopped playing with his chin, satisfied it was not broken. "I would like to show you around first, then perhaps you can decide if you want to go back or not. But before that, I just need to go out there and tell my guards and my people that they can expect you. Then you are free to roam around." Jaimis gave her a look of a boy pleading for sweets. "Do we have a deal, Emme?"

Emme inhaled slowly, thought carefully. "Very well then. Go and tell people I'm here."

"Wonderful." He clapped hands together once. "Oh, and no more hitting me. You could be killed for doing that here."

"You'd have to catch me first."

Jaimis laughed. "You are feisty, aren't you." He studied her face a moment, the smile still touching his lips. His eyes took in every detail, then seemed satisfied with something. "It will take me a while to get used to you."

"Why do you have to get used to me?"

He smiled secretively, waved the comment away, then walked to the door. "Make yourself at home." His fingers reached to a small hook beside the door. A fat, black key hung on its circular head from the rusted hook. He took the key in hand. "Now – I'm going to lock the door. Not because I don't want you getting out, but because I don't want anyone to get in and discover you before I tell them about you. A lot of people walk in here. Maids, guards, my advisor, my chamberlain. But if I lock the door and take the key, people know they are not to try to enter. So don't be alarmed if you hear the door lock, okay?"

Emme's eyes narrowed with fleeting suspicion, then she shrugged. "Whatever."

"Good girl." He turned before he caught Emme's scowl at his patronising praise. The door opened, and he closed it behind him. Emme heard the key scratch at the lock, the soft click as it turned. Metal gently grated metal as the key withdrew from its socket, then footsteps disappeared down what she guessed was a stone hallway.

She put hands on hips and studied the room. Despite swirls, colours, and richly woven tapestries, it felt dull, detached. She imagined more character lay in one corner of her dinner table than existed in this entire room.

A crusty parchment and thick book with browned edges lay on a turned-leg table. An inkwell with a protruding pure white feather, a mound of red wax, and a candle sat beside the parchment. Her village had one book – the book of the law – but only the chieftain and his smug family could read it. Served them all right having to sit for hours and hours learning the boring skill of reading and writing. If that was part of being the village leaders, they could have the job. What good was reading and writing amongst trees, rivers, squirrels, badgers, deer, or birds? And what could the book of the law teach them that oral tradition had not?

A prince. Jaimis was a prince. She had heard of princes and their castles – those strange rock fortresses they insisted on living in. Her country had a prince, but they never actually heard from him. He didn't care about the outlying forests of his province. She knew the prince was rich though, and powerful. But he could be the cruellest prince in the world and she wouldn't care. As long as he left the forests alone, the rest of the country could do what it liked.

She wondered what nature of prince Jaimis was. A good prince? He must have been if he had abhorred Wendaya's beatings. Any prince who was against a beating, had to be a good prince. No wonder he didn't fight back when Emme punched him. The village boys would be all over Emme by that point. Of course, she could give as good as she got, but they often won with numbers. But she could outrun them – all of them – and they knew if they called her a coward, she would find ways to prove them just as gutless. A chunky spider down their shirt, or a dagger aimed to fractionally miss their heads, would always force them to retract their insults.

Emme smiled to herself and drifted over to the open window. She wouldn't have to put up with them anymore – not if this city was a worthwhile place to stay.

She leant against the wide stone sill, peered down at a dull grey courtyard. She jolted. Snow. There was snow on the ground, and no leaves on a drab tree tapping the nearest windowpane. A severe chill swept up into her face, made her hair stand straight as straw. Tiny bumps rose along her entire bare arms. Winter?

Was it winter here? How could it possibly be winter?

She watched people shuffle through the snow. Some dragged deep furrows with sliding feet. Others punched black boots down into the fine grey powder, lifted legs high, then punched down again. Emme noted clothes not nearly as impressive as Jaimis' outfit. Jaimis had patterned colours, fine fabrics and tight knits. These people wore rough weaves, thick knits, browns, greys, and dirty beiges. Some clothes had stains and rips to match weatherworn faces and coarse, aged hair.

She wondered why they did not wear thick furs and skins for warmth. Instead they clutched cloaks about their bodies. Woollen caps and white bonnets protested the wind. The women waded through the snow in impractical fat skirts and tight bodices of drab colours. Stiff aprons, smeared with the dirt of labour, wrapped their waists.

Some carried stacks of firewood, others baskets of laundry or winter root vegetables. One carted a weighty vat Emme supposed contained alcohol. A metal bucket holding scrubs, brushes and rags, swung from the closed hand of another.

Curious, she listened as some stopped to talk to each other. Voices, as dull as the weather, discussed the mundane. A garden needed tending to. Washing, left in a strategic spot, awaited collection. The chamberlain had given a certain order that morning. A particular room had not been cleaned in a while.

A beautiful slender woman in a textured red cloak stepped from a side building. She flowed around the ice-compacted courtyard edges. The cloak parted when a breeze tugged at it, revealing in full, her glossy-green, stout skirt. Long honey-blonde hair, neatly brushed and shiny, fell to her petite waist.

The village women wore dresses at celebrations. Other times they worked in loose straight skirts and unadorned angora tops. Even at their best, with draping dresses and plunging necklines, the village women never looked as striking as this woman. Emme had never seen such an ornate or full dress before. She wondered what was stuffed up the skirt to make it sit so wide. Emme chuckled quietly with the thought that maybe the woman's thighs held the skirt out.

An elderly man, greying but upright and strong, exited a door on the other side of the courtyard. He wore no cape or woollens as if he did not expect to be outside. He seemed as well dressed, as impractical as the woman. The two noticed each other, and the man waved a gesture to bring her closer. They met in the middle of the courtyard beneath the grey smudged sky.

The man bowed subtly.

"You have news for me?" the lady asked.

"Yes, My Lady. Your brother has returned. He has asked to see you, urgently."

Brief alarm flitted across her pale, sculpted features. "Is Jaimis all right?"

"Fine, My Lady, apart from a bruise forming on his chin. He says it is a matter of great importance. He's in the library."

"I'll see him at once then."

The two walked towards a door opposite Emme's window. Their footprints meshed through many trails made since the last snowfall.

Emme straightened. Sister. That was Jaimis' sister. And she looked nothing – *nothing* – like Emme did.

Emme had short, shaggy rough-cut hair; always totally unbrushed. Her hair and eyes were the colour of autumn acorns, and her brows were dark, thin on a tanned face. That woman was blonde, feminine, pale as the snow, with light-pink lips and a tiny, curvy body.

"Lady Ennika; my Lord Chamberlain; please wait," a man called from the other side of the corridor. Wearing clothes of a lesser quality, the man possibly held the position of a high-ranking servant – like the ones who waited on Emme's chieftain. The chamberlain and the lady stopped, turned.

"It's all right, I've already told her," the Chamberlain said. He and the lady went on their way.

Ennika – her name was Ennika. Not Kara. Emme felt her heart thump in her thin chest. If Jaimis had lied about that, what else had he lied about? Maybe he wanted to kill her, or worse, violate her. Damn it. That's why he had locked her in his bedroom.

Fear shocked Emme into action. She had to get out of here. Fast. She tried the door, but it was securely locked. She kicked it hard several times, but the rusty lock refused to give.

She spun to face the room. Her eyes darted for anything that would pick the lock. A feather maybe? Too brittle. She frowned. Even if she found something suitable, picking locks was the least of her skills.

Think, Emme. What are your skills? Climbing. Climbing was one of her skills. She loped back to the window and peered outside. *I need a way to climb down that wall. Jutting stones – anything.*

She scanned the wall for irregularities, but the large stones of the wall were smooth with very little grouting. No – wait. A vertical strip of square stones extended out from the rest like flat steps. Odd. If she could put her toes on each one, and hang onto ones above with fingertips, she could probably scramble her way to the bottom. Eyes measured the horizontal distance. The stones seemed within easy reach.

She waited until most people had cleared the courtyard, then swung over the window ledge, reached out a foot to the nearest overhanging block of stone. Bravely she let go of the ledge and held onto the block above her. Beyond the warmth of the room, biting cold hit her.

She glanced up at the enormous wall that rose, grey rock to grey sky. Up close, she could see grooves and gashes of stonemason marks on the carved blocks. She realised the room was part of a square tower, four storeys high. Beside the tower, to her left, a wide roofless corridor branched from the square courtyard. A possible way out.

Surprised by the ease of the vertical pathway, she swiftly climbed down the blocks. From a leap, she landed in snow. The icy powder closed in on her ankles. She jumped out from the foot holes pounded into the snow and ran left. Astonished, several people watched her flight.

Too bad if they had seen her. Let them try to catch her. Angry fear made her fast despite the hindering snow.

Emme followed the left edge of the stone tower. The courtyard expanded to more outdoor areas between buildings, towers and rooms. She shot through open spaces until she reached the castle's outer wall. A quick decision, and she turned left. With her right hand on the stone slabs of the wall, she ran, hoping to make it to an entrance or exit. The stone beneath her fingers felt cold, coarse, like sand particles.

Five guards, with fancy red pinafores over shirts and trousers, and flamboyant rapiers, stood at a colossal half-raised timber gate studded with iron spikes. It arched up into its rock frame. A hefty metal chain dangled from one side. Was that how the gate opened? Beyond the gate, she could see a snow-covered slope down to a vast, overwhelming array of houses and buildings. Able to see a great distance, she realised with a jolt of alarm, that this place, this city, was entirely alien to her.

The guards openly gawked at her, their eyes freely roaming her body. Her tanned arms began to flush red from lack of cover. Angora singlet-tops were for summer, not this wintry cold. Her deer-hide pants were a strong contrast to their coarse cotton pants. She knew about cotton, but only the important wore it – never as pants. Not when animal skins were so protective and comfortable. And her tough pigskin boots looked entirely different from the guards' velvety boots. Their boots, tops folded over, reached their knees. Their wide-brim hats possessed a useless feather, and their tunics had a strange animal on it with big teeth, a mane and sharp claws. Each wore a well-groomed goatee as though an essential part of the uniform. They looked more like they should have been performing plays at village feasts, not guarding anything.

Emme's fists tightened. "What are you all looking at?"

One of the guards stroked his black, pointed chin beard as if pondering a decision. "What in the devil are you wearing that for?"

Emme glared at him, then realised she had no time to explain. "I'm going to the city, and this is what I want to wear." Was that an adequate excuse for leaving this place? Maybe they had already heard about her and would make leaving difficult. She glanced again at the rapiers. Although the hilts swirled in excessive shiny patterns, she doubted the thin blades were as impractical.

They only laughed at her. It seemed they were little concerned about those leaving, and more concerned about those attempting to come in. One of the guards turned to interrogate an old man bearing a lumpy sack over slumped shoulders.

Upon request, the man opened up the sack to reveal knobbly dirt-crusted potatoes. With gnarled spotted hands, the old man produced well-worn papers from a pocket. The guard waved permission to enter the castle, and the old man shuffled through the gate, his back humped under the load.

Emme squared shoulders and marched through the snow past the chuckling guards. She forced herself to walk, not run, down the long slope to the city. Large housing blocks, richly carved, lined the road. Each rose two, some three storeys high. Although joined by a single roof line, occasionally a slim covered lane separated buildings. The lane of steps led down to more buildings behind.

She caught glimpses of plush furniture behind jutting, lead-lined windows. People milled in their houses. Some sipped steaming drinks. Others in simple clothes carried baskets and trays through rooms. Could everyone afford servants here?

Expensively dressed people clustered quickly at their diamond panes, and gossiped and gaped at her as though she were a play for their benefit. Two young women with glittering gold ribbons through neat hair, pointed at Emme, then turned to each other and whispered, giggled. They watched Emme with amused disdain. She wanted to run to their glass window and threaten to smack the smug looks from their faces, but knew now was the worst possible time.

She neared the bottom of the slope. Shouting made her turn. Someone yelled, pointed to her.

Damn it! It was Jaimis.

The guards started to run towards her. She turned, loped down the street until a side lane offered itself. She swiftly turned onto it and ran down its winding slope. The tall, old buildings rose up like a carved rock corridor.

The lane levelled out to an ancient, grand staircase. She took the stairs then pelted down the street beyond. Through the timber panels of a high fence on either side of her, she glimpsed a substantial garden area where people bent over snow-drowned vegetable patches, tended to unruly goats that kicked snowballs, or gathered eggs from elevated chicken pens. Several looked up as she ran past. They stopped to stare, faces blank.

Steam gushed from her mouth as she ran. She knew the bite of cold would sting her when the warmth from her run dissolved away. The snow tried to stick her feet to the ground, but her long strides fought against it.

The streets began again, these not so opulent as the ones leading from the castle. Smoke poured from multiple chimneys on the stretches of rooftops. She rushed into lanes and streets crowded with passers by. She knew that everywhere she went, she left an impression on people who would be asked if they had seen a strange woman running past. She had to get into the back streets. But where? This place was enormous.

In the snow, one stone building looked like another. Shops, houses, halls, streets, alleys, lanes, all faded into a blur of grey and dirty, sludgy snow.

She heard a commotion behind her. Without even looking, she knew the guards tried to push through the crowd. Damn it. Her lack of knowledge of this place had allowed them time to catch up. No more tactics. It was time just to run.

She fled through the snow, pushing anyone, old, young, male, female, out of the way. She darted around creatures and carts being pulled through the snow. A man sidestepped her, and a basket of firewood scattered at her feet. Her long legs took her over it with ease. The man bawled a curse at her. She ran on.

The wind began to pick up and rush down through the corridor of the streets. The words, "Stop her," caught up with her, then general shouts and animated conversations closed in on the distinct command.

A dutiful citizen reached out, trying to grab her. She swung her fist. It contacted with something on the way past. A face maybe? She heard a string of curses from the man, but he did not chase her. His curses began to fade, then the wind swept the last of them away.

I need a building to hide in. She glanced at every shop, every house. All seemed too obvious, too open. And there was a risk that someone inside might hand her over to the guards behind.

She turned left down a narrow lane. The houses began to look older, drabbier. Dull colours, rips, stains and dishevelled, greasy hair indicated that poorer people wandered the streets. The snow made everything look clean, but she knew, in summer, the streets would be dirty and unkempt.

She flung into an alleyway with a dead-end. A wide stone staircase ascended to a narrow side door. A body lay in the snow beneath the stairs. How long it had been there, Emme could not tell. The chill of cold preserved it in its blue slack-jaw state.

She quickly studied the corpse. The clothes were tatters. A green alcohol bottle lay in his arms. His beard was long, scruffy. A stuffed sack hung at his back. Perhaps the man was a forgotten citizen, left to die in the cold.

She winced at the idea that flashed into her mind. She made a mess of prints in the snow in all directions at the alley entrance before going up the stairs and sliding down the rail. Then she propped the body to cover the lower wedge behind the stairs, and ducked down into shadows. There she sat, waited.

Time seemed momentarily suspended. She longed to peer around the edge of the stairs and see what was happening. The dead man in front of her, blocking out light and view, made her shiver more than the cold.

She began to make out voices that suggested a disturbance of some kind.

"This way. I think she went this way," a bass male voice said.

She heard voices at the entrance to the alley. "Only a dead street serf down here."

"Lots of prints though," a second voice said.

"Going up the stairs. Come on. Let's try the next alley."

Emme waited an achingly long time. They could be roaming every street, checking every shop. She would have to be patient. Soon her fingers grew numb. The cold crept into her thin boots and made her toes sting. She felt if she stood, the brittle bones in her feet would snap. The cold made her sleepy. Heavy eyelids slid down, and she snapped them open with an angry thought.

She noticed again the sack the dead man carried. She tugged it off his snap-frozen shoulder and rummaged inside. Just dirty rags, an untouched bottle of alcohol, and a moth-eaten jumper.

It would have to do. She pulled out the jumper, noted the rather large hole on the back and down the left shoulder. Stiff from the cold, she worked it on. It clung to her skin. Clearly this was a jumper stolen from a child. In that moment she felt grateful she was thin up top. Of course, the bandages that wound her breasts helped with that – bandages that held the bruised rib Wendaya had given to her a few weeks ago.

Emme shivered and thought of her mother. Wendaya would probably be hand-sewing more of those garments she bartered for food at the village. She would be sitting in the warmth of the summer sun, sipping hot tea and wondering what she could yell at Emme about that evening.

Wendaya would be watching the people go by, lamenting her outcast status, and the life that Emme so cruelly took from her.

Right at that moment, Emme did not miss Wendaya, but she missed the forest and the sunshine. She missed the familiarity. Early that morning, she had been moving through the forest, tracking strangers. Now she was sitting under a cold stone stairway, her bottom in slushy, biting snow, a dead body her only protection from a large gathering of soldiers who wanted to find her. Why would Jaimis possibly bother to bring her here? Maybe this was the man those six weird men had warned her about. She shivered against the cold. Not that the six strange men would have been the better choice to trust, that much was certain.

Emme waited patiently, then warily exited the underside of the stairway. She peeped around the edge of the alleyway. The street was clear of all movements but a woman in a knitted shawl and bonnet turning down a nearby street. She scanned as best she could from her position. Perhaps another alleyway would be her safest choice.

She wished she had warmer clothes. That dead man could have chosen a better jumper to steal.

Emme spotted a break in the buildings. Was that a tiny passageway between the houses? It was worth investigating.

She made a decision and stepped from the cover of the alley, then broke into a run. She heard a little bell tinkle as a door opened.

"There she is," a man's voice said.

Emme glanced over her shoulder to see two red guards exit what looked to be a shop. She broke into a run. She dashed down the main street, past the alley she had hoped to investigate, and aimed solely to pick up speed. Her cold, aching legs hindered her run, but she managed a speed still faster than the guards behind her.

She turned down a side street. A quick glance behind told her she had one chance to hide before the guards rounded the corner and saw where she went. She flew down a thin side alley. Slime covered the walls on either side of her, and the stones of the buildings were rough-cut and odd-shaped. Thick, cheap grouting filled the gaps the irregular rocks left.

A cat jumped out of her way. Clothes flapped from a clothesline above her – just a stick that jutted from a tiny ice-frosted window. She followed the alley. A building stood at the end of it, but the alley turned sharply right. She took the right-hand turn, then swore. A dead end.

The sound of shouting on the street made her realise she had left clear prints down the alleyway. They would quickly find her down here. And if she turned back now, the guards would see her. She would have to climb the wall ahead and go into that narrow window at the top. A gutter edged the roof above her, two storeys up. It jutted out far enough to prevent snow reaching the thin edge of the tiny corridor between the houses. A grated drain sucked down snow spills.

She turned and backtracked a few steps, making sure she left clear prints in the snow, then leapt to the cleared, cobbled edge. Her boot clanged as it struck the drain's metal grating. If lucky, it would seem she had turned around, then followed the edge all the way out of the alley. She slid against the cleared stone, her belly to the wall. She felt the chill of the stone through her angora singlet and the newly acquired jumper. The biting cold stone made her arm-hairs stand and teeth chatter.

She continued sliding sideways along the wall. Shouts close by made her pace quicken.

She neared the far wall and looked quickly for the roughest stones, hoping that handholds and footholds would stand out. The gutter and drain ended, leaving no cleared edging; just three paces of snow between her and the wall. She would have to leap across the snow to vertical slabs of grey sandstone in an attempt to climb.

"Down here," she heard a voice call out. They had found her prints. She had no more time to squander. She had to clear the wall before they found her.

With a lunge of all strength and speed she had, she leapt to the wall hoping against hope that her feet and hands would grip something. She braced herself for the smack of the wall against her bruises.

The instant she jumped, a concealed door opened up in the wall, and she crashed into half-darkness on top of someone who yelped in surprise.

"Shut the damned door!" Emme scrambled to her feet.

She grabbed the edge of the thick stone door and swung it shut. It boomed in the gloomy space. A single candle on a wall bracket guttered and nearly died. When it recovered, it illuminated a tiny, empty room with no other doors than the hidden one.

The young man, flat on his back on the seamless stone floor, sat up, blinked once, eyes wide. "Who in the name of the Almighty are you?"

"I should ask the same about you. What kind of a ridiculous house is this?"

Voices outside forced them into momentary silence. Both watched the doorway guardedly.

"She must have back-tracked out of here," she heard a man say.

"No prints," a second replied.

"She must have slid around the side to avoid making prints."

"Let's go then."

The snow muffled the steps of the guards. The two waited quietly in the room until sure the guards had gone.

The sandy-haired, young man finally stood. Shorter than Emme first assumed, he stood a head height below her. Emme stared at the young man for the first time. He straightened his drab but tidy brown jumper with fastidious attention. He smoothed every crease as if expecting important visitors, then seemed to remember Emme again. The grey eyes locked onto her.

The two just stared at each other until the young man's pink cheeks turned red. He gripped his left and only studded wristband in his other hand, turned it over and over whilst he looked down at the floor as if confused by it. "How did she find our door? I mean, it's very well hidden, and she's not one of us, but she might be new, but then Kye would have told me about her, and –"

"Who are you talking to?" Emme waved a hand in front of his face. "I'm right here. You can ask me directly, you know."

The young man seemed not to hear. "I was going outside, wasn't I? Yes, that's right. I was going outside. And then you . . ." He looked up at her. "Then you came in the door. How did you find the door?"

"I didn't. I was jumping onto the wall, and you opened the door at the right time."

"Jumping onto the wall? Why would you jump onto the wall? There's nothing out there." He stared at the floor again, still trying to piece bits together. He continually turned the treated animal-skin wristband.

"I don't see what the problem is," Emme said. "It's not that hard to work out. I was about to climb up a wall to escape the . . . And what do you have that secret door there for anyway? It's not like there's anything special in this room."

The young man looked up again. "Who was after you?"

"People."

"What people?"

"None of your damned business."

The young man let go of the wristband and swiftly held up palms. "I don't mean any harm by the question. I just might be able to help you. That's what I do. That's what we all do. Were they city guards?"

"What does a city guard look like?"

The freckled, sandy-haired young man blinked. "You don't know what a city guard looks like?"

"Just answer the damned question."

The young man seemed confused about who was questioning who. "City guards wear blue."

"Blue what?"

"Pinafores over their uniforms, and tall suede boots, and they have rapiers too. They like their rapiers."

"These wore red."

"Red? You mean the prince's own guards were chasing you? You must have done something really bad. Are you from the castle?"

"Maybe. Would it matter if I was?"

The young man looked her up and down. "Is there any reason why you're wearing those clothes?"

"I always wear these clothes."

"But women always wear . . . well, they wear modest dresses, not pants. I mean, men wear pants, and not those skin pants you've got. And certainly not tight pants like yours. I mean, not that they look bad or anything, quite good actually." He leered.

Swiftly Emme walloped his stomach with her knuckles.

A whoosh of air escaped his surprised mouth. He doubled over, winded. "What –" He sucked in air. "What was that for?"

"For staring lewdly like that."

"I only meant –" he sucked in more air, "I only meant to be nice." He blushed bright red.

"Well don't bother. Now tell me how to get out of here."

The young man caught his breath and slowly straightened. "It depends on whether you want to go back out onto the street or not."

"Of course I want to go back onto the street. There's no other way out of here."

The young man grinned. "Ahh, looks are always deceiving." He looked her up and down again. "Of course, I would like to show you how to get out of here, but you might be a Black Band, and then I'd be letting in trouble. But you don't look like a Black Band. They'd never dress so obviously. And a city spy wouldn't either. So maybe you're safe."

Emme rolled her eyes. "Stop prattling, and tell me what you mean."

"I suppose if I take you to our quarters and you end up being one of them, we'd have to imprison you."

"Whatever. Just please help me to get out of here. I'm new here, I don't know anything about the city, and someone is after me, and I don't know why."

The young man nodded once, firmly. "Yes – you're exactly the sort of people we try to help. Or should that be 'person'? Well, follow me then." He spun on his heels, took a single step towards the back wall, and traced a hand down a track of stones. His hand contacted a rough protrusion, and he pushed it. A thin, hidden door swung towards them, revealing a dimly lit passage beyond.

The boy blew out the candle on the wall and walked through the deep doorway.

"Well, well. Looks can indeed be deceiving," Emme said. She followed after young man. He hit a button on a nearby wall, and the solid door closed behind them, leaving them alone at the landing of a candle-lit staircase. Their shadow stains shifted along the walls as the candle guttered briefly.

"By the way, I'm Dusty."

Emme stared at him blankly. The young man waited for some recognition. Finally Emme said, "Oh, I see; that's your name. I thought you were telling me you had dusty clothes or something because I leapt on top of you."

The young man let out a laugh that lay between amusement and relief. "No – I was called Dusty because when Kye found me on a dirt-pile as a baby, that's what I was – dusty."

Emme raised a brow fractionally. "Found?"

"I'm an orphan. Most of us are. And your name is?"

"I'm Emme, spelt E double-M E."

The young man, Dusty, watched her curiously for a moment, seemed about to say something, then changed his mind. "Follow me." He headed down the stairs.

"So tell me about this place," Emme said as they stepped.

"We're the street kids – the street rats." His tone belied a belief that Emme would know exactly what he meant.

"The who?"

"You haven't heard of us? Well, we used to be Black Bands, or heading for it, but Kye pulled us out. He's an amazing guy. I'll take you to see him because he'll know if you're one of them or not. He's clever like that."

The stairs met another landing, then veered right. At the bottom, Emme could see the beginnings of a hallway.

"Black Bands?" Emme said. "Who are the Black Bands?"

"Goodness, you are from far away. When did you get into the city?"

"This morning."

Dusty stopped swiftly, stared at her. "This morning? There's no way you could have walked the entire city in one morning. It takes me nearly a full working day from here, but I know all the shortcuts."

"One day? I thought you people used those black void things."

"What black void?"

"Never mind. So tell me about these Black Bands." The two started down the stairs again.

"They're the people that society rejected; the orphans, the abused, the poor. The tough ones, the skilled ones, join the Black Bands, and they steal and murder for a living. They don't choose the Black Bands; the Black Bands choose them. They're responsible for just about all of the city's corruption." The stairs reached a T-intersection. "They practically own the place."

"And this Kye – he pulled you out?" An unsealed doorway to their left guarded a large room crowded with rows of tables and chairs. A display reminiscent of her village square at a feast, Emme decided as she stepped into the room.

She had a brief moment to notice the spacious kitchen area straight ahead, partitioned by a bench below a square arch, before Dusty moved to a second door two paces to her right.

Dusty opened the chipped door for her. "Yep. He teaches us things. Teaches us to read and write in the hope that one day we'll get back into society. Helps us make an honest living."

Emme stepped into the junction of dim windowless corridors stretching directly ahead and left. Straight ahead, uniform doors lined the left of the passageway; a boot-scuffed straight wall marked the right. Several children, tidy despite drab clothing colours and styles, entered and exited the doors. Some stopped to observe her, then went on their way.

Dusty took her down the shorter passageway, empty but for one left door. No windows, only half-used candles lit the cold space. She realised she was underground in an immense, sophisticated furbished basement.

"Honest? If it's so honest, why are you hiding?" Emme tried to peer through the gap in the door on their left before being forced to continue past it.

"The Black Bands stop us from going out much. They try to kill us because we try to stop *them*. We try to sort out the Black Band issue, and until we do, we have to hide down here. But we don't kill, and we don't steal anymore."

The straight path of the shorter corridor met a rough white-painted corner, then resumed right. She turned with Dusty and followed him along a mirror image of the room-lined corridor. "We have to be quiet down here. Red and Timus are sleeping."

They drifted down the hallway. Emme soon realised the rooms behind the time-scarred doors were bedrooms with rows of bunks. "So, this Kye – was he a Black Band?"

"No one knows, and he doesn't say and so no one asks. We don't really care, you know. He's a good guy, and it doesn't matter what he's done in the past. Kye always says that to us. That it doesn't matter what we've done in the past; it matters what we try to do with our future."

"Sounds like a bit of a bore," she muttered.

Dusty seemed not to have heard. "Hey, Lydia." A lithe girl with golden curls stopped before she entered her room. "Where's Kye?"

"Gone up top with Davis. Some problems with the Black Bands. Who's that with you, Dusty?" The girl looked Emme up and down.

"Emme. She needs our help. Did Kye say when he'd be back?"

"Not that I know of."

"Thanks."

The girl nodded, her lustrous curls bobbing, then entered her confined room. Emme briefly heard a group of giggling girls, then the closed door sealed in the sound.

"He's gone up top – to the city," Dusty said.

"I do believe I was standing right next to you when the girl said that."

Dusty blushed bright red. "Yes. Silly me. I'm a bit scatter-brained sometimes, you know."

"I noticed," Emme said dryly.

"Well, I'd best show you around for now, I suppose. Would you like to see it all?"

"I guess so."

Dusty turned to retrace steps. "Follow me then." As they strolled, he pointed to the identical hallway doors, now on their left. "These are the bedrooms. There are two corridors of bedrooms. That room at the far end of this corridor," he thumbed behind him, "is Kye's office. His bedroom is off that."

"How many people live here?"

56

His chest puffed out slightly. "Sixty-two, and we grow every year."

"And you all used to be Black Bands?"

"Not all. I wasn't. Kye found me as a baby – but I said that didn't I – and he brought me here. Kye and I are like brothers. He practically raised me."

"No wonder you go on about him."

"Oh, I'm not the only one. We all like Kye. He saved us all and gave us a new life. There isn't a single person down here who'd speak badly of him. Not a single one of us. You'll like him too. It's hard not to like him."

"Why? Is he made of gold?"

Dusty's brows dipped; his lips flattened, thinned out. "You don't seem to like people, do you? I don't have Kye's keen eye for these things, but I can at least tell that about you."

"People are nothing but trouble." Emme's brown eyes flickered darkly.

"*You're* a person."

"Yes, and I bring nothing but trouble. Just ask my mother."

"So you're not an orphan?"

"Why would I be an orphan? Is it only orphans who get in trouble with the guards?"

"I just wondered why you were in the city alone, that's all. It's not an insult down here to be called an orphan. Maybe up there in the real world, but not down here. It's a badge of honour. Is your mother in trouble too? If she is, Kye will go and find her. He's good like that. He'd send whoever it took to see that people were safe."

"My mother is just fine. In fact, come tomorrow morning, she'll be the happiest woman alive."

"Why tomorrow morning?"

"When she realises I've gone."

Dusty's brows shot up. "Did you run away?"

"Yes – no. Well, it's complicated. So what's this place?" They re-entered the room with disorderly rows of diverse tables and chairs.

"This is where we all eat. Kye insists we all eat together. And we play games in here too, and talk. Sometimes we dance. Some of the people here play instruments. We're all a big family in here. It's not often we get to eat but when we do, we all share the food. No one is to be selfish and keep food to themselves, and the weakest of us get the food first if there isn't enough to go around. Kye makes sure of that. Kye's always –"

"You do talk a lot don't you," Emme cut in.

Dusty merely grinned widely. "Yes, I'm always being told that. You'll get used to it. Everyone else has."

Emme stared at the long timber bench separating the dining area from an enormous dull stone kitchen. Tarnished copper pots hung from a chopped ladder suspended from the ceiling. A vast fireplace sat empty, neglected. Beside it, a fire in a smaller hearth licked at a generous pockmarked, black pot hanging from a hook in stone bricks. Wicker baskets of onions and garlic sat on timber shelves opposite the bench.

"Anyway, I'll show you the rest of this place." He took Emme out the other door and down the first corridor, past the base of the stairs. Beyond the staircase, the hall stretched straight, the right side adorned with nine timber doors. Dusty opened each one. Three held baths and washbasins, two tight rooms were latrines, and one room contained sheets, towels, spare clothes. The rest were storage areas heaped with weapons; rapiers, daggers, whips, broadswords, spears and barbed metal balls on chains. Heavy iron hats, metal replicas of the guards' feathered wide-brim hats, sat in stacks. An open chest of dangerous three-pronged spikes rested nearest one of the doors.

Emme wondered that they could afford so much iron here. Although used by her village, bronze and bone remained the most common.

"All confiscated from the Black Bands," Dusty explained. "We try to stop them getting weapon supplies."

Dusty led her to the door at the far end of the hallway. They stepped inside a large muggy laundry where two young boys and a girl Dusty's age worked over open vats of boiled water to wring out clothes and sheets. Another young woman beat a rug that hung over a thin piece of rope strung from one end of the room to the other. Dust plumed from the rug, momentarily visible before heavy steam camouflaged it. The smell of pitch, used to seal the timber wash barrels, clashed with lemon and caustic soda. A large fire in an enormous hearth to Emme's left, scorched the base of three colossal iron pots.

The damp heat of the room contrasted with the dry chill of the corridor beyond, and Emme felt fingers and toes begin to defrost and sting.

Dusty took her back down the chilly corridor, through the empty dining hall, then out the second door. There he turned left and left again through the next door. They entered a room full of bookshelves, most empty. Tables met into squares, totalling seven squares, each with its own black candelabrum of candles burning low in their sockets. An empty, sooty fireplace, framed by black stone, sat on the far wall. The room held a single damaged tapestry of a feast of fruit against a backdrop of hills. Green, blue and red rags converged in a thick rug that blanketed the middle of the room.

Children and young adults intently read books parted beneath candles. Four girls giggled and gossiped in a corner, books covering their faces where hands might have been. Their animated conversation ceased abruptly when they noticed

Emme. They whispered whilst their eyes peered secretively at Emme from above their books.

"This is where we all learn and read," Dusty said. "It's our quiet area for anyone who is studying or discussing things."

"What are you looking at?" Emme said loudly, and the girls jolted, startled. They hid faces behind books, pretending sudden interest in the words on the page. All other heads flicked up from books to stare.

"You'll get a lot of stares dressed like that, Emme," Dusty said, then swiftly took a step back, hands raised. "Don't hit me." Emme's hands had not moved. "I only meant to explain. But you'll need to forgive people. No one here judges others, really. Well, some might, but we've all been misunderstood by people up top at one stage, and so we know what it's like."

"What else do you want me to see?" Emme said, face tight. She pushed past Dusty and out of the room.

Dusty showed her the other corridor where doors lined the left wall. "All just rooms. In case you're confused, beyond that wall there," he pointed down the corridor, "is the laundry. We access it via the hall on the other side of this wall." He patted the solid white wall to his right. "And in the laundry, there's another hidden door and another staircase leading to a room at the top. We have three of them. The one you came in, the one in the laundry, and one off the library. I would have pointed it out but you marched off so quickly."

"And that's it?"

"That's all we need. Just a library, bedrooms, eating area and laundry. And the storage and wash areas."

"It's more than I have. So I've seen it all then?"

"Actually, you haven't seen Kye's office. Or his room. His room is the door at the end of the other sleeping quarters. I was taking you there, but then Lydia told me that Kye had gone up to the city and . . . but you were there of course."

"So what now?"

"Well, we sit and wait for Kye to return. He could be hours; he could be days. Depends what the trouble was. Maybe I should show you to a room; you could be here a while. And would you like some warmer clothes? We're on wood rations here, so we only light the fires at night. It does get cold down here, doesn't it?"

"Not as cold as up there."

"Yes, well, that's true. Winters are really bleak here in the city, in this part of the country. So would you like a hot drink? One thing we always have in abundance is hot drinks. We have hot mint and tea."

"Tea. I would kill somebody for a tea."

Dusty's brow arched faintly. "I hope you didn't mean that literally."

"Of course not."

"Thank the Almighty. Follow me." He led her back to the kitchen to the tiny fire smouldering in its socket.

"If you're on wood rations, how come this one is lit?" Emme asked.

"Kye insists on having it running all the time for hot water. That and the laundry fires for baths. We may not always have lots of food but Kye insists we stay warm with hot drinks and hot baths. He won't have anyone freezing to death for the sake of a few bits of wood."

"Makes sense, I suppose."

Dusty opened an under-bench cupboard, drew out two honey-coloured timber mugs. He placed them on the bench, then retrieved a large metal canister of mixed tealeaves and sugar. He put a generous pinch in each mug, then ladled hot water and

61

handed a mug to Emme. "We don't have strainers here, so it'll be lumpy."

Emme took the mug, grateful to the tea for its existence. "I'm used to it."

"Have a seat anywhere you like." He gestured to the many mismatched chairs and bench-seats beyond the kitchen counter.

Emme chose a hard-backed chair closest to the weak warmth from the fire and inhaled the fragrant steam drifting from her drink. The mug's heat began to defrost her fingers; the slow sting made her wince.

Dusty attempted questions about her home, but Emme ignored them pointedly. He soon ceased probing. Slowly they sipped tea whilst Dusty nattered about some of the people living in the strange semi-darkness of this headquarters, as Dusty called it. Emme stopped listening to him whilst she savoured the warmth and aroma of her drink.

A few sips of the tea remained when the golden-haired girl, Lydia, burst into the dining hall. "Kye's back," she puffed, "if you still want him. He's in his office."

Dusty stood at once, his drink forgotten. "Let's go," he said to Emme.

"Wait a minute – I haven't finished my drink."

"Well hurry up then," Dusty said with an excited impatience.

"Anyone would think you were about to catch a glimpse of the Almighty you keep mentioning. Sit down. I'm going to finish my drink at my own pace."

Dusty plunged hands into a fold over his chest and slumped onto the bench-seat with a childish scowl.

Let him think what he liked. Emme needed time to sort her thoughts before she went to visit this mysterious Kye. Too many strange things had already happened to her today. The last thing she needed was to meet one more enemy unprepared.

3

Dusty halted before the narrow iron-decorated door at the corridor's end. "I'd better go in first." He knocked lightly on the scratched oak. A polite male voice called out permission to enter. Dusty opened the door partially, squeezed through the gap and secretively closed it behind him.

Emme allowed Dusty his clandestine indulgence without comment. She heard unintelligible voices, one animated, the other calm, quiet. The voices spoke for some time, and impatiently she began to pace. A little way down the hall, two older boys strolled from their room, hands stuffed into pockets. They stopped swiftly, stared at Emme until Emme's return stares unnerved them. They hurriedly feigned brave disinterest and made their way to the library.

At last Dusty opened the door; put his head around the thick timber edge. "You can come in now."

Emme shoved the door back and, shoulders squared, stepped into the room. Her eyes locked with a pair of soft blue-green eyes. Dark red lips sat flat, unresponsive, but those blue-green eyes watched Emme curiously. His eyes did not roam her body as every other pair had. He simply gazed at her face.

Emme felt a shock of betrayed expectations. Nothing like she had imagined, he was young, possibly late twenties, calm, gentle-looking. She had visualised a rugged, middle-aged male with a bulky frame, hoards of weapons on his belt, and a scruff of dark stubble or a thick beard. Only an elegant rapier sat against a wall in its casing with a brown sword belt still attached to it; and his defined jaw was entirely too smooth, his softly curled dark, almost black hair too neat, his hands too well-kept, to be a man of action.

"Come in, Emme," he said calmly. His steady, kind voice blew away the last of her presumptions. "Have a seat." His flat, upturned palm pointed to a high-backed chair opposite the desk his legs were tucked under. Two bookshelves, with mismatched collections of books, guarded his back. A lantern, hanging from a ceiling hook, illuminated the desk and its globe and neat stacks of papers. The lamp gently lit a sizeable, detailed brown map on the left wall. A closed door to her right, probably leading to the bedroom Dusty mentioned, sat mostly in shadows.

Emme hesitated. Dusty excused himself and left the room, closed the door carefully behind him. The soft click of the metal latch sent a prickle over Emme's skin. She could run if necessary, but she would have to waste time on the door first.

"I just want to talk to you," the handsome, dark-haired man said. "Nothing sinister."

Emme scraped the chair as far back from the desk as possible without creating suspicion, and sat down. "So you must be the Kye that that Dusty boy keeps prattling about."

The man's lips curled into a faint smile. "I'm Kye, yes." He offered his hand, thumb up. Unsure of what to do with it, Emme slowly mirrored his movements. He gripped her palm and shook it. She swiftly retracted her hand as if he had burnt it. Unperturbed, he said, "I hear you're in trouble, Emme. Do you want to tell me about it?"

How much should she tell him? Just enough. He could be the enemy. "I arrived in the city recently. I ended up at the castle – it's a long story – and then these guards with red tunics on started chasing me. I ended up here. Another long story."

"I'm going to need to hear that long story, Emme. My advice to you is to just be honest. There isn't much that shocks me anymore, and I can't help you if I don't know the full story."

"And you just expect me to trust you?"

"Do you have anyone else you can trust?" The question was genuine. "Perhaps I can help you get to some people you feel more comfortable with."

Emme weighed his apparent authenticity with a critical squint. Jaimis had been more than convincing – for whatever reason he chose to lie to her. Nothing had been as it seemed all day.

"I – I don't know anyone here."

"What about outside the city?"

"I don't know anyone outside the city either."

"Where do you come from, Emme? Can you at least tell me that?" His tone held a tremendous amount of patience. He did seem to really want to help, but then, Jaimis had too.

Emme sighed. "I wish I knew where I was from, but I can't tell you that until I find out where I am."

Kye's eyes narrowed slightly. He seemed to be considering her statement. "You're in the city of Endoria."

"What country?"

"Kildes. Have you had an accident, Emme?"

"No – why?"

"I was wondering about the bruises on your hands and neck, and you seem to have lost some of your memory."

Emme found herself feeling self-conscious. She reached up to attempt to cover the bruises on her neck but only exposed the ones on her wrists. A flush of hot pride stiffened her. She had not felt self-conscious since childhood and was not about to start now.

"Tell me something," Emme said. "Do you like your prince?"

Kye considered his response. "I don't have a love for him, no. Not many of us do. He isn't an honourable man."

Emme warily assessed Kye's face for honesty. "You're not just saying that?"

"You could be killed for saying that in this country. We don't mention his name unless we're prepared to take the consequences. And we certainly don't say it in context of not liking him. It's too dangerous. I'm telling you this because I'm hoping it means you will trust me."

Emme relaxed back into the chair. "He's the pig who brought me here."

"Who? The prince?"

"Yes. Prince Jai –"

"Don't say his name, Emme," Kye cut in. "It's too dangerous. Just call him the prince."

"Why? Is Dusty going to report you?"

Kye's brows dipped fractionally. "You're really not from around here, are you."

She shook her head.

"So how did the prince bring you here and why?"

"How? Through one of those black portal things you use. And why? I haven't worked that out yet. This morning I was roaming around in my forest, tracking intruders, when I came across these six strange men, and they kept going on about 'him' finding me, whoever 'him' was, and how they would keep me safe. I ran away, and then I found Jai – the prince, and he said he'd help me run away from my mother, who gave me the bruises. Then he opened up this black hole and pushed me in. I ended up at the castle. He locked me in his room, but I ran away." Emme took a breath to chase away welling indignant anger. She deflected with, "I'm starting to sound like that Dusty boy."

Kye took a moment to think over her words. "Okay, let's go back a little. You came from a forest. Do you know which forest?"

"No, but it's summer there; not this cursed winter."

Kye's brows rose slightly. "Now you've surprised me. You must live very far away indeed. Do you know anything about the world and how the seasons work?"

"No."

He stood, showed Emme the faded globe on the end of his desk. His index finger tapped his country, a large brown spread across the sphere. Slowly he explained how the winter in the northern hemisphere occurred at a different time of the year as the southern hemisphere. He pointed to the unmapped seas below the globe's midline. "Your country must be down here somewhere. To sail it by ship would take months, possibly years."

Emme gaped. "No – you must be mistaken."

Kye shook his head and sat down neatly in his chair. He shifted the chair into position at the desk. "I'm not mistaken. I don't know how the prince got you here, or why, but it troubles me very deeply that he was able to. I will have to look into that. So do you know the name of your country?"

"I once heard it was called Saschuwa."

"That doesn't mean anything to me. It must be the uncharted lands. Do you have a prince or country ruler?"

"Yes."

"And do you know his or her name?"

"No. Why would I need to know that?"

He watched her curiously. "I take it politics don't touch you where you live."

"Politics? You mean like when clan chieftains war?"

"Something like that." He seemed to be thinking to himself for a moment. Then he leant elbows on the table. "Now, tell me about those other six men."

Emme described them, their clothes, mannerism, hand tattoos. "And one of them was called An-something."

"Anderson?"

"That's it."

Kye leant back in his chair and exhaled slowly. "The Ashrones – high priests of sorts. Also very bad men. You did the right thing to run away from them. So you don't know what they wanted with you?"

"I haven't got a clue. I was just minding my own business this week, and then the strange prints appeared. They seemed to materialise from nothing. All week I tracked them, and now this –" She gestured to the room around her.

"So do you want to go home?"

Emme considered briefly. "Not necessarily. I don't like home very much. My forest, yes, but home, no."

"Why did your mother beat you?" Kye seemed more concerned than curious.

Emme remained silent. Oddly, her fingers began to fidget in her lap.

"So tell me what happened when you arrived in the city." Emme knew Kye had tactfully changed the subject.

"Well, I arrived in the man's bedroom. He told me he had to go and tell others I was here or guards might try to kill me. Then he locked me in his bedroom. I knew something wasn't right when I looked out the window and saw Jai – the prince's sister. Are you sure I can't say his name?"

"He'll know it if you do."

Emme frowned, puzzled. "What's that supposed to mean?"

"I'll explain in a minute. Go on."

"Well, the prince described his sister one way, but she looked totally different. I knew he was lying and wondered what else he had lied about. I thought maybe he'd brought me to his room to violate me and that's why he'd locked me in there. So I escaped."

"Well, I'm not sure what all of that means, or what you mean by his sister, but I'm sure I can get to the bottom of it. So how did you end up here with Dusty?"

"First tell me how the prince will know it if I say his name."

"He's the heir to the throne of Kildes, an Endorian – a family who've ruled Kildes for centuries. The eldest child of each family has the ability to hear when others talk about him or, in some extreme cases, think about him. It's enough of a risk to mention the term, 'the prince', but Kildes has many princes, and as Kildes has about ten-million people, there are probably many people every day who use the word 'prince', and it can often confuse him. His name, however, is a very different matter. Down here, in this place, we are not in too much danger because the thoughts are buried a bit in this basement. But we never risk it. And you would do well to try and not visualise his face – especially if he's looking for you."

"Why would anyone need a ridiculous ability like that?"

"It's a very valuable ability if used properly. Now, tell me about how you found us here, Emme."

Emme briefly explained, and Kye smiled his soft smile. "A humorous story." He ran the story around in his mind before adding, "Now, is there anything else you can think of that you should tell me?"

"No. That's it."

"Maybe you'd better tell me about yourself, then – your home and your family or background. Perhaps there's a clue there."

"There's not much to tell. I come from a large village. My chieftain is the most powerful out of all the forest chieftains. I don't know my father, but my mother isn't very popular in the village."

"What about your mother's background?"

"My mother used to be the daughter of an important couple in the village. They died of a fever when I was a little girl. She was very well liked and beautiful. She was supposed to marry someone in the village. I don't know who. But she's alone now."

"Why?" The blue-green eyes followed Emme as she pretended interest in the features of the room. "Well, perhaps when you get to know me better, you can trust me with that story."

Emme met his gaze again. "So what should I do now?"

"Well, I can find you a room. Are you a good sleeper?"

"Yes."

He watched her face briefly, seemed to search for truth as if it really mattered.

"I usually sleep on a thin mat in front of the fire or under a tree in the forest. I can sleep anywhere."

"Good, because I was going to give you the room next door to this one, and the room on the other side of it is full of young girls who giggle and chatter throughout the night. The walls aren't very thick between the bedrooms."

"So how are you going to find out about me and why I'm here? Do you know the prince?"

"I have some connections in the city. If anyone will know what's going on, they will. Would you like me to get you some sheets and blankets so you can set up your bed?"

"I guess so."

Kye stood, then halted briefly when Emme said, "I have nowhere to go, you know. I don't know how long I'm going to be here."

"You can stay for the rest of your life if you need to. The rest of us probably will. Although my aim is to have most of the young ones back into society before they're too much older."

"But you can't because of the Black Bands?"

Kye nodded. "Yes, that's right. Dusty told you about them did he?"

"He did."

"Well, there's probably a lot you're going to have to learn about this place, but I won't tell you all about it now. It will only confuse you. Perhaps you'd like to meet again tomorrow when I get back, and we'll talk some more?"

Emme shrugged. "Whatever." She stood, then stopped, eyes

narrowed. "Why – what are you doing this afternoon?"

"I think I might go talk to my contacts. Some of them are an inn-stay away."

"An inn-stay?"

"One of those many things to explain." Kye moved around the desk and gestured politely to the door. "After you."

She moved out of the room, waited just beyond the doorway in the dim lantern-lit hall. Kye opened the door to the nearest bedroom for her, and she peered into the darkness.

"I'll have Dusty bring a lantern for you. The beds are comfortable, but you might want to dust them off a bit. They haven't been used for a long time. I'll just go and get you some sheets."

Emme nodded and watched Kye walk away down the hall. He was tall, taller than he had seemed from his sitting position. Over six foot, with strong, wide shoulders and a straight body. His long legs took almost graceful strides, not the robust strides of the village men. But then, the men of the village walked like they had something to prove, as if their manhood depended on it. They would walk, chew grass roots, and spit out the excess.

Emme might prefer to dress like a man and engage in men's jobs and men's fights, but she abhorred the spitting. That and the drinking.

Emme noted Kye's clean clothes, the buttoned white shirt, the brown pants, the black boots. How different he was from any male in the village with their rugged skins, furs, and food-stained clothes over bulky frames.

Emme tugged at the ragged jumper on her body. She knew she did not fit in here, but it would have to do. It was home now. At least until Kye worked out what she was doing here.

Dusty turned up with a bright lantern and slung it on a rusted hook near the door. It lit up a very narrow room, long, with just a double-bunk on the left wall and a cupboard beyond that. Between the bunks and the wall, Emme had just enough room to walk the length without touching anything. Beyond the cupboard with its back to the left wall, was a narrow space, unfilled despite room for at least a second bunk. She might be able to bring one of the dining room chairs in here so she could sit somewhere without anyone staring at her.

"Not bad, getting a room to yourself," Dusty said. "Of course, Kye does, but the rest of us don't. Not that we mind." He placed a flintbox and a bottle of lamp oil on the floor beneath the lantern. "We're used to sharing. It's nice to have people to talk to. I could imagine it would get very boring down here if we didn't."

"It's not very fair that Kye gets his own room."

"Well, Kye's always up late and having meetings and the like, and some of the meetings are private, and we wouldn't want to interrupt them by walking through the office all the time to get to our room. And Kye doesn't come out of his office much during the day. He's always reading and thinking. We'd get distracting for him. No, we'd *be* distracting. Kye's always teaching us to speak properly. Anyway, so Kye doesn't really like anyone taking this room so he doesn't keep anyone awake when he comes and goes a lot."

"Do you ever have a sentence without Kye's name in it?" Emme ran a hand along the bunks. She lifted her palm and inspected it. Not too much dust.

She heard Dusty laugh, then say, "I'm just so proud of him. He's like my brother, you know. But then, I did say that earlier, didn't I."

Emme walked to the cupboard. "How old are you, Dusty?" She pulled back the creaky mahogany doors and peered inside. The shelves lay empty.

"Nearly seventeen. Why?"

"You don't act it." Emme closed the cupboard and examined the space beyond it. Dust and a dead cockroach lay on the floor.

"Well, they do say that to me a lot. But none of the girls seem to mind. I still attract the girls, you know. More than the others do."

Emme turned and peered at Dusty from beneath her brows. Dusty blushed brightly and grinned.

"How old are most of the people down here?" Emme went and sat on the lower bunk and bounced a few times to test the softness. It gave a little, then held with the timber slats underneath.

"The youngest is five. She's a sweety. The oldest is Halder. He's fifty-five. He helps Kye a lot. There are six around Kye's – your age. The two girls teach us. They live in the building in that alley you first came down. That means they're the only ones who see us coming and going. One of them has a boyfriend." He smiled to himself. "It's very sweet. The four guys go with Kye a lot. The rest of us are my age – under twenty. It's only ever the younger ones that want to get out of the Black Bands or don't want to get involved in the first place. The older ones are too set in their ways. And too risky, as Kye would say. They could easily be spies. Black Band spies who could tell them where we are and give us away."

"You don't think the younger ones could possibly be spies?"

"They have to go through some pretty tough tests before we let them down here. Of course, they don't know they're being tested. But Kye's really good with that sort of thing. He just seems to know if someone's a spy or not. He's very streetwise – for someone of his social class."

"What social class? He's down here too, isn't he?"

Kye returned, ending the conversation abruptly. He placed sheets, blankets, a pillow, and a fresh jumper on the bed. Emme stared at the pillow. She had never had a pillow in her life – a luxury her mother refused her.

Emme ran her hand over the striped pillowcase. She had often wondered what it would be like to sleep with one. Now she would find out. In that moment, it struck her that she was finally free of her mother – no more of her mother's cruel ways and unreasonable demands.

"Dusty can help you make the bed," Kye said. "Then I might get him to continue what I sent him up top for in the first place." The statement seemed a gentle reminder.

Dusty slapped his forehead. "I clean forgot. I was supposed to be buying food. We're a bit low at the moment," he explained to Emme. "Some of the young girls earned some money with some cleaning work they did yesterday, and Halder was paid some money he was owed."

Kye was watching Emme. "I'm going to see what I can find out about you, Emme. I hope to return tomorrow with some news. Don't worry, we'll get to the bottom of this."

"Whatever," Emme said with a casual shrug.

"You're most welcome." Kye's lips turned into slight smile. His eyes danced at her briefly then he disappeared down the hallway.

Emme scowled after him.

Dusty grinned at the space left by Kye as if the man still stood there with his teasing eyes.

"And what are you grinning at?" Emme glared at him.

"He doesn't often joke like that, you know – he's so serious all the time. No, not serious. More just thoughtful. He always seems to have something on his mind, but that's perfectly understandable with all the things going on in the city at the moment. Well, better get going and get us some food or we won't have any dinner."

Emme watched him go, then gratefully closed the door behind him, leaving herself alone in the dimness. The smell of musty mattresses and dust swelled in the confined space.

She held the woollen jumper up to lantern light. Weighty and a little oily with lanolin, it was neither feminine nor masculine in fawn. It would suffice.

She yanked off the shredded jumper, made a brief inspection of her bruises. Stale, yellow-green bruises interspersed with fresher blue-tinged stains. New or old, now that the numbing cold wore off, each reminded her terribly of their presence. She shrugged and worked the new jumper on, felt the instant warmth of the prickly wool. She rolled down the tall neck of it, then flattened onto the bed.

She lay, completely bored for what seemed hours, until a commotion carried down the hallway – voices, scurrying. Someone pounded on doors and shouted into rooms. She lay very still and listened as the bellowing voice worked its way down the hall. Finally someone banged with the padded side of a fist on her door. It rattled in its loose socket. "Dinner's up," a deep, gruff voice shouted.

Emme sat upright and listened warily for further sounds. "Did you hear me?" the voice called loudly. "I said, 'Dinner's up'. Dusty asked me to bring you to the dining hall."

Emme got up and opened the door, stared up at a giant man dressed entirely in black. A black head of shaggy hair flecked with grey, and a stark black beard on white skin, added to his burly appearance. She wondered if she had been tricked and this was the Kye she had imagined.

"I'm Halder." The man grabbed Emme's hand, smothered it totally it his expansive one and shook it roughly, warmly. He reminded Emme of a bear turned into a man – tame but not harmless. "Good to meet you, Emme, spelt E double-M E." He broke into a huge grin of large, yellowing teeth and spun on his big feet. "Follow me."

Emme blinked and watched the man's heavy departing steps. She could almost see the air part in his wake.

He did not seem to have noticed she was not following. She shrugged to herself, ran to catch up.

Animated people, laughing and gesturing excitedly, quickly crammed around the old, scratched tables.

"Any table will do, Emme," the man-bear said. "You can sit with me if you like." He swung tree-trunk legs over the bench-seat and slid to the middle, patted the space next to him.

Emme sat down cautiously, knowing that people in the room stared.

"They always stare at newcomers," the man announced to her. He smiled a large, warm smile. "You'll be fine. Just be yourself."

She turned a cold face to him. "I don't intend to be anything but."

The man slapped Emme playfully on the back. Her body lurched forward under the force of it. "Good for you," he said loudly, then turned to the kitchens, roared, "Bring on the food." Several boys exited the kitchens and positioned baskets of bread and timber trays of boiled potatoes beside dishes of butter on the tables. Rutted metal plates were swiftly passed around, and people dove for the food. Laughter and intense excitement filled the room.

"They don't get much food," Halder explained loudly in her ear. She flinched at the volume.

"You don't need to shout," she said, face sharp.

Halder seemed not to have heard. He reached for the bread and tore off a generous chunk from the nearest loaf. He peeled the portion into two. With a crooked fork, he skewered a potato and shoved the potato between the halves of bread. Using the same fork, he dunked it into the butter and scooped a substantial slab of it. He wiped it onto the hot potato, jabbed the fork back into the potato pile as if killing it, then sat down and bit through the huge sandwich.

"Help yourself, Emme," he said with a mouth engorged with food.

Emme pushed a youngster out of the way and repeated Halder's movements. She hungrily ate every last bit of bread, then launched back for seconds. She matched Halder's movements when he went back for seconds by groping for thirds.

"My, my – you have a massive appetite for a girl," Halder said, eyes grinning. "Good to see. Although you might find it a little tough down here with irregular meals."

"I can cope with irregular meals, just not small ones." She bit into her thirds.

Several older girls began to stack plates, and Emme swiftly grabbed another wedge of bread before they whisked the basket away.

"Fourths. I'm out-eaten." Halder's lips parted into a huge grin that showed potato in the gummy corners of his teeth. "I haven't been out-eaten in here before."

Emme held her bread close to her chest as if any minute one of the servers would try to take it away. She tore chunks and stuffed the portions in her mouth. Minutes after the last of the food had been consumed, Halder belched noisily. Emme laughed at the open disgust on several girls' faces at the table. She might not belch like a man, but she at least refused to be so alarmed at their table habits.

Halder's after-dinner manners set off a crude competition amongst the boys at the table that quickly spread through the room. Not much changed from country to country, she noted with a roll of her eyes. Halder guffawed and outranked them all with a second belch.

A symbolic rhythmical tapping on a metal plate swiftly silenced the room. Emme peered around to see who made the sound.

All eyes seemed to be looking at Dusty and his table crowded with young girls. Dusty stood, and the many pairs of female eyes at the table gazed up admiringly at him. He cleared his throat. "Ladies and gentlemen," he said formally, and a chuckle broke out. His eyes smiled as he said, "I wish to introduce to you our newest member. She has come to us from very far away and could

77

be staying with us for quite some time. I want everyone to make her feel welcome. Her name is Emme, spelt E double-M E." Dusty gestured to Emme, and she glared at him for the attention.

The room broke into a mix of applause and the sound of implement butts banging against tables.

"Okay," Dusty said, "bring on the drinks."

The room launched into an uproar of cheers.

"Cider," Halder bellowed in her ear, making her jump.

"Will you stop doing that," she snapped loudly. "I'm right here; you don't need to shout."

He only grinned, his large, slightly crooked teeth showing in all their yellow splendour.

"We don't get cider very often," the boy beside her said. "It's a real treat when we do."

"Only wish Kye is here," another boy said.

"Was," the first boy corrected. "Was here."

"No, *were*," a sharp-eyed girl put in haughtily.

The two boys shrugged it away.

"They're all learning to speak correctly," Halder said not so loudly. "It helps them up there." His eyes flicked upwards as if the ceiling were the city.

Hands eagerly passed around metal mugs and flagons of cider. Even the youngest of them held up dented mugs for some of the mild alcoholic drink.

"Not having any, missy?" Halder asked when Emme declined.

"Don't touch the vile stuff."

"Good – more for me." He poured himself a generous amount, then filled her mug and slid it over to his. He seemed little concerned for her reasons, and Emme felt momently grateful she did not have to evade.

Dinner ended, replaced by conversations that continued long into the night. Emme left early, disturbed by the number of people wanting to talk to her, to ask her questions. No one in the village had ever wanted to talk to her other than to utter snide remarks or impart important information to their forest tracker.

She began to grow wary of their niceties and interest in her. She wandered back to her room, heard her lonely boots on the untreated pale oak floor. The sound unsettled her, reminded her that her boots should be crunching the dirt road to her cabin, not clacking on a timber hallway.

She entered her cold room, heard voices through the thin right wall – young, female voices – but could not distinguish words. The girls had returned to their room before she did, and, it seemed as she listened a little longer, had invited male guests.

She lay down on the unmade bed, inhaled dust discharged from the mattress by her movements. She stared at the bunk above and immediately a whirl of thoughts flooded her mind. Had she done the right thing to talk to Kye? No one was ever nice to anyone for no reason, at least not to her. That prince had been no exception. The cool green eyes of Jaimis flashed from her memories, and she quickly tossed the image away. If he could sometimes sense when people thought of him, then she did not want to be the one who alerted him to this place.

No wonder the man had known of Emme's presence behind the tree in the forest. She had been staring straight at him, and he could hear her thoughts. With no one else in her country that could possibly be thinking of him, bar the six disturbing men, how could he not hear her thoughts.

No, she shouldn't be thinking about him like this. She tried to think of other matters, but the mystery of her strange arrival in – where was it? – Endoria? – kept pushing into her mind. The more she tried to suppress it with other thoughts, the more it longed to rise to the surface like an apple in a water barrel being held under by a hand.

She hoped Kye would find out something. There had to be a simple explanation for it all, although it escaped her why a man would travel through a strange black gate all the way to the bottom of the world just to get her. For that matter, why would six men – Ash-somethings – be bothered to come and get her too?

It must have been a mistake. They must have been looking for someone else and grabbed the wrong girl. They probably got lost in that black tunnel and found themselves in the wrong forest. Yes, that must have been it. Mystery solved.

But did they know that? Would they keep looking for her thinking she was the girl they wanted? Or perhaps they had realised their error and she was safe to move about the city again.

She decided tomorrow she would go up to the city and see, maybe listen a little. If it seemed the guards were still looking for her, she could run back here. If they weren't interested in her, she would know they had realised their mistake. Simple. She was sure Kye would return to confirm her words.

She patted the dagger in the rarely removed pouch, then tucked hands under her head and sighed. Yes, tomorrow she would go out to the city and look around. She just might find out something for herself.

4

Emme woke to an alien darkness, the sound of laughter. She sat up abruptly, sensed the confines of something above. Groping, she felt slats of timber overhead. The laughter swelled, then dissipated to grating high-pitched giggling. Nothing smelled right – the rank odour of mould, dust and stale mattress fused with fresh linen.

Memory returned, and she fumbled from the bed to the door, almost smacking the dead lantern off its hook in her careless haste. She felt for the handle, then flung open the door and gasped as though just discovering air in the room. The pale light of sickly lanterns spilled into the doorway where sunlight should have been.

The sound of the giggling increased. The group next door, she realised. What time it was, she could not tell. Her senses stumbled in confusion. Eyes longed for a sun or moon, anything that could tell her how long she had been asleep.

The space confined, suffocated. She fled down hallways, through the dining room where people startled from leisurely hot drinks, along the echoing second hallway and up the flight of stairs. At the final landing, she pounded every stone until one forced the door open. She dashed to the next door, slapped her palm against the rocks, ignoring the stab of stone protrusions. The door creaked open. She stepped out into icy snow, inhaled deeply and felt faint early morning light on her eyes. Her mind screamed that the sun had it wrong; that dawn should have spread across the sky two hours ago. Perhaps time played differently in this place.

"You all right, Emme?" A voice behind her made her spin, fists ready for action. She released her fingers.

"How can you stand the darkness down there?" she said to the unfamiliar black-haired boy.

He shrugged unusually broad shoulders for one so young. "You get used to it. There's an hourglass in the library that helps us keep track of the time. Do you want me to show it to you?"

"I want to stay right here."

"Well, I'll have to ask you to close the door. We can't leave it open for long, or someone might discover it."

"Fine. Close the damn door then."

The boy shrugged again and shut the door behind her, leaving Emme to the cold and silence. Fresh snow had fallen on the alleyway, concealing yesterday's prints. Only a cat had wandered the alley since the snowfall; it sat under the eaves licking its mottled fur. The tabby watched her briefly with icy green eyes, then returned, disinterested, to its cleaning.

Emme leapt to the snowless alleyway border. The cat flinched, ready to flee. Briefly she squatted to smudge her deep footprints, then stood, caught her balance on the jagged cobbles. She scraped along the drain's grate, and the cat skittered away down the alley.

The cold bit through exposed skin. Breaths of air visualised with each exhale. The new woollen jumper kept out most, but not enough of the chill. She would have to go for a run later to warm up.

She slid to the alley entrance and peered around the sides. All was quiet, still. The dawn had only just turned the black sky to a dark-grey smudge.

Smoke rose lazily from many chimneys. A light flickered on down the road, and in the distance a dog barked. Further down the street, lantern light squeezed between shutter slats. People were rising to begin the drudgery of a new day.

It seemed a perfect time to investigate the city, but for the fresh snowfall that would highlight her lone tracks. She wondered if, even at this hour, guards traversed the streets. She supposed crimes did not confine themselves to the waking hours, but rather, flourished under the blanket of darkness.

Oh well. If she left it any later to find a concealed place to listen, too many eyes might note her – eyes that would know how alien she was to this vast city.

Emme calculated the risk, then with a flush of bravery, straightened, stepped from the alleyway and jogged down the street. She spotted the tabby cat that padded carefully across the snow, barely making a dent in the powder. Perhaps she could follow it and discover some of the quieter alleys the creature was sure to know.

The cats in the village, immigrants from outer forest lands, knew where to laze unseen without drifting too far from anticipated dinner summons. Cats in this foreign world would surely be no different.

She shivered, less from the chill than from nervousness of the unfamiliar scene. Her feet crunched down into powder like boots over glass shards. The buildings were dark grey monoliths watching her in the dawn quiet.

The cat turned down a side street, and she followed it. Large metal bins sat empty in the lane, a possible sign that the street's inhabitants could afford to waste little.

"Falling!" The cry shattered the stillness.

Emme jolted to a standstill and stared up at the noise's source just as liquid muck surged from an open window to the white snow. The yellow fluid quickly stained the snow, then dissolved into it. An unseen person retracted a white pot through the window, worked closed a rickety glass windowpane, then yanked down a blind.

"That's disgusting," Emme yelled up at the unknown individual behind the glass. "Don't you people have proper hygiene in this vile city of yours? I should make you come down here and clean this up."

Everyone knew that if you didn't bury it, you got sick. Surely these people weren't that stupid.

The blind recoiled, and the stiff, painted window jerked upward. "What you yelling at?" a woman asked as she curved out the window.

"You, you foul woman. You don't throw that sort of thing onto the street."

The weatherworn woman's lips curved into a sneer, revealing several black teeth. "And who might you be? Prince Jaimis himself?"

A chill loped down Emme's spine. "Damn it. Why did you have to go and say his name? Do you know what you've done?" He might hear his name, might know the woman looked at Emme.

A gruff man's muffled voice squeezed around the stout woman. "Who you yelling at?"

"Bitch in the street complaining about the way we dump our waste."

"You want me to go down there and give her a walloping?"

"Yeah, just you try it," Emme yelled, but knew now was not the time to settle this. She had to get out of here. Fast.

She turned and walked calmly from the street. If she ran, they would think she was a –

"Coward," the woman bawled and slammed the window shut against any reply.

Emme felt her fists tighten. She hated – *hated* – being called a coward. For twenty-two years she had endured Wendaya's beatings, the villagers' cruelty, the pranks, the abuse. No coward could do that.

When she reached her own prints at the lane's entrance, she glanced over her shoulder, noted that the woman had pulled down the blind. She waited patiently, then when sure the woman would not look from her window again, Emme turned and fled the other way down the street. If pressed, the vulgar couple might point guards in the opposite direction.

Emme began to find the labyrinth of streets overwhelming. This place had no logic or pattern to it. Everywhere there rose three-storey buildings of grey rock with dark oaken doors. Occasionally the line of joined houses broke, revealed an alleyway or street, but where those convoluted alleys or streets led, was nearly impossible to tell. Some were dark corridors of stairs leading down to lower levels of the hilly city, or up to the elevated districts. Others were streets and alleys that curved sharply into the unknown, or split into more streets.

She needed a wider view than the closest houses or bend in a road. She glanced up to rooftops, and a crafty smile curled her lips. *What I need is a way to get to a roof.* Up there she could listen to conversations, avoid notice and get her bearings.

She cleared a bend in the narrow road and stopped still. It was all too easy. A white ladder reclined against a dirty, dark grey wall. At its top, it tapped the eaves. She investigated the ground at the ladder's base, but no recent prints spoiled the snow. The ladder looked new, the white paint unworn by boots. Sharp, translucent icicles did not dangle from the rungs as they did the gutter above. Oddly, the recent snowfall had not buried the base of the ladder, yet no prints existed to indicate someone had put it there after the night's flurry. It all seemed somehow unnatural, yet no sinister explanation could be conjured.

She tested the first rung with the toe of her boot. It seemed sturdy. Warily she climbed the ladder. It sank swiftly into the snow under her weight. She waited until it settled, then continued to climb. When she reached the top, she peered, eyes just above the gutter, for any signs of use, but the pitched rooftop lay empty of people and prints. Not even a feline print marred the snow. The gentle incline stretched, snow-covered, for the expanse of the entire housing block. The other side of the roof fell away along the narrow width of the rectangle. Chimneys, irregular shapes and sizes, jutted, and filmy smoke from stale fires filled the air with a tang.

She climbed onto the roof, careful to not slip on the ice. It seemed a perfect vantage point to watch the streets. Right foot higher than the left, she manoeuvred across the slope and positioned herself at the apex beside a fat square chimney. Warmth emanated from the bricks. She pressed palms to it to fight the chill, but no warmth emanated from the bricks. Cold seeped into her trousers. If only she had her warm winter furs and skins on, then she wouldn't feel a hint of this cold.

The frigid air and snow competed heavily with the vestiges of her body heat. Soon billowing smoke replaced the dribble from the chimney beside her, and she knew the owners were awake and stoking their fire.

From up here, facing east, she could see a vast array of rooftops and a few streets. The city rose quite steeply to the south. Row after row of buildings stretched up the rise before disappearing over the other side. The north seemed just rooftops and chimneys. A break in the northeast rooves, filled by the stick branches of treetops, suggested an area of vegetation, but whether practical or for some rich person's private viewing, she could not tell.

As the sun lightened the dreary grey sky, the street started to come alive. Lights flickered on, smoke thickened within chimneys, and blinds and curtains retracted. People bustled from their doorways, some with empty bags, others carrying loads.

Some turned metal-plate signs around that hung from their front doors; possibly shops indicating they were open.

Emme scowled as the cry of "Falling" echoed all too often, followed by the unwholesome removal of refuse. *Barbarians, all of them.* For all their fancy buildings and clothes, they had a lot to learn about health.

Before long, a troop of soldiers in blue pinafores exited a nearby building through a timber door that had flat wrought-iron fixtures. Emme wondered if the troop had spent the night drinking like the village warriors did, or if the building was a communal lodging. The last in the group closed the timber door, then jogged down the stairs to the snow. A second band strolled from somewhere down the street. Their casual disorderly gait did not deceive Emme; the many eyes were alert and ready for duty.

From her elevated position, the large feathered hats looked ridiculously impractical. When the first group passed directly beneath her, the hats almost obscured their entire body, so that it seemed six blue hats went by. She wanted to laugh out loud, but knew it would be folly.

Emme listened for mention of her, but the troop said nothing as it passed. It seemed more concerned with making its way somewhere.

The second troop progressed slowly. It knocked and conversed at many doors. At some, people produced and exchanged papers; at others, people answered questions. What questions, Emme could not tell until the troop came closer. The troop did not ask about Emme; they assessed the city's daily concerns and the honesty of its citizens. Still, she would not relax until she was sure.

Soon merchants with open cartloads of goods, pulled by sturdy horses, moved down the street. Briefly Emme conceded that the prince had at least not lied about horses tamed for labour, then pushed the dangerous memory from her mind.

One merchant delivered bottles of milk to most doorsteps. Another called out, "Timber. Buy some more timber. Good dry timber." A third steered a cartload of frozen carcases around a side street, then pulled up at someone's front door. Before the wagoner even dismounted, another man, thickly built, opened the door from the inside. A mound of snow, caught by the lintel, splattered at his feet. He glanced up, uttered something Emme could easily guess at from his dark expression, then stepped down snow-covered stairs to the newcomer. The first alighted, and the two spoke briefly. Soon the two dragged the carcases off the wagon, slung them over strong shoulders and offloaded them somewhere inside the building. When the entire load had been relocated beyond the door's shadows, coins changed hands, then the wagoner went on his way. The remaining burly man stared down the street briefly as though expecting someone, then went inside and closed the door.

Moments later, two women wearing bonnets and full russet dresses, turned up at the man's doorstep and entered. A short time after, they bustled out with brown paper parcels tucked under their arms. They hastened into the house next door. A few minutes later they exited with more string-tied packages. Chatting all the while, they visited the building beneath Emme. Emme caught a drift of fresh oven pastries and suspected she sat above a baked-goods house of sorts.

Before long, the whole street thrived with activity. More carts rolled deep furrows through the snow or navigated the slushy dirty edges of the street. Some stopped at houses to unload goods; others continued to distant destinations. People scurried in and out of houses, their parcels growing more numerous with each stop.

For a few hours Emme watched, then a group of children appeared in padded jackets and earmuffs, carrying grubby satchels on their shoulders. They threw snowballs at each other, before a gloomy-faced adult yelled at them to move on. They scurried away like scolded dogs and darted into a building up the street. Soon more children carrying small sacks appeared from nearby houses and streets and entered the same building. Emme wondered what they would be doing in there. An elderly female appeared in the doorway and waggled a bell. The crisp ringing seemed to attract children from all over who ran as though risking a beating if they did not. They jostled for space in a congestion that squeezed through the doorway, then the elderly woman shut the door.

Curious, Emme decided to investigate that one later.

A group of redcoat guards appeared. Emme stiffened. The prince's guards. They rapped on doors and asked pointed questions of residents that had some shrugging and others waving fingers down the street. A second unit of redcoats advanced down the road. Eventually the two met in the middle close to Emme's post.

"Found out anything?" one of the left redcoats asked. He caressed a pointed chin beard that did not distinguish him from the others.

"Nothing. The prince said she was around here somewhere though. He had a lead this morning."

"Someone is bound to have seen her. She's hard to miss."

"You would think so. Well, we'd best keep looking then, before the trail runs cold."

Feathers bobbed as the two men politely inclined heads to each other, then the troops passed, rapiers swinging by their side and pompous knee-high boots soundless in the snow.

Damn it! Surely the prince had realised his error by now. Maybe she should go to him, make him see that she was a nobody of a nothing lineage, from a forgotten forest in a country that according to Kye, wasn't even charted yet.

Curiosity satisfied, she stood up, clambered across the rooftop to peer over the other side. Nothing interesting; just more of the same thing.

"Hey!" A voice startled Emme. "This is *my* territory. What are you doing here?"

Emme spun to a black-clothed kid whose hand clutched the pole of a massive wire brush. Blue eyes peered out from his sooty face – a stark contrast.

"That your ladder?" he asked sharply. "This is my street. Go get your own."

"Go get my own? To do what?" Emme remained unsure if the kid posed any threat. The sturdy, long-poled brush could easily push her off the rooftop, but soft fresh snow might catch her – if carts and feet hadn't already compacted it to ice.

"*I'm* doing these chimneys here. You can go and get your own customers."

Emme scowled at him. "Do I look like a damned chimneysweep?"

"You don't look like you're out for a weekend picnic. Now, is that your ladder back there? 'Cause you can just go and remove it."

"No, it's not my ladder. I saw it and chose to use it. You can have it, for all I care." She waved her hand as if shooing the boy back to the ladder.

The boy's sternness dissolved instantly to mild curiosity. "So what are you doing up here?"

"Looking around. Is that a crime?" Emme addressed the boy with a cold gaze.

"Looking around for what?" Something lit in the boy's face. "Almighty save me. You're that woman they're all looking for.

You exactly match her description."

Emme tensed. Eyes darted for the nearest escape route. The boy still blocked the path to the ladder. "No one is looking for me. I don't know what you're talking about."

The boy half-jumped, half-jiggled. "I found you. I found you. They're offering ten gold for any news about you. That's five years of my wages." He turned, sped to the gutter of the roof, hollered over the edge. "Guards, she's up here. The wild woman – she's up here."

"Wild woman? I'll give you wild woman, you little brat." At the nearest crossroads, a group of red-tunic guards turned, came running back. "Damn you, you little bastard." Emme whirled away from the boy, fled along the rooftop. The boy lowered his large brush, swept it horizontally. It collided with her feet, dislodged them from the roof. She slapped onto her chest. White snow mashed against her lips. She felt a shock of pressure on bruises and her damaged ribcage, then her vision fractured as roof and sky blurred to one. She felt snow on her shoulder, then her back, then her other shoulder. She was tumbling. A moment when her stomach pushed up into her throat and air left her lungs, then her back slammed down onto the compacted snow of the street below.

"Down there," the boy cried out. "She's down there. And I want my money. I'm coming down."

Several people began to cluster around her, peer down at her as though inspecting a dead animal.

"You all right, miss?" the only kindly face amongst them said. The elderly man knelt beside her.

"Yes – fine." Emme sat up swiftly. Her head spun momentarily, and she gasped again for air. If she didn't have so many, many bruises and a healing ribcage, that fall would not have been nearly so difficult to recover from.

"She's hurt," a woman said. "She's got bruises on her."

"What a revolting outfit," a wealthy, snooty, pointy-nosed woman responded. "Who is she? A troubadour?"

"One of bad-taste if she is," her equally snobbish companion responded.

Emme stood just as the redcoats raced around the corner, their feathers trailing back in the icy breeze that howled down the corridor of houses. She pushed roughly through the crowd gathered at her expense, and fled down the street.

"Stop her," she heard someone yell.

"Hey, that's the girl worth ten gold," someone else yelled.

The crowd rose to a greedy frenzy and hurtled after Emme in the street. More people joined in the chase that swelled to over twenty.

Grateful that the same snow that hindered her hindered them, Emme's speed seemed her only advantage in this city of enemies.

A group of large, strong men appeared as if from nowhere up ahead. Shoulder almost to shoulder, they formed a solid barricade across the street, their eyes sharply trained on her. Damn it. She would be trapped. She stopped, looked about quickly and saw her only chance – a thin side alley leading to the city's higher levels.

She fled down the rank print-scuffed alley. Without warning, an arm snaked out from what seemed the very wall itself, yanked her backwards through a secret door edged with ragged stone as if random stones had parted to make an opening. The wall-door swung shut with a hollow boom leaving total blackness. Emme turned to face her attacker but could see nothing. She swung fists, but someone faster, someone with strength, caught each blow, then snapped her around, away from him, grasped her from behind to thwart her desperate retaliations. His unyielding arms enclosed her, compressed her own arms at her side, impeding contact with her dagger. Emme lurched back to force him off her. Her assailant off-balanced and, still joined, the two fell backwards to their bottoms. His tight body locked in a sit to prevent momentum smacking them back to the hard floor. Speedily the aggressor adjusted position, and she found herself tangled up in a prison of her own arms and legs held down by her assailant's arms and legs. She yelled curses, but a hand clamped over her mouth. "Be quiet or they'll find you," a stern, quiet voice said in her ear.

She knew the male voice, but who? She lay still, every joint locked ready to strike out. For long minutes they sat there, the heat from her assailant pressing through to her chilled back, her mouth turning hot and moist from the hand clamped over it. She could feel the assailant's calm breathing, feel his hot breath on her hair, and knew that her own erratic breaths outnumbered his.

She heard the frenzy of the crowds. Above the excited babble of her pursuers, she heard, "This way. She turned down this alley."

"That gold is mine," a young voice exclaimed loudly. That damned chimneysweep kid.

The noise died away down the alley, then a voice said in her ear, "I'm going to release you and light a candle. Don't kick out or yell."

With the hand still over her mouth, Emme could only nod. Slowly the assailant unwound his legs and arms from her. She stood swiftly and spun around ready for action.

The shadow slowly rose, felt in his pocket for something, then struck a flintbox to a fat candle on the wall. Instant light defined a tiny cold stone room with no markings, no furniture, just a single candle on its flat iron candleholder and a large stack of candles on the floor beneath it – like logs for a fire. She glared venomously at the face of her attacker, then softened.

"For goodness sake, Kye," she said exhaling. "Why didn't you just say it was you? And where did you come from?"

"I was coming back from my visit to my contacts," Kye said. "I saw you fall off the rooftop and knew what was happening, so I organised those men to barricade the street to force you down this alleyway." He looked around at the walls. "We have lots of these secret rooms in the city for moments like these."

"Why didn't you just say your name and I wouldn't have swung at you?"

"I wasn't sure if you thought I was the enemy or not. I can imagine you don't know who to trust right now."

Emme felt a small stab at the truth in his words. Who to trust? Probably not a single soul in the city – not even Kye. When he found out who the prince thought she might be, he might turn her in himself.

Kye sat down onto the stone floor, rested against a wall. His easy mannerism suggested she was safe, but it could have been a ploy. Did he know about her? What would be his next move if he did?

"Now, what were you doing out in the city? I gave strict instructions to Dusty to keep you out of sight until I could find out what was going on."

"Dusty probably doesn't know I'm out here. Well, he does now, but I went out before everyone got up."

Kye's brow rose fractionally. "Were you leaving?"

"No, I just wanted to look around." Emme slumped down ungracefully against the opposite wall.

"Emme, you strike me as someone intelligent. Surely you could see that was an unwise thing to do."

Emme glared at him. "It was better than –" She stopped. Admitting weakness was unnecessary.

"Than the darkness?"

Emme shot up straight. "I'm not afraid of darkness."

"No, not afraid; but the darkness is hard to get used to at first. We all went through it. Even burly Halder, and he's probably the bravest man I know – *and* he lives upstairs."

Emme relaxed back against the wall. As long as he didn't think her weak because she was a woman, she could probably admit it. "I just needed to see light, real light."

Kye nodded but said nothing.

"So what now? Should we go back?"

"No. It's too dangerous. You're very obvious out there – even if you had my cloak on. We'll have to wait until nightfall, and then go back."

"Nightfall?" Tension tautened her body again. "You want me to wait in this tiny room until nightfall?"

"Or we could go out there and find out what the prince wants with you and make someone ten gold pieces richer. That's the alternative." Despite the sharp words, his tone remained gentle, his eyes soft as they watched Emme carefully.

Emme sagged. "So you didn't find out anything?"

"No – no one has a clue as to who you are or what the prince could possibly want with you. Or for that matter, why the Ashrones are after you." Emme's eyes narrowed. It was difficult to tell if he lied; his face remained calm, confident. Would he tell her if he knew? Maybe it advantaged him to keep it from her. "Although one did offer a rather unsettling suggestion."

"Which was?"

"To go and ask the Black Bands. Whenever there is something going on in this city and with the prince, the Black Bands usually know about it."

"So let's go and ask them."

"It's not that easy."

"Why not?"

"If I send any one of us to the Black Bands for information, my street kids will end up dead or followed – and either way, we won't know any more than we do now. The only way to get information from them is to find one of them, capture them, and force them to talk."

"Then let's do that."

"It's very rare to go up against a Black Band and come away alive and with information. Finding them is difficult, subduing them is even harder, and getting them to talk can sometimes be nearly impossible."

"But worth the risk, surely."

"I'm still trying to decide that."

"What – don't you want me to know why I'm here or why my whole world has been turned upside down? Maybe you know about me and don't want me to know what you know."

Kye seemed totally unruffled by her tone. He watched her with steady, calm eyes. "Maybe – maybe not. Sooner or later, Emme, you're going to have to pick who you want to trust. You won't last if you're alone in this city. Now – I have shared my home with you – a home that most don't see until after a lot of investigation on our behalf. I have shown you a world I have spent a lifetime building. If I expose you, you could expose me. I would say we have a mutual basis for trust, even though it is a forced basis."

Emme considered his words for some time.

"Do we have a partnership, Emme?"

She eventually nodded.

"Good."

Silence replaced words briefly, making the walls seem suddenly heavier, closer than before. Emme began to fidget restlessly and peer furtively at the walls.

"So tell me about your homeland," Kye said, and she suspected he attempted to distract her from the oppressive space.

"Well, I live in a forest." She stopped and watched the walls. Her heart began to beat faster in her chest. Her hands grew clammy.

"Describe it to me," Kye said, his eyes, his face, a steady presence in the room. "I want to know everything."

Emme began – distracted at first – then memories flooded and she conversed eagerly to a perfect listener. She described her favourite lofty, broad trees; painted word-images of the generous river that coursed by their village – a river she often swam in on idle summer days. Her mind raced to the myriad of tracks she would follow; to the dark, dry caves; cliff edges where she could see the whole world – *her* world.

She told him of her large village with its neat tree and ground cottages, and her passionate dislike for the people in it.

"And then there's the chieftain and his family." Emme expressed mild disdain as she explained about the chieftain, the nearby villages, and the fights that sometimes took place between them. "I'm in charge of tracking the forest, reporting suspicious behaviour, reporting when other villagers are out of their territory and hunting on my village's land. Every village owns lands; mine owns the largest."

At that, Kye offered up exhaustive questions, seemed to want to know everything he frequently labelled 'politics', then settled back to let Emme continue.

She described the chill of winter that did not seem to bite as deeply as Kye's winters. Her furs, the thick round fur hat, tough skin pants with fur turned inside, and fur-lined boots, all kept her so beautifully warm in winter. Even the coldest days, going into the forest remained a pleasure. She pictured out-loud the winter-bare trees, the white gleam of snow on the tracks, the thick ice that set across the river and sometimes in the well if the villagers were not diligent with pouring boiling water down it. Children made flat shoes out of polished timber cuts and slid playfully across the river's ice. Emme never joined in, although she regularly investigated the ice's scratches, for in winter, crossing the solid river was an easy way for other villages to breach territory rules. And in winter, other villages grew hungry enough to take the risk.

The village relied almost solely on meat, salted and smoked in the smokehouse, to survive the winter. Occasionally they found nuts, and ground down an abundant sweet bark to mix with goat's milk and honey. Emme recalled one winter when the smokehouse supplies dwindled dangerously, and the chieftain had ordered two meals to be replaced with the sweet drink. They had all grown thin and irritable that winter, and Emme had never really put weight back on after that.

Kye listened with an interest that initially produced scepticism. At first Emme supposed he had nothing better to do than listen, but his questions were numerous and detailed, and she realised he took in every word she said.

"Your home sounds beautiful," he said when the descriptions slowed.

"I don't know how you can live in this place. Just grey sandstone and dirt and filth. And you people throw your refuse out the window. That's just disgusting."

"The poorer people do – those who can't afford to build latrines and connect to the main sewerage system. We get charged a hefty tax for the privilege. A lot of people illegally dig their own connections to the city pipes like we did, but it requires skill and knowing who to ask to supply you with black market city maps."

"The Black Bands?"

"Connected to them, but not direct members. Only selected people in the city get to talk directly with the Black Bands. It keeps them anonymous."

"And the Black Bands make money from the sales, I suppose."

Kye nodded once. "You can pay a lot of money for those maps, but it's less than a lifetime of taxes."

"Is this the poorest end of town?"

"No – this is one of the main business districts. You always get a mix of poor and moderately wealthy. The really wealthy live in their own pockets of town, and the terribly poor, the ones not living on the streets, live on the outskirts of those pockets and beg for scraps."

"And the prince does nothing to help them?"

"No – why should he?"

"Because loyal happy subjects will serve him in times of war with other villages – cities. Even our arrogant chieftain knows that." Emme's brown eyes flickered darkly. "And you agree with him do you?"

Kye regarded her coolly. "I strike you as someone who would agree with the prince, do I?"

Emme glanced at her hands. Heat rose to her cheeks. "No. It just sounded like you were saying . . . Well, you know what I mean."

"I was merely pointing out that when our hard-hearted prince has no personal gain to help anyone, he doesn't. The prince has his King's Guard to help him in times of war, and the City Guard defend the city during sieges. The people know they depend heavily on the prince for protection during those times, so no matter how much poverty they're living in, they'll support their prince during times of war."

"Do you fight much with other cities?"

"Not for over a hundred years. All trouble is internal now, but we won't talk about that here. We'll wait until we're underground."

99

"That gift the prince has?"

"Partly, and partly because you never know who is listening to us."

"Even in here?"

"Walls are never as safe as you think in this city. You will need to remember that."

"So how did you end up with the place you've got? Did you build it yourself?"

"Ours is not the only one, and they've always existed. They were built for times of war to hide or shelter people but were long forgotten. I was fortunate to come across someone when I was a young man, who knew about them. She told me about them before she died – it was a secret handed down to her by her family over many generations." Kye seemed lost in thought for a moment before he continued. "It took me six months of scouting to realise they were well and truly abandoned."

"Don't the people in the house above you hear you all making noises and wonder?"

"The houses down the street were abandoned shops and warehouses, destroyed by a fire that swept through the whole area. When I met Halder – did you meet Halder?"

Emme nodded.

"Halder agreed to help me rebuild parts of the street, and he lives in the house above us. Now anyone living down that street is loyal to us. Our two teachers – Illina and Ada – live in the building that guards over the alley you first came down. Our contacts down the street help with duties in the city and report Black Band activities to us."

"Were they all Black Bands?"

"Some were, but not all of them."

"Was Halder?"

"No – there's a lot to Halder, but I probably shouldn't go

into it here." Kye reached into his pocket and pulled out a cloth-covered parcel. He unwrapped the cloth to reveal a segment of half-eaten cheese. "Would you like some cheese?"

"I never say no to food." She leant over and took a portion of the cheese, swallowed it hungrily. "How much longer do we have to wait?"

Kye smiled faintly. "We've only made lunchtime."

Swiftly the walls became oppressive again. "Can't I just go outside, just for a few minutes?" She pleaded with her eyes.

Kye pondered an idea for a moment. "I could probably find a way to get you back on to the rooftops. We could sit up there for a while. But it *is* cold out there."

Emme leapt to her feet. "Let's go."

Kye's gentle smile widened fractionally. Double smile lines appeared around his closed lips. He watched Emme until his stares caused her to fidget. At last he said, "Will you be all right if I go outside and scout for a while to work out the best place to sit? We'll need to pick a roof where chimneysweeps have finished their job."

Emme sighed. "Well, if it means getting out of here, then do what you must."

Kye nodded, stood and placed his ear to the cold wall bordering the alley. He listened carefully for any echo of disturbance. He turned an eye to a crooked crack in the wall. Kye seemed in no hurry to open the door and many seconds passed before he finally pushed the false stone, activating the switch. The door parted partially at the grouting between the stones, leaving an edge like an unfinished brick wall. Kye pulled the door the rest of the way.

"Please don't go anywhere," he entreated before he disappeared behind the door.

Long minutes elapsed. Emme paced restlessly, felt as if the air diminished with every breath until she would suffocate in here.

Her palms grew sweaty, and her legs trembled. She had never felt like this before – never known this curious, invasive fear of confinement.

The walls became torturers waiting to close in on her and pin her down to inflict hideous cruelties. She almost thought she could see eyes, faces, leering at her from the irregularities of the grey stone.

"I have *got* to find a way out of here," she said to the silence. The thick door behind her swung open. She turned to the door, lips parted to express gratitude that at last Kye had returned, but the words fell unspoken. Apprehension shot the hairs up on her arms. "Kye?" she whispered to the empty doorway. "Kye – are you there?"

No reply came. Emme crept to the doorway, anticipating an impending ambush. She propelled an arm beyond the doorway and snapped it down in a chopping motion, hoping it might stir the assailants beyond the door. But no one moved.

"If this is some kind of joke, Kye, then it's not funny."

No response, just the cold quiet of the alley beyond.

Warily she peered around the jagged edge of the frame, but the alleyway and the street on either side stretched empty, devoid of even shoppers scurrying away to the next store. Frowning deeply, she stepped from the doorway to the snow just as Kye rounded the corner from the street to her right. He saw and stopped, eyes staring, then sprang into movement. He bolted down the alley and thrust Emme back into the room. He forced the thick stone door closed. Crisp air propelled from the door movement to the tiny space. The candle fluttered on its base, causing the long shadows in the room to jump until the flame steadied.

"What were you doing?" Despite the demanding tone, his eyes held no anger or malice.

"What do you mean, what was I doing? You're the one who

opened the door, then ran off."

"I just got back to the alleyway then, to find you standing in it."

Emme's jaw and fists tightened. "Well I was minding my own business when the damned door swung open on its own."

"That's impossible," Kye said genuinely, a faint frown on his face.

"Is it?" Emme's eyes seethed. "Well it happened so it's not as impossible as you think."

"Did you see anyone run past?"

"No – no one. I heard no one, I saw no one. It just opened."

Kye looked beyond her to the back wall, thought carefully. "I think maybe we'll have to stop using this area for a while until we can find out what happened. It might be a faulty mechanism."

"It's going to give things away a little if it swings open again of its own accord and shows everyone these spaces exist." Remnants of anger still tainted Emme's tone.

"Yes. I'll have to send people to keep checking it for a while." His eyes returned to Emme's face. "Are you ready to go?"

"What sort of a question is that?"

He smiled at her, yet to himself. "Then let's go." Kye took off his thick russet cloak and handed it to Emme. "You'll need to wear this or you'll definitely be spotted."

Emme raised a hand to take it, hesitated. "But you'll get cold."

"My jumper is thicker than yours, so I'll be fine. This city is always cold, even in summer."

Emme wrapped herself in the cloak and flicked up the hood. They waited at the door, one still and calm, the other fidgety, until Kye indicated it was safe to go. Emme let out a long, unambiguous sigh as they exited the building.

Kye took her along ancient, seldom-used lanes that twined up and up to the city's summits. They hurried up a wide pathway of stairs that ascended the breadth of terraced houses either side of it. At the top, they encountered a road that followed the back of those terraces, making the three-storey apartments, built against rock, appear single story. After turning left, they stopped at the very last terrace, faced the back wall.

"Most chimneysweeps in this area get onto other rooves via this lane," Kye explained. "You'll need to climb those bricks there, but I don't think that will be a problem considering you got onto that other roof earlier today."

Kye went first, up the jutting stones. He pulled himself easily over a solid stone railing rimming the roof, landed lightly onto the flat rooftop beyond. He turned to help Emme.

"I can do it," Emme said stubbornly. "I don't need help."

Kye retracted his hand and said nothing. Emme hauled herself ungracefully onto the thick fence edge and leapt off onto a level roof.

"Why the half wall around the roof?" she asked Kye.

"It makes this useable space; although the weather tends to ruin that idea."

Emme followed Kye to the opposite walled edge of the building. They stood near two chimneys that exuded clouds of light smoke. Kye leant wool-wrapped elbows against the snow-coated wall and peered over the edge.

"How do you know the chimneysweeps won't be back?" Emme asked.

"If they were still working in this district, they would have climbed on this roof at dawn to get to other areas. But as you can see, the snow is smooth."

Emme rested her waist onto the wall and gazed out. She could see so much of the city from this place. Rows upon rows of white-dusted rooftops stretched further than she imagined she would see from up here. Smoke, pouring from countless chimneys, muddied the air.

Kye pointed to the distance. "Can you make out the city wall?"

Emme nodded. The bulky, towering wall, soaring above the three-storey houses, wrapped around the city's distant edges. Beyond that, she could just make out mountains shrouded in mist.

"And behind us," Kye turned and Emme followed, "is the castle."

Emme's brows rose, an indication the mighty fortress on its high rock ledge impressed her. The highest structure in the city, it stood higher even, than the great protective wall enclosing the city. Behind it, the city still stretched out, vast and overwhelming until it met the city wall. Beyond the wall, more mountains materialised through the smoky haze, these closer and clearly snow-covered. The sky seemed vast and grey from up here, endless in its dreariness.

To her left, a line of bare-branch trees on the other side of the street, partially overlayed the view of the city where it rose to the castle road – the lavish street she had first fled down.

"Would you like me to point some things out for you?" Kye asked.

"Of course."

Whilst they faced the castle, Kye pointed. "That road leading from the castle is where all the prince's officials, and the major players in this town live. The closer you are to the castle, the more important and wealthy you are."

"I see," Emme said. "I remember that road very well."

Kye pointed to the furthest edge of the castle. "That natural rock wall at the back of the castle is one fourth of a mile high. Do you know what a mile is?"

"Of course," she said haughtily, but she didn't. Well, she did now. It was as long as four of that vast, sheer rock wall at the castle's rear.

"At the base of that rock wall are the worst of the city's slums. Apparently in times of old, kings used to throw down lavish food wastes over that wall, and the poor people used to pick up anything worthwhile and take it home. The slums grew from that." Kye's outstretched pointer finger moved left to the huge garden area beside the wealthier castle road. "That's one of the city's agriculture areas and parks. It belongs to the prince, and his servants tend it for him. In summer, the wealthy get out there and have their picnics and their social gatherings, and the prince sometimes wanders down there to get out of his castle grounds. The prince has no shortage of castle and city gardens he's claimed for himself." A hint of bitterness edged Kye's voice. "Guards swarm those parks at night to stop thieves from helping themselves to the vegetables."

"How does the rest of the city get vegetables?"

"Merchants come to the city every day from the farmlands beyond the wall, or from other states. There are three main entrances." Still facing the castle, Kye pointed straight ahead, to his right, and behind him to the distant mountains. "The one behind us, or south, is the closest gate to us. They deliver the food to the shops and the shops add their profits and sell their goods. Only firewood vendors are allowed to sell directly to people as no one wants to own a firewood shop. The poorer people usually go out and get their own firewood, sleep out in the farmlands, then return the next day."

"Who forces merchants to sell to shops?"

"The prince's law does. It's too hard to control food and supply taxes when you don't know how much vendors are selling. When the food arrives in shops, the guards regularly check shop inventory, and the shop sellers are required to pay a tax on all the money they make. I've heard a few reports of people paying guards to look the other way on some earnings, but I don't know how true that is."

"We don't pay taxes back home," Emme said. "We don't have money or shops, although the village next to us does. We all do our share, and if we do, we get to eat the food the hunters bring in. If we don't, we get smaller shares, or none. We can barter goods and services with those who have chickens and vegetables and useful things if we don't grow our own."

"Sounds fair. Although, it would be a little tricky to do in a city this size." Kye turned to face south. Emme followed and looked out to where his gaze fell. "That," he pointed to a large spired building, "is the main cathedral."

"The main what?"

"Cathedral, church."

Emme looked at him blankly.

"Place of worship."

"Oh right. That Almighty you all keep mentioning."

"That's right. What do you call him?"

"Creator."

"And you don't worship anywhere?"

"We worship everywhere and anywhere. All of life belongs to the Creator, not just a building like – what did you call it?"

"Cathedral. Or church. So you don't worship together?"

"At festivals we do. Or *they* do."

"They?"

Emme waved the question away. "Never mind. What were you saying about the cathedral?"

"Ah yes. The ministers – you probably don't know what a minister is. They're the ones who teach people the ways of the Almighty. The ministers answer to the Ashrones, and the Ashrones are supposed to be the guardians of religion." Again a hint of bitterness edged his voice. "But not many go to church nowadays since . . ." He glanced at Emme briefly. "Ask me to tell you about it later."

Curiosity would demand it from him, Emme was sure.

He spoke on, his finger all the while pointing. "There are many lesser churches over the city. You can see their spires jutting up above the rooftops. And you'll probably see many breaks in the city – more park areas. Some are for people to just go and see nature for a while; others are more of the prince's agricultural blocks.

"This area just below us is one of the many commercial areas in the city. Most people run their business from their house. This area is the food centre. Beyond that, you start to get the tailors, the blacksmiths, the tallow makers, the builders, the bankers, the taverns and inns and other such businesses. There are many divisions within the city, each with a different name, like a separate town or village within the same city. Each division has its commercial area, its own wealthy, its own poor, its own barracks, and its own boundaries."

"Barracks?"

"Soldiers' quarters – housing for guards. We're in the Royal Centre – that's its name. Most goods are not as cheap in these parts because the very wealthy live here and merchants charge a lot of money because they know most people can afford to pay it." He lowered his arm to his side and leant again on the edge of the balcony.

"You said something about an inn-stay. What did you mean by that? What's an inn?"

"Even from here, the middle of the city, it's a long trip to the city gates and beyond – mostly because of all the winding roads and limited routes to the gates. If you want to make it to the city gates and back again, you either travel all day, or you do half a day, stay somewhere overnight and travel again the next day. There are places set up that offer beds and a bath for a fee. Then you can get a meal and a drink in a tavern. Many merchants rest at inns before moving on to other areas of the city or back out again. And often farmers have to come to the city for business and stay over." Still leaning over the edge of the balcony, he looked at Emme. "I take it you don't get very many visitors to your village?"

"We got one once when I was about ten. He came to the village and said that he wanted to rest for a while. The chieftain had him over at his house. He told us about the prince and the castles and some of the things that were going on." She realised he had taught her much of what she understood, but had never seen about this kind of place – this city. "He said he wanted to live in our village, to build a home. And everyone thought that was great because he was new and exciting and had so much information about the outside world. But then he got to know me and was actually nice to me, and the villagers didn't like that at all. So they threatened to stone him if he stayed in the village, and he had to go. He was the only visitor we had until those Ashrone men and Jai – the prince arrived."

Kye watched her carefully, his blue-green eyes focused on every expression. "Why would your villagers not want him to be nice to you?"

"They don't like me. They never have." Her tone was casual, unaffected.

"Why?"

"They just don't. You got any more of that cheese?"

Kye continued to watch Emme for a moment, but she held her hand out expectantly, determined not to answer his question. "I only have a little bit," he said, and handed her the remaining slither.

Emme took the cheese and turned away, studied the city. Kye seemed to respect her, to acknowledge her as a valuable human being. She was not going to spoil it with her past.

"How old are you, Emme?"

"Twenty-two winters; but sometimes I feel so much older than my years." From the corner of her eye, she could see him study her expression. She misread his face and said, "Yes, don't worry; I know I'm a bit immature sometimes. It's just that sometimes I feel old, deep in my bones, like I've lived another few years inside my mother's womb that haven't counted to my age."

He leant back over the brick railing and stared at the city. "Strange," he said to the scenery.

"No, not strange. Rather stupid really." She faced him. "And how old are you?"

"Twenty-eight. And yes – I guess sometimes I feel older than that; like I have a lifetime of weight on my shoulders."

"At least *you* act older than your age." She turned from him to the cityscape.

The two stared silently out over the city, the chill wind blowing their hair and making faces cold. Together they watched all day whilst people roamed the streets, cartloads came and went. Then the last of the people hurried inside and locked doors as the darkness fell very early in the evening.

◉

A hooded figure walked down the spacious stone corridor. Early evening light, the last of the endless dismal grey, drifted through glass-enclosed, arched windows to his right before dissolving into the unlit corridor.

"My apologies," a startled servant said as the cloaked figure floated by. The servant's flintbox spark roused the nearest wall candle. "I'm late to light the candles this evening."

The hooded figure did not reply but continued down the corridor, his cloak billowing like a black sail behind him.

The man stopped at a heavy, timeworn door and rapped on it with a deliberate and complicated pattern.

"Come in," a muffled voice called behind the door.

The man entered, briefly stopped by the brightness of the

room, then spotted his target – Jaimis, sitting in one of the prince's plush reading chairs with a thick, leather-bound book in hand. The newcomer closed the door, sealed the two of them in the room.

"You're late," Jaimis said. "I sent for you yesterday."

"I was on business – you know that." The tall, straight-backed man drew off his hood with gloved hands to reveal close grey hair, a neat grey beard, and slender, grey brows – a stark contrast to his sharp, dark-brown eyes and lean, harsh nose.

"Did you hear I found her?" Jaimis asked, keen green eyes watching the man expectantly.

"Right before I heard you lost her."

Jaimis shrugged. "Not for long, now that you're here."

"Do you think that one of my skills?" the man demanded sternly. "If I could find one woman in a city of hundreds of thousands, then I should be able to find our street rats who keep eluding us."

"It's only because you refuse to use your power."

"Yes, and you know very well why. And now without my power, the girl might get away."

"Relax. She won't get far. She's entirely too obvious."

"And what fool of a person put it into your head to go and find her ahead of time?"

"I thought now was the perfect time with you distracting the Ashrones on that futile expedition to the southern kingdoms."

"Well, we left behind just enough Ashrones who could try and stop you. Your use of the travel gate over and over gave them enough time to know that power was being used, and not by them, and to try and impede you. And now they know that there is a traitor amongst them." The man pulled off his thick gloves to reveal a distinct tattoo on his right hand. He muttered to himself, "I should never have shown you how to use that

111

travel gate." He tossed the gloves on the royal bed and took long, elegant strides to the padded, red chair beside Jaimis. He tucked his cloak to his flesh and sat down, then smoothed the legs of his pants with meticulous care. "And what did you hope to do when you brought her here? You couldn't do anything without me."

A sly grin spread across Jaimis' face. "I hardly think I'll need your help with *that*."

"Idiot," the man snapped, and Jaimis' smile abruptly faded. "There has to be witnesses, and there is a lot that needs to be done before you can use her. There is protocol. There always has been. Didn't you listen to anything I said?"

"You did say a lot more than is normal for a man to take in," Jaimis taunted.

"And now you've gone and alerted the Ashrones. And if we drag her in ahead of time, it gives the Ashrones more time to find a way to stop us. Not only that, but no one will be able to leave the premises without being watched. It will no longer be easy for me to come here and instruct you."

"Then maybe it's time you left them. You've avoided using your power for years to prevent them discovering the truth. Why not stand up and announce which side you are on. Your power is stronger than theirs. Be proud of it."

The man stroked his grey beard. "Perhaps I might. After all, we're all looking for the girl now. There is no point in hiding our plans any longer. And we may need my power to stop the other Ashrones getting to her first."

"Good," Jaimis said. "Then it is settled. You can come and stay with me, and start to use your powers to the full. And you just might find a way to track down this girl before she dies out there on the streets."

"If I use my power to track her down, I will track her down just enough to make sure she *doesn't* die on the street. If she is safe, we will leave her there until the time is right. We must wait for a full moon – a visible full moon."

"Damn that for a joke." Jaimis slammed the book pages together. "That could be months in this cursed grey city."

"Yes, Jaimis, months." The man regarded Jaimis coldly. "Which is exactly why we must leave her where she is and have her think she is safe. She will not expect our attack when it comes and she may surface, making it all the more easy for us to go and pick her up when the time is right."

"So I should call off the guards and the Black Bands?"

"After I find her, yes. And retract that ridiculous price you have put on her head. Do you want the Ashrones to hear of her every whereabouts when the villagers cry out that they've seen her?"

Jaimis' face darkened. "You have to remember, old man, who is heir to the Kildes throne. Do not treat me as an idiot. I am well aware that the people have less love for the Ashrones than they do for me. And even if they did have love for the Ashrones, they have more love for gold. They would not let the Ashrones come in and take her, when they can turn her in to me and receive a tidy sum. The Ashrones might hear of her whereabouts, but I own the soldiers who will ultimately capture her when the people find her and turn her in."

The newcomer picked a piece of fluff from his trousers. "I do see your point. But you do see mine, I hope, that pulling the price from her head and letting her relax a little is exactly what we want. You can instruct your Black Bands to make sure the Ashrones are well-watched and distracted from any attempts to find her – at *all* costs."

"Ruthless," Jaimis said with a sly grin. "I will concede to your plan. And who knows, we may just find a street rat or two in the process."

"Oh, we will find them; I have no doubt about that. When they catch wind that the Black Bands and soldiers are after a strange girl, they will be sure to try and find her for themselves and unwittingly reveal themselves to us."

Jaimis rubbed his hands together. "Very good. I will have all my desires at once. I will send word out to the city tonight." He reached up beside his chair and yanked a tassel. Somewhere in the castle, a bell rang. The grey-haired man replaced his hood to hide his face, tucked the hand tattoo within the cloak edge. Shortly after, a servant arrived. "Get me Captain Toussen." The servant nodded and disappeared into the dimly lit hallway.

The captain arrived, a bit of food still in his goatee from the dinner he was enjoying when the summons came. The captain bowed his feathered hat to the prince. As he straightened, his eyes fixed momentarily on the shadowed stranger. He scanned for possible danger, then turned to his prince. "You wanted to see me, Your Highness?"

"I want you to send word tonight to the King's Guard and the City Guard, and to the Black Bands." Jaimis quickly outlined the retraction of the monetary reward and a change in directives.

"Very well, Your Highness. I will send it out at once." The captain waited, hoped for more.

"You're dismissed," the prince said, and brief disappointment played on the captain's face. For two days now, the guards had been hoping for an explanation of the girl. But they would not get it; not until the entire plan had been carried out. The captain turned and left, shutting the solid door behind him.

The grey-haired man flicked back the hood with mild relief. "So, Jaimis, do your Black Bands know who she is?"

"No. And it would be highly foolish of me to tell them. I doubt they would serve me so avidly if they knew."

"I doubt they would believe you if you told them. People will have to see the results before they accept the truth." The two men regarded each other briefly, then the grey one continued. "Tell me about her. Tell me everything, and don't leave a single thing out. It may be important for when we have to break her."

Jaimis nodded once and began.

◉

When total darkness shrouded the landscape, with no signs of movement for some time, Emme and Kye, who had sat close to each other all afternoon to fight off the terrible chill, left the rooftop and headed back down the alley towards home.

"I really don't want to go back, you know," Emme whispered to Kye's back in the thin, dark passageway.

Without turning, he said, "Just think of a hot tea, hot bath, and a warm bed."

"Okay, so that all sounds rather good. But only if I can wake up outside in the morning."

Kye stepped beyond the thin passageway onto a connecting lane, then stopped, waited for Emme to catch up. "I always wake early. Maybe I could wake you and we can go outside and watch the dawn."

"You'd do that for me?" Emme asked before she realised the weakness that sentence carried.

Kye smiled in the quiet darkness. "Anything to stop you running off into the path of soldiers."

The two continued down the laneway whilst dark clouds swirled above them. Soon snow began to fall. Kye shivered, and Emme knew how cold he must be without his heavy woollen cloak. He refused to take it – had refused all afternoon. What kind of a man put a woman, put *anyone* else, before himself? She couldn't think of a single man in the village who would do that, not even for their wives and children. Emme had protested, saying she was no weak woman that needed a man's cloak; but he had told her it was to stop her drawing attention to him. He had made it up; she knew it. No one would see them on the rooftop. But the lie allowed her to save face, and she was silently grateful for it. Still, he puzzled her. There must have been some underlying sinister reason for being kind to her. No one was ever nice to her without some thought of return.

Maybe it was the deal they had struck – he didn't expose her, she didn't expose him. If he were nice to her, she would be less inclined to betray him. Maybe – but she doubted that would go as far as a cloak donation. It was entirely unnecessary.

Kye directed her back to the headquarters via a path she did not recognise. "We never take the same way twice consecutively," he whispered to her. His cold hand on her back guided her quickly to a thin laneway on their right. Several tabby cats sat licking themselves on rows of bins. The wind briefly swept the stench of garbage into her nostrils, then away down the alleyway after two of the less brave cats.

"Disgusting," Emme said. "Don't they know to bury their rubbish?"

"We pay to have our rubbish collected by special farmers," Kye explained quietly as they wandered past the large metal canisters. "Once a month the farmers take the rubbish to the farmlands and bury it in big holes. The poor –"

"I know, I know. Do it themselves."

A shadow flitted across the end of the open laneway. Kye stopped, his hand tight on Emme's arm, a warning to make no sound.

He leant close to Emme. "Wait here. I'm going to go and look."

"Not without me," Emme whispered.

Kye swiftly shook his head. "Two are more easily noticed

than one. Wait here – please." He stole away before Emme could protest, his hand on his rapier hilt.

She watched as Kye dissolved to a silhouette in the darkness. Then the silhouette peered around the edge of the alleyway before disappearing beyond it.

Four men sprang from behind the large bins. The cans clattered and tumbled, spilling rubbish onto snow. Cats hissed and skittered away in fright. Emme yelled, bolted. She dashed down the alley after Kye, but a leg launched from the last bin. Her feet snagged on the human log, and she smashed down into the bitter snow. Emme cried out, enraged, as a man dove on top of her and wrenched her arm up her back. She bucked and struggled. More hands, uncountable hands, pinned her to the snow. Her hood was ripped from her head and someone meshed taut fingers through her hair, yanked her hair backward to tilt her head. A gag was stretched around her mouth with pinching tightness. She heard a dagger whisk from a pouch – she knew that sound all too well. Then an echoing crack like a breaking bone in a cavern. Her head exploded. Darkness.

5

Firelight, flickering in the small, windowless room, stabbed into Emme's mind when she opened her eyes. She winced, pinched lids tight, then opened them to slits to filter the stinging light. Her head pounded with all the ferocity of a mallet fracturing rock. She felt tender, aching, where rough handling had awakened every bruise on her body.

She peered through squinting eyes around the stifling room. A stranger in pitch-black clothes sat on a padded bench-seat to her left. She realised she was on a chair, hands tied behind the hard chair back, feet strapped to the chair legs. The rollneck of her jumper felt moist against her throat, her chin wet, possibly from drool. She licked her lips, and an acrid taste made her wince. No – not drool. Whilst unconscious, a concoction had been poured down her throat. Its remnants sat on a spindly fold-up table in front of her. White pills rested in an open porcelain jar. Whether she had been fed them or was yet to be fed them, she did not know.

Gradually Emme relaxed narrowed eyes and took in more light. She realised the firelight, initially stinging, was merely a weak yellow glow in a gloomy room.

The stranger regarded her curiously, his pale silver-grey eyes eerie on a handsome face partially shadowed from the flickering flame. Who was he? No tattoo ornamented his hand; nor did a white skullcap cover his ash-blond crown. So he wasn't an Ashrone. Tar-black clothes, glossy black boots, and a smooth chin told her he could not be a guard. And a commoner wouldn't have set that elaborate trap by the bins. That only left the Black Bands.

At the conclusion, hair bristled along her arms and scalp.

Emme yanked violently at her ropes. The throbbing pain in her head flared at her sudden movements, but she persisted against the cords. "Damn you, you cowardly pig. Untie me and fight me like a man."

The man's neat left eyebrow arched as he regarded Emme calmly. Gradually the brow lowered, and a dark humour stirred in his pale, cold eyes. "Well, well. We have all been anxiously waiting to hear what language you speak. It seems you speak King's Tongue and very well at that."

"I wouldn't want you to miss out on all the insults you deserve." Emme glared at him, her hands still twisting inside the ropes. She noted that her pouch had been removed from her waist, and with it, her dagger. Not that it would do her any good in this position.

"So, you pig's backside, are you going to violate me?"

"Is that what you think I would do? Bother to expend my men's energy dragging you in here, when I can have a whore for a fraction of the cost of that medicine I just gave you?" He gestured calmly to the tray.

Emme wanted to kick the tray to the far wall – smash that bottle of expensive liquid. Watch the pricey fluid splash across the floor and up the sides of the walls, and see his face twist in horror.

The ropes at her feet refused to give. "Then, what are you going to do with me? And what have you done with Kye?"

"Kye – who is Kye?"

"The man who was with me."

"He is probably still wandering the streets looking for you. Say, what would gutter trash like you be doing with a gentleman like him?"

Emme snorted. "Kye? A gentleman? Hardly."

The eyebrow arched again. "You have a lot to learn about social class in this city. But then, I am told that you are not from around here – that you are from a country far, far away."

"So what do you want with me?"

"It is not what *I* want with you; it is what Prince Jaimis wants with you."

Emme scowled. "Don't say his damned name."

"Oh, there is no danger in doing that. Prince Jaimis is well aware of our operations. He is the one who instructed us to find you."

"And what does *he* want with me?"

Emme almost thought she saw uncertainty alter the man's face, but his voice remained impassive as he asked, "You don't know?"

"Of course not, you stupid pig. I'm not from this country. How could I possibly know?"

He seemed to be thinking, to be weighing up her words. "You know, you may as well not bother to tug on those ropes. The Black Bands know how to tie up their victims."

"I'd be a fool if I didn't try."

The man shrugged slightly. "Suit yourself."

"So when is the prince coming?" She felt hot blood trickle down her hands. The flesh of her twisting wrists eroded beneath the ropes.

"He's not. We were just waiting for you to wake up so we could take you to him. I'm sure he'll be glad to see you. And pleased that we saved him ten gold pieces." A commotion echoed in the hallway outside. His head turned swiftly.

"Open it," a male voice beyond the door said sharply. The door swung open, and Kye stepped into the room, his dagger blade pinned to the throat of a little pale-eyed boy backed against Kye's chest.

The man in the room launched to his feet, dagger in hand. "Drop it," Kye warned, and instantly the man discarded the weapon. It clanged on the floor like a death toll.

Kye's foot flung out behind him and slammed the door shut, leaving brief tense silence in the stuffy room.

"Sorry, Papa," the little boy whimpered. Only his eyes were the twin image of the other man in the room.

The pale-eyed man fixed Kye with a level stare, seemed almost to recognise Kye. "What do you want?"

Kye regarded the man with cold speculation. "I've come for the woman. I'll let your son go when she's out and safe." He glanced at Emme. "Are you all right?"

"Fine. Just get me out of here."

The pale-eyed man nodded once to Kye, eyes still sharp. "I know you – you're the leader of the street rats. You choose poor company for a man of such well-breeding."

"My company is none of your concern, and if you hurt any one of them, especially this woman here, my blade will go *into* your son's throat."

"Tough words for a gentleman. But are you all bluff?"

"There's only one way to find that out."

Again the two men regarded each other as though their frosty animosity went beyond that tiny, hot room. The lingering, hostile silence made the room feel even smaller.

Kye's dagger pressed harder to the boy's pale throat. "Shall we test it?"

The cool-eyed man did not even flinch. At last he said, "All right, I'll let the woman go – for now. But don't think she won't be caught. You'd do well to advise her to change her clothes and grow her hair if you don't want her to be caught again."

"Thank you for the advice," Kye said, tone cold.

"Of course, we know what she looks like now, and she is not going to be safe – not anywhere. And neither is the man who threatens my son."

Kye's face remained steely. "It took one man tonight to rescue her – just one. Imagine what I could do if I send all my men after you."

The Black Band's eyes narrowed. He showed no sign of fear as he calmly considered the threat.

"Now untie the woman," Kye said. "No daggers, just your fingers on the knots."

The man stepped to Emme's back and worked briskly on the wrist knots. Kye moved from the closed door and pressed his back against a stone wall near the bench-seat to protect against surprise from behind.

"My, my," the Black Band said to Emme, "you did do some damage back here." He seemed almost amused.

Kye expressed nothing, but watched intently.

Whilst the Black Band still worked on the secure knots, the door opened a mere hand span. An arm snaked around it, waved a white handkerchief as a sign of peace. Then the heavily shadowed Black Band in the hallway opened the door a little further, knelt, pushed a hollow tube of parchment across the floor to the pale-eyed man. It skidded over timber and contacted with Emme's chair. "You both might want to read this," the messenger said through the gap in the door. The door hurriedly closed.

The Black Band's eyes questioned Kye. Kye considered it, then nodded approval. The man knelt, picked up the stiff curled parchment and read. His expression showed intense curiosity. "Well, well, well. It seems this whole evening has been for naught. It appears the prince does not want this woman after all. She is free to go. Your efforts to rescue this prize have been in vain – she is worthless to you and to me."

"Why did he want her in the first place?" Kye asked. He positioned his blade tip beneath the boy's ear. "Tell me."

"Ahh – now that I do not know."

"*Tell* me." The dagger sliced the child's face from ear to chin – a cut designed to scar, not kill. Blood seeped from the superficial trail. The child gasped, eyes wide and lips trembling. A slow spread of wetness moved down the boy's trouser-leg.

For the first time, the Black Band began to lose his icy coolness. He held up hands. "I promise you, I do not know. We were told to look for a woman dressed like this one, and failing that, for a woman with a strange birthmark on her wrist."

Emme stiffened. That snake. She should never have shown him her wrist mark.

Kye looked at Emme, his eyes questioning her. The two regarded each other for some time.

"Untie her," Kye said at last, breaking eye contact with Emme.

The Black Band returned to the knots. Emme's inflamed wrist flesh tore as the Black Band ripped the ropes from the sticky wounds. Hands finally free, Emme worked furiously on the lower legs. Blood from the wrist wounds trickled down her hands and onto the ankle cord. At last her shaking fingers tossed the bloodied ropes into the fire. The fire hissed and spat maliciously at her.

"Now – she is going to walk out of here," Kye said. "We are all going to walk out of here, together. You will command your Black Bands to stay well back."

"Why do you still want her? She is not worth any money, and you will not be stopping any of the prince's plans by taking her."

"People are worth more than what we can use them for."

"Except little boys, it would seem." The man let the irony settle, before he added, "You and I are not so different; we both choose who we value."

A muscle tightened in Kye's jaw. "You are playing a game you have forced me to enter. Now *walk*."

The pale-eyed man nodded. Emme stood. The room spun from the pounding in her skull as the three moved slowly across the room. Emme sidestepped to the dagger dropped by the Black Band. She gripped the cold silver handle, felt the impressive weight of it in her palm. A well-made weapon, she could tell at a glance. She waved it angrily at the cold-eyed man. "This is for stealing mine, you thieving pig."

"Keep your back to the wall," Kye ordered when they moved into the hallway, "or they'll knife it when you're not looking."

With slow, tense movements, their backs dragging along the abrasive sandstone wall, the four of them progressed down too many dark corridors, uncontested by other Black Bands who stayed as far back as their pale-eyed leader commanded. They passed many stairs leading to secret city entrances, but Kye disregarded them all as though wanting one in particular. Kye seemed as knowledgeable of the maze as he did of the Black Band leader's one weakness – the frail son.

They stopped when Kye ordered Emme to gather up a torch blazing on the wall. Emme worked it from its tight socket, withdrew a little from the oily heat, and then pressed back against the wall.

At last they took a flight of stairs to a trapdoor. The leader led them out the trapdoor, and into a deceptively ordinary tailor shop closed for the night. The leader unbolted the shop door latch, pulled the door open into the shop. A mound of snow tumbled onto the shop floor when the doorbell tinkled, loud on the still night.

"You – back to the trap door," Kye ordered the pale-eyed man.

When the man stood at the trapdoor, Kye turned to Emme. "Gather up some of those bolts of cloth. Place them in a line between them and us."

With the hand not clutching the spitting torch, Emme dragged over the stiff, heavy rolls of fabric and spread them out in a flat, rough wall.

"Now come back to the door," Kye ordered Emme.

As Emme reached the door, Kye thrust the little boy away from him, back towards the square hole in the floor. The boy hurried over the wall of cloth to his father.

Kye snatched the torch from Emme's hand. "Hurry out of here, Emme. Run out that door and wait for me down the street."

Emme bolted out the door into freshly falling snow. She rushed down the street. Behind her, she heard the bell tinkle. The slamming shop door silenced the bell, then glancing over her shoulder, she saw Kye run after her. Hungry flames licked at smoking windows of the tailor shop. The eerie orange flames swiftly turned to rampage through the room beyond the imprisoning glass.

Emme slowed until Kye caught up. She felt momentarily bewildered by this man she had so underestimated until now. "You burnt the shop?"

Kye did not answer. He pulled her through a dark alley. Down confined streets they wound, then into an insignificant passageway. Kye pushed on a stone. A jagged door swung open. He hastily tugged Emme inside after him, then shouldered the door closed. Utter darkness closed in on them, and Kye fumbled for his flintbox. She heard the scuffle of his feet on rock, and then heard a hand explore a wall. The flintbox struck, lit a mounted candle, then Kye turned to her.

"Are you all right, Emme? Really?"

"I'm okay. My head really hurts and –" She held up wrists to the light. "And my wrists are cut but I did that myself."

"Let me see."

"I'll be fine."

"Let me see." His tone left no room for argument. "Wrist cuts can be lethal."

She presented wrists to him, and he inspected them in the pallid light. His palms held the back of her hands, and his thumbs traced lightly over the wounds. "They'll be all right once we get them washed and bandaged."

"Told you," Emme sighed. Her voice just sounded as weary as she suddenly felt.

"Is that the birthmark?" Kye looked at the blood-crusted brown design on her wrist.

"That is *a* birthmark. It doesn't mean anything. I showed it to the prince when I first met him. And you heard the letter. The prince has realised he made a mistake."

"I doubt that. There's more going on than a major mistake."

Emme sighed and looked around at the thick walls. This room, a different location to the last, was almost identical inside – the wall candle, the stacks of spares, the irregular stone walls and floor, the brick-edged doorway. "Why in here? Why not go back home?"

"Trehn, the leader – that was the leader in that room – will be very swift to send his Black Bands after us. Not to kill us but to follow us and find out where we live. We need them to lose our trail. They'll give up in a few hours. I know them and their ways."

"So you didn't kill them tonight? The leader and his son?"

"No – I made sure the two were down the hatch. They would have torched the shop tonight anyway and caved in the tunnel to destroy their secret entrance. I saved them the trouble so we wouldn't be followed for a while."

"How did you know about that man's son?"

"If you're going to play a game like this, you need to know your enemy's weakness. Trehn thought no one knew about the boy, and I knew I would only ever be able to play that advantage once. He'll keep the boy underground with him now."

"He wasn't already underground?"

"He lives in the city with his mother. I wouldn't have even made it past the first Black Band I saw without the child."

"How do you know all of this?"

"I just do."

An evasion. Emme sighed deeply and slumped to the floor.

Kye squatted in front of her but kept his distance, eyes almost sad in the pale light of the candle. "I'm so sorry that happened, Emme. I really am. I know better than that. I've survived for twenty-three years on the streets. I should know how to recognise an ambush by now."

"It's all right," Emme said, too tired to insist she did not need the help of a man.

"No, it's not all right. That will never happen to you again. I promise you, as long as you are in my care, I will never let that happen to you again."

She believed him. In that moment, without knowing a thing about him, she believed him. The sincerity was more real than anything she had encountered before. Even the prince's clever lies that had tricked her into coming to this city, seemed totally artificial compared to those two sentences. Why would Kye make such a promise to her, a mere stranger from another world?

He awaited her response, and Emme slowly shook her head. "I was the one who ran out this morning. It all started then."

Kye sat back onto his bottom and rested shoulders against the wall. "It doesn't matter to me when it started; I should have known better." His whole being suggested a man sternly berating himself. "I'm just so sorry. I always protect my people better than that."

"*Your* people? Is that who they are? Do you really believe you're personally responsible for each one of them?"

Kye watched Emme silently. She knew she had touched on something very personal, very profound about him, but the exact truth of it escaped her. Was she one of his people now? Is that why he was so kind to her? Because he felt it was his duty to protect her? She didn't sense it was pride that drove him; pride at losing a prize in his collection. She guessed it was a genuine feeling of responsibility – but where it came from, and what sins he felt he was atoning for, she could only guess at.

She watched his eyes slide from her face to the floor, and there he sat in silence for some time. Was he reliving the night and going over his mistakes? Was he dwelling on her questions? She longed to know; then suddenly longed to know why she longed to know.

She sighed again, a tired sigh, and rested her heavy head against the wall. It throbbed all over and stung in a distinct line across the back where the dagger handle had smacked it. Her wrists burned where rope fibres and infected blood had burrowed into the shredded flesh. In that moment, she could count almost every bruise on her body, just by concentrating on where she hurt.

The acrid taste of the medicine, probably given to shock her awake and remove any groggy effects of the dagger handle, still contaminated her mouth.

She shut eyes and imagined a big meal and hot tea awaiting her when she finally got back. In that moment, the dark underground home of the street kids seemed the most inviting place in the whole world.

Emme guessed the time to be more than two hours past midnight when she and Kye finally stepped into the well-lit dining hall of the street rat headquarters. She noted, with faintly visible surprise, the number of people still awake.

Halder, the big bear-man, surged to his feet at the sight of them. His echoing triumphant roar silenced all agitated conversations and murmurings. Dusty shot to his feet and dashed to them as though they had been away for years. Halder strode resolutely behind.

Dusty hugged Kye roughly before throwing arms around Emme and sobbing like a child onto her shoulder. He did not seem to notice that her arms remained stiff at her side, nor notice her glare of horror that he even touched her at all.

"I – I thought I'd killed you," Dusty said between sobs. He seemed to gather himself and finally stepped back from Emme, leaving her shoulder damp with tears. His eyes were puffy, bloodshot. He had sobbed a few more times that evening. His hand went to his studded leather wristband and spun it over and over, a nervous gesture. "I thought you'd gone and the guards had you and they'd kill you and we'd never see you again." He drew a crinkled, well-used white handkerchief from a trouser pocket and blew his nose loudly. "And I wanted Kye to come back so he could go and find you but there was no way to know where he was or when he'd be back. And I waited and waited and waited for him, and I wanted to tell him –" He sniffed. "Tell him that I'd lost you and it was all my fault. I was to keep you down here, make sure you didn't go out. I should have told all the others not to let you –"

"Oh, stand back, boy," Halder said, his bulky arm sweeping Dusty aside. "Can't you see they're injured and tired?" His face and tone were not nearly as rough as the words.

"Yes, injured and tired," Kye said. "Dusty, go and get the medicine kit. Emme has a nasty bump on her head and gashes on her wrists."

"I'll be all right," Emme said quietly.

"*I'll* tell you when you'll be all right," Halder said with gruff kindness. "Come sit down and show me those injuries." He grabbed Emme by the shoulder, his hand a tight, aching pressure on her thin bones, and pulled her roughly across the room. Afraid her collarbone might snap if she resisted, she obeyed the bear-man and sat on the chair he kicked out for her with his feet. Kye moved to a short distance behind her.

Halder inspected the wrists. "Hmmm – bad cuts and a rope burn. Treatable." He looked from the wrists to Kye and sent silent questions to him.

"Tomorrow, friend," Kye said wearily. He sat down on the nearest chair.

"You – Jackson," Halder roared. "Get them drinks and food. The rest of you, go to bed. You're not needed here anymore."

Chairs scraped noisily along the stone floor, then ten younger people scurried from the room. As though breaking from a daze, the instant the children's feet struck the timber beyond the doorway, animated conversations set off between them all. Excited babbled questions gushed from their mouths and could be heard all the way down the hall until one-by-one their bedroom doors locked out the sound.

"You can give me my wrists back for now," Emme said, disarmed by the continued contact of Halder's hands on hers.

Halder released them. "Just don't run away from me."

Emme doubted anyone would attempt to run away from the big man, unless they were already ten yards away from him.

The older boy, Jackson, returned with tea and remnants of the previous night's potato. He deposited the tray on the nearest table to Halder, then left the dining hall just as Dusty raced into the room clutching a large sack in his bloodless fists. He hurriedly dumped the sack on the table in front of Halder, then stepped back behind the big man. Dusty paced, wringing his hands as if waiting for Emme to die.

Halder could hear Dusty's irregular steps on the boards and rolled his eyes a little. He turned attention back to the wounds, picked up Emme's wrists again.

Dusty inhaled sharply. "Good Almighty, that looks awful," he said loudly to Emme's wrist wounds.

Halder turned his shaggy head to the boy. Emme did not see the look Halder gave Dusty but could easily imagine it from the way Dusty stiffened. "Go to bed," Halder ordered.

Dusty scuttled from the room.

Halder refused to let Emme touch the food until he had finished picking thick rope fibres from the wounds, washing the injuries, lathering them in salves and bandaging them. Then Emme tucked into the food with ravenous vigour.

She swigged the lukewarm tea as though water. Kye picked quietly at the cold potato, then sat back in his chair. "I'm going to rest now. Do you want me to wake you in the morning, Emme?"

"Leave the girl to sleep," Halder said.

"I promised Emme I would do something tomorrow morning." Emme noted that he tactfully left off details.

"Yes, wake me," Emme said. "I might go to bed now too. I'm so tired."

The three stood and parted. Halder tramped down the storeroom corridor towards the laundry stairs to his apartment. Kye and Emme drifted silently down the far left corridor to their rooms.

"Goodnight, Emme," Kye said before she disappeared into her room. He bowed slightly from the waist. "I hope you sleep well."

Emme smiled thinly, and shut the door to her room. Judging by the oil left in her lantern, someone had recently lit it and made the bed. The tatty jumper, taken from the corpse in the snow, sat neatly folded at the end of her mattress. Who would bother to do that, she wondered.

She tugged off excess clothes and slid between the freshly straightened sheets. The tip of the new dagger, tucked down into her trousers, pricked her hip slightly, and she adjusted it, patted it once, a reassurance that it would be there if she needed it.

Moments later she was in an uninterruptible sleep.

Emme whisked the dagger from her trousers, pinned the point to the throat of a heavily shadowed male leaning over her. She slowly released it. "Damn it, Kye – you could have just knocked on the door."

"I did, but you didn't answer. You must have been in a deep sleep." Kye straightened and stepped back.

Emme replaced the dagger into her trouser top. "I'm sorry about the dagger but you need to be careful. I may not always be able to protect you if you come in here like this. Especially if I can't see who you are."

Kye's lips turned up in a slight smile. "I'll remember that."

Emme yawned, sat up and stretched. She kicked off the heavy blankets and swung her legs over the bed, then looked expectantly to the source of the light. This time the lantern still burned but her eyes longed for sunlight, and within seconds her heart began to pound with irrational fear.

"Let's get out of here," she tried to say calmly.

"We'll go up to Halder's house and to his rooftop."

"Let's just get there quickly."

"Here." Kye handed her a weighty woollen cloak.

132

She took the olive garment, wrapped herself in it, then followed Kye out of the room. He led her swiftly through the building, to the hidden door in the vacant laundry and up the steep flight of stairs. It led to a stone trapdoor cut into Halder's floor.

With his left ear slightly upturned to the door in the ceiling, Kye listened for a while. "The sound of Halder's voice usually means it's not safe to enter."

Emme opened her mouth to ask what that meant, when Kye pushed at the weighty trapdoor, forced it back. The trapdoor, stone underneath, treated timber boards on top, came to rest on a sharp angle, prevented by a tight hinge from laying flat. The parting in the floor led to a cavernous timber-floored space with a colossal empty central fireplace open on two sides. A staircase on Emme's right spiralled to an indoor balcony. Other than a stocky table and chair, only a room sealed by an unstained timber door sat beyond the balcony's crude wire railing. The vastness downstairs, canopied by a ceiling two storeys up, did not come close to being filled by two bulky couches, an empty desk and a solid dining table.

One entire corner was set up with an enormous active urn-shaped fireplace, blacksmith tools, and clever metal creations that Emme imagined only the rich could afford – Halder's trade. His coarse, grubby aprons hung down the wall from rough metal hooks beside the only window – the window that let out heat from the huge fire and let potential customers see in. She realised the curtained window was positioned so that at any time of the day, passers-by would not see street kids appear mysteriously from the floorboards. The enormous central fire, and a rack of metal wares for sale, blocked the view of the trapdoor.

The last structure in the room, dominating an empty corner, was a steep, spiralling black staircase that coiled right to the ceiling, then uselessly stopped.

"How do we get up?" Emme asked quietly.

Kye pointed to the twisting staircase in the far left corner. "Most factories like this have staircases leading to flat rooftops."

"Is that Halder's bedroom up there?" Emme pointed right, to the only door off the loft.

Kye nodded and strolled towards the far staircase. Emme followed behind, her gait not nearly so relaxed. She stepped hastily up the staircase, eager to see the light.

Kye pushed open the roof hatch and climbed up over the edge. He remembered not to offer a hand to Emme, and she suddenly wished he would. Her bandaged wrists burned as she dragged herself out of the hatch.

The cold hit her face as she stood and surveyed the flat, snow-covered rooftop with the two solid brick chimneys rising from its floor. The generous space discontinued just beyond the second chimney, and Emme guessed that the warehouse below had once been two. The high walled edge, almost to Emme's shoulders, divided Halder's space on three sides from long-gone neighbours. It looked out at a beautiful dawn on the remaining side. The sky, no longer a conglomerate mass of grey, had divisions in the thick clouds, and from one of the divisions, the pale sun shone. It rose just above a sea of rooftops, and over the arches of some of the city's trees – green pines and winter-bare branches.

"Sunshine," Emme sighed. She raised her face to it and longed to feel its warmth on her cheeks, but only the breeze met her skin.

A long metal bench-seat was bolted into part of the unshared balcony edge. Tiny slits, like arrow holes, parted the bricks where people might sit and peer through them. Kye guided her towards the bench, but the two stood and leant shoulders against the wall.

Emme saw black sooty streaks in the bricks. She ran her hand along them and inspected her skin, but the black streaks were permanent, burned into the stone by the fire that had ravaged the warehouse many years ago.

Kye watched her movements. "How are your wounds?"

"They don't bother me." Emme had learned long ago to live with pain.

Kye turned from gazing at the bandages to the dawn. "We don't often get the sun in winter here. When we do, it's for a few hours at the most."

"I don't know how you can stand it. Even in the middle of winter in our forest, we can have days where the sun blazes so bright it reflects off the snow and burns your face."

"I wish I had seen your homeland. It sounds very interesting."

Emme took a moment to guess whether his words were polite protocol or genuine. She figured it didn't matter. She was not so attached to her homeland that a lie about being interested in it would hurt her feelings.

"I don't think there will be anything for breakfast this morning," Kye said after a significant silence. "There are a few potatoes left, and a bit of stale bread. That will have to go to the younger ones."

"Does Halder's business pay for most of it?"

"A lot of it. But it's hard funding sixty-two people with one business. Many of the younger ones have chimney-sweeping jobs and do irregular cleaning of the wealthier houses. Some of the kids do busking in the summer. Do you know what busking is?"

She nodded. The stranger had been a busker. He recited poetry – though no one in the village understood his poems. She assumed that was why he ended up in Underoak. He couldn't find an audience anywhere else.

"And some of the older ones travel to the farmlands for a few weeks work, but they don't get paid much. So when we get desperate, we send kids up to wait for the scraps that taverns and wealthy homes throw out. The taverns will usually give their wastes to the poor who wait at their doors. This winter though, the poor are numerous."

"Why?"

"The prince has increased a lot of taxes."

"Does he do that a lot?"

"Only when he's trying to pay for things that I won't describe here."

"It's not right." Emme scowled at the sun as if it were the cause of the problems. "You should be able to eat whenever you are hungry, and none of you should have to search rubbish piles."

"That's life for us," Kye said calmly. "I wish we could all own a plot of land and work it like your villagers do – or have a forest we can forage in without being taxed, but our world doesn't work that way."

Her brows knitted in anger. "Well I don't like the way your world works."

"Do you wish you were home in your forest?"

Emme considered his question. No. Somehow the hatred from the villagers and the beatings by her mother, weighed as heavily as all the injustices and darkness of the city. It made little difference where she was. She shook her head.

"Well then this is your home now, and if you hope to survive, you're going to have to learn its ways. Would you like me to teach you? To help you to survive here?"

"Whatever," Emme said with a shrug. "I seem to have done all right so far." At the left boundary of her vision, she saw the slow smile spread across Kye's face. She sighed. "Yes, that was a stupid thing to say. Teach me, then. But I'm not wearing those hideous dresses that your women wear."

"I can only teach you, Emme. I can't make you change."

"So when do we begin?"

"Well, today I'm going to go to some other contacts I have. I want to tell them about your birthmark and see what they know. I should be back tomorrow, and we can begin then."

"Whatever," Emme said. Then the two quietly watched the dawn until the sun finally surrendered to a patch of cloud, casting a grey veil over the landscape.

Emme argued with Dusty and two other boys in the dining hall.

"I'm coming with you," she said again, hands folded stubbornly over her chest.

Dusty spun the studded leather wristband around and around his wrist, shifted from one foot to the other. "I don't know, Emme. I just don't know."

"I am not going to sit by and watch everyone starve to death. I'm coming with you, and that's that."

"But your appearance," said Jase, the younger but taller, leaner, blond-haired lad.

"Just give me some of your clothes," Emme said to Jase. "I'll fit in if I wear your clothes."

Jase gave a snorting laugh. "You'd never pass for a boy."

"Why not? I have short hair." She tugged the short, tufted strands of her dark brown hair as if pointing it out to them for the first time.

"Yes, but your face is too pretty, too girlie."

Emme curled fingers into a fist and slugged Jase's stomach. He doubled over with a startled gasp. "What was that for?" he asked, more stunned than injured.

"I am not girlie," Emme said hotly.

"What's wrong with looking girlie?" He straightened, arms across his stomach protectively.

"I am *not* girlie."

"Fine, you don't look girlie, then," Jase snapped back.

"Thank you," Emme said, anger gone. She looked from one to the other. "Now, who is going to lend me some trousers and a shirt?"

"I will," Dusty said. "We're about the same size."

"And I'll need boots too."

Dusty shook his head slowly. "Kye is going to be unhappy about this. He trusted me to keep you here while he was away."

"The prince doesn't even need me anymore," Emme said. "Just ask Kye."

Jase's eyes widened. "The prince was after you?"

Emme ignored him. "I'm in no danger and I want to go and help you carry as much food back from the taverns as I can. Now stop arguing with me, you three." Emme glared at each in turn. "Go get me the damned clothes."

The three scurried off, evidently frightened of being thumped. "And an extra backpack," she called after them.

They returned a short time later with a bundle of clothes. Emme took the pile into the kitchen and ducked behind the bench. She commanded the three boys to turn around, and swiftly slipped on the new clothes. The garments felt odd against her skin. The white, lace-up shirt that she tucked into snug, brown corduroy pants, rippled and tickled. The stiff black boots with the weighted soles made her feet feel bigger than they were. She yanked the bootlaces tight, levered her thick jumper over the top of her shirt, then draped Dusty's cloak over her shoulders.

The three boys were grinning when she exited the kitchen. "You look very sex –" Dusty jabbed Jase's ribs; shot him a warning glance.

"Like a guy," Jase finished safely.

"Let's go, then," Emme ordered. She followed Dusty, Jase and the black-haired, black-eyed boy, Jerris, out the door and up the flight of stairs first used when she discovered this place.

The four worked their way through the city maze, Emme at the mercy of the boys' sense of direction. Darkness had fallen many hours before, and most citizens were tucked in bed. Very few lamps burned behind curtains. Most windows were dark eye sockets staring blankly at the silently falling snow. The snow-coated streets stretched grey, dull in the darkness.

Dusty assured her that now was the hour most taverns finished cleaning up after guests. Having washed mounds of dishes, taverns would be preparing to dispose of any foods they could not reuse.

As they trudged through the thick snow, Emme began to wonder if she would ever memorise some of the streets. No matter how many times she wandered this city, nothing seemed familiar.

After twenty minutes of walking, they approached a building with a large, curtainless, ground-floor window. Bright light flooded onto the street, as did a few last citizens staggering towards their houses.

"Drunken pigs," Emme muttered to their backs. "Are we early, Dusty?"

"No, dinner is always finished early. People often stay late for drinks until they get so drunk the tavern owner throws them out."

"Vile habit," she said with a deep scowl.

Jerris tugged on her cloak and pointed to the alleyway she had overstepped. She followed them to the back of the old tavern, up to the flaking painted kitchen door, and there they waited in the freezing cold.

"No one else here," Dusty said.

"I told you there wouldn't be," Jase said as if he had just won a competition. "It's too cold for people tonight."

"I would think that would make them more desperate," Emme said, then shivered as a burst of icy wind shot through the gaps in her cloak. She wrapped it cosily around herself. The wounds on her wrists began to ache in protest. The salve Halder had applied twice that day, had long since soaked into the bandages, leaving nothing but thin, wind-ravaged rags between her raw, damaged flesh and the cold.

"Poor people can't afford to get sick," Dusty explained to her. "They won't go out on really cold nights. It's safer for them to skip a meal."

"Tragic," Emme muttered. "I'm beginning to really hate this place." But she knew it was the cold weather and the ache of her motley collection of bruises making her grumpy. "And you people have got to learn to dress better for the weather. These clothes wouldn't even keep me warm in summer."

"What do you wear?" The quiet black-eyed Jerris asked her.

"Furs. Lots and lots of furs. Fur in our boots, fur in our coats, fur on our heads, even fur in our underpants."

Jase giggled boyishly, and Emme turned a neatly arched brow to him. "Is that necessary?"

He did a poor job of smoothing the smile.

"Now what?" Emme asked.

"Well, we either wait, or we knock and ask," Dusty said. "Sometimes taverns don't like people asking. They hate being pestered all the time."

"Well they'll just have to get used to it." Emme pushed Dusty neatly aside and sauntered up the four stone steps to the back doorway. She peered through the little glass window and surveyed the spacious kitchen area. She sniffed once. "Chicken.

They've had a roast dinner tonight."

Without knocking, Emme flung open the door to the kitchen. It slapped against its wall, the sound muffled by the kitchen bustle.

"Emme, what are you doing?" Dusty whispered loudly.

She ignored him, threw back her hood and stared boldly around the room. The five staff members stopped swiftly to stare, pots and soiled plates frozen in their hands.

"I need enough leftover chickens for sixty people, wrapped in leak-proof bags," she called out. "And all the vegetables you have left."

The kitchen staff stared, blinked at her for several moments, then burst into laughter.

A portly man put down his carving knife and approached her whilst his hands cleaned themselves on his grubby apron. "Well, look what we have here. A woman dressed as a man who thinks she's Lady Rich and can order us all around."

The room laughed again. Emme merely watched them with a calm expression. "I'll have the chickens, thank you."

The man chuckled darkly. "And what makes you think we'd be so careless with our money as to cook enough chickens for sixty *extra* people, when our room only seats thirty?"

"I want the chickens now please," Emme said.

The sardonic smile still curved the man's lips. "I can't give you what isn't here."

"If you had them, would you give them to me?" Emme's eyes narrowed shrewdly.

The man considered her for a moment. "If I had them, then I guess I would."

"Everything you've got left?"

"I'm telling you, there *is* nothing left."

"I want your promise that you'd give them all to me if you had them."

"Fine. For what it's worth, I promise that if I had them, I'd give them to you."

"Good – now look."

"Look?"

"You heard me; I said *look*."

"You want me to play your little game? Okay, I'll play." He turned, enjoying the laughter of his comrades, and bent to the open shelf under a large workstation in the middle of the room. "Under here? No – no chickens here. In here?" He stooped over a hefty food-stained pot. "No – not here." He played with a stack of loose carrots. "Maybe there are chickens hiding under here. No – no chickens." His staff behaved as though he supplied the best amusement they'd had for days. Emme merely watched.

"Emme, come away from there," she heard Dusty snap behind her. "Stop it at once."

The man stopped at trays of leftover food – a few drumsticks, some roasted chunks of potato, a few wilted carrots. "Chickens in here? No. How about we try the oven."

He walked over to the enormous oven that sat at the apex of an urn-shaped clay structure. A fire roared underneath it, and a chimney rose from the back of it past the oven space. He opened the large clay door and stopped, stared. "Good Almighty, will you look at that." All traces of mockery were gone.

The room gathered close to peer inside. Rows and rows of chickens, spitting and browning, packed the oven space.

The portly man's face surged to deep red and he whirled, roared at his staff. "Who bought this food and cooked it up? What a shameful waste."

The staff looked to one another with silent questions as though it deflected suspicion of their own guilt.

"Don't lie to me," the man shouted hotly. "One of you did it. And I'll find out who it was before the night is over and deduct it from your pay."

"Before you do that," Emme said calmly, "can you package the chickens please? My friends are getting cold."

The man's scarlet face snapped around to Emme. His chubby finger shook at her. "You'd better not have done this." He seemed to realise the stupidity of the statement and turned, flustered, back to his staff. He punched a gesture at them as if sentencing them to the stocks. "Bag the chickens for them."

"But we could use the chickens tomorrow," one man protested.

The portly man's face grew hot again, and he spun at the brave objector. "A promise is a promise," he snapped. "Just bag the chickens." He added as an afterthought, "And any left-over vegetables and loaves of bread."

The staff scurried about and within minutes were loading the four canvas backpacks with food. The packs overflowed, forcing Emme and the boys to carry the surplus in sacks at their sides.

"And we'll be back later this week," Emme told the confused kitchen staff before she finally shut the back door behind her.

As the four of them hurried home, the three boys laughed hysterically, recounting the story over and over until Emme fixed them with a level stare. "I was there, boys. Remember? Must I hear about it that many times?"

A few loud snickers and a snort escaped, then the wind hastened their stifled laughter away.

"How did you do that, Emme?" Dusty asked after minutes of quiet contemplation.

"Do what?"

"Know about the chickens."

"I could smell them."

"You knew there were that many?"

"I could tell they had quite a lot left. I just made sure they'd give us everything they had. If I hadn't said a high number, they might have only given us a couple and kept the rest."

Black-eyed Jerris snorted sourly. "It's amazing that they even gave us one. You can't demand anything from anybody in this city unless you're rich."

"Do you think they knew they were there?" the blond-haired Jase asked Emme.

Emme glanced at him. "Knew what were where?"

"The chickens. Do you think they knew they were there and were pretending they didn't have them?"

"Of course they would have known about it. You don't forget putting thirty chickens in the oven." Emme shrugged. "They just didn't count on me having the good sense of smell I developed back home."

"For what?" Dusty asked.

"For tracking. I was a forest tracker."

The boys' eyes lit with interest.

"Really?" Dusty asked excitedly. "What did you track for?"

"Intruders mostly, and I kept watch of the wild herds so we didn't over-hunt them."

"Tell us about it, Emme," Jase said.

For a few minutes, the cold and the dark were forgotten as Emme unwittingly entertained the boys with descriptions of her occupation.

"Wow," Jase whispered into the darkness when the crunching of stiff boots into snow replaced Emme's voice. "Sounds really exciting."

Emme shrugged. "It's not that exciting."

Jerris shoved fists down into his pocket; kicked a bit of snow with his boot as he walked. "Sure sounds better than begging for food."

Emme glanced at Jerris, saw the misery on his face and felt aching pity for them all. They walked for a time in awkward silence.

"Everyone is going to be so excited to eat," Dusty said at last. "This was really worth waiting up for."

"Yeah," Jase said, a grin on his cold face. "We haven't had meat in months. Not since summer."

"Have you ever had times you've all waited up and you guys have come back with nothing?" Emme asked.

"Heaps of times," Jerris said. "But you get used to it."

Pity merged with anger as Emme made a vow that they would never again feel the desperate pangs of hunger.

That evening they feasted joyously on the roast. Swiftly the story of the night's adventure was passed around, the favoured topic of the evening. Emme knew the exact moment Halder heard the story. Although at the furthest table from her, his roar of laughter resounded above all other chatter in the room. Emme flinched at the volume, whilst everyone else seemed immune to it.

At Halder's table, four men, roughly Kye's age, stared at her with annoying constancy while they conversed. One winked at her, and she glared back at him. Unusually, her first impulse was not to leap up and smack her fist into his jaw. If he had been a villager, he'd be on the floor under her foot by now, but she put the wink down to gratitude for the food she had delivered, and felt content to let it be.

Emme realised she had been designated some sort of hero. She was regularly passed the roasted meat and the bread, and people hurriedly filled her empty cup with water as if she might deal out a monetary reward for the service.

When scraps of chicken remained on her table's platter, Emme was the first to be offered it. She desperately wanted to take it, but her eyes drifted over the faces of the younger gaunt children in the room, and for the first time in her life, she declined food offered to her. "Give it to the younger ones," she ordered quietly.

When Halder let out a loud rumbling belch at the end of the meal, it sent up roars of male delight as if he had just won some special prize. Within seconds, most boys were trying to out-belch each other.

Emme sadly ruminated that it didn't take much to amuse the minds of the people down here. No doubt confinement, lack of sunlight, no food and little to do, left them starving for something – especially a hero.

When Emme left the table to go to her room, seven little girls began to tag along, some trying to hold her hand. She snatched her hand away, but relented to them following her to her room.

"Goodnight," the little girls said at her door, their shiny, smiling eyes watching her.

"Do me a favour," Emme said to them. "If any of you see Kye in the morning before I do, tell him to wake me again." She placed her hand on her door, ready to close it. "And make sure you tell him to knock on the door this time."

The girls giggled as if she had said something delightfully naughty. They whispered to themselves, then the swish of skirts and aprons mingled with laughter as they dashed away down the hall to their room.

"Thank goodness that I'm not like that," Emme muttered and closed the door to her room. Then a tiny smile betrayed her.

Kye sat in the wingback chair in the small study at the wealthy boys' boarding school. Large, overflowing bookshelves wrapped around the entire windowless room but for where the door stood. The pile of books Kye returned rested neatly on the desk in front of him. He was yet to peruse the study, and the vast library the school shared with the city's wealthy, for the next assortment of books for the street kids. His contact at the school, the head teacher, surreptitiously donated to Kye all the books the school ordinarily tossed into furnaces to make space for up-to-date volumes. Any other required reading matter had to be discreetly borrowed.

Kye watched the lanky head teacher tap long, bony left-hand fingers on the desktop. The man's right hand played with a trim brown beard on an almost gaunt face.

The head teacher looked at, yet beyond, Kye whilst the man carefully considered Kye's words. The drumming on the desktop finally ceased. "No – the birthmark means nothing to me," he said at last. "Although I've been thinking a great deal since your last visit."

"Tell me about it." Kye reached for the last of the pastries – a late meal.

"Well, is it possible that our prince went to that barbarian girl's world to stop the Ashrones, instead of the Ashrones going to stop the prince?"

"Possibly, but I doubt it. What would the Ashrones want with her that they don't already have?"

"Well, I know they don't have the hearts of the Kildarians. The sacrifice all those years ago hasn't exactly endeared them to the people."

"Sacrifice. I despise that term as if it were some noble act. I call it murder."

Russen regarded Kye closely. "I'm well aware of what you would call it, and you are becoming entirely too vocal about it of late."

"Meaning?"

"I've heard you have been openly calling it murder to the others. We may all share a dislike for the prince, but we don't all agree with what was going on in the girl's head. The reports say she consented."

147

"She was *tricked*."

"Yes, and that is one side of a very volatile debate."

Kye's eyes sharpened. "And what side of the debate are you on?"

"I may use the word 'sacrifice', but it is only because it is the least hazardous word I could choose – a word that could imply I rest on either side, or none at all. You don't have to consent for something to be a sacrifice. It could mean her own personal sacrifice, or a ritual slaughter." The man reached for his unfinished pastry on the neat, white plate before him. He took a small bite and chewed. Crumbs dusted into his beard before he brushed them to the table. "As for personally, I believe the sacrifice was done *to* her, not *by* her. On the one hand they managed to remove her to stop their enemy; on the other hand they used her to buy their dark powers. She bound them to a bargain with the devil." Russen watched Kye for a moment. "So how long have you doubted what I believe?"

Kye allowed a grim smile to pass his lips. "About two minutes."

"I don't know what it is about that event that disturbs you so much, Kye. I may be wrong, but it seems a trace of anger leaks out whenever we raise that ghost."

Kye considered briefly whilst he chewed on the pastry, then chose to ignore the veiled question he always evaded. "So how could Emme possibly help the Ashrones win the support of the people?"

"I admit that's where my mental scheming breaks down and I realise it is a little far-fetched, although my mind does wander to some bizarre ritual that she could be used for. If they did use a dark ritual once, they could do it again."

A chill passed through Kye's insides at the memory, but he remained outwardly calm. "Why would they go all the way to

Emme's country to get her? Why not choose anyone from here for some arcane ritual? Why not someone the country would really love to lose?"

"Yes, that I don't know."

Kye returned the pastry to the plate. "No – it doesn't explain why they chose Emme. Why not any girl or guy?"

"That's a question you should ask the Ashrones. It's *their* black ritual, and only they know what they need for it." He picked up his glass of red wine and took two deep swallows as if for courage.

Kye shook his head. "No – the Ashrones went to stop the prince. I'm sure of it. Emme told me the Ashrones tried to warn her about the prince, that he was coming for her. And remember, when I was captured by the Black Bands, there was that letter delivered – the prince called off the search, not the Ashrones."

"Ahh yes, the letter." The man traced his finger around the rim of the fine glass.

"And the prince would not let Emme go from his clutches if he thought the Ashrones were still after her."

"Maybe they weren't after her anymore," the man suggested calmly. "Maybe there were alternatives for their new sacrifice."

"I don't like this line of thinking. I really don't."

"Why? Because there could be a grain of truth in it?"

"No, because it's rubbing against my mind like a pebble in a shoe. Something isn't right about it."

The man sat back into his winged chair. "Well, if there's one thing I have learned over the years, it is to trust your instinct."

Kye observed Russen's expression for a moment. "There's something else you want to tell me."

Russen smiled slightly. "Yes. I was debating whether to mention this or not until I had thought about it a bit more."

"You know I don't act rashly on anything. Tell me your thoughts."

"Well, if it wasn't a case of the prince going to stop the Ashrones, then there is a possibility I have been considering – especially now that we know it's not just the Ashrones who can use a travel gate." Russen paused briefly, leant forward. "You told me the girl doesn't know her father, right?"

"That's correct."

"Did she mean she never knew him because he died? Or did she mean she doesn't even know who he is? Is it possible she's illegitimate?"

Kye shrugged lightly. "I don't know. Why does it matter?"

"Well, what's the one thing the prince needs to ascend the throne?"

"Obviously a gifted Hunston girl."

"And what if Emme is a Hunston girl? What if one of the Hunstons went through a travel gate at the prince's doing and fathered Emme?"

"I don't even know where to begin to tell you what's wrong with that."

Russen sat back, casually gestured an invitation to Kye. "Try."

"Firstly, why send one of the Hunstons all the way to Emme's country? Why hers?"

"Furthest away, maybe?"

"Secondly, Emme said that the village only ever had one visitor, and that visitor came after she was born."

"Maybe that's the only one she knows about."

"Thirdly, why send a Hunston to a forest on the other side of the world on the slim chance that the child is born a girl and a girl with the gift. It's a totally random gift. You never know which branch it's going to come from."

"True, but maybe Emme's forest is not the only place the Hunston male visited to impregnate a woman. And maybe more than one Hunston went through the travel gate to other worlds."

"What one Hunston do you know of who would do that for our prince, let alone many Hunstons?"

"We can't know the mind of every Hunston, but I see your point."

"And then there is the timing of it all. A child born with the gift usually occurs once every generation. Emme told me she is twenty-two winters. That's too soon for another gifted Hunston girl."

"Okay, I concede to that."

"Not only that, but Emme bears no resemblance, none at all, to the Hunston family."

"They *are* fairly distinct," Russen said with a slight nod.

"Emme is dark-haired, really brown eyes with long black lashes, tanned skin, very tall and straight with very defined mature features. The Hunston girls are pale, gold-haired, short with curvy bodies, almost childlike in their faces."

"She might take after her mother."

"Which leads me to my next point. The Hunstons certainly marry outside their family but for a girl to have the gift, the mother must be of the Hunston line. The gift is passed through the women. It's impossible to hope that a Hunston male might sire a girl with the gift if he joins with a foreigner."

"Of course." Russen stared at the desk, shook his head. "I do know that. My logic has been slipping lately."

Kye sighed and leant back. "You could be forgiven for it with all we have to think about at the moment." He picked up the glass of red wine, enjoying the thought of drinking more than the taste. It had been so long since he had consumed wine. "The more I uncover about what is going on in this city, the more I get confused by it all. The Black Bands, I have worked out. The prince, I mostly understand, but the friction between him and the Ashrones and our brutal past, I don't understand."

"Not many do, and that is why we strive to uncover the truth." The man waved his finger at Kye and spoke as if a teacher instructing his class. "Knowledge is power."

Kye nodded. As many times as Russen said that to him, it still impressed him with the truth of it.

"So are you going to interrogate her to make sure she isn't holding the truth from you?" Russen asked.

Kye shook his head. "Poor thing. She has absolutely no idea why she is here. She really doesn't."

The man's thin lips curled. "Ah, you pity every poor soul you come across. That's why you have that motley collection of kids you risk your life for."

"Compassion is not a wasted sentiment, Russen. Those streetwise *kids* have saved my life many times over."

"Well it doesn't sound like this new addition is going to save your life. From what you've told me, she's been a terrible risk to it. Not that I blame you for taking her under your wing. Anything the prince is after is well worth our attention."

Kye took a sip of his wine, felt the spicy liquid heat his mouth and throat. "It's not always about how you can use people. That's always been the difference between you and me."

"It was my job to work out ways to use people," the man said wistfully.

"I know." Kye smiled gently. "And mine to decide whether to use the information or not. Not much has changed."

"No; but I will not sit in this insufferable job forever, you know. I am better than this. You *and* I are better than this."

"This is our world now," Kye responded. "We make the most of it, and we do not lament what could have been. If we do, we may not survive."

The man nodded slowly. "You have become very wise despite your circumstances, Kye. I'm proud of you."

"Thank you. That means a lot coming from you."

Russen ran fingers through grey-flecked brown hair. Age was beginning to turn his middle-aged face to the edges of elderly. Brown spots, pale and wide, flecked his thin hands. "Anyway," he said after a while, "you really must bring this girl to see me sometime. I would love to learn about her world."

"You'd be fascinated by it. It's almost primitive yet somehow their ideals are more advanced than ours. They believe in sharing the workload and hence the spoils of the forest. If you don't do your share, you get less of the meat that the hunters bring in. It's not a bad idea."

"Anarchy for a city this size," the man said, regarding Kye from beneath his brows.

"I suppose – but it is interesting to learn of a different way of doing things. I can imagine it's what we used to be like before civilisation built us up to the poverty and drudgery we live in now." Kye took a sip of his wine and stared at the dark red liquid as he spoke. "And she's this fascinating mix of barbarism and civility, of roughness and gentleness, of strong independence and yet need. She attempts in every turn to be tough and boyish, to defend herself against something – some hurt that has been given to her that I cannot work out. Yet the more she tries to cover up the hurt with bravery, the more you realise how needy she is. It's a very curious mix."

Russen's brow arched neatly. "Indeed, you will definitely have to bring her to see me. At least to meet the girl that has put that look in your eyes."

"What look?"

"And managed to blind you to it."

The two men considered each other briefly.

"Don't go getting any ideas," Russen said. "You know you can't have her."

"I don't hope to *have* her, Russen. I don't hope to *have* anybody – especially not someone I've known for three days. I *am* well aware of my past."

"Good. Because the future is unpredictable but for one sure thing – she will ruin everything we have worked for."

"Yes – and you don't need to worry. If there is any look in my eyes it is because I am curious about the knowledge in her head, not what she'd be like in my bed."

Russen laughed merrily and slapped his hand on the table. "I do like your level-headedness. You've always been like that, ever since you could talk."

Kye let a smile of fondness creep to his face, then he concentrated heavily on the spicy, mellow wine. The heat from the school's main furnace pumped from a wide floor vent into the room, making Kye sleepy. He rarely felt this warm, this relaxed, or for that matter, sleepy.

Soon a lighter conversation started, and then Kye took his leave and began the all-night journey through the driving snow to his home.

◉

Kye did not come for her that morning, but the fear did. Emme raced through the building and up to Halder's balcony. The torrent of driving snow and rain, and the harshest cold she could remember, did not repel her from the view of sky and pale morning light. Halder poked his head out of the roof hatch and stared at her.

"I was wondering who went clomping through my house this morning," the large, shaggy head said. "You all right, Emme?"

"Fine. Just catching some fresh air and light."

A knowing look crossed Halder's broad face before he went back down the stairs pulling the latch closed behind him. Some time later, she heard his hammer pound out a shrill, metallic ring. The hammering stopped a short time later.

Emme was peering over the wall's edge to the street below when Kye returned with his thick cloak about him. She recognised his brown pants, dark-green jumper and the rapier that swung at his side. Even in the thick snow, his long strides were even, smooth. He entered Halder's door.

She half expected him to come up to see her, but long minutes went by and she remained alone.

Finally she conceded that the driving ice and cold against her jumperless, coatless skin was doing damage, and made her way back to the underground world of the street kids.

Kye was sipping hot tea, staring intently at a table knot, when she entered the dining room. He did not look up from the table surface, and she wondered briefly if he had discovered something about her that made him ashamed to look at her. Her heart punched her chest. Did he know about the circumstances of her birth?

She shook the thought from her head. How could anyone in this rotten city know that? Sullen, as if Kye had openly insulted her, she ignored him and headed for her room.

When she reached the dining room doorframe, Kye broke as though dazed, from his tea. "Emme. How long have you been there?"

Emme spun on heels to face him. "Long enough to know you're ignoring me."

"I don't ignore anybody. Not even my enemies. Come sit down if you like. I was just lost in thought."

Emme watched him, sceptical.

"You look cold," he said.

"I am. I should go and get changed."

Kye appeared to notice her outfit for the first time. "Are they Dusty's clothes?"

"They are."

His lips curled slightly. "He won't like it that you got them all wet and dirty. He's very fastidious about his clothes."

"It wasn't his choice. I might go and get dressed into my own clothes. Better still, I might go and run a hot bath and get warm."

"Will you meet me in my office when you're finished?"

"That doesn't sound too good."

"I just want to start our lessons, that's all."

"I don't particularly like that word. One of the boys in the village had to take lessons, and he was an arrogant bastard."

Kye seemed faintly amused. "What would you like me to call it, then?"

"Discussions."

"Discussions it is," Kye said, and Emme turned before she could see any hint of apprehension on his face over whatever it was he had discovered from his contacts.

6

Emme seated herself comfortably on the hard-backed chair opposite Kye's. A wealth of cloth-bound books lay open before Kye on the desk, and a map stretched just beyond them. He wordlessly closed each one and stood to replace them.

"I take it the books are for someone else," Emme said. "I can't read you know."

Kye turned after placing a thick book onto the nearest shelf. "No, but we can change that during our discussions." He paused briefly. "How do you know how to spell your name?"

"The traveller who came to the village taught me – the one the villagers sent away. It's all just sounds though. I couldn't recognise it if you showed me."

"I see." He put another book on the shelf, his eyes perceiving some sort of order that Emme could not. "You'll find that in this city, being able to read is a very valuable thing."

"I haven't seen any of your students use it so far. Not up there anyway." Emme's eyes pointed to the ceiling.

Kye continued to place the books on the timber shelves, his back to her. "Reading maps, reading street signs, reading shop signs, reading prices, reading city notices and new tax laws, reading contracts or job descriptions when they are posted – these are all ways my students use their readings skills. Without those skills, young people only have the option of prostitution, thieving or begging."

"So are we going to start that today?"

With the desk cleared, but for the map, Kye finally sat down and folded his hands in front of him at the table. "No – I thought we might start with some history. It might be time for you to learn a little bit about this city and how it's run."

"Sounds fascinating," Emme mumbled.

"It will be fascinating, I can assure you. It's a story of betrayal, murder, and dark magic."

"Well, let me hear it then." Emme sat back in her chair and watched Kye expectantly.

"There are many cities and many states all over Kildes." Kye spun the parchment map around until it faced her. He showed her the shape of Kildes, traced his finger around the brown outline. "Every territory has a prince, and every prince is ruled by the king who is, if the Almighty wills it, from the Endorian line – a family who have ruled Endoria, our city, and Kildes for centuries." He tapped the rough, lumpy circle that divided Endoria from the other states. "As long as the Endorians keep having sons, the Endorians keep ruling." He retracted his finger from the map. "In just my lifetime we had a king and a queen, and they had four children – four sons. One of them is our current prince who, for today's discussion, we will call Jay."

"Is this safe to be talking about?"

"I've instructed Halder to make a lot of noise above us in his blacksmith shop. It would be rare the prince could hear us down here, and even rarer that he could hear us through the noise Halder is capable of making."

"Strange. Go on."

"The queen died when she gave birth to her last son. The king was killed five years later by a strange sickness that overcame the nation – a plague – although some suggest his death could have been made to look like the plague, so none of us to this day know if it was natural or murder."

Emme shifted in her seat, sat a little straighter. "This is getting good."

"I'm glad," he teased lightly. "I wouldn't want to bore you."

"So, what happened after the king was murdered? Who took the throne?"

"No one has. Not yet."

Emme frowned, puzzled.

"I'll explain it to you. In this country, we have a law – a very ancient and unbreakable law that is above all other laws. It was once called The Asher, which we now just call the Kildes Law. It was written by the Ashrones and the Almighty at the dawn of our world, and it's guarded by the Ashrones to this day. The Ashrones were given special powers to be able to uphold that law. The laws stand above all princes, all kings, all churches. Each country can do what it wills with such things as taxes and trade, but they must comply with the Kildes Law."

"We don't have anything like that. We don't need it. We just live by the land and obey the land's laws of seasons and sharing and survival."

"Yes – a concept that does fascinate me." He did not speak for a while, his mind seeming to take a tangent.

"So about this law . . . " Emme urged into the silence.

"Yes, that law. Now, according to that law, even though Endorians – the heirs to the throne – are in line to become king, they can only become king when they have the Gift of the Asher."

"The what?"

"The Gift of the Asher. It's a strange name for a special power that a king must have before he can rule."

"How does he get it?"

"Ahh, there is a good question. There is another family in Kildes. The Hunstons who own Hunston Valley." He pointed to the territory once removed from Endoria. "Since the beginning of time, once every generation, one of their daughters is blessed

159

with the Gift of the Asher. She is a carrier of the power, and when she marries the prince, she passes the power to him. Only then can he become king. Of course, one always goes with the other. The heir always marries the Hunston woman, and the Hunston woman always gives the power to the heir. That way there is never a deadlock. The Hunstons can't bribe the Endorians and visa versa."

"So the previous queen who died in childbirth was a Hunston and a carrier of the power."

"Exactly."

"So what happened?"

"Well, let's just take a little tangent for a moment. The Ashrones are supposed to be the keepers of both the Higher Law and the ways of the Almighty. They guard the king's conduct, and they make sure the heirs to the throne are worthy of their calling. The Ashrones instruct the future leaders to be honourable and fair, and that way no one ever resents the law that the heir to the throne will unite with the daughter of the Hunstons. The Ashrones also rule the country in place of the king after a king's death and before the next coronation. All has worked successfully for many, many centuries, and then things started to go wrong – although no one knew what started it."

"What happened?"

"Well, the Ashrones became greedy for power. They wanted the power to rule totally, not just be in charge of guiding kings and future leaders."

"And?"

Kye smiled at her open curiosity. "And one of the four sons of the king decided that he was not content to be third in line. People say that the Ashrones instructed the prince to betray his family as part of their plot. No one really knows who affected who, but the prince struck first. He murdered all three of his brothers, leaving himself the only one in line for the throne."

"No cousins or distant relatives?"

"None. The Endorians have always had a small lineage and the plague wiped many families out. So we had just those four young men, and now there is one."

"Jay." Emme's jaw clenched, and she punched a fist into her open hand. "That sneaky snake. So what did the Ashrones do?"

"Well, once Jay had murdered his brothers, he set his sights on the Gifted Daughter of the Hunstons who had been betrothed to the now dead eldest son."

"But he didn't get her right?"

"No, because that's when the Ashrones made their move. They killed the Hunston girl. Without her and the Gift, there was no way Jay could become king – not by lawful means."

"That's awful."

"Yes, that is awful because in the absence of a king, the Ashrones rule Kildes as regents. That's the law. So Jay rules only Endoria but the Ashrones have all of Kildes, and the people and other princes must follow them until such time as a king returns."

"Which is never, right?"

"No, not exactly. Jay must marry and have a son or grandson, and then that son or grandson will be heir to the Kildes throne, and hopefully one of the Hunston families will have another girl with the Gift."

"There are many Hunston families?"

"Yes. They are a large family. You never know which branch of the family tree a girl with the Gift is going to come from."

"So why doesn't Jay marry then?"

"Ahh, there is Jay's dilemma. If he marries, he instantly gives up all right to the Kildes throne. He can never have the throne. Remember, to have the throne, he had to marry a Gifted Hunston girl, but the Ashrones killed her. The only thing left is for him to take a girl of noble blood, and then he'll remain the prince of Endoria until he dies. He'll never be king. Even if he's the father of the heir to the throne, the Ashrones overrule him."

"But he can't have the throne anyway, because there is no Hunston girl left, so he may as well marry and do the right thing by everyone else."

Kye smiled grimly. "I do wish it were that simple. You see, partly Jay's waiting for another daughter to be born with the gift, but in the meantime, he's trying to win the right to rule, and he's doing that through power. At the moment, he's bringing in masses of weapons and recruiting a large army so he can conquer other lands and rule them through strength. He'll never technically be king, but he'll still rule."

"Let me guess – that's what the Black Bands do for him."

"Yes, the Black Bands smuggle in weapons for him – in an underhanded yet obvious sort of way. Huge supplies of weapons. They also gather information for him, control the black market and are involved in a lot of the corrupt, devious dealings Jay has with other officials. Mostly they oversee the weapons though – especially this year."

"So then tell the other states about the weapons," Emme said, "and have them rise up to stop Jay."

"They know about it."

Emme's brows shot up. "And they don't stop him?"

"Ahh, but it's not that simple. You see, there are other Kildes laws, and one of them is that the Endorian prince has every right to defend his homeland. And according to the law, any nation conquered in the process comes under Jay's rule. That law and the law about Ashrones ruling as regents are there to stop other nations rising up against Endorian princes before they're given the Gift. When a king dies, the land is very unstable for a while, and it would be a very good time for other countries to try to destroy the Endorian prince if they were desperate for the throne. You see, if an Endorian prince is not crowned, he does not control all of Kildes' armies. As king, he does control them all. So Jay is given the right to defend against any state or prince that tries to take his city. On the other hand, according to the Law, Jay has no right to go out to other states and conquer them if unprovoked. That's to ensure that Endorian princes don't conquer the land with might, but rule with fairness. So if Jay marches on other nations with his weapons and army, when he is captured and brought before the Ashrones, he will be sentenced to death. And he *will* be captured because he is not powerful enough yet. And therein lies the terrible deadlock."

"I don't understand."

"Okay. Let me explain as best I can. If Jay marches on other lands, other lands have every right to fight against him and to stop him. When he is caught, he is sentenced to death. However, if the states suspect that Jay is making moves to conquer them and that he might eventually get an army big enough to defeat them, they can decide to march on the prince before his army gets so big that he is able to march on *them* and win. But the prince can claim he was just defending his home, conquer them and bring all the other states under his rule. And he and all his descendants are allowed to keep waging a war until they win. It could begin a war that could last for centuries."

"So they should just execute Jay for murdering his family."

"No, see there's the deadlock. No one wants Jay to die. He's the only heir to the throne and the only one who can provide them with a son, or at least with more Endorians. If he dies, the Ashrones rule forever, and remember, the Ashrones murdered Kildes' beloved Hunston daughter. The princes are afraid of the Ashrones and Ashrone power, and they hate that the Ashrones are currently ruling."

"I see. So the princes won't attack Jay, or they'll be ruled by him. Jay won't attack the other states or he can't rule under Kildes Law. And the other princes won't provoke Jay to come and get them, or accuse him of the murder of his family, because they don't want Jay to die because then the Ashrones will rule forever."

"Exactly, Emme. Well done." There was no hint of condescension in his voice. "We know the Ashrones want the Kildes heir – Jay – dead, but not at their own hands and without good cause. If they kill him themselves, Endorian Law states that they rescind all right to power. There will be no true ruler, and there will be anarchy."

"Then the Ashrones should accuse Jay of the murder of his family."

"Ahh, but the murders were so subtle that it took a while for the Ashrones to gather proof that Jay had done them. And by the time they had the evidence, they knew every prince had turned a blind eye to it, so they had no grounds to accuse him of it. Executing an Endorian prince is very tricky, and the majority of states must support the decision for the Ashrones to go ahead. So instead, the Ashrones are trying to incite the other princes to rise up against Jay before it's too late – before Jay is actually able to defeat them. But the others won't move. The princes are hoping the Ashrones kill Jay and hence give up the right to power – after Jay has produced heirs. If the Ashrones kill Jay without majority support, the Ashrones must be sentenced to death. Meanwhile, Jay is hoping that when the time is right for him, the Ashrones and his obvious collection of weapons and fighters stir the other princes to move against him. In short, they don't want to come and fight Jay, Jay doesn't want to go and fight them, and everyone is hoping that something will break the deadlock – a marriage, a new heir, a murder at the hands of the Ashrones."

"Totally barbaric," Emme said. "Totally."

Kye smiled gently at her choice of words. "Yes, I guess in a way it is barbaric."

"In my country, you hunt outside your own territory without permission, the tribes have a fight to sort it out. And if you fight the other tribes, they fight back. And if you hurt or attack any individual of any other village for no good reason, all villages agree that you should be killed. That's the law. Other than that, every village does what it needs to do to survive."

"Your world does have many advantages over ours, I have to admit that."

"So it wasn't against Kildes Law to kill the Hunston girl with the Gift, I take it," Emme said.

"Ahh, no. You see, it was all very cleverly done. It's only murder if the person doesn't consent to the death, and the Ashrones had the Hunston girl convinced that the only way to stop Jay was for her to die and end her power. While-ever she lived, Jay could take the power by force."

"How?"

"Rape."

Emme felt her whole body tighten. "Vile pig."

"Anyway, so the Hunston girl willingly went to her death, not knowing the terrible deadlock her death caused us. But, to be fair to the girl, nothing like this has ever happened in history. I don't believe it ever occurred to us we'd be down to four brothers of the Endorian line and one would go and kill the others. This has never happened to the country before. I'm sure she just did not know what else to do."

"How long ago did this happen?"

"When I was a young boy. I remember seeing the Hunston girl – she was a woman then, probably about seventeen – when she was brought into the city. She passed by us in her carriage –

a stunning, dignified woman. Very beautiful. It seemed like the entire city turned to the streets to watch her go past as if somehow she might save us. Not one of us knew that she was being brought to the city to be ritualistically sacrificed."

"So how do you know she consented?"

"Well, the truth is, a lot of it is speculation. There's the fact that she was brought to the city. She could have easily been murdered at her home – poison, a dagger through the heart, an assassin. But they brought her to the city, to the place of their High Temple and their magic gifts, and they kept her here in a secret location, and then they butchered her. They had five scribes, five witnesses, record her words, her consent to the barbaric ritual, but many believe the documents to be a lie. But no one has any right or courage to protest it and the scribes never changed their story before they died."

"Died?"

"Either murdered by bitter citizens who were outraged at the tragic death of the Hunston girl, or possibly by the Ashrones themselves before the witnesses could change their stories. No one knows. There are many views on everything that has happened. Some say the Ashrones murdered the Hunston girl and in doing so, sold their souls to the dark powers – that their powers are from an evil source now and so the Ashrones are to be greatly feared. One of the witnesses' accounts suggests the possibility of evil powers – it paints a much darker picture of the night. Others say the girl's consent gave them a loophole with the Almighty, that it could be argued they had done something noble – stopping the prince – and hence the Ashrones have retained their place in the joyous afterlife, and not in the fires of hell."

"And you don't know which one to believe?"

"No, and it doesn't really matter. What does matter is that she died and it could be many more years before we see the Gift of the Asher appear. And we would still have to wait for the girl to grow up to a marriagable age, though I doubt that Jay *would* wait for it."

Emme gasped. "You don't mean he'd . . . to a *child*?"

Kye's faint nod made her stomach convulse. She wanted to smash something and be sick at the same time. "That – that . . ." 'Pig' wasn't even the right word anymore. The prince was a vile man who deserved to rot in the stocks, not sit on a throne. If anyone, *anyone*, even looked at an Underoak child in that way, he would suffer a long, slow death at the chieftain's hands.

"Now we just wait to see what happens," Kye finished. "Will our prince marry and produce an heir and right the wrongs? Will he march on the other states? Will the states march on him? Will the Ashrones succeed in having the prince killed without it being on their hands? We all wait with baited breath."

"Is that all you do?" Emme almost accused. "Wait?"

"Not the street kids, and not my contacts. We try to stop the Black Bands bringing the weapons into the city so the prince has no power with them, and then we pass word to contacts in other cities, that we have confiscated the weapons. Jay hopes to force the other princes to move by scaring them with his army and weapons, but the fewer we make those weapons, the more time the other princes have before they need to make a move against him or come up with an alternative. It stalls everything."

Emme scowled. "What good is that?"

"The longer we stall, the more chance we have of getting our prince to see reason and take a wife. And it gives us more time to think of ways to deal with the Ashrones. Either that or come up with some totally obscure solution that has so far escaped us all. At the very least, it prevents a war that could throw Kildes into chaos for centuries."

Emme locked eyes with Kye. "And how did you get caught up in all of this?"

Kye went quiet and sat back in his chair. "I am just another player, that's all."

"Were you a Black Band?"

Kye sighed and watched Emme with eyes that were looking at her yet through her to something only he could see. "I'm just another player," he said, "who isn't content, like I can see you wouldn't be, to do nothing."

She didn't believe him. Not entirely. There was more to him than that. But she would not get an answer from him and didn't particularly care to try. She didn't want him knowing about *her*. She'd hardly berate him for not telling her about *him*.

"And then the prince brought me into the country and made things even more complicated," Emme said.

"Yes. You are the mystery. You are the total surprise, in fact. Not one of us can figure out what you could possibly be here for or why the prince went so far to get you. Or how the Ashrones know about it and why they want to stop him. You are a really strange twist in the whole convoluted story."

Emme shrugged with feigned disinterest, but curiosity burned hotter inside now. Her only peace was in knowing that whatever she was brought here for, she was no longer needed. The prince had either realised an error, or missed his opportunity.

"So why can't the prince's sister rule or produce some heirs?" Emme asked after a while.

"The prince doesn't have a sister."

"Yes he does; I saw her. Her name is Lady Ennika."

"I can assure you he does not have a sister." He noted Emme's stubborn set of jaw. "Trust me." He watched her, and when she refused to relent, his brows dipped in a puzzled frown. "What makes you think he has a sister?"

Emme described the conversation held in the castle's courtyard.

Thoughts flitted across Kye's face until realisation sharpened his focus. "Of course. Ennika must be his lover. He knows he cannot marry her or he'll relinquish the right to the throne of Kildes. I did hear a rumour he was seeing someone. It seems he has no intention of marrying after all. If he's openly declared her his sister, he will not go against Kildes Law and marry his own sister or show himself to be a liar. But she can forever be by his side, even in his room and no one will think twice about it. I will have to tell my contacts about this."

"Pig," Emme said. "All men are pigs."

Kye's brows arched. "All?"

Emme hesitated. "Well, most," she conceded for the first time. "There's possibly an exception to the rule. Although, when it comes to relationships with women, all men are pigs."

"All of us?"

"Yes. No exceptions there."

"I'm curious to know why you think that."

"Because all men violate women. They either do it before they get married or they go and violate their wives."

"Is that standard village practice?" Kye's eyes stayed locked on Emme's face, searched it as if discovering something about her.

"Yes. And here too. No men are different."

"I have to say I don't agree with you."

"And men always lie about it too. Always deny it. My mother taught me that."

"Well unless I am mistaken about the way every single man in your village behaves, your mother has a lot to answer for."

Emme's shoulders squared. "My mother was living proof of it. My mother is many things but she's *not* a liar."

Kye watched her quietly for a moment, seemed to be taking in the vehemence in her face and tone. He finally said calmly, "I wish there was a way I could prove to you that you're mistaken."

"Don't go getting any ideas."

"I wasn't volunteering myself," Kye said, the faintest trace of mirth in his tone.

"Oh." Emme's shoulders loosened. She wondered at the odd way that last statement hurt her.

Kye turned the table map to himself and began to study it, perhaps to alter the mood. Without looking up he said, "So have I convinced you that the prince doesn't have a sister called Ennika?"

Emme considered it, then snapped straight. "Maybe the prince wasn't lying after all, because if Ennika isn't the sister, then Kara must be."

Kye's head jerked up. "Where did you hear that name?"

"Jay told me his sister was Kara."

Kye's brows plunged into a deep frown, the strongest expression she had seen on him since she met him. "I have no idea why he would say that." He seemed intensely puzzled for a moment, then the frown smoothed slightly. "Just trust me, Emme, the prince does not have a sister."

Emme shrugged. "If you say so."

Kye poured over the old brown map again, then looked up. "By the way, I heard about your exploits last night."

Emme rolled her eyes. "It was hardly worth mentioning. I just didn't want people to starve and I made it my mission to bring home something. That's all."

"I must admit there are four different, four rather wild versions being passed around and a fifth version that's a little tamer – Dusty's. His is probably the true one. He's quite reliable for passing on information, even if he does get a bit absent-minded sometimes."

"Did you really find Dusty as a baby?"

Kye locked eyes with Emme for the longest time until Emme

began to wonder what he was seeing in her face. "Yes. Why?"

"Just wondering if that's another far-fetched story."

"No, that one is true."

"So you're practically family right?"

"Yes, I guess so."

"So why don't you share a room together? Don't you feel it's a little greedy, a little arrogant, to have a room all to yourself?"

"You have a room all to yourself," Kye replied, a trace of mischief in his voice.

"Only because it's the old dirty one no one wants."

"If you do ever share a room with others, then you can come and ask me that question." He folded the stiff map and placed it in a drawer. "Now, I should probably head off to the library and hear where everyone's lessons are up to. I still teach, but only one to one. The other older ones do most of the group lessons now. Will you join me?"

"I guess so."

"Good. And then let's see if you can't conjure up another thirty chickens for our lunch today." He smiled gently at her.

A pounding knock on the door made Emme twist abruptly in her chair.

"Come in," Kye called out calmly.

Dusty flung his head around the partially open door, his cheeks flushed and his breath ragged from running. "Weapons merchant sighted on Tailor Street."

Kye shot to his feet. "I've got to go, Emme. Dusty, go tell the team to get ready."

Dusty darted away down the hall, leaving the door open behind him. Cold, damp air from the hallway seeped into the confined room. Kye hastily buckled his weapon belt to his waist. The magnificent curved rapier handle swung like silver jewellery near his trouser pocket. He drew his thick woollen cloak from the back of his chair and wrapped it around his shoulders. "I could be away a few days, Emme. Dusty will look after you, and no more expeditions to get food. Leave that to the others." He reached into his drawer and took out a folded map. He tucked it into his back pocket and walked to the door as he spoke. "I'm not convinced the prince doesn't want you anymore, and until I'm sure, please stay out of sight. I can't protect you if you stay out of my reach." He stopped beneath the doorframe, turned to look at her. "But feel free to go up and watch the sunsets or sunrises when you need to." Kye strode quickly down the long hallway, leaving Emme alone in his office.

Emme smiled almost wickedly to herself. Kye had not extracted her promise that she would stop helping to find food. It would irk her to sit by and do nothing. Perhaps she would be more careful than the last time, but she would not sit and wait.

Emme scraped the chair backwards across the floor and stood, stretched. She turned to leave the room, then stopped as her eyes met the door that always remained closed – the door to Kye's room.

She wondered mildly why no one had shown her the room, then her eyes narrowed as the questions swelled to an intense curiosity.

She arched back a little until able to discreetly peer down the shadowed hallway. The doors down the corridor remained still, and only faint male voices issued from one of them. Seconds later, a door burst open at the end of the hall and two of the older men, dressed in travel clothes and adorned with weapons, disappeared swiftly around the farthest corner. No doubt members of the team Kye gathered.

She watched a moment longer and when satisfied Kye would not return to discover her, quietly closed the office door and crept to the bedroom door. She turned the bulky, dimpled copper handle and carefully swung ajar the peeling door. She peered once to check for dangers before opening a wider gap.

Light from the study spilled into the room to illuminate a small space. She noted with one glance that the windowless room was fastidiously tidy. The blanketed bed was made to perfection as if it had never been slept in.

A beige wing-backed reading chair filled the far right corner, and a large pile of old books, stacked in order of size, leant against the chair's left edge. A lantern decorated a wide chest of drawers, positioned so that when lit, it would illuminate both the chair and the headboard on either side. A mahogany cupboard to her left covered almost entirely the portion of wall that joined the door. She stepped over to the cupboard, pulled the wrought-iron looped handles. The clothes were arranged in colours and order of height.

She raised a brow. No one needed to be that neat. His pristine black boots were polished, in their pairs and evenly spaced. A spare rapier tilted into one corner of the cupboard.

She closed the cupboard. There was nothing terribly suspicious about this room. She moved to leave the room, gripped the doorhandle, then halted. A lock. There was a bolt lock, and a very solid one at that, on the bedroom door. No other door in the building had a lock. Why would Kye need a lock on his door in a place like this? If anything should have a lock, it should be the stores of weapons in the hall off the laundry.

Curiosity fired up again, and she crossed the room back to the chest of drawers on the far wall. She lit the lantern and opened the top drawer to see his personal items – his shaving implements, hairbrush, toothbrush, bars of soap, a small hand mirror – all tidily displayed. Two slim books sat at the back in shadows, but she saw no point in picking them up. They would mean nothing to her anyway.

She opened the next drawer. Undergarments were nothing spectacular. The third drawer, taller than the rest, contained thick jumpers folded and arranged. The last drawer surprised her with the disorder of it. The spare linen sheets and towels were dumped in a tangled, unironed mass in the drawer. Faintly suspicious, she tapped the pile with her foot and felt something bulgy underneath.

She bent to get a closer look, peeled back the top layer of towels to reveal six lumpy black pouches. She picked up one of the pouches by its bunched top and noted how heavy it was. Very heavy. At its base, it spilled just over her supporting palm. It chinked slightly as she lifted it to the top of the chest of drawers. She worked open the drawstring and peered inside, gasped. More gold than she had ever seen in her life. She pulled the other pouches out and opened them. Gold. Every pouch brimmed with small round imprinted pieces of gold. Real gold.

She tipped the contents of one pouch onto the bed. So many gold pieces tumbled onto the grey blanket. A finger-sized piece of waxen parchment fluttered onto the top of the small mound. She picked it up, turned it over. What she supposed was writing on one side, meant nothing to her. She tucked the scrap of parchment back into the empty sack, and spread the mound into a thin layer across the woollen blanket. Quickly she estimated each sack contained about one hundred and seventy gold pieces. What was it that chimneysweep had said? Ten pieces of gold were five years wages for him. This would be over five hundred years of wages for the boy. Five hundred! She may not be able to read, but she could count. Years of counting animal prints to keep track of wild herd numbers had taught her that. What was Kye doing with that much money? And for that matter, how did he get it?

Anger scorched Emme's insides. Those young kids beyond

that door were starving, and all the while Kye was hoarding money to satisfy greed. No wonder he had that damned lock on the door. And no wonder the bastard slept alone.

Emme began to feel as if the betrayal had been to her, not to the sixty-one other people who lived down here with Kye. Wendaya was right, so right. All men were pigs, and right after she had confronted Kye about it, she would let the whole headquarters of the street kids know.

She scooped up the shiny coins, funnelled them back into the empty pouch. She returned the sacks but one to the drawer, snuffed the lamp, then headed to her room. Back in the narrow musty room, she scouted for a place to keep the money. She wrapped the tatty jumper, taken from the corpse, around the moneybag and tucked the bundle in her empty cupboard.

When Kye arrived home, no matter what time of the day or night it was, she would know about it. And then *he* would know why she was sleeplessly waiting for him.

◙

Kye returned late in the night two days later, but Emme was awake and ready for him. Lying there in the pale lantern light, she heard him return alone, enter his room, then heard the study door close. She knew he would not be expecting anyone to be awake at three in the morning. Even the giggling, gossiping girls next door managed to settle by midnight each night.

She had to act swiftly before he locked his door. She got up, grabbed the sack of money from the cupboard and hurried from the room.

Without knocking, she burst into the office, half expecting him to be there, then a few steps across the study and she flung open the door to his bedroom. His bared back was to her, a black-button shirt dangling from his hand. She caught a glimpse of a solid tattoo on his lower back just above his trouser line before he spun in seconds, startled, his exposed muscles flexed for action. He quickly flung the shirt onto his torso and with it unbuttoned, said sternly, "What are you doing here, Emme? You should always knock first."

"Why? So you can quickly hide all that money you've been keeping from everyone?" She jiggled the heavy black sack of coins at him.

Kye clasped her arm and pulled her into the room with a strength that caught Emme off guard. He snapped the door closed behind her and bolted it. The echo of metal clacking in the lock made her stomach cramp.

Emme glared at him, felt her heart begin to pound for the first time. "You'd better not be thinking of violating me." Of course he wasn't, but she could think of nothing else defensive to say.

"Sit down, Emme."

"Why? So you can have your –"

"*Sit down.*"

Sweat broke out on her body, and a shadow of a memory darkened her mind – Kye permanently scarring a young child, the son of a Black Band, to accomplish a purpose. She met his eyes defiantly. "Not until you do."

"Very well." Kye sat down on his narrow bed, shuffled back against the wall, and gestured to the chair in the corner. "Sit there if you like."

Emme took the corner chair that sat half-shadowed where the wing blocked dim lantern light. Her eyes never left Kye, cautious of every movement, aware that his eyes did not move from her face.

She thought she could almost hear his calm breathing in the tense silence. Her feet shifted on the patternless taupe rug, the scratch of socks against coarse fibres loud in the stillness.

"You've been going through my room," he said at last.

"I knew there was a reason why you insist on sleeping alone, why you have that lock on the door. What will your street kids say when they find out you've been starving them to death while you hoard all the gold? I knew all men were pigs. My mother was right. You're no different than the rest."

Kye remained frustratingly calm. "I'm sorry you think that, Emme. I'm sure nothing I could say would change your mind about that, but I can at least clear your mind about those coins you're holding."

"I'd love to hear you try."

"They're King's Gold. Look at the imprint on the back of the coins."

Emme hesitated.

"Go on, have a look."

Emme dared to take her eyes from Kye and fumbled with the drawstring, silently cursing her shaking fingers. She drew out a coin and glanced at the back of it.

"Do you recognise the likeness?"

"No."

"It's not the prince you met, is it?"

"No, but so what?"

"Every new king, or failing that, prince of Endoria, has his likeness stamped on the back of the currency of the time. That gold is out-of-date and worthless."

"Then why do you have it?"

"I can't tell you that, but I can tell you this – many people down here know about that gold. They may not know how much, or why I keep it, but that I do keep it is no secret to them. I am betraying no one by keeping it in here."

Emme looked at him with open scepticism.

"And Halder knows about the gold. He loves the children down here and would never let me betray them by hoarding wealth while they starve."

The unconcealed suspicion remained on Emme's face.

"Think about it, Emme. That lock on the door doesn't stop people coming in when I'm not here. It bolts from the inside."

Emme faltered at the logic, then stiffened. "Well then, if everyone knows about the gold, why were you so quick to shut the door just now? You were afraid everyone would hear about the money."

Kye's blue-green eyes watched Emme calmly. "No, I closed the door because I wanted to talk to you about something else."

"Me going through your room?"

"I'm not disappointed with you for going through my room. It's natural to be curious, and I had nothing to hide."

"Then what?"

Kye seemed to be thinking up an answer, putting words together in his head. "I want to talk to you about what you saw tonight."

"Saw? What do you mean? I haven't seen anything."

"On my back."

"Oh, the tattoo. What about it?"

"Emme, I'm going to have to trust you with one of the very biggest secrets of my life and the reason why I have that lock on the door. You must not, under any circumstances, tell anyone about the tattoo on my back. And I implore you to forget about it."

"Why?" Emme put the coin back in the pouch and pulled the drawstring. She watched Kye expectantly.

"I'm afraid to give you this answer, but I just can't tell you what that tattoo means or why you can't tell anyone about it."

"Typical."

"But you mustn't tell anyone, Emme. It is so important." Kye paused, took a slow breath. "How can I impress upon you how important this is?"

Emme shrugged casually. "It's all right. I didn't even see what it was anyway."

Kye seemed to analyse her for a moment, to weigh up how trustworthy her words were.

"Who am I going to tell secrets to? I've never had any friends. I still don't."

"I'm sorry you've never had friends."

Emme jolted. In a moment like this he was pitying *her*, not focusing on himself and his predicament.

"It doesn't bother me."

Again that look where Kye seemed to be deducing if her words were true.

"I shouldn't have gone through your room," Emme said, knowing it was the closest she had come to an apology before. "I won't do it again."

Kye smiled. "I think you've seen all there is to see anyway. If you snoop through my room again, you're going to get terribly bored."

Emme found herself smiling with amusement, and unusually Kye's smile spread to show teeth.

"That's the first time I've really seen you smile," he said.

"Yes, I think it's the first time I've smiled like that. At least since I was a child."

Silence returned, less oppressive than the last.

"So is there anything else you want to ask me?" Kye asked after a while.

"Why are you so neat? You don't need to be so neat, you know."

Again the closed-lip smile. "Everybody is different, I suppose."

Emme shrugged. She stared down at the black sack that suddenly burned her with shame for having so mistreated the man who twice saved her life. Heat seared her cheeks. She held up the sack. "Here, I should give this back."

"Just leave it on the chest of drawers if you like."

Emme placed it on the bedside drawers as if it were a sack of hot rocks about to scorch her. "I should go," she said hurriedly. "I should go and get some sleep."

"You do look like you haven't had much sleep lately."

Emme felt her cheeks grow even hotter, and she rose swiftly, ashamed that her lack of sleep was from her desire to strike out at Kye. Emme fumbled on the bolt. It was stiff, jammed. She swore under her breath and tried to yank it harder. Kye stood beside her, leant almost over her, his arm outstretched above her shoulder. She grew flustered by his proximity, by the heat from his half-bared chest and the breath that exhaled just past her hair as he said absently, "It's an old lock and takes a bit of fiddling." He effortlessly tugged back the bolt.

As soon as the lock parted, she snatched the door open. "Goodnight," Emme said without looking back, and with the little dignity she had left, fled the room.

7

Emme flipped open the hatch to the roof and inhaled sharply as fresh biting air struck her face. Even after five weeks, Emme still could not get used to the disturbing darkness of her room. Every morning, the same fear – the terrible sense of confinement, disorientation – surged through her. The darkness drowned her. She would kick and force her way to the surface of Halder's balcony.

At the edge of the balcony, Halder spun towards her, his enormous feet carving craters in the fresh snow. "Thought you'd be here soon."

His presence no longer startled her. Used to her flights through his home, Halder often joined her. He noticeably enjoyed her visits, and she grew used to his loud voice and boisterous mannerisms. Rowdy men did not perturb her, but Halder's rough friendliness differed with the village men's undiluted aggressiveness. At first Emme had struggled to know how to respond to it.

"I've got some breakfast here for you." Halder removed a chunk of cloth-wrapped meat from his pocket. Emme approached him and took the offering. "Someone left it in my shop yesterday, and as it didn't have a name on it, I cooked it up."

Emme peeled back the wrapper, picked two cloth filaments from the chunk of lamb. "Shouldn't we share it with the kids?" She took a bite.

"I thought about it, but if the owner came back, I doubt I could explain how I managed to eat a whole leg of lamb myself overnight."

Emme smiled slyly and eyed him up and down. "I think they could imagine it."

He gave a hearty laugh and thumped her on the back. "You're probably right."

She sat down on one of two metal stools Halder had constructed on the balcony after she complained the bench-seat faced the wrong way.

Halder slumped his bulk on the other one. "You know, it occurred to me yesterday that I hadn't finished telling you the story about Sir Diamond Plumb."

"Is that really his name?" Emme had already asked, but hoped for a more satisfying response.

"There are plenty of stupid names amongst the aristocracy in this city." Halder turned a grin to her that never matched his gruff voice.

The same answer. Still, she suspected, as she had the day before, that Halder changed names to protect either himself or those involved.

Halder was not oblivious to her scepticism; he was entirely too perceptive for that. But he feigned ignorance and continued. "Anyway, as I was saying yesterday, Sir Plumb's brother was having an affair with Sir Plumb's wife. Sir Plumb found out about it and decided he would get back at his brother in a most creative way, so at first he did not let on that he knew. Around that time, his brother was thinking of investing a rather large sum of money for . . ."

Emme listened to the gossip, fascinated more by Halder than the tale. Despite Halder's keen observational skills, and hence knowledge of the dirtiest of the city's stories, he seemed not to notice Emme's discomfort with him, or perhaps was exceptional at pretending, as he half-shouted away about the town's gossip. He would loudly laugh about some of the pompous pretentious customers he had, and told her many a brow-raising yarn.

"How do you find out all of this stuff?" Emme asked when the long tale finally concluded.

Halder laughed heartily, dark eyes gleaming. "Oh, it's a skill I've always owned. I can find out just about anything about anyone in this city. You just need to be able to read people, listen at the right time, and have all the right connections."

"And you're just a blacksmith? What a waste."

The gleam in his eyes faded. That masculine gruffness – so at odds with his feminine love of scandals, his artistic metal creations, and keen perception – replaced the friendly chattering briefly. "Yes well, we all do what we have to."

Despite the steel in his eyes, Halder replaced the gruffness with a wide smile, reminding Emme why she was never entirely comfortable around the contradictory man. Not for the first time since she had met him, Emme realised that there was more to Halder than a creative blacksmith trade, yet what other dark training the man had received, alluded even the knowledgeable street kids.

Halder's gleam returned. "I must tell you what my neighbour heard last week." He plunged into the story with gusto, telling it with all the creativity of a master talesmith. Emme pretended interest in it whilst she studied the expressions of the big man.

What was going on in this place? Kye had saved others who openly confessed their past and yet Kye, who used to be a Black Band, couldn't admit it. And then there was Halder, a perfect candidate for some high position within the Black Bands. And yet when Emme had asked Kye recently about the big man, the only statement she received was that there was much to Halder but it was Halder's story to tell. And yet every time Emme came close to bringing it up, Halder dove into another bit of gossip. Perhaps she should try a trickier method. Halder loved secrets, and she could certainly present one.

Halder roared with laughter, and Emme snapped to attention, realising the story was over. He slapped her heavily on the back as he concluded, "And let that be a lesson to you; greed will always make you miserable."

Emme forced a smile despite not having heard the bulk of the tale. The obligatory smile gave way to a deliberate look of someone with much discomfort to hide. She refused her usual response of questions.

"What's the matter?" he asked after a while. "You're not yourself today."

"I'm just thinking." Emme feigned a sigh.

"About?" His thick brows rose above dark, almost black eyes.

"Probably shouldn't say."

"Oh, come on," he half-shouted jovially, "you can tell me anything. I'll only tell ten other people that I trust."

"Actually I was thinking about –" *You.* "Kye."

"Of course you are. There isn't a girl down there who doesn't." He winked at her. "What about him?"

"No – *that* I definitely can't say."

He frowned, disappointed. "You can trust me."

Trust you? She certainly knew she couldn't trust the bizarre, gossiping man. She waited moments, pretended to make some decision. At last she spoke. "I was just wondering – how did you meet Kye?"

"Saved his life once."

"Really? How?"

"Long story."

An evasion, but the game was not over. "But you love long stories."

He chuckled, his whole chest moving. "That I do, but it's Kye's long story."

"Ahh, I see. You saved him from the Black Bands."

Halder shrugged noncommittally. Her rich brown eyes watched him closely. It did seem as good as an admission, but she couldn't yet be sure.

"And were you one of them?"

Halder's dark eyes narrowed slightly, then he turned back to the city. "My past is not a good one, Emme. It won't do to drag it up."

She felt a tug of annoyance, then her mind flashed to a scene of her own unhappy past. "I understand." She meant it.

"I did something bad once," he said to the city. "No – a lot of bad things. But a few particularly bad things that I'm not proud of and one day will have to pay for. Until I do, I have to live with it." As he stared out at the rising dawn, he stayed silent for a long time; something he had never done.

The trapdoor to the roof flipped open, cracking into the stillness. Dusty's freckled face rose above the snow. "There you are, Emme. All the kids want to continue their dagger-throwing lessons."

Halder gave a crooked smile. "Dagger throwing, eh? Good luck with that, Emme. You'll need it with that no-talent lot." He grinned broadly at her.

"We're doing very well, thank you," Dusty said. "We might not all be as good as Emme, but we at least hit the tea chests now, and we haven't had a dagger break against the wall in weeks. Mind you, not many of us get the dagger *into* the tea chests, but we at least don't hit the wall and that's the main thing because Illina would probably wring our necks if we broke another dagger. Not that she would hurt us. Illina's too gentle, too sweet. She's lovely. We all like Illina . . ."

Halder turned to Emme whilst Dusty continued his seemingly endless chatter. "Better not disappoint them, then, if they're all waiting."

Emme nodded, stood.

"I'm sorry I'm too mysterious for you, Emme," Halder said in an unusually low voice.

Emme felt a chill at his perception, the same perception that won him large quantities of gossip. Perhaps the same perception that allowed him to know more about herself than she realised.

"It's just that sometimes secrets protect others too."

Emme nodded, a slight frown on her face. Not entirely sure what he meant by that curious statement, she turned from him and followed Dusty through Halder's house.

The clack of their boots on the timber echoed around the dark warehouse. The scent of wood smoke and remnants of roasted lamb drifted through the cavernous space.

"Dusty?"

"Yes?"

"Do you know much about Halder?"

"Lots. Why?"

"About his past?"

"Ahh, now that's something I don't really know. But then, no one really knows, actually. None of the street kids. We don't really ask, like we don't ask about Kye. All anyone knows is that Halder understands more about weapons and weapon supplies – black-market or otherwise – and where to get them than most Black Bands do. He's really quite amazing like that. Kye knows a bit, but Halder knows most of it. Between the two of them, they work long hours trying to find large safe areas within the city to store the huge amounts of weapons they confiscate each year." They reached the second trapdoor and wandered down the stairs to the laundry door. "And Halder knows lots about the Black Bands too. Or so Red says."

"Red?"

"The red-haired guy who goes into the city every day with

the others. The one courting Ada. Of course, Red is his nickname. 'Cause of his hair colour and –"

"You were saying?" Emme said before Dusty whirled away on some other tangent.

"I was saying?"

"About Halder and the Black Bands."

"Oh yes." The storage room doors drifted past as they headed down the cold corridor to the dining room. "Most of what Kye knows about the Black Bands, he learns through Halder, but no one really knows how Halder knows what he knows. Did that make sense?" Dusty seemed to be reworking the complex sentence in his mind, his lips silently moving over the words. At last he shrugged. "Probably not. Anyway, what was I saying?"

"You said that Halder knows more about weapons than Kye does."

"Oh, that's right. Halder knows the most, but that doesn't mean Kye doesn't know much. Kye knows lots too. Kye's pretty street smart for a man like him."

"Like him?"

"His social class."

"What is it about these social classes?"

Dusty flung open the dining room door and the conversation ended abruptly. A room full of young and slightly older faces turned to the open door expectantly. Emme felt a smile tug at her lips.

The children, clustered in the middle of the room, watched her whilst she surveyed the room. The mismatch assortment of timber chairs and tables had been peeled back against the edge. Large printed tea chests, gleaned from shop rubbish heaps, were stacked against the wall, chalked targets on their front. The shop owners happily disposed of them to Emme, saving them the cost of collection for reuse. The faint tang of tea, indelibly soaked into the tea chests, drifted above the scent of honey used on oats that morning.

In return for her own lessons, Emme had educated others about her forest, about much of her ways and politics, taught basic wilderness survival skills, and now she trained them to throw daggers.

Emme enjoyed the excited anticipation in the children's eyes. They admired her abilities. Their own attempts to use the weapon – the daggers usually skittering across the bumpy stone floor or flicking off slabs of sandstone in the walls – made her want to burst out laughing. The kids would stare wide-eyed at the accuracy of her throws. Even Kye would sit for lengthy periods, watch whilst she threw over and over with a lethal aim.

"It's very easy," she had told them in the beginning, then after seeing many failed attempts, began to wonder if she had a talent for the weapon. In time, she gave up on the throwing and turned to teaching them the best way to quickly whisk a dagger from a pocket or boot and stab something. This morning, they would continue this more appropriate training.

"Okay everyone, listen to me," Emme said. "You in the corner – Saran – are you listening?"

The young boy broke from his conversation with his friend. Emme saw Illina, the tall elegant head teacher of the children, smile sweetly from the opposite corner of the room, and wondered what lay behind the smile.

"Okay, Saran, you'll do. You and two friends, go to the kitchen and fetch all the butter knives. I don't want anyone cutting their bellies."

The three boys swiftly obeyed.

"The rest of you, put your daggers on the kitchen bench for now."

Children scurried across the room, deposited their weapons

onto a growing pile and rushed back to get the best view of Emme.

The three boys returned with stretched handfuls of the metal implements and distributed them.

"Everyone take one and shove one into your trouser pants or up your sleeve, or down your dress top. Wherever you would feel most comfortable wearing a dagger. Be careful to put it flat against your skin – not on an angle where the edge can cut you – as practise for when we use the real thing."

The room eagerly did as instructed.

"Okay. Today we're going to learn to pull out a dagger quickly and have it ready to throw or pin to someone's throat. This is different to pulling it out ready to stab." She held up her right hand. "With whatever hand you write with, or throw your dagger with, you grab the dagger handle with your thumb pointing down like this, and the back of your hand facing you. Your fingers curl around the dagger handle away from you." She demonstrated. "If you grab it like this . . ." She took the dagger with fingers curled around it, thumb up in the air, and fingernails facing her. "Then it won't be in the throwing position when you pull your hand back. The other way . . ." She turned her hand around again. "The dagger is ready to curl back over your shoulder and fling through the air." She whisked out the dagger and pitched it to the tea chests. It skilfully missed heads and punctured a tea chest beside other holes. The room launched into applause and animated dialogue.

"Now, let me show you one more thing. Issy, can I borrow your butter knife?" The little girl gladly handed over the crooked tool. Emme tucked it into her trousers. "Now, I need a volunteer." All hands instantly shot up. "Maybe a boy for this one. Randle, come to the front and walk towards me." All arms lowered and eyes watched expectantly. The thickly built older boy approached Emme and when he reached her, she whisked out the knife and swiftly pinned it to his throat. Randle stiffened with a sharp inhale, then relaxed and grinned at her. Emme lowered the makeshift dagger, and again the applause broke out. "Now, you practise. But no throwing and no thrusting it into each other's throats. I just want everyone to pull out the dagger and have your arm back in a throwing position. Do it until you get fast at it."

She observed briefly and drifted to those who needed personal demonstrations. She gave pointers and tips, then wandered to the back of the room and took a chair. Lulled by the sounds of young murmuring and butter knives clicking against belt buckles, she watched, eyes smiling and betraying her thoughts. The street kids had begun to grow on her.

Prior to the dagger throwing lessons, she had spent time with others Dusty's age learning their strategy and card games, and helping to piece complex wooden puzzles together.

It fascinated Emme that people would invent these games just to pass the time. The only adult pastime in the village, besides music and dancing, was drinking. The village children invented games using rocks and sticks, and as a little girl, Emme had longed to join in. Even then they had rejected her and called her names. It had hurt her – made her cry herself to sleep. But not anymore, and never again. Emme would never cry again – not ever.

Emme studied the faces in the room. The clusters of children practised and practised with an eagerness so absent within any of the village children. Illina stood in the doorway, arms folded across her breasts, and smiled fondly down at the children as though each one belonged to her.

Despite Illina's friendly, delicate countenance, Emme took great pains to avoid long contact with the woman and the woman's friend, Ada. Adults of the village, the women especially, had always been nastier than the children. Even the soft ones, the doe-eyed ones, had gossiped cruelly about Emme, creating most of the rumours that produced Wendaya's beatings.

Emme knew Illina could not possibly guess at Emme's illegitimacy, but the presence of Illina and Ada produced a flood of dark memories that made Emme insecure when the two were close by.

As practise time wore on, Emme noted warily that Kye was not in the room. It meant he was away – again.

Emme had feared to look at Kye after her night of shameful behaviour, but his easy, yet always aloof, mannerisms did not alter in her presence. She quickly deduced he was unconcerned about her conduct, and whilst the fear did enter her mind that he expected just as much from a barbarian like her, an in-pouring of knowledge soon swept it away.

She and Kye spent long hours on lessons. Initially she learned more of the history and politics of the city, which all sounded unnecessary although interesting. Later she impressed Kye with her ability to count, and devoured the maths he taught her. She quickly amazed him with the complex formulae she conquered.

Not so easy for her, or enjoyable, was the reading. She began to sound out small words and simple sentences but felt like a child as she toiled over the strange letters and their confusing formation as words. Despite the struggle, soon she was reading basic shop windows visible from Halder's balcony and from the streets themselves on nights she defied Kye and brought back food for everyone.

Emme never failed to acquire food on the expeditions, and soon whole groups of children went with her to carry back fare the inns threw out. Her methods rarely changed, and taverns soon knew her and began to have a fondness for her, overcooking

191

just for her scheduled visits. She instructed people in her team to keep silent about it. If Kye knew citizens were coming to recognise her, even getting to know and like her, he would fear for her that news would reach the Black Bands of the strange girl who dressed as a man.

But Emme thought Kye needed to let it go. She was sure if the prince still wanted her, he would have grabbed the chance to get her when the Black Bands had her. If that letter had not arrived, she and Kye would not have made it out alive that night. At least not Kye.

Kye at first spoke to her with stern but calm words about disobeying him, but the joy on children's faces at the food she salvaged and the way they looked up to her as some hero, a spark of light in the dark underground of their world, made him turn a blind eye. He never openly condoned it, but his silence was enough.

Emme noted that the men Kye's age, frequently came and went. They seemed to be there solely to assist Kye in aboveground duties. They had given up a life, an existence, to be available at any hour Kye needed them. The five took shifts, aided by random members of the team living down the street. Three scouted the city all day for signs of Black Band activities; the other two disappeared with their team at night, leaving the first team to sleep. According to Dusty, Kye had seventeen other informants positioned throughout the city to keep vigil over the city's outer reaches. Disguised by respectable positions within society, these associates supplied information, not action. Originally street rats rescued and educated by Kye, the seventeen differed from the other information-mongers Kye continually mentioned. The children rarely saw these seventeen adults, or even the twelve down the street, outside of occasional meetings or music nights at the headquarters. As for those other contacts, they were anonymous to all but Kye and Halder.

As Emme sat contemplating the last few weeks, the children still cheerfully whisking blunt knives from belts, Illina approached. Furtively, Emme glanced about for an excuse to escape but realised it would be too obvious to everyone in the room. Emme refused to be labelled a coward.

Whilst the woman drew near, Emme regarded her with an open scrutiny that time now afforded. Illina had white, flawless skin with the tiniest flush of pink on her cheeks. The neat, soft bun she wore on her head of wispy brown hair, made her slender white neck long. The woman did not just walk anywhere, she glided, and again Emme wondered what a woman like that would be doing in a place like this.

When Illina had almost crossed the room, Emme pretended to be engrossed in the practise of a nearby child.

"This is a good lesson, Emme," the tall, elegant woman said. "And they all love you. They really listen to everything you say."

"Thank you," Emme said with affected vagueness, still staring at the child.

Illina's small hand held out a dagger, drawing Emme's attention to it. "I thought I should return this to you."

Emme took the weapon, noted for the first time that Illina's hands were a striking contrast to the rest of her body. Usually gloved, today they were uncovered to reveal the pucker and dimple of burn scars. Emme wondered how far up the arms the burn scars went. A slight shift of the woman's clingy sleeve showed unblemished wrists.

"I'm sorry we haven't spoken before now," the soft-spoken woman said. She clutched the back of a chair, spun it around to face Emme and sat. "It seems I'm always rather busy teaching the children."

Emme held back open suspicion whilst the woman only looked at her with a regal genuineness. Emme knew it was entirely her own fault the two had never conversed.

Illina's friend, Ada, chewed her lip as she crossed the room to them. Without a word, Ada took another chair and positioned it close to Illina's. Not as composed as Illina, Ada seemed at least more refined than the street kids. Ada did not suit the mischievous strawberry-blonde hair plaited down her back, soft freckles, and blue eyes made bright by strawberry-blonde brows. She stared at the floor, her chalky lips thin and pressed.

Illina turned briefly to her friend. "Is Red back yet?"

Ada shook her head.

Illina gestured a damaged hand to Ada. "Ada's courting one of the men who go aboveground during the day – the one we call Red."

"Yes, I just heard that today," Emme said to Ada. "What's his real name?"

Ada merely blushed.

"Jon," Illina said, and Emme wondered that Ada could not speak for herself when for countless hours Ada dictated lessons, or issued scoldings to the street kids. Emme studied the woman who had not yet acknowledged Emme with eye contact or words, and saw a second slow blush spread across Ada's freckled face. Intensely shy, Emme realised.

Illina noted Emme's unabashed scrutiny of the two newcomers, almost seemed to guess that Emme questioned if the two really wanted to be there. "Do you mind if we sit awhile? Talk, perhaps?"

"No, I don't mind. As long as you don't."

Illina laughed sweetly. "We've been looking forward to it."

After a brief awkward silence, Emme asked, "So how did you two end up down here?"

"I was the servant of a wealthy family until they dismissed me after my accident," Illina said. "Kye found me wandering the streets injured and took me back here and helped me to heal." Her eyes shone slightly at a private memory.

The implications of Illina's words shocked through Emme. "They tossed you out when you were injured?"

"They didn't want to pay the doctor's fees for me, and I wasn't a lot of use to them with damaged hands." Illina cursorily examined the scars. "I've healed well though."

"Bastards. They had no right to do that." Emme detected Illina's faint surprise at the simmering rage. "How did it happen?"

"A falling broom handle knocked a pot of boiling oats onto my hands. The sticky oats just kept burning."

Emme watched Illina for the longest time, detected something that Emme felt was inappropriate to mention. Emme turned to Ada to deflect the lengthy silence. "What about you? How did you get here?"

"Ada was the governess where I worked and my good friend," Illina answered. "It was a very unhappy place to live, with terrible abuse, and they kept stealing her wages so I pulled her out. Now she helps me to teach the younger ones."

"Governess? What's a governess?"

"Private teacher and caretaker for the children. Some wealthy families prefer to hire governesses who can teach the children in school hours and care for the children after school so they don't have to."

"Usually the wealthy who didn't want to have children in the first place," Ada said in a whispery voice, eyes to the floor. Her cheeks reddened a little as she spoke.

Emme stared, curious that for all Ada's sophistication, the woman could be so painfully shy. Illina noted the staring, sensed what lay behind it. Gently, tactfully Illina explained that Ada had been a child of high birth tortured by terrible shyness. With little else to do with her, her parents sent Ada to Teachers' School. "She excels at it," Illina said, affection dancing in her eyes. "The children of Kildes would be sorely at a loss without teachers like Ada."

Ada's freckled skin, from neck to ear tips, exploded into crimson.

How ever did Ada fight shyness to form a relationship with Red, Emme wondered? And why expend the effort in the first place?

"And the men? What did they used to be?"

"They were once Black Bands," Illina explained with no discomfort or resentment for the fact.

"Don't tell me – Kye," Emme said.

Illina nodded. "And Halder. So tell us more about yourself, Emme."

Emme frowned slightly, not sure of where to start. Two clumsy sentences formed, then words flowed effortlessly to the captive audience. She wrapped the morning in tales of her dearest memories.

"So do you all dress that way?" Illina asked as the morning drew closer to lunch.

"No, just me."

"And the others don't mind?"

"They're used to it."

"Why did you choose it in the first place?"

Emme felt her stomach tighten. "I can't be a forest tracker in women's clothes."

"I see. So tell us about your parents," Illina said.

"There's nothing to say about them," Emme said tightly, then the bell for lunch produced visible relief.

Lack of time prevented the three from conversing much beyond that moment. The occasional greeting in the hallway, a short conversation before dinner or before lessons, seemed all time afforded them. The necessity of avoiding suspicion called Illina and Ada regularly to their home and meant the two hardly ever shared meals with the children. Anyone watching the upper floors might notice that the two seldom came and went, or were unnaturally delayed in lighting lamps each evening. Local vendors might also notice the two rarely purchased enough food for themselves, or did not work to support themselves yet still survived. In the hours the two did not teach, they dwelt in their home, shopped, and repaired clothes to make enough money to keep up the facade.

Although Emme spent little time with them, the cruelty that had brought the two women to this place occupied much of her thought. Memories of the stories, Illina's in particular, made her burn with an anger that she could not explain and could not escape.

◘

Kye disappeared several times during those five weeks, sometimes to answer the challenge of some new threat, other times to talk to those contacts he frequently mentioned. During those times, Emme sat in on group lessons, or went to Halder's balcony and looked out over the city.

Emme lay awake late one night dwelling heavily on the mystery of Halder, the terrible injustice of Illina's burns, and the strange aloofness and all that was unknown about Kye. The lantern, kept on throughout each night, gave its soft yellow glow. Shadows lingered where the light would not reach. Scratchy woollen blankets protected her from the moist chill of her room. That damp night, the odour of the musty mattress above seemed particularly strong.

Quiet footsteps down the hall interrupted her thoughts. The girls next door had long before ceased their gossiping, telling Emme it was well past midnight. She supposed it was probably close to two in the morning, although who really knew the time in this endless underground monotony?

She heard the office door open and knew Kye had returned from a two-day journey. She lay there, listened for the sound of his bedroom door, but instead heard rustling within his office. With her room closest to Kye's, she often heard his movements; seemed the only one to know he rarely slept, and wondered if perhaps he was awake more than even she realised, for she usually fell asleep first.

She got up, peeled the top blanket off the bed, wrapped it snugly around herself for warmth and left her room. Quietly she knocked on Kye's office door. She heard the shuffling of papers cease. Silence crept by. Finally she heard him call for her to enter.

"Emme," he said from behind his desk, his collection of papers scattered across it as though about to be sorted into some important order. "What are you doing awake at this hour?"

"I should ask the same thing about you."

"I thought you were a good sleeper."

"I mostly am. But down here I sometimes think a lot and can't sleep."

Emme saw the slightest dip in his brows, the faintest narrowing of eyes and detected that her response bothered him, but could not tell why. It was not concern for her; that much she perceived.

"So what can I do for you?" he asked after a while.

"Well, I'm guessing that you're going to be awake for many more hours. You usually are. So I thought we could probably have a discussion on one of those subjects I find boring, and hopefully I'll get sleepy."

A drift of a smile touched his lips. "Such subjects as?"

"I don't know – geography maybe?"

"You don't like learning about our geography?"

"Well, it's all right, I suppose; but I'd rather see it. Hearing about it isn't much fun. The best way to learn about geography is to be out there experiencing it. It's how I learned about my forest."

"I see." Again the faint amused smile. He reached into his drawer and pulled out a tube of parchment. He unrolled it, positioned an inkwell on two edges. The corners of the map curled around the inkwells. He smoothed the corners back, bent them under a little until they sat straight enough for his satisfaction. "What did we get up to last time?"

"You told me about Endoria, about the farmlands and hills beyond the city in the south and the snowy mountains in the north. You mentioned about the sheep farming and that grain called barley. And you told me about the southern forests along the Endorian border. I liked that bit."

"Ahh yes." He looked down at the map, different to the plain Kildes map. His eyes roamed markings that indicated population numbers, landscapes, terrain levels and bodies of water. Finally his mind formulated an outline for her lesson, and he spoke on through the night about Kildes' industries. He explained how each state produced a wide range of agricultural goods giving states a degree of self-sufficiency. However, by law, and in some cases geographical necessity, each state also specialised in at least one agricultural product and several industrial products not present in other states, giving the states a unity of trade. Endoria had vast northern factories that produced piping. Endoria also owned the mint, specialised in barley and made whiskey.

He explained how the land grew warmer as travellers moved south, and colder as people progressed north. From the map, Emme could see that more land lay south than north, and wondered that Endoria had not chosen a more central position for a ruling state.

"When princes first established themselves on pockets of land," Kye explained, "the Endorians chose the rocky fortress for their royal castle. It was the best-defended position in all of Kildes, and to this day, even with a history of overseas invasions, it has never been taken. It's the heart and rock of Kildes."

"Which is why it's awful that the enemy now owns it, so-to-speak," Emme said.

"Exactly. You have a fast mind for learning."

"So you've said." Emme stretched and yawned. "Yes, I think I'm sleepy now. Thank you for my discussion."

"You're welcome."

Blanket tight about her body, Emme shuffled to the edge of the chair, then hesitated.

"What is it?" Kye asked.

"Well, I was thinking tonight about Illina. About her hands."

"And?"

"It wasn't an accident, was it?"

"No."

"So not the broom handle?"

"There was a broom handle, but the broom was attached to someone else's hands."

"Was she – was she illegitimate?"

"No." Kye's brows dipped into the fainted gesture of puzzlement. "Why do you ask?"

"Are you sure?"

"Quite."

"Did she do something wrong?"

"No – Illina would never do anything wrong. She's too honest – too genuine."

"Then what? Why was she treated like that?"

Kye thought over his response. "Illina was never very good at basic labour. You've seen how she is – very elegant, very regal, very intelligent. She was born into a wealthy family and sold as a servant to pay a gambling debt. She was always a little slower, a little less apt at her tasks. The owners just thought it was about time to replace her."

Rage smouldered inside of Emme. "Then they had no right to treat her like that."

"No – no right. Although it doesn't matter what the circumstances of her birth were."

"Does it happen often, that kind of treatment?"

"Yes. Maybe not physical violence, but the rich constantly abuse their servants. Sometimes they don't pay them. Sometimes they overwork them. Sometimes they sell them like possessions. Sometimes they beat them. That's our world's social classes and our biases at work."

"Somebody should do something." Her eyes flashed.

"Yes – the prince should. But his way of ruling is to thrive on corruption and class systems. There isn't much anyone else can do until the prince changes the law or makes economics fairer."

Emme shrugged, a useless attempt to get the anger from her mind. She should have smacked more than just the prince's jaw when she saw him last. She should have cracked some sense into his royal, arrogant skull.

Kye watched her quietly for a moment. "It has really bothered you."

"Yes, and I don't know why. I really, *really* want to do something about it, and not being able to makes me burn inside. It makes me so angry I can't sleep."

Kye nodded once, and in that moment, Emme realised he felt the same. Perhaps that was why he slept so poorly. No – he *never* slept. Or so it seemed.

"Don't give up wanting to make a difference, Emme. Even if

you save one person at a time, like I did for Illina, then that's one less person who suffers."

Emme nodded. "Well, I can at least keep getting everyone food. And maybe not . . . maybe not avoid Illina and Ada so much."

"So do people in your village get treated like that if they do something wrong?" Kye asked.

"No. Not like that. Why?"

"Earlier you seemed to offer me two situations where that treatment would be acceptable – illegitimacy and crime."

Emme shifted slightly. Kye was a little too intelligent sometimes. "If you commit a crime, you go in the stocks."

"The stocks?"

"Hands and head in a vice and pelted with vegetables for the lesser crimes, whipped for the bigger ones."

"And if you're illegitimate?"

Emme shifted again. "You deserve what you get."

"Which is?"

"You know, I think I might go to sleep now. I'm feeling very tired."

"I see."

Emme felt a chill at his words. What did he see? That she was tired, or that she had given away her secrets? She stood hastily, loosened the blanket around her waist, and hurried to the door.

"Oh, and Emme?"

Hand on the doorknob, Emme turned. "Yes?"

"Don't tell anyone that I don't sleep so well."

"Why?"

"Because they'd worry about me, and they don't need to."

Emme nodded and left the room, but the frown stayed on her face even as she slid under the thick pile of blankets on her bed. Kye's response had been entirely too quick, too rehearsed, for her liking.

8

___

At the end of the sixth week, Dusty knocked loudly on Emme's door with a musical rhythm.

Brow arched, Emme opened the door. "Was that necessary?"

"Yes. Totally appropriate." Dusty's boyish grin spread across his freckled face. "It's to remind you that tonight is our monthly music night and you absolutely have to come to this one. You missed the last one."

"Illina put you up to this, didn't she?" Emme said flatly.

"She did mention that you were refusing to go, but it's going to be a really great night, and you'll be missing out on a lot of fun if you don't go. We don't get to do very many enjoyable things down here but music night is one of the things we all look forward to, and I think that if you could just come for one night you'd see that it's a lot of fun and –"

"Stop talking for a minute, Dusty."

Dusty snapped his jaw shut and waited expectantly.

"Getting dressed up and doing some dancing just isn't something I'm comfortable with."

"It's not all dancing. Some of us perform plays, and some of us sing or do an item, and then we have dancing at the end. Maybe you could just come for the first half, and you don't have to get dressed up. No one would expect you to wear a dress or anything, so just come as you like, and if you don't come we're all going to be really sad because we've written a few plays and songs in your honour that you'll –"

"Mine? Why me?"

"Because since you arrived, we've never gone a day without food and because we've never come this close to being liked by the city folk before. But they're starting to like us all now so even if you go away, we'd still probably always be able to get food. And you know those girls got a regular job in some of the kitchens because of you. And the city folk aren't the only ones who love you, Emme. All the little kids love you too. You're their hero, and they're always talking about you, and they'd hate it if you weren't –"

"Dusty – please stop prattling."

Dusty grinned. "You did ask."

"All right, I'll come. But just for a little while and strictly no dancing." She scowled playfully at Dusty. "Now I know why Illina sent you. Because she knew you'd prattle me insane if I didn't go."

"That was the idea."

"Say, shouldn't you be on laundry duty?"

"Yes, but I got Lydia to replace me."

"How did you get out of it this time?"

"I told her I had to do preparations for tonight. Lydia will do most things for me."

"Dusty," Emme scolded. "I have never known anybody to get out of jobs the way you do. You have got to stop using people to get out of your responsibilities. And I've seen the way you hide at the back of groups when Illina and Ada are handing out the list of chores."

"I admit I'm a little bit lazy, but I do go up with the groups that go for food every week."

"Not good enough, Dusty. If you're given a job, don't use girls' attractions to you to get them to do things in your place. It's wrong."

Dusty shrugged. "It's all harmless." He winked at her and

took off down the hallway before she could further berate him.

"Come back here, I haven't finished," Emme yelled at his back, but Dusty ignored her and disappeared down the perpendicular corridor. She slapped the door shut to her room. It cracked through the empty hallway beyond, then all was still and quiet. She flopped back on the bed and glowered at the bunk above her. The humorous thought of poor Lydia's adoring eyes having to look at dirty washing all day, made Emme's irritation dissolve. Lydia was a smart girl. It was as much her fault she was off in the laundry doing Dusty's duty, as it was Dusty's. What was it that made those girls lose all sensibilities when it came to men?

She began to think about the evening's music night and realised Dusty had just used all his boyish charm to get Emme to consent to something she had aggressively refused for weeks. Who was the weaker fool here – her or Lydia? Emme felt a smile tug at her lips.

More smiles had pulled at her lips in the last few weeks than in all the years previous. She had often smiled from her treetops at newborn forest creatures. Or smiled maliciously as some cruel village joke aimed at her, came to haunt the perpetrator. But she had never smiled because she found some light-hearted joke funny. Or because she had won some recreational game of strategy. And especially not because she found some good quality about someone enjoyable.

She wondered at the gentler, freer Emme that was surfacing. Was she being set up for some hurt? Was it some big sting to get something from Emme they all knew she had? Or was it because she was worth something to important people in the city, and the street kids wanted to make sure she was on their side?

Maybe there were people in the world who were genuinely friendly to others, with only the hope that others would be friendly back. Or maybe the street kids just belonged to the family of desperation giving them a unity that produced a reasonable tolerance for each other.

Emme shrugged. As long as she didn't get too close to anybody, she couldn't be hurt, and what did it matter if she enjoyed a few weeks of her existence. It didn't have to be forever. She knew she could cope with the hurts and disappointments of life – she had for twenty-two years.

Emme sat up and went to her cupboard. She tugged the creaky timber doors. Dust clouded the air briefly. She grabbed her towel and spare clothes donated by some of the young men. She banged off the edge of dust against the dull grey wall, then headed for the baths. She might not dress up, but she could at least be clean.

She entered the bustling laundry where a group of boys and girls stirred large boiling pots of whites and plunged colours in separate cold tubs. The pungent smell of lemon and caustic sodas assailed her senses briefly. In striking contrast to the cold, dry corridor, the air hung hot, moist.

With a shudder, Emme remembered all too well her own day on laundry duty. She would much prefer the job of tracking the city with the other men, but the suggestion did not fare too well with Kye. Especially not whilst Kye sent his men to track for signs soldiers continued to pursue her.

"Hello there, Emme," the golden-haired beauty, Lydia, said. "You're not on laundry duty, are you?"

"Thank the Creator, no. Have you got any hot water left for a bath?"

"Some. That smaller black pot over there." A pockmarked cast-iron pot hung above coals. "It's just boiling now."

"Can I take it?"

"I guess so." Lydia pushed clammy blonde locks from damp cheeks, then hurried to the black iron left amongst coals for pressing clothes. "There's been a rush on hot water today.

Everyone gets clean and dressed up for tonight. The smaller bathroom is free. No one has used it today."

"Of course they haven't," Emme muttered, imagining her long legs in that tiny, unpopular tub.

"Have you changed your mind about coming?" Lydia used a thick towel to remove the metal iron from the slumbering coals, and drifted over to the padded ironing bench where crumpled white shirts waited.

"I'll come for a while, but not long."

"You'll love it," Lydia assured her. "And there are some surprises for you too."

"Dusty told me – those songs and plays in my honour."

Lydia looked up sharply from the first shirt, the sizzling iron hovering just above the linen fibres. "Oooo, that Dusty – When I get my hands on him. He's absolutely hopeless at keeping a secret." But her eyes sparkled even as her tone scolded. She pressed the iron to the fabric again, her free arm smearing away more clinging curls from her face.

Emme took the weighty black pot, careful not to let the metal touch and burn her legs. She entered the nearest bathroom and tipped the hot water into the small copper tub. She turned the thick tap jutting from the cold stone wall above the bath. Water did not flow.

"Damn pipes are frozen again," Emme grumbled. For all the convenience of these alien services – taps, pipes, latrines – it was still more unreliable than a bucket dipped down a well and other methods considered primitive by this world. "I want cold water, damn it." Seconds later, water spurted in uncertain bursts from the tap. When the water gushed in a thick even stream, she quickly turned down the pressure and let the frigid water drain into the bath whilst she returned the pot.

Back at the bathroom door, she turned a flat metal plate and chain to its red side, the signal the bathroom was in use. She entered the room, noted with satisfaction that the chill already dissipated as steam took its place. She waited patiently until the water reached the perfect temperature, then turned off the tap.

She began to unbutton the donated pants, looked down at them. Her fingers halted on the buttons. No, it was time to put *her* clothes – her forest clothes – back on. She dashed back to the room and pulled them from the bottom of the cupboard. One of the little girls had neatly folded the garments for her, and they had been left to gather dust. She had not worn them since the night she first went to find food. The necessity of being ready to go to the city at a moment's notice forced her to remain in borrowed clothes.

She soaked leisurely in the tarnished copper tub, rigorously dried off and stood in front of the cracked, gilded mirror – a mirror one of the street kids had discovered on a wealthy family's rubbish pile.

She stared at cheeks no longer as brown as she remembered them. Days of no sun had begun to turn her cheeks to a common white – a feature that made it easier to blend amongst the city folk.

The boys were right, Emme admitted – her face was entirely too feminine to pass for a man. None of the men had defined crimson lips or long black lashes, or the fine, curved eyebrows. But then, none of the women wore that scowl she could see pointed back at herself. She smoothed the scowl; tried out a smile. Her teeth were white from the charcoal the villagers used to keep their mouths healthy. Here they used those tiny brushes and that unusual soda that made cakes rise.

She closed her lips, afraid of the alien look on her face when she smiled. She scrutinised her hair. It was a little longer now, didn't sit nearly so ragged as it used to. It was definitely time for a cut. She should probably see to that before tonight.

She shook her head and saw her reflection shake back. Why was she going to that ridiculous dance? That was the last thing she wanted to do. She had plans to wander the city tonight. Despite being the middle of winter, the weather had eased off the last few days, creating the perfect time to go exploring. She hadn't been out for a while and needed to see some sky, to have a sense of space. More importantly, she longed to climb a tree, to feel its uneven branches beneath her hands and feet, and to hear it creak and tap in a breeze.

She didn't miss the village, or the people, but she missed the forest. Mostly she missed the trees. She loved those trees. They were family – sheltering her, holding her, raising her, teaching her about the world she watched from their branches.

She wondered what the village thought about her absence. Wendaya would be thrilled, and had probably been reinstated a little into village social life. The chieftain, although glad she was gone, would be cursing the loss of his best and only tracker. The men would grow bored with having no one to victimise, and would soon find someone else. The next thug who picked a drunken fight and lost would probably become the latest brunt of cruelty – although without the same degree of hatred they felt for Emme.

And although deprived of their malicious gossip, the women would never cease to find things to meddle in – who was attracted to who, what husband wasn't nearly up to standard, provocative stories from nearby villages. No, the women's tongues would never be bored. Although their vindictiveness might not find a home for a while.

Emme had always dreamed about running away, but to freedom, not into more confinement. She was sure she was safe to wander the city alone and free, but Kye insisted on keeping a tight leash on her movements. How was she to really learn about city life and ways if she couldn't be up there living it?

Emme looked her bruises over. They were just about all gone. The cuts on her wrists left faint scars, but she had so many other scars anyway, and smooth, unmarred flesh had never been her desire.

She almost didn't like the long patches of unbruised skin, for it looked a little more feminine without the marks of her lifelong war.

She quickly covered over the skin with clothes, put a warm jumper over the top, then rustled hair loose to let untangled strands dry. Droplets of water sprayed across the walls and mirror from the vigorous movements.

She bundled up her wet towel and strolled to her room where she put on thick socks and shoes, then sat on the bed to pass time until evening. She at first occupied herself with a slate of maths problems Kye had given her. She looked at the separate parchment marked with his neat, flowing, almost beautiful writing; took the maths problems into her mind; then scratched out the solutions onto black slate with white chalk.

The maths filled her head for hours until she started to feel nervous, jittery, about the evening to come. She delved into more puzzles, then angrily threw the chalk to the floor. It cracked into little pieces against a brittle timber floorboard. How could she concentrate with all those anxious flutters in her stomach?

Why was she so disturbed? She would just go, eat the meal, listen to a few songs, and then leave.

Her mind began to trace back to village feasts and dances – such as the one that celebrated the coming of spring, or gave thanks to the Creator for the forest harvest, or ones held at weddings and births. On a warm night, tables would be set out in rows through the grassy village centre. Ribbons, soaked in dyes from the forest, would be strewn from tree to tree. Candles, placed on each table, illuminated large platters of forest fare.

Then the women would turn up in their silky, draping dresses that showed hips, full bust-lines and browned backs. The men managed to wash, shave, comb, and don their best leather jerkins and silk shirts. Children, bounding behind their parents, arrived in their neatest clothes and managed to stay unstained until at least the meal began. The children would sit at their own table and stuff down mounds of luscious foods reserved solely for feasts.

Villagers would eat, drink honeyed wine, and talk into the long hours until several villagers took up hand drums, seed rattles, and bone flutes. Then the dancing would start. Even Wendaya would go to the dances, and in those moments, Emme saw glimpses of her mother's former glory. Wendaya would shine, turn heads, and laugh as one whose life had never known bitterness. The next day, all would go back as it was. Wendaya would remain on the edges of town, mostly within her hut, using long fingers to sew those clothes the villagers had displayed the night before.

As a child, Emme used to watch from the trees and longed to be down there amongst them all, laughing, sipping honeyed-wine, and dancing in those shimmering dresses. The aroma of sweet-burning candle wax, roasted meat and freshly picked forest flowers, reached her branches and intoxicated her mind like an alluring perfume. But one year they caught her, found her watching. In their drunken, frenzied state, they dragged her down from the tree and beat and kicked her until she bled. Every bone in her body felt smashed. Her arm crumpled under her, and the bone in it had never set right. One eye had completely closed, the other puffed to half-shut, making it difficult to see as she sobbed, staggered and vomited her way into the forest for safety.

It was the spitting that she hated the most. She was covered in alcohol-drenched spit, issued from mouths that had despised her. It was worse than any jeer or any bruise they had given her.

When she got older, and could out-fight most of the men in the village, they left her alone on music nights, but she never went to the dances. Several times she defiantly crossed the town square, cutting through the dancers, to some important destination on the other side, but no one touched her. Admittedly many were too drunk to even care that she passed by.

Emme felt a stab of sickened anger at the memory. Maybe that was why the thought of tonight distressed her so much. Music nights always did – for they reminded her of that terrible time long ago, when instead of welcoming an excited little girl to the dance, they had beaten and kicked her until half-dead.

Emme placed hands reassuringly on the skins she wore. That's why she needed to wear them – because they stood for the Emme that had fought to be left alone amidst villagers who wanted to see her dead. She had never won respect or friendship, but she had won the right to be left alone. Only then did the chieftain give her the job of forest tracker. At first he aimed to get her out of the village for long hours, sometimes days at a time, but after a few years, he had to admit she was very good at her job.

Emme had been well used to forest tracking before that. At thirteen winters, she had come of age and village custom demanded she be given a job. She had to work to get her share of the meats the hunters caught and crops the land tenders grew; it was no longer her right to receive the food without earning it. But the villagers had cruelly denied her a job, and Emme had been forced to go out to the forest and find her own food. There she became strong, independent, unattached from the hurts of life. The trees had taught her that. They even taught her to fight. Knuckles against the trunk of a tree ensured those knuckles would not smart at contact with a man's jaw. And she had learned to dodge and thrust – punch even – with legs in a way that no other man could master.

Tired of silence and maths, Emme went to the kitchens and grabbed the sharpest knife she could find. She took the knife back to the mirrored bathroom and slashed at the lengthy bits of hair. She cut back the unruly ones, then tussled the hair to the shape she liked it – a neat mess, like hair that just needed to be brushed. She stood back. She would never cut her hair as cropped and close as the men did, but then, she would never wear it long and silky like the women, either.

That was her life – a strange half-world where she stood in the middle of everything, never belonging to anything beyond the middle ground she had claimed for her very own.

Emme shrugged and took the knife back to the kitchen, poured herself a hot cup of tea and returned to her room. More time, more anxious flutters passed.

The knocking on her door indicated the night had begun all too soon. Emme followed Dusty down the hall, a cold, uncaring expression on her face. The room was already nearly full when she entered. A few girls looked up at her expectantly, then after noting with disappointment that she had not worn a dress, went back to their conversation.

The jumbled nattering of the crowd had a feverish pitch to it – an intensity not usually present at mealtimes. The large fire in the kitchen had been stoked to brightness, and the ever-present chill in the room slowly dissolved away. Emme could smell the wood smoke and an intense blend of perfumes, soaps and colognes. Excited eyes, and teeth bared by animated smiles, glimmered in the light of numerous lanterns – more lanterns than usually adorned the dim room.

Emme noted warily that several unfamiliar adults filled chairs in the first two rows. Dusty forewarned her that outer-city team members often stayed over for music night. Ordinarily Emme did not fear strangers. Tonight, however, their new faces chilled her.

Emme sat up the back, as far from the cleared performance area as she could. Although at first she had the row to herself, it quickly began to fill. Tables had been stacked against the back wall, and semicircular rows of chairs faced an area of musical instruments and props.

Emme heard Halder roaring out some conversation up the front, a huge toothy grin on his face. He said something lost to Emme's ears and slapped the man next to him on the back. The man laughed, and Halder turned to the woman on his other side and engaged in conversation with her.

Kye entered soon after Emme, and most faces turned to him expectantly. Emme saw the way every girl lost their eyes for Dusty when Kye walked in the room. The older girls became almost childishly silly and flustered when Kye was around. He charmed them, Emme supposed, with his polite bows, flattering words, and the way he kissed their hands before he parted company when he walked them to their rooms.

Always, though, he remained aloof, mysterious: an enigma that Emme wanted an explanation for. She had kept her word, and not mentioned Kye's secret to anyone, but she suspected that if she did, someone just might know what that tattoo meant and give her a clue to Kye's history. Had he been a Black Band? Possibly a leader of them? Or was he a rich man who had been cast out of society? After all, he did have six bags of King's Gold in his possession – only a man with a rich past would have access to those.

Kye scanned the room as if looking for someone amidst the familiar faces. He seemed the best dressed out of all of them with a flawlessly pressed green button shirt and black pants. His gently curled hair had been washed and brushed to neatness, the stubble from the recent trip to his contacts, gone from his chin.

Despite poverty, everyone presented neatly. Men tugged at sleeves of their dressiest shirts, and wide skirts swished as girls breezed into the room and swept to their seats.

Emme remained unimpressed. Fancy clothes were all too often worn to please the opposite sex – a waste of time.

Emme noted that Kye's eyes had reached her row. He saw her, nodded his head once and took his seat in the front row.

The last of them arrived, and soon trays of bread and drippings were passed around. No one minded that bread and lard was all lack of money allowed. All eyes were fixed on the musicians who took their place on the stage area.

Emme knew their instruments – had been taught what they were and what sound they produced. A violin, a guitar, a flute and a – she focused her mind on the last one, the oversized violin that sat on the floor, but couldn't remember the name.

The musicians played, and two young girls sang a cheerful tune. The street rats joined in on the chorus. An older boy beside Emme nudged her with his elbow and whilst his mouth moved in time to the song, gestured with his head towards the stage. "Come on, sing," he whispered, then continued with the chorus.

Emme gave him a scorching look that went unnoticed. She did not know the song; she did not want to know the song.

The song finished. Whistles and a huge applause broke out. The two girls sang another song, then sat down as a second group of singers took their place. The mixed group sang more tunes. Although admitting to herself she enjoyed the tunes, Emme thought the words were mildly annoying – songs about love, requited or otherwise.

Emme found herself growing more and more uncomfortable. She shouldn't be here, watching this. It was forbidden back home. Maybe if they knew about the circumstances of her birth, they would forbid it too.

Then the plays began. Young people performed plays written by famous playwrights Emme had heard about. The longer the evening went on, the more restless Emme became. She slid about in her chair and tugged at her clothes. Should she go now? No, she should wait until the plays had finished so as not to be noticed when she left.

Then the student-written plays commenced. Some were tragedies; most were comedies that had everyone laughing but Emme. And then the play in her honour came on – a re-enactment of her exploits in the city, performed with a heavy dose of overacting. The play sent everyone into fits of laughter, but Emme sat there deeply troubled, her heart pounding like a hammer against her ribs. They were laughing at her. Or were they? She could hear laughter beyond the laughter, but where was it coming from? And why did it sound so cruel?

She felt her clothes start to restrict her, and sweat broke out beneath them. Then the faces all around her became the twisted faces of the villagers glaring down at her. She saw legs kick, heard smacking echo repeatedly through her body as knobby fists tenderised her flesh. She felt the hot rancid spit drop down her face and soak through her clothes. She could smell the alcohol on their breath, smell the stench of sweat and fear – her own. Heard the whimpers of her mouth, felt her salty tears sting the cuts on her face. They made her stand, stabbed booted feet into her shins, fists into ribs and face until she buckled, then dragged her to her feet again.

"Go home," they yelled over and over.

She heard laughing, a whole crowd of people laughing, and

she snapped back to the room where people glanced at her, hoping she would laugh too. The room was hot, thick, stuffy. No one seemed to notice. They just kept on laughing.

The laughter was loud, cutting to her ears like the shrill scrape of nails on slate, but they did not notice, they just went on and on with the laughing, with the mocking rendition of her exploits.

She felt her breath start to quicken, could suddenly hear it in her ears. Sweat trickled down her hot burning cheeks. She burst. Snapped to her feet and pushed through a tangle of legs and boots. She fought her way down the row of chairs. Could everyone hear her ragged breaths, smell the sweat on her neck, back, stomach? Could they see her shaking hands, her unstable knees?

Heads swung her way at the sound of chairs scraping back for her. Faces stared, wondered that she got up. The play paused and the sudden silence mocked her louder than any laughter. Didn't they know that the walls were pressing in on her, that there were faces all around her jeering and spitting and telling her to "Go home, devil child. Go home."

She fled down the corridor, the longest corridor in the world, to the laundry; fought her way through a sinister maze of suspended sheets that flapped and bit to stop her getting through. She pounded every slab of cold stone in the wall until the door swung open, then ran up the longest flight of stairs she could ever remember. She snapped back the trapdoor, heard the loud thumping of her feet in Halder's vast warehouse. Or was that a thumping in her chest? Up and up the coiling stairs. The stairs tried to leap at her at every turn. They kicked into her shin as she stumbled onto a sharp edge, but she fought against it, pushed her feet up and up, stomped on each step to subdue it.

She punched back the second trapdoor and climbed out, belly first, onto cold snow. She pushed to her feet and thrust through the recently fallen snow to the edge that peered out at meagre streetlights and dimly lit windows – and sky, vast black-clouded sky.

Trees. She longed for her trees. Her trees had sheltered her, cradled her that night as a child. They had nursed her in their long wooden arms night after night until she was brave enough to return home. The leaves had caught and mopped her tears, her blood, and the birds had come each day to sing her the celebration songs she had been cruelly denied.

She sucked in air, cold refreshing air, and felt sweat cool her, soothe her. Wind pushed through her hair and reminded her, her thin arms were bare.

"Emme?"

Emme flinched, turned to the voice, fear all too apparent in her eyes.

"Are you all right?" Kye asked.

How did he get that close without her hearing? Had he followed her the whole time?

"I'm fine." Emme entirely lacked conviction.

"Did we upset you in there?"

Emme turned away from him, looked out over the city. "I shouldn't have gone. I wasn't welcome there."

Kye came and stood beside her against the lower balcony edge. Whilst she looked out to the vast darkness, he watched her, his right side leaning and arms folded. His silence seemed to invite her to talk, but she didn't want to tell him anything.

"I've never been welcome at village dances," Emme said, weakness overruling resolve. "I was never invited."

Again Kye just watched her, his silence patient and expectant.

"They beat me, you know."

"Who did?"

"The villagers. I escaped my house once when I was a child and watched the dancing. I just wanted to be there with all the other children." She recounted the story in its graphic ugliness until she saw Kye's jaw tighten. He said nothing, but that jaw movement, so slight, spoke volumes about the anger he felt.

Her story spent, Emme silently surveyed the city, drowned the memory in its vastness.

"Why do your villagers hate you, Emme?" Kye asked, eyes still on her.

Emme look at him, almost through him. What did it matter if he knew? All pride had gone now. She had shown weakness tonight the moment she fled the room. His eyes were watching everything she did, every facial movement, almost seeing every word she said. Expression stony, she turned back to the city. "Mistake," she murmured.

"What mistake, Emme?"

"That's my name. Mistake. Not Emme. I gave myself that name. The letter M short for mistake, that I made E double-M E. My mother called me Mistake. I was her one mistake. She got drunk one night and a man took advantage of her because men are pigs and that's what they do. She got pregnant with me." She looked once at Kye, but there was no disdain on his face, only a strange kind of sadness. "I lied to you. We do have a higher law like yours. It's from the Creator, and that law is that children must only be born in wedlock. Anyone who is born out of wedlock is the lowest of the low. If someone had claimed responsibility for what he did to my mother, owned up, the two could have been married. I could have been spared. But no one owned up. And my mother was ostracised, and I was hated, passionately hated, from the moment I was born."

"And she used to beat you."

"Yes. Every day nearly. There was always something that would set her off. I got used to it, but I still wished that one day she would just . . . " *Tell me she loved me.*

"I am so sorry."

"Don't be. I don't care anymore." She dared to look at Kye. "Why would you be sorry anyway? It's not your fault it happened."

"I'm sorry *for* you – that you've been treated so cruelly all your life."

Emme searched his face. He seemed to really mean it. "I was only treated with what I deserved. I was an illegitimate child. That's how I *should* be treated."

"Well, I don't know who your people think the Creator is, but I know our Almighty wouldn't allow you to be treated that way. He might not want children born out of wedlock, but He would never ask people to be so cruel to any child who was."

Emme did not, suddenly could not, respond. She looked back out into the darkness.

Kye turned and leant his chest against the roof railing, stared across the rooftops. "It's all making sense to me now, Emme – the way you are. You've grown up trying to protect yourself. And your mother has made you think that because one man could take advantage of her, all men would. So you try to stop any man thinking of you as a woman they can abuse."

Quietly, lifelessly, Emme muttered, "Are you finished?" The wind replaced conversation. The streets were cold, empty, and quiet – just how she felt inside. "So do you despise me now? You may as well. Everyone will eventually when they find out."

Kye said nothing for a while, then turned to her. "I tell you what, Emme. How about we go back in that room and you experience the first dance in your life you've been invited to, welcomed to, and actually been the guest of honour for."

Emme faced him with a puzzled frown. "Even after what I just told you?"

Kye bowed debonairly, straightened and held out his hand. "Will you do me the honour of the next dance?"

Emme thought it over carefully, stared at his outstretched hand. "I'll come back down. I don't know if I'll dance though because I don't know . . ." Her voice trailed off.

"How to?"

She felt her cheeks burn, and was silently thankful for the darkness.

"Then consider tonight one of your lessons or discussions. Come with me and learn to dance."

Emme opened her mouth to object, but Kye cut her off. "I insist and that's all there is to it." He took her arm, pulled her to the trapdoor.

"All right, I'm coming." Emme yanked her arm free, scowled at him playfully. She saw the gentle smile on Kye's lips as she walked past him and down the flight of stairs to Halder's house.

Lively music was playing when Emme entered the brightly lit dining room. The flurry of movement momentarily dazzled her. Chairs had been stacked up against the wall near the tables. Pairs and groups swirled within the centre to the spirited tune.

Others stood along the edges drinking hot drinks, chatting. Halder was swinging a flushed giggling girl from the floor like a cherished rag doll, and a smile longed to turn Emme's lips. She suppressed it and stepped from the doorway.

No one seemed to care about her return, let alone her hasty departure. Kye stood beside her, studied the room. The music finished on a staccato note, and everyone applauded loudly. The musicians sipped glasses of lemon water, then discussed amongst themselves the next song choice.

"Glad you're back, Emme," red-cheeked Dusty puffed on his way to returning a girl to her friends. As soon as Dusty's arm uncoupled from the young woman, another girl attached herself. He led her to the dance floor.

One of the musicians announced the name of the next tune, then settled his violin on his shoulder.

"This one will be a slow tune," Kye said. Emme glanced up at him. "It's perfect for learning to dance."

The tune started at half the pace of the previous song. Kye extended his arm, poised for guiding her somewhere. "Link your hand onto my arm. It's the way I lead you to the dance floor."

Emme wondered if it was just the heat of the room that made her cheeks feel warm. She hesitantly tucked her hand around his arm, and he escorted her to a clear space near the second door. "If you get overwhelmed, the door is right there," Kye said quietly.

Emme nodded, grateful for his forethought.

"Now, put your left hand here." He took the hand and positioned it on his shoulder. "And hold my other hand like this." With an arm bent close to his side, he held her hand in his. "Now, I put my hand on your waist like this."

Emme stiffened as his hand contacted her waist. "Is this necessary?"

"Very," Kye said, and she knew mischief lay in his tone. "Think of it as another learning experience."

They stood locked in that stance whilst other couples twirled around them. "Now what?" Emme asked.

"I lead, you follow. That means that I'm going to take steps, and you follow where I step."

"Just don't do anything surprising. I'm not a mind-reader."

Kye's slight smile widened. "You'll be fine, Emme. Now follow me." He began stepping and Emme looked closely down at his feet, watched exactly where they went.

Several steps later, whilst Emme still concentrated on his feet, Kye said, "Can you see that it's forming a pattern?"

"Yes." Emme smiled at the maths of it, the precision of the steps with the rhythmical counts of the music. "I didn't know this could be so mathematical."

She heard Kye chuckle softly, then he said, "Do you think you could be brave enough to look up from my feet now? The idea is to be enjoying your dance partner and the other people in the room."

Emme nodded and levelled her gaze at Kye's shoulders. She glanced once at his feet, then closed her eyes and visualised the movements. She overstepped onto his toes and felt panic flutter in her stomach. Hastily she stared down at his feet again, but he put a finger under her chin, lifted it. "You're doing fine," he said.

She looked up again and around the room, found that she *was* doing fine. She beamed at Kye and he smiled down at her. The beat of multitudinous feet pounded deep within her chest. She could feel the rhythm swell in her mind, flood to every limb. "I didn't know this could be so enjoyable."

"Are you ready to take bigger steps, then?"

Emme nodded, and Kye converted small steps to sweeping strides. Something small bubbled inside her stomach – joy. She actually laughed – felt the laugh escape before she knew what it was. She almost felt she was flying as she stepped and spun around the room.

She realised she was right away from the door, the centre of the room like star dancers surrounded by secondary dancers. Many pairs of eyes fixed on her, female eyes that watched the two of them curiously as if wondering what was happening between the dance partners.

She didn't care. She was enjoying a dance and that was –

Goodness – what was Kye looking at her like that for? She

noted the way he watched her, wouldn't take his eyes from her. Something significant was going on in his mind, but what?

When the music stopped and partners separated to applaud, Kye remained locked in the dancers' embrace. Emme's cheeks burned. Suddenly she felt like the eyes around the room had seen something she had not and were waiting for her to discover it.

Kye seemed to snap back to the room. Swiftly he let go of her. "Thank you for the dance, Emme," he said with detached politeness. He bowed stiffly and without warning, turned, walked through the crowd and left the room.

Emme stood there, suddenly alone, angry and hurt all at once. The whole room whispered and pointed to her. She had been an idiot to come back here. She knew why Kye had left like that. It was because of her past, because of who she was. He had suddenly realised it, had regretted the way he danced with her, the way he had looked at her.

Bastard. As the music started up again, Emme took the opposite door to Kye, headed to the haven of Halder's balcony. Once there, she no longer felt anger inside, only a strange emptiness.

◙

Emme woke the next morning to news that Kye had left some time in the night without giving any reason to anybody for the disappearance. All anyone knew was that he had taken his travel pack with him, hence he intended to be gone for several days.

"He doesn't usually do that," Dusty said to her over a plate of leftover bread and drippings. "He usually tells at least one of us that he's going, or leaves a note or something. It must have been urgent and important. Not that this would be the only time he's done anything urgent or important, but this must be even more urgent and important than usual."

Emme glared at him to silence him, the effect lost, for his

eyes were fixed on Lydia across the room. Lydia, nose raised slightly, made moves to look keenly interested in something else.

"She's not talking to me, you know," Dusty said, eyes still on Lydia. "I promised her the last dance and then Kit cut in halfway through, so she's not speaking to me."

"Good for her. It'll save her a lot of pain in the long run." Emme scraped back her chair across the stone floor and stood.

"You haven't eaten your food," Dusty said, noticing Emme again. "That's not like you."

"You can have it." She pushed the bread to Dusty and left the room.

She moved into the library's silence, strode past people reading, and flopped into the furthest wingback chair. Protesting rough treatment, the chair springs creaked and the cushions puffed in the stillness. In the opposite corner, Illina and Ada glanced up from tutoring the three youngest students. They returned to the quiet lesson.

Emme picked up a slate from a stack on the tea table beside her, and selected a piece of chalk. She scribbled numbers at random, then scrutinised them for patterns, any formations that might distract from sullen childish thoughts.

Close by, two girls whispered behind hands, eyes roaming pointedly to Emme.

She glared at them. "Well let's hear it, then. If you've got something to say about me, just say it."

The two girls' faces paled. They launched to their feet. Books from their laps thudded to the floor, pages flapping like broken wings. They scurried from the room.

The rest of the room stopped, stared. Not even the swish of a turning page could be heard. Emme slapped the slate on the pile angrily and slumped back in the chair. She was right. She had been setting herself up for hurt. Why did she think Kye was different to every other person who despised her for her birth?

Unsettled by the awkward silence in the library – disrupted only by her shifting feet on knotted floorboards – she went back to the dining room for hot tea to take to her room. She stepped into the empty kitchen, heard a young man in the dining hall covertly utter, ". . . and he says her real name is Mistake."

Emme whirled, stormed to the boy. She curled fists through his linen collar and yanked him from the chair to his feet. The chair pitched unsteadily, then tumbled onto its back, legs jutting helplessly.

"Who told you that?" she demanded loudly in the boy's startled face.

"Dusty did."

"Right – he is going to suffer." She abruptly released the boy's collar. He rocked on his heels, then landed heavily on his bottom. "And so will the next person who says that."

"I tried to tell you she was behind you," Emme heard the other boy mutter as she stormed to Dusty's table.

"Get to your feet," Emme demanded hotly.

Dusty blinked heavily, gaped up at her. "What did I do?"

"I said *get to your feet*."

Dusty stood clumsily, straightened his shirt as if about to be inspected. Lips pressed thin, he met her blazing eyes.

Her words came low, dangerous. "Who told you my real name?"

"I – how did you –"

"Did Kye?"

"I haven't seen Kye all night."

"Liar!" Emme gripped Dusty by the shirt, lifted him almost from the floor. She smacked his back down onto the tabletop; his shoulder blades thudded against the timber. With fists full of his shirt, she pinned him to the table, leant over him. Tone ominously quiet, she said, "Tell me."

He gasped, winded.

"Leave him alone," Lydia shrieked from the edge of the room. She dashed to Emme.

Emme shot up a warning hand. "Stay back, little girl." Lydia jolted to a standstill. "This is between me and Dusty." Emme looked back down at Dusty. "Tell me the truth and I'll leave you alone." Dusty winced, gasped for breath whilst Emme waited, muscles tense, for the name she knew would issue from his mouth. She saw Dusty's boyish, pleading eyes stare up at her, fear swirling in them. Sweat seeped along his hairline. He wheezed again whilst Lydia whimpered at a safe distance.

Dusty – her good friend. What was she doing? This wasn't the village anymore. These people respected her. It wasn't the frightened boy's fault Kye was an untrustworthy bastard. Shame burned her cheeks, and she knew Dusty could see it. She slowly released Dusty's shirt, hands spread and retreating as though stained with blood. She straightened, stood back. "Are you all right?"

Dusty nodded, coughed a little and tried to sit up.

"Dusty, I'm sorry. I shouldn't have –"

Her apology severed from her lips as an arm hooked around her throat. "Hey, I was apologising," Emme called out, but was jerked to the floor. Swiftly she found herself tussling and kicking one of the older boys whilst voices hollered, "Fight, fight, fight."

Within minutes the room swelled with people, and Emme took on three boys, then four. With one gang defeated, more vigilante boys leapt in to try to stop her, unaware she defended, not attacked.

She glimpsed Illina and Ada rushing into the room. They attempted to push against a flood of children to the fighting circle.

They stopped halfway, shocked at how many crowded around for the fight, and how many they were fighting – just one. Illina turned swiftly to Ada, ordered something Emme could not hear above the shouting mob.

Emme fought off more boys, felt a fist in the stomach. Her face tore as a knuckled hand struck it. A solid boot in the shins made her wince, but she flicked the boy's legs from under him, saw him fall onto his tailbone against the hard floor. Desperately she wished the crowds would go away, or at least take the little children to a safe distance. The proximity of the weaker little children hampered Emme's movements, making her less efficient than in a village fight. She took great pains not to injure any of them. An assailant tripped on his own lace and crashed against a small child. Emme grimaced, longed to pick the child up and dust her off. The distraction allowed a knuckle to crack against her ribs. She knew she had just forfeited her advantage, but she fought on. More boys flooded in to profit from her failing movements.

At the edge of vision, she noted Timus and Red in the doorway, woken from their daytime sleep, and now trying to shout over the swarm. They started dragging back a child at a time, but the mob, pushing to get a look, continually thwarted them.

Nothing had changed. Nothing. They all knew about her now, and she was just as despised as she had always been.

Her fist contacted with a jaw and one of the boys step back defeated, but a second filled the gap. She kicked, struggled, but the numbers quickly corroded her resistance. She felt a rigid boot bruise her calves. Numerous hands shoved her downward. Her kneecaps bashed the stone floor, sent a shock through her legs. Fleshy fingers gripped her wrists, wrenched her arms up her back until her shoulder sockets burned. Fingers matted into her hair, yanked her head back. She saw a fist draw back ready to contact with her face. She braced every muscle against imminent pain.

"Enough!" an enormous voice roared from the back of the room. The fist aimed at Emme, froze mid-air.

In the haze of sweat, she saw the crowd part in the wake of Halder followed by Ada. "Let her go," Halder demanded, and the boys peeled back, frightened. Halder glared around, eyes angry for the first time since Emme had known him. He saw the blood on Emme's face, the lump on her cheek, surveyed the damaged boys in the room. "What the devil happened here?"

"She started it." One of the boys jabbed his stiff pointer finger towards Emme as she stood on shaky legs. "She threatened Dusty."

"It's my fault," Dusty said. Emme stared at him, blinked. No one had taken the blame for her before. "I told people something very private about Emme and I hurt her feelings."

"She was apologising," one of the witnesses said, "then the other boys jumped on top of her."

"Is that true?" Halder asked Emme.

Emme glared at him. "What does it matter? I'm not welcome here anymore. I'm leaving."

"There's no need for that," Halder said, anger dissolving.

"I know why you all hate me now." Emme defiantly engaged the crowd. Illina watched Emme with what seemed to be pity. "Because Kye told you about me, about my name being Mistake. Well go ahead and hate me. I'm used to being hated." She felt an ache swell inside, briefly pushing words away. "And you all mean nothing to me anyway." The final sentence lacked the conviction she had hoped for.

"Emme," Dusty said quietly. "Can we talk – in private?"

"Talk away, Dusty. I have no more secrets to hide."

"It was . . . " He shifted weight from one foot to the other. "You see it was me who . . . I started it. Not Kye. Last night I went up to Halder's to see if you were all right, and I overheard your conversation and I . . . I'm so bad at keeping secrets."

Emme's eyes sharpened. "Is that true? You're not just trying to protect him?"

Slowly Dusty nodded, eyes and ashen face to the floor.

The ache swelled even larger inside Emme until she almost thought she could feel a stinging behind her eyes. "And now, thanks to you, nobody is going to want me to live here anymore."

"Nobody cares about that sort of thing down here, Emme," Halder said. "We've all got our stories. All of us were hated by society at one point. Most of us have done things we regret."

"Then why did they fight me?" Emme gestured brusquely to the gang of bruised boys. "Tell me that?"

"Because the boys down here are like bulls that charge when a red flag is waved in front of them." Emme didn't understand what Halder meant by that but she let him go on. "You show any signs of a fight, and they'll itch to jump in. We've had more fights down here this year amongst ourselves than run-ins with the Black Bands." Halder fixed the closest boys with a level stare, then the crowd. "Everyone, get back to your rooms. This is over. Illina, Ada, take the kids to the rooms and shut them in there until supper as punishment for their behaviour."

People obeyed with swift movements, squeezed out through the doorway as though afraid to be the last. She now knew she had been right about Halder – he was frightening when angry. Yet in that moment, she realised: Kye might have been their leader and their hero, but Halder was their father – the big man who fondly watched over them, and if necessary, disciplined.

Dusty remained in the room, Lydia fretting at his side.

Halder turned to two. "Lydia, go to your room. Dusty, you go to the library. I'll deal with you in a minute."

Emme was sure she saw Dusty's face pale before he and Lydia hurried from the room.

Halder looked at Emme, totally unruffled by her fiery stare. "Emme, don't let this affect you. I've seen boys fight until they were black and blue, and then share their food with each other the next day. When bellies are full and life seems to be good, the boys get bored and complacent, and their silly little boy pride needs to kick and punch something."

Emme's fire dimmed a little.

"By the way, Emme, that was some of the best fighting I've seen in my lifetime. Where did you learn to fight like that?" He grinned at her. "Go and get cleaned up, Emme with an E-double-M E, and I promise you, by dinner time, this will all be forgotten. But I'll tan the hide of Dusty, you can be sure of that. He knows better than to spread cruel gossip." He spun on large heels and strode to the library.

Emme marched through the empty dining hall to the bathroom. She filled a small washbasin with chilled water and splashed blood – her blood – from her face. A gash made her left cheek look red, angry. One of the boys must have had a ring on.

She looked at her reflection; marred by cuts and bruises just as it used to be. Recognisable but for those large, dejected brown eyes where angry, proud eyes would once have been.

She didn't belong here. Who was she kidding? She would be despised, teased, and tormented until her dying day. Only this time, her forest would not help her. She had abandoned it for a dream, for a better life she had foolishly believed possible.

She needed to go somewhere she could be anonymous, somewhere secret. And this time, she would not, in a moment of weakness, tell others about her past.

She left the bathroom and walked down the hallway to the fourth door. She grabbed a travel sack from the storage area and filled the bottom of it with seven of the best daggers she could find. Then she headed back to her room.

Illina talked earnestly with Ada and Red in the dining hall. Illina swiftly looked up when Emme entered. "Are you all right,

Emme? That was just terrible. I've never seen them fight a woman before."

Emme regarded Illina with an empty expression. "I'm fine. I can defend myself."

Illina's sad eyes made Emme hurt inside as she walked away from the caring woman. It was yet to occur to Illina about Emme's past, it seemed. A last vestige of kindness remained in the woman's eyes, but not for long. Illina would come to hate Emme, just as all the other women in the village had.

She passed the library, heard Dusty's quiet apologies through a gap in the door, but did not stop to listen. In her room, she pounded clothes into her sack and put on a thick jumper and woollen cloak. She crept down the empty halls to the dining area now abandoned by the older ones. Free to leave unnoticed, she exited the building via the very first route she had taken. Once outside the building, she tapped the disguised mechanism, closing the hidden door that had miraculously parted for her on that first day. Sheltered partly by the wide overhanging gutter, she trundled down the roofless corridor, followed it where it bent at right angles past Illina and Ada's home. The buildings and the gutter ended. Beyond it lay the joining street. If she took that step, beyond her meagre shelter, there would be no turning back.

A moment of hesitation, then Emme stepped out into the driving snowstorm. Emme noted across the way, a tall grey-haired stranger in a grey cloak with gloved hands and an unrecognisable face. From an unused alleyway, the stranger steadily watched the street. She almost supposed he was watching her, his shadowed face pointed in her direction, yet it was impossible to tell where those hidden eyes wandered.

For a split second he seemed to flicker, as though not quite there. Emme stopped, squinted at him. Propelling snow stung her face. The man seemed to waver again, then turned away from her and strode down the alley, his cloak billowing behind him like a grey sheet on a clothesline. At last the alley's shadows shrouded him from view. She wondered about him briefly, about the illusion of him being there yet somehow not there. Then with a shrug, she put it down to the fierce snowstorm. She moved on down the street.

Kye scanned every book on the shelf within reach from the top of the ladder in the expansive library.

"I wish you would tell me what you were looking for," Russen, head teacher of wealthy boys' school, called from the bottom of the ladder. "Then I could help you find it." He searched the empty room, a man hoping not to get caught. Knowing all the students were in classes did not lessen his apprehension. "Could you hurry it along? You know I shouldn't be letting you look at those."

Kye knew. Although strictly for those with a pass, Kye had looked through the collection many times – never at this time of the day when he could get caught.

Kye spotted the volume he had been looking for – a volume noted on a visit here long ago. He slid the bulky, brown tome from the shelf.

Book in hand, he sped down half the ladder, jumped the rest, and strode beyond the black metal security gate to the nearest table. He put the book on the polished tabletop, sat down. He parted the covers of the volume. The ancient brown pages crackled as he peeled them open.

"Careful," Russen said, taking a seat opposite Kye. He placed the hefty gate key on the table. "That book is one of the original hand-written volumes from the ancient Endorian scribes. It's very valuable."

Kye ignored him. He had been travelling all night for this. Something in his dealings with Emme the night before, the moment they had danced together, had stirred a dark idea in him – a possibility he had never considered before.

He scanned the ancient text. The elaborate calligraphy was hard to read, despite its meticulous strokes. He flipped the pages. Each page described a new topic. He barely noticed the beautiful coloured pictures highlighted by gold leaf, or the heavily designed illuminated first letter of each page.

He turned one more page, scanned for key words, then stopped. His eyes flicked back to the beginning of the page, and he read slowly, carefully. When he reached the bottom, he looked up, eyes darting about, looking at nothing in particular, as strange pieces started to fit together in his mind.

"It can't be," Kye said to the air.

"Can't be what? What have you seen?"

Kye read the page again, faster this time. It was a thin link, but a link none-the-less. His eyes roamed the illuminated T on the page. Small, crudely drawn men sat at sloping tables within the tail of the T. They scribed words onto books propped against the tables, their brown robes neat across their laps. Gold leaf rimmed the pages of the miniature books, and there on the tiny pages of one of the books, was an image that activated a pounding in his chest. No wonder the prince had sent that letter to the Black Bands.

He leapt to his feet.

"What is it?" Russen asked, bewilderment drawing his brows down. He turned the book around to see what Kye had read.

"I've got to find Emme. She's in trouble."

"Why? How?" Russen asked Kye's fleeing form.

"Read that page," Kye called back as he sprinted from the library, determined to run, all the way if he had to, back to Emme.

9

"Where is she?" Kye demanded from behind his desk, and Dusty shrank back at the dark urgency on Kye's face.

"We – we don't know." Dusty's fingers swirled his studded wristband around and around. "We haven't seen her all day. She left this morning after –" He stared at his feet.

"After what?"

"After the fight."

"What fight?" Kye managed to conceal alarm.

Dusty shifted from one foot to the other, unusually silent.

"*What* fight?"

Dusty gave details, skirted his involvement, before adding, "And we think she's run off, because all her clothes are gone."

"Look at me, Dusty." Kye locked steely eyes with the red-cheeked young man. "What caused the fight?"

Dusty fidgeted, shifted, but finally confessed.

"Dusty – do you know what you could have done?" No – that wasn't fair. Of course Dusty didn't know. Kye exhaled slowly. He was acting totally out of character and needed to be calm. "Has anyone gone looking for her?"

"Halder went. He took Telier and Davis with him."

"How much did you overhear last night?"

"Only the part about the name, and about her mother."

Kye leant onto the table, hands folded in front of him. He knew his expression looked stern enough to be meaningful to the young man. "What she told me, Dusty, she told me in private. I am absolutely ashamed of your behaviour today."

Dusty hung his head, and Kye knew that one reprimand from himself weighed a thousand of Halder's. Kye watched the pout on Dusty's face, then, when sure the words had achieved their purpose, added, "But I forgive you, Dusty. Right now, we just need to find Emme."

Dusty perked up. "I'll help you."

"No – I'm going out to look for her myself. I want you to stay here in case she returns. People have treated Emme very cruelly all her life, and right now she thinks that we're all going to treat her exactly the same. The treatment in her world for being a child born out of wedlock is being despised to the point of utter cruelty, and being beaten nearly every day of your life. Did you know that?"

"No. I had no idea."

"And right now, Emme thinks that that's the way we're going to treat her. That's why she was so angry with you for telling everyone. That's why she didn't want anyone to know, and that, my boy, is why she has acted so tough since she got here. Standing up for herself was literally a matter of life and death."

"I – I didn't know. If I'd known . . ."

"Well until you do know, Dusty, secrets are secrets, and you never pass around something you have overheard until you find out from that person if it's private or not. Are we clear?"

Dusty nodded. His freckled fingers wrung his wristband nervously.

"So when Emme returns, I want you and every other person in here to go absolutely out of your way to make sure she knows she is still accepted and liked. No matter how nasty or tough or cold she gets, that's what you need to do. Do you understand?"

"Yes."

"Good. Go and tell the others what I've said, and make sure they know why it's important Emme sees that in our world we don't treat illegitimate people the way her villagers do."

"Okay."

Kye stood and moved to the door. He opened it for Dusty. Fresh, cold air blew in from the hallway beyond. Children moved in and out of their rooms. Some stopped to peer nervously at Kye. Kye knew no one had seen him as urgent, as insistent, as when he came in tonight. That, along with fear of Kye's disapproval of their behaviour, made the atmosphere tenser than it had been in a long time. Kye needed people to retain a degree of that tension to understand the gravity of what they had all done to Emme. But Dusty needed Kye's reassurance too.

People had heard Kye's door open and were spilling into the hallway. Whispers in rooms hushed the instant they stepped into the quiet hallway to watch what Kye would do.

Kye's face softened. He flicked his head to the slowly crowding hallway to indicate Dusty could go. "Dear boy, what am I going to do with you?" Kye tussled Dusty's sandy hair on the way past. No matter what transpired in life, Kye would always see Dusty as his younger brother. One day Kye hoped to be able to tell the truth about Dusty. For now, the story of a baby on a dust pile remained the only safe story to give. "Go on, get out of here," he said lightly. Dusty drifted to the crowd.

Kye surveyed the young faces that watched him for even a sliver of forgiveness. "The rest of you: I want you to listen to Dusty. Gather everyone together and join him in the library. He has something he needs to tell you. I want you to listen to him as if they are my words. Understood?"

Children nodded. Some scurried to the library, others poked heads inside dorms to pass on the message.

Kye calmly shut the office door, sealing himself from watching eyes in the hallway. There he allowed emotions to flood his face. *Emme, please don't do anything foolish. You have no idea what you are up against.*

He picked up his recently cast-off travel bag from the office floor and entered the heavy shadows of his room. Without the usual care, he upturned the contents into a messy pile on the floor. Disregarding wrinkles and order, he stuffed a fresh lot of clothes into it, prepared to travel for as long as it took to find her. He may not be right about her, but if he was – *if he was* – then she was the most important thing to happen to this country in his lifetime.

Emme stood at the back of the tavern kitchen and patiently awaited the food to be brought to her. The spicy bean and barley stew, simmering in its black cauldron, scented the entire room. Freshly baked yeasty bread had been pulled from the oven, and kitchen staff cut it into slabs with serrated knives. Workers filled dishes with soft yellow butter and piled plates with slices of gold cheese ready to be taken to customers beyond the swinging kitchen door.

Emme's stomach growled but she remained unenthusiastic about the thought of her coming meal.

"Here you go, Emme," Roul, the kitchen overseer said as he passed her a plate of stew edged with buttered crusts. "I'm surprised you're not asking for food for the rest of them tonight." He spied Emme's overstuffed travel bag. "You leaving us?"

"I'm thinking of it. What's the best way to get to the nearest city gate?" Emme took a mouthful of hot stew and found it disappointing to her tongue. Her stomach wanted the food more than she did.

Roul's unruly grey brows dipped as he thought it over. "I think I've got a map somewhere. No, not here – back home. But I can try and point you in the right direction."

Emme tucked into the peppery stew, as much to quickly fill her annoyingly empty stomach as to give herself something to distract her mind. She shrugged. "Whatever."

"You all right? You don't seem yourself tonight."

"I'm fine," Emme lied. "Just wondering how to get out of the city."

"Getting out isn't so hard, but if you want to come back in, you'll need to see a city official first to get some papers."

"What do I have to do to get the papers?"

"Answer some questions, show a birth document if you have one, allow the officials to run a background check on you. It generally takes a few weeks."

"That's okay – I'm not coming back anyway."

Roul frowned sadly. "That's a pity. We all like your visits." He wiped his hands on his apron and turned his head away from her. "Hey, everyone – Emme's leaving us."

The staff ceased their nightly task of preparing food for customers and approached Emme.

"Where are you going? What are you going to do? Must you go?" they asked over the top of each other.

"You got anywhere to stay tonight?" Roul asked.

Emme shook her head.

"You can sleep in front of the fire tonight if you want to, then head off tomorrow."

"Are you sure you trust me in here?"

"I doubt you're going to fit any pots and pans in that full bag of yours." Roul grinned, then added, "You're welcome to stay."

"Thank you." Emme finished her meal in silence, washed up her own plate and sat by the fire whilst the kitchen staff bustled about her. When the oven was needed, she stood to let them pass, then sat back down on the floor.

"Listen, Emme," Roul said after a while. "Why don't you go out to the main area and we'll bring you a nice glass of wine. Then we won't keep disturbing you."

"I don't drink alcohol," Emme said quietly.

"Then a hot tea?"

Emme thought about it briefly, then nodded.

"It's pretty quiet out there at the moment – mostly the wealthier travellers looking for a meal. You won't find it too rowdy."

Emme stood, brushed floor dust from the back of her trousers.

"You go in," Roul said. "I'll bring the drink in."

The swinging door clacked on hinges as she pushed past it and entered the dining area where people chatted over half-empty dinner plates and chalices of wine.

At first, no one looked up, then one spotted her, and soon all the wealthy clientele were eyeing her boyish clothes with disdain. The women especially seemed to have a silent opinion of her outfit.

For the first time, Emme did not care. She did not even feel inclined to glare at them. She gazed above them all to the large, frost-edged window near the front door. Beyond the window, light from the well-lit room spilled out onto snow. A man in a velvet jerkin cut across the street and peered through the glass. He spotted someone he knew, waved to them once and came inside. With a smile of hello, he settled at a table of well-dressed friends and ordered a drink from the serving staff.

Emme took a table in the corner and sat quietly, her blank

expression meeting eyes that regarded her as some kitsch curiosity. Several men leered crudely at her tight pants, but all soon gave up stares in the wake of Emme's indifference.

The room smelled faintly rank from alcohol and unwashed travellers. The pleasant aroma of the stew soaked into it.

Roul brought out a glazed mug of hot liquid and placed it on her table. "There you go." He watched her for a moment, yellow-flecked hazel eyes soft with concern. "That will cheer you up."

"Thank you," Emme said quietly.

Roul's saddened eyes tarnished the smile on his lips. With a barely recognisable shrug, he turned and left the room.

Emme slowly sipped her sweet, milky tea and stared at the darkness beyond the window. Snow began to fall, and she watched it, mesmerised. It drifted in thick sheets that fluttered and floated like leaves on a breeze to the brown dirty snow of the street. An ice pile stood to the height of the windowsill, created when staff dredged snow from the low doorway to a mound now compacted to grimy ice.

A hooded man walked past the window, his grey cloak white-specked with snowflakes. He opened the tavern door, shook snowflakes from his cloak, then stepped inside. With the door closed behind him, he fastidiously flicked off every crystal of snow, and brushed off excess wetness with gloved hands. Finally he pulled back his hood and peered around.

Emme noted his harsh nose and intent brown eyes. The dark grey of his neat hair and beard softened an otherwise severe face. He selected a table near Emme. His back to her, he sat down to wait for service. Briefly Emme caught a scent of his cologne that drifted in the wake of air dislodged when he sat. He peered out at the snow as if expecting someone. One of the serving staff approached him and offered him some stew, a cold or hot drink, asked to take his cloak and gloves, but the man only ordered a glass of dry red house wine.

The chill of the air, let in by the newcomer, filled Emme's half of the room. She stood, moved to the fireplace where she sipped her hot drink and stared down at the flames. Time became inconsequential as her tea slowly drained. Any other night, the tea's mellow aroma would have comforted her, but tonight she barely noticed it.

In the eye of her mind, she saw faces of the street kids, those she had come to know well. The absent-minded, incessantly chattering Dusty with his boyish grin and easy acceptance of everyone. Lydia, the golden-haired beauty who adored Dusty even more than the other girls did. Halder, the great beast of a man who had an open friendliness entirely at odds with his rough physique. Kye, the aloof gentleman who watched all and knew all, yet shared little. Then there was Illina and Ada, Red and Timus, and the other four men her age who taught her board and card games, helped her with her reading.

Of course, she wouldn't forget the silly boys Jase and Jerris, her constant companions on visits to taverns. An honorary boy, they called her, and often tried to emulate her – a thought that would bring a smile to her face as she lay in her faintly lit room each evening.

She knew every face now, and although she had very little to do with the young ones, could remember every name, knew almost every surface personality.

They would go back to being hungry without her if people like Roul were not generous beyond their contact with Emme. She felt regret at the thought, regret that swelled so large inside, it almost compelled her to march out of the inn and endure scorn just to know the street kids survived. Then images of the future stole into her mind, quietened her. They wouldn't *let* her go on missions with them anymore. People would hate her from now on, and she had no forest she could run to when things became severe. Confined in that space, she would have to suffer through fight after fight after fight – and cruelty. And she could not bear it – not with them. Not with the faces that had once looked at her with respect and even admiration. Her villagers, she could tolerate. She had never been accepted by any of them; did not know what that was like. But these people were a glimpse of friendship now lost.

"Cold night isn't it." A voice startled Emme from sullen thoughts. She stared up at the imposing sharp-eyed, grey-haired man. He placed his wine goblet on the pale marble mantle.

"I guess so."

The man extended gloved hands out to the fire.

Emme watched him waggle leather-coated fingers, heard the faint creak of stiff leather above the brilliant fire's crackle. "You know, you'll get your hands much warmer if you take those gloves off," Emme said. His foolish attempts at warmth rubbed at her threadbare tolerance.

"Oh, I won't be here for long. I just came to get a glass of wine." He curled long fingers around the full wine goblet, extracted it from the marble mantle and took the tiniest sip. He replaced it and extended hands out to the fire again. "You must be new to the city are you?"

"Relatively," Emme replied stiffly. She smiled grimly to herself. That would be a word Kye would use.

"Are you here on business?"

"I guess so."

"Staying at one of the inns?"

Eyes slightly narrowed, Emme scrutinised his face. "Probably."

"Well, if you need someone to show you around – I'm Rastin, by the way." He extended his gloved hand to her.

243

Carefully she watched the hand, then with a light shrug, took it. The instant her hand contacted with his, she felt a shock of something rise from her feet to her head. Her lungs constricted, and she gasped for air. She jerked her hand from him and took a step back, tense fingers on a dagger hilt protruding from her trousers. The man's sharp eyes watched her keenly, but he offered no help as she struggled for breath. Her lungs finally released, a sudden thrust that thudded in her ears. She inhaled a loud raspy breath that disrupted a nearby conversation.

"Weather shock," the man said. "It happens all the time in this city. It must have been the gloves."

Emme puffed heavily, doubled over slightly. Eyes at the nearby table watched her curiously as if she were choking. Some noted her hand on the dagger blade and tensed as if anticipating a fight. Within moments, their curious silence infected everyone in the room.

When her breathing levelled, and concentration returned, she wanted to be anywhere but here talking to this man. Tea mug in hand, she went back to the kitchens and with a sigh of relief, watched the swinging door divide her from the stranger. She took a deep breath, hand over ribs, to assure herself her lungs still worked. Slowly conversations began beyond the door again, these more animated as people offered their conjectures on what had just transpired.

She put the tea mug on the closest bench top and moved towards the oven. Hand outstretched, she examined it. She had received weather shocks before – those faint zaps in the finger when the weather made clothes crackle. That wasn't like any weather shock she had experienced. That had been a jolt preceding a vibration through her whole body. And her lungs, she had never had that feeling of being unable to breathe from a weather shock.

No marks appeared on her hand, but she vowed she would not shake any stranger's hand from then on. Who knew how this city worked?

Curious about the grey-haired man, she went back to the kitchen door and peered through the tiny glass pane to the tavern's main room. Her eyes scanned the room, but despite less than a minute passing, the stranger had gone. She looked to the fireplace, and her eyes narrowed with angry suspicion. The stranger's full glass of wine had been left sitting on the mantel.

"Back again already?" Roul asked pleasantly as he bustled past to the pockmarked cauldron of stew. He ladled a helping into a flat metal bowl and handed it to a serving woman who took it through the swinging door.

"Roul," Emme said, "can I ask you something?"

"I believe you just did." Roul's eyes bent into mirthful crescents. When Emme's frown of thought did not dissolve, he replied, "What about?"

"Weather shocks. How strong do they get here?"

"How strong? Well now, that is an odd question. They can send a jolt right through your hand."

"But not your whole body?"

"Well, I doubt there would ever be one that strong, although I did touch a metal plate one night and felt a zap through my fingers and right through to my head. That was the strongest one I'd felt."

"Do they constrict your lungs? Stop you breathing?"

Roul laughed. "What a silly question." The laughter faded when he saw something in Emme's face. "Why do you ask?"

"There was a stranger out there who . . . Never mind."

Roul shrugged and went about his business.

Later that evening, Emme busied herself in the kitchen helping the grateful staff to finish the cleaning and go home.

The last to leave, Roul blew out all but one lantern, waved his final goodbye and shut the door behind him, leaving Emme alone in the space.

Emme tucked down in front of the fire, patted her bag into a pillow shape, then lay down on the cold stone.

She heard the fire crackle and pop, saw its light even through closed lids. Tomorrow she would leave early before the tavern staff returned to prepare breakfast. She could head for the southern exit – the one Kye had said, that day on the rooftop, was the closest – and to the forest. How she would get there, or how to get to the forest once she had passed the city walls, she did not know.

As Emme lay there, she recalled sleeping in front of the cottage fireplace back home. She had a new location now – buildings and streets replaced trees and tracks – yet she was lying in front a fire, on the floor, an outcast again, despised for her birth.

It didn't seem right that she could be so hated for something out of her control. It wasn't her fault someone had abused her mother, and it wasn't her choice to be conceived from it.

Oh well. That was life. That was the way of things. And she had more blessings than most. Too many dead bodies lay in the snows of the city. The poorer parts of the city were slums of despair and isolation. It was little wonder many of them consumed large quantities of cheap, bitter alcohol to forget their misery and ended up dying alone on the streets.

If she owned this place, she would make some big changes – share the wealth. Instead of pouring money into weapons, she would feed the poor and the hungry.

Emme considered the idea briefly. Maybe instead of running and protecting herself, she should steal some of that wealth from the snooty rich people, and give it to the poorer people.

No. She needed to avoid the prince, and being caught by

unscrupulous guards and hauled into prison was sure to bring her to the prince's attention. But maybe when she was older, when this was all over, she would return and start to make some changes. It wasn't right for human beings to suffer like that. To live in filthy, bitterly cold houses. To float around the city in thin rags. To have to endure terrible diseases and hunger whilst the rich threw out huge quantities of waste, and spent money on lavish, extraneous furniture.

Emme sighed, suddenly wearier, heavier than she had ever been. She patted the dagger in the top of her pants once as she always did before sleep. She felt the reassurance of solid steel, the heavy perfectly balanced handle. Comforted by it, the protection it offered, she allowed herself to fall into a deep slumber.

"Well?" Jaimis asked the grey-haired Ashrone, Rastin. "If you're back, it means you found her."

"I did." Rastin flicked out his grey cloak to flatten it before sitting in the wingback chair. He took his seat beside Jaimis in the library, spotted a wrinkle in the leg of his trousers and smoothed it away. "I knew she would surface eventually."

"And?"

"It seems she is running away, which is even better for us."

"But did you make the connection?" Jaimis asked with impatience.

"Yes. That was never going to be difficult."

"So we can bring her here whenever we want without her consent?"

"Well, that is the idea, but remember, this is a new power I have asked for. It is yet to be tested."

"Now why would Altha –"

"Don't say his name, you fool," Rastin hissed.

"Why would you be given a power that was useless to us? He works on our side in every way he can."

"It's not about him. It is about the power of the Ashrones. You just never know how the other Ashrones are going to try to stop this."

"How would they know to stop this?"

"Because tonight I announced to them who I am."

Jaimis' eyes lit up. "I would have loved to have been there for that."

"No – I imagine you wouldn't have. Two Ashrones died in the struggle that issued to try and imprison me. The two did not stand a chance against my protective wards, and it was not a pretty picture, even for you."

A shiver passed over Jaimis. "For all your claims of ancient laws and morality, you are all rather barbaric with some of your rituals."

"I believe that is to ensure that we take them seriously and use them only when we must."

"So did you get a chance to delve into her mind tonight?"

"For the weakness?"

Jaimis nodded.

"I saw enough, yes."

"Was I right?" Jaimis asked.

"Yes – it should all be very easy if you can just be patient enough to do things my way."

"You don't have to worry about that. It would be my pleasure."

Rastin's brow arched neatly. "Yes, I should have guessed that it would." The brow lowered. "Now, onto another matter – did you send those letters I asked you to?"

"Of course I did. Like you just ever-so-tactfully implied, I'm the impatient one. Right now I would jump off the top of this castle the second you asked me to, if it meant getting this all done faster."

"And have you heard back from them?"

"They have agreed to at least hear us. They are all rather curious now, although suspicious at the invitation of course."

Rastin rubbed hands together, sharp eyes dancing. "Good. Then it is time to pay a visit to the Kildes princes."

Emme struggled to wake, but obstinacy made her get up and move heavy, aching legs. She filled her pack with a small selection of durables from the kitchen stocks – salted pork, wrapped cheese, sacks of crackers, a pouch of nuts. Although given permission to take a little food, Emme still felt guilty as she squashed it all down into her overfilled bag. They would not be nearly so kind to her if they knew what the street kids now knew.

Careful to acknowledge the kindness, Emme spelt out the word 'thanks' on the large central bench-top with butter knives for anyone who could read. She left then, making sure to lock the door behind her.

She had thought the weather cold when she first arrived, but began to realise how bitter it could turn as she pushed into the driving storm. Her lungs, afraid to suck in the cold air that smarted her face, seized up momentarily. She forced herself to inhale, felt the instant ache in her chest and throat. The wind pushed deep into her ears, making her head throb where the jaw met the neck. Gusts of steam rose from her gasping mouth like smoke.

Not even her stiff woollen cloak gave her protection from the driving wind. She would have to find shelter this evening, or face the possibility of death.

Emme wandered streets that were an illusion of busyness as everyone ran through the snowstorm to their destination.

Not one person noticed her, except to avoid running into her. Although her hood concealed her face from recognition, she peered furtively at every person she passed. The incident with the stranger the night before left her wary.

Around lunchtime, she ducked behind a wide stone staircase, planted her bottom in snow and nibbled on crackers. The supplies would not last her long, but once she cleared the gates, she could forage for food in the wild as she was used to.

She felt stiff, sore. Her toes had long ago stopped aching but her fingers still smarted, throbbed. She felt heavy somehow with a strange pressure in her head. The snow she had waded through all morning no longer seemed powdery; it felt thick with the resistance of mud.

Pains stabbed at random through her body, and her eyes felt weighted. Still, she had chosen to leave now, and she would have to deal with it. She could have waited, endured their scorn and abuse for several more weeks until the weather died down, but pride had forced her onward. Well, now pride would just have to try and find a way to keep her warm.

"What are you doing?" a voice barked at her. "Get out from under my staircase, you filthy beggar." A stout man in pompous red clothes, about to ascend to his plush house, glared at her from the staircase edge. "I won't have one more drunk dying under my stairs."

"Just go inside you arrogant pig," Emme said unemotionally.

"How dare you." His face swelled red and round like a tomato.

She threw a cracker him. It struck him between the eyes. "And next time it won't be a cracker I'll waste – it'll be one of the daggers in my bag." She was entirely too cold, too grumpy and too weary to avoid drawing attention to herself.

The man straightened, his large belly jutting out like a stiff, frilly pillow. "Well I never." He shot his nose into the air and marched up his stairs. "You had better be gone by this evening," she heard him say at his doorstep through the stone stairs. Then the door slammed with a loud obnoxious bang that cracked against the door on the other side of the street.

Although ready to move on, Emme stayed beneath the stairs a while longer just to spite the arrogant man. Not only did the wealthy wallow in their riches, they couldn't even donate unused space beneath their stairs to shelter the poor and dying from the cold. How dare the poor be so inconsiderate as to die from starvation, isolation and frostbite beneath his stairs. Childishly, she wanted to knock on his door and empty a big inconvenient barrow-load of snow into his house, right on his polished timber floor against expensive tapestried couches.

She moved out and pushed on, trying to take any turn that seemed to be heading south – a direction difficult to guess at in this sunless place. She cursed several times when dead-ends forced her to backtrack. The place was so random, so convoluted, that Emme began to wonder how anyone found their way, even after a lifetime of living here. Why would anyone design a city with such lack of forethought?

She passed a group of children who ran from a building with books in hand. The noisy chatter and laugher made her stop momentarily to watch. She knew what those children did all day now – their lessons. She remembered being told about a large boarding school in the city for wealthy children. The less wealthy met in small schoolhouses, whilst the poor were considered fortunate if their parents plied a trade to be passed down.

Emme would miss her lessons. She had surprised herself and others with how much she enjoyed the lessons and how quickly she learned. The reading remained difficult, but being able to trace a finger over black scribbles on pages and know what some of those scribbles meant, was an accomplishment that made her proud.

The history fascinated her – so many stories. The villagers orally handed down histories of great chieftains of the past, but little else. Kye had taught her of people who had invented great things, of famous kings, champions, of invasions from other continents that shaped the nation. Three-thousand years of history – two-thousand before man tallied the years, and a thousand after. She wondered how far back her village could trace its roots.

Emme smiled sadly as the last of the children passed. Yes, she would miss the lessons.

She peered through the window at the teacher who rubbed chalk from an enormous slate board on the wall. Emme briefly wondered what the children had learned that day, then pushed on.

Darkness began to descend. The heaviness inside of Emme grew oppressive. The pressure in her head, the stabs of pain, intensified.

She no longer felt cold but hot – achingly, stiflingly hot. She felt sweat on her chest and back despite the snow. She drove herself on – she had to find a tavern and beg to be let in, in front of the fire. She knew she was well beyond the boundary of people who knew her. Would the tavern owners in these parts be so easy to win over?

Final darkness overtook dull grey light. The streets were nearly empty now, but for people hurrying home. She noted where the largest crowds went and followed them. Everyone seemed so fast tonight. Her weak legs could not catch up.

Snow had long ago stopped falling but Emme did not notice. Everything looked blurry, disturbed, like it had when the snow was falling. She still felt hot as though her whole body were burning up. That wasn't right, she told her fuzzy mind. She should be cold. Snow made you cold.

She drifted to the back of a tavern, but when the door swung open at her knock, Emme could not think of anything coherent to say. She could only stare at the hard-faced woman who watched her. Emme opened her mouth but all she could think about was how heavy and hot she felt. She watched as everything became distorted, like a chalk drawing slowly being smudged across slate.

"Get away from here you filthy drunk." The woman slammed the door in Emme's face.

Emme knew she should be saying something, but she was too weary, felt too odd inside to respond.

She turned away, followed the housing corridor to the street. Her body moved without her now. She saw her feet walk in front of her, each step falling down into deep snow. But she did not hear anything; could not hear the footsteps, nor the wind, nor the calls from the tavern. Everything was quiet, as though she no longer walked with the living, but into the arms of death.

Adrenalin gave Kye energy to push on through snow and darkness. He hoped Emme had found a sheltered place for the night. Already it was proving to be one of the coldest nights of the year.

After examining the cityscape from the rooftop he had taken Emme to, he suspected where she would head. To the south gate – the gate he had told her was the closest. And if he knew Emme, she would be longing for trees, for the southern forest he had described to her – anything but this wasteland of buildings and streets.

Kye frowned deeply. Finding Emme was nearly impossible in this city. If she had been a local, he could guess the paths she would take – either the quicker thoroughfares, or the quiet backstreets. But Emme knew nothing about this maze, designed originally for protection against intruders who might hope to speedily access the fortified castle. By the time intruders navigated the streets, the army would be gathered to stop them.

Emme – please Emme – find somewhere sheltered tonight. People die on nights like this. He was well aware that he could be one of them, but he was used to the cold, and was thickly rugged up against it. And finding Emme was so important – more important than anything he had done in his life.

He felt a small surge of excitement at his discovery. If he was right – if he was *right*. The excitement died. If he was right, Emme's perils tonight were more than just the cold, so above all, he needed to find her and get her somewhere safe. But where? Back to the street kids? No. Somewhere even safer than that – for he had given his face to the Black Bands the moment he went to their headquarters to rescue her. And he was sure he would have been followed – with a prize like Emme, he definitely would have been sought out and followed. He could not risk taking her one more time to a place that the Black Bands most likely knew about.

Kye saw a nearby tavern and hastened to the back of it. He knew Emme had a gift for getting people to give her food. She was not there. Heavy prints led to the doorway, possibly another beggar. He peered beyond the wet window in the door and saw staff cleaning up for the night. It was very late, he realised – possibly midnight.

He knocked on the kitchen door. He had knocked on every tavern door he had passed since sundown. A man opened the back door and stared with open surprise at Kye. Kye felt heat exude from the warm kitchens onto his cold face, could smell the faint trace of the roast they had served for dinner.

"What would a gentleman like you, be doing begging for food?" the man asked.

"Forgive me this intrusion, good sir, but I was wondering if you have seen a woman come by here to ask for food. She is tall, about to my shoulders, has very brown eyes, short brown hair and wears the clothes of a man."

The man nodded, igniting a spark of hope inside Kye.

"She came by several hours ago. Drunk."

Kye suppressed a facial response at the curious statement. There would not be any chance Emme would touch alcohol – not with her passionate hatred for it. "Which way did she go?"

The man shrugged. "Don't know. She just left."

"Sir, may I trouble you with one more matter? Why do you say she was drunk?"

"Don't know. Marin just said a strange-looking drunk came by. You'd have to ask her."

"Never mind," Kye said. "You have been most helpful, sir. I thank you for your time." Kye bowed formally.

The man shrugged and closed the kitchen door, shutting in the warmth.

Kye noted the deep footprints that headed to the kitchen door and then from it. They had to be Emme's. The prints did not look right, almost like a dragged stagger, not a step.

Kye followed them until they meshed with a mass of prints from late-night tavern goers. He frowned as his mind worked quickly. He would just have to follow every set where they parted.

He followed the main south-heading conglomerate of steps, then spotted several that were more distinct than the rest – ones that swayed a little over the street, most likely drunks'. As he stared at them, the odd pattern of Emme's prints began to stand out, different to the tottering of the drunks. Deeper, stretched, like one wading, not walking.

255

He picked up the trail and followed it down the street. He noticed a heavy indentation in the snow where she had knelt, perhaps. He glanced ahead a little. The snow seemed widely scuffed, like she struggled to rise. A second heavy indentation, longer than the first, marred the snow further along. She had not knelt; she had fallen. His chest began to pound with suspicion. He took off at a run.

The tracks took him down several side lanes and to a dark dead-end alley. He could see a crumple of clothes at the end where a wide, overhanging gutter had shielded a cobbled edge and grated drain from the worst of the snow. He took out a candle and lit it. It sputtered slightly in the breeze but settled when he stepped into the shelter of the confined alleyway. He glanced up once at a high window, but no light or movement stirred beyond the shutters.

He walked cautiously towards what still looked like a pile of clothes, then realised what it was. "Good Almighty." He ran to the end of the alley. "Emme." He poked the candle into the snow just beyond the cleared patch of cobblestones and touched Emme's body. "Emme, can you hear me?"

Emme did not move. He rolled her from her side to her back. He could see a bruise and lump forming on her forehead where it had struck a jagged cobble. Had the cobblestone knocked her unconscious after a slip? He felt her forehead, expecting her to be frigid, but burning flesh met his hand. He quickly felt for a pulse. It was rapid. She had a terrible fever. The fever had caused her to collapse.

"Emme," he said to the lifeless form. "Stay with me, Emme. We can't lose you now."

He took off her cloak and jumper. His hands worked on the buttons of the shirt. She would hate it if she knew what he was doing, but he had to bring the fever down. He pulled off the shirt, leaving her angora singlet, and scooped up a handful of snow. He rubbed it quickly over her face, her arms, her throat. When the snow melted to water, he scooped up more.

For what seemed hours he worked until at last her forehead felt cooler. Now he had to move fast. She would go from one extreme to the next, and quickly. He had to get her out of the snow.

He dressed her, wrapped her cloak around her like a blanket, then scooped her up. With her dangling from his arms, he headed back out onto the street. He glanced about to get his bearings. He could stay at an inn, but Emme needed special care and tonics to bring the fever down.

He spotted a familiar church at the end of the street and realised where he was. He took off at a rapid pace for Endoria's largest, wealthiest school, praying fervently that the helpless woman in his arms would not die.

◙

"How is she?" Russen asked as he brought in a tray of fresh cloths and pungent tonics.

Sitting on the hard-backed chair beside Emme's bed in the isolated guest room, Kye glanced up briefly. "She's very sick. Her temperature still keeps going up and down. I've given her the tonics, but it's not helping."

"Well, try these ones." Russen placed the tray on the wide bedside drawers. He handed a spoon and small green bottle to Kye. "They're the most expensive ones I could find."

Kye took the bottle and spoon, placed them on his lap. He put a hand on Emme's brow. It was just beginning to warm up from a cool spell. Soon they would have to strip her down to the minimum again and take the heat from her body.

Russen took a chair from the corner of the room and dragged it over to sit beside Kye. "I've heard of a few fevers going around this winter, but none this severe."

"She was in a rather nasty fight before she left yesterday. Her body would have been very weak."

Russen's brows shot up. "A fight? With who?"

"Some of the boys. *Many* of the boys." Kye fought to hide a scowl.

"Your boys fight girls?" Russen seemed darkly amused. "I thought you were training them better than that."

"They see her as one of them in a way."

"I'm not surprised with those clothes she insists on wearing." He waved to the pile of men's trousers, jumper and button-up shirt on the floor beside the stiff lace-up boots.

"Clothes don't define our value as human beings any more than that head-teacher's badge says anything about who you really are or who you've been."

Russen tilted his head slightly, considered the comment, then shrugged. "I suppose that's true."

Kye watched Emme's face with a gentle fondness. "She works very hard to fight the fragile female image, but it's just a cover for how hurt and alone she is. No one has treated Emme very well at all. If you knew some of the stories . . ."

Kye straightened to pull himself from dark thoughts. He read the label on the bottle and tipped the required amount of medicine onto the spoon. He opened Emme's mouth and angled the liquid in. He watched as the body's reflex forced her to swallow.

She moaned and tossed her head away from him, then the head flung back to face him, eyes still closed.

Kye returned the lid to the bottle and placed it and the spoon back on the tray. "We'll have to wipe her down again soon. Her temperature is rising."

The two stared down at her for a while.

"Pretty," Russen said almost to himself.

Kye seemed to snap from a daze. "What was that?"

"I was just thinking that she's pretty – in a way. She'd look better without those boyish clothes." Russen studied Emme's face for a moment. "I read the page in the book."

Kye glanced over at him. "And?"

"It's a bit far-fetched. Almost preposterous in fact."

"But did you see the image in the illuminated letter?"

"Yes."

"The book the illustrated men scribed onto?"

"Briefly."

"Then look at this." Kye leant over Emme's body, peeled back the blanket and removed Emme's right arm. He turned her limp wrist until the inside with the birthmark faced Russen.

Russen's brows shot up briefly. "I see what you mean."

Kye tucked the arm back under the blanket and patted Emme's forehead, silent thanks.

"It's not as precise as the image in the picture, but it's very close." Russen shook his head with wonder. "If you're right, Kye – do you know what this means?" He seemed to be talking more to himself, then his eyes, wild with thoughts, focused back on Kye. "But what made you suddenly think that? I mean, of all the obscure things to think up."

Kye turned back to Emme to hide emotions on his face. "Something I was told as a boy. Do you remember that prediction the Ashrones gave me?"

"I remember the day, but you never told me what they said."

"Well, the clue to my thinking lay in something they said. I don't particularly want to say more than that – not yet."

"So what now?"

"I need to confirm it when she wakes." Kye saw movement

beneath the blanket on the edge closest to him. He pulled the blanket back a little and grabbed Emme's twitching hand to steady it. He wrapped it totally in his hands. The restless movements persisted, then steadied.

"Are you going to tell her?" Russen asked.

"If it's true, then yes, but not here. I need to take her somewhere safe. If I tell her, they'll find her; and right now the only thing that is keeping her safe is that she doesn't have a clue what she's here for. As soon as the prince suspects she might find out, he'll hunt her down."

"So where is somewhere safe?"

"I don't know yet. I'm no longer sure what is safe and what isn't in this city. If I'm right about her, then I've been wrong about so many things, and that's taking a little bit of adjusting to." Kye looked from Emme to Russen again. "You do know to try and push the thought from your mind, don't you. It's dangerous enough that we are thinking what we are."

"Of course, but it's not easy. It's a very exciting and very frightening thought."

Silence took over for a while, filled by the small crackling fire on the other side of the room. Russen cleared his throat. "Kye, has it occurred to you that she might die from this?" He gestured to Emme's still form.

Kye felt his throat tighten, and a slow ache spread through his stomach. Calmly he said, "Of course."

"And then what do we do?"

"Let's just get her from one hour to the next. That's all we need to think about right now."

Russen nodded once, awkwardly.

"Why don't you go to bed," Kye said to him. "I can handle this."

"I'm well aware of that. I do wish I needed as little sleep as you do."

Kye reached a hand to Emme's brow again. "She's all right for now. You go."

Russen nodded and stood. "I'll bring you in some breakfast in the morning. I've left the medicine cupboard unlocked in the kitchen if you need more supplies."

"Thank you." Kye nodded to Russen, then watched as the respected friend closed the door behind him.

Emme moaned, and he swiftly turned back to her. "It's all right, Emme, I'm here." He took her hand again.

For an hour he stared, so many thoughts swirling in his head.

Sweat broke out on Emme's brow, and she tossed fitfully again.

Kye reached for the thick blankets. "Please fight this. You're strong enough to win this." He peeled the blankets back. He took a cloth from the tray on the dresser, dipped it in lavender-scented water and squeezed out the excess. He turned back to Emme. "I know you, Emme – you're the most courageous woman I've ever met." He ran the cool cloth over her face. "You've never let anything defeat you, so don't give in."

But even as he said it, Emme's temperature began to rise to dangerous extremes.

◉

Russen entered late in the morning of the next day, a tray with steaming oats beside a hot drink in his hands. Kye could smell the sweet cinnamon honey from the oats, and the light scent of the tea as soon as Russen entered. It briefly replaced the strong lingering odour of bitter herbs and garlic tonics.

Russen shuffled the tray to a careful balance on one arm, then pushed the door closed with his free hand, shutting out fresher, cooler air. Russen placed the tray on the floor near Kye's chair and looked down at Emme's sleeping form. "Well?"

Kye shook his head slowly. "She's still feverish. This is a really bad illness."

Russen sat down on the single timber chair dragged over the night before, and almost seemed to slump. "If it hasn't broken by now . . ."

Kye's chest tightened painfully. He held an outward appearance of calm. "No, she's stronger than this. She can fight this."

Russen shifted restlessly in his chair. Finally he said, "I can't stay long. The students' breakfast will finish soon and lessons will start." He hesitated before adding, "And the last thing I need is to get sick too."

"I understand."

"I've told the kitchen staff you are here. I've also told them you are parents from one of the Endorian cities come to investigate the school for your recently born son. They're aware one of you got ill on the long journey and they're not to disturb you."

Kye nodded once, eyes not leaving Emme's face.

"Do you need more supplies?" Russen asked.

"Yes."

Russen picked up the tray of medications and returned a short time later with fresh lavender water, cloths and more tonics. Russen moved to the neglected fire and poked it, threw a thin log onto it. He took skeletal sticks and began to feed the faintly glowing ashes with wooden food.

"It wouldn't be right for her to die this way, you know," Kye said whilst Russen reworked the fire. "After everything she's gone through, after everything she did, after everything she's given up, after all the confusion. It wouldn't be right. She's come too far to die this way."

Russen stood, exhaled slowly as he straightened. He wrung hands momentarily. "Well, like you said, she's a fighter." But his words lacked conviction. Kye looked at Russen's face briefly, could tell at a glance it had just occurred to Russen she might die whilst he watched. The thought clearly frightened the man of mind, not action. "I'd better go. I'll come see you at lunch."

He hurried from the room leaving Kye alone to watch Emme slowly give in, little by little, to the raging sickness.

10

Imren sat at his long desk, opened the top drawer and reached for his ornate gold-coated letter opener.

Firelight played on his white hair and partly weathered face. Although younger than most of the other Ashrones, he seemed one of the eldest with his premature white hair. Still, as the most powerful Ashrone, the burden of leadership had always forced him to be wiser, more mature than the rest. And never did he feel the burden of leadership so keenly as he did now with the gory deaths of his close friends fresh on his mind.

What made their deaths harder to bear was that it came at the hands of one who had been with them all the longest – one who had seemed among the most trustworthy.

Indeed, when Prince Jaimis had first opened the portal to the other land, making them aware of a traitor, Rastin had been at the very bottom of the list of suspects. Imren ruminated again how thin a line it was between loyalty and betrayal.

Fiercely weary of the deadlock, or so Rastin had told them the night he announced his identity, Rastin had changed sides to join the very prince they all worked so hard to stop.

Imren again wondered when Rastin had changed, had crossed over to the other side. It could have been years ago, and Imren supposed Rastin had bided his time all these years until he had discovered the whereabouts of the girl. Only four of them knew the location. Thank the Almighty that Rastin had never been one of them. But the time had been drawing near to go and find her, and believing it to be safe, Aller had begun to work on a portal to the girl's world. Rastin, with access to those parts of the Halls of the Asher, must have overheard Aller working on it, for no sooner did Aller complete his portal, than the Ashrones felt the pull of power as another portal, illegal, opened at the Endorian Castle.

Imren allowed brief anger to pass. The small fire, as if in response, flared up bright and hot over some sap and popped loudly up the sooty chimney. It had all been too soon to go and get her, but they had to try and stop the prince claiming her first. It had gone terribly wrong – in their haste, they had not made allowances for the girl's culture and nature. And they had lost her, possibly forever.

Poor Aller. He had been the first to die. And due to working so tirelessly on the very long, very complicated portal, he had not put up the necessary precautions of security. But who suspected the traitor would come from one so high up in the Ashrone as Rastin? He could have been the next leader. All knew that Imren was contemplating stepping down from the role. Rastin was one of the favourites to take the position.

Imren shook his head. He really thought he knew Rastin. They all did. Now he wondered at the mind that had worked so patiently, so craftily against them. And he wondered what Rastin's next move might be. Perhaps this intercepted letter to the Saltorin prince might offer some insight.

Imren worked on the envelope, grimly noted the Endorian prince's seal. Whatever the prince wrote to the southern states, one could hardly help but be suspicious. It was little mystery that not one prince had a love for the Kildes heir.

Imren paused as a surge of power went through him. Another portal had been opened to some mysterious destination. He felt them all the time now. They all did.

So many portals had been opened and closed in the last week, that Imren had known something quite significant was going on, and had set up some portals of his own to his contacts down south. There, he had discovered the letter he now held in his hands. The poor courier, mauled by some rather hungry wild animals, had not made his very important delivery, but a small group of peasants had discovered the bag and taken it home to glean out any valuables. Thank the Almighty they could not read, or they might have seen the contents of the letter before Imren did.

Imren felt the portal close and shook his head, cross that he could not trace the destination. He could track it if Rastin played on the same side with the same power they did. But Rastin had changed the stakes of the game – had enacted a ritual of his own that no Ashrone had executed in three-thousand years. Imren sighed angrily that all this had to happen in *his* lifetime, under *his* leadership. But who was to know that three years after Imren's appointment to leadership, the then young Prince Jaimis, that seemingly innocent man, would turn and slaughter his own family, his own brothers, and set into place a chain of events that would change Kildes forever.

Imren levered out the paper – a thick, quality parchment embossed with the royal symbol. The prince had spared no expense for this correspondence, making Imren even more certain it was not just one of the usual reports and trade updates.

He scanned the letter briefly. It always amazed him that such a scoundrel as Prince Jaimis could have such beautiful writing. Imren always thought that writing should reflect the true character of a person – sharp and angular for a man like Jaimis, soft and flowing for the wise and beautiful person Jaimis' father had been. Such a tragedy the way Jaimis' father had died. And not one Ashrone suspected for one moment that it was the fever that had killed him. All the money in the world had been sent to buy the cure that would save the king – the cure that the Tynecians had discovered – yet no cure had ever arrived, even after the king's death. And the Tynecian prince, loyal to the crown in every way, swore on his life he had sent it. Without doubt, someone had intercepted it, and most even wondered whether the tonic would have actually cured what the king had. Certainly some subtle symptoms had been puzzling. Whatever the truth, intercepting that cargo prevented the king's death being revealed as a poisoning.

Logic would dictate that Imren suspect the eldest son in line for the throne. He knew a few who had, but Imren knew Lian's gentle, pleasant nature, and the way the Hunston Daughter had adored him.

No – following the king's death, it had not surprised Imren in the slightest that Jaimis had been the last son standing. Still, Jaimis had not counted on how ruthless and determined the Ashrones could be – nor how deep and dark their rituals could go. Jaimis had not at all expected to be in the deadlock he was in now. Imren clearly remembered Jaimis' open shock and outrage when Imren had told the prince that the Hunston girl was dead. Imren had deposited copies of the testimonies of witnesses in Jaimis' lap – copies of testimonies that meant Jaimis had no moral or legal right to strike out at the Ashrones for the atrocity.

Imren savoured the memory of Jaimis' face that day, a smile tugging at his lips. Then he sighed. That victory had been short-lived, or so it seemed. My, how the years since had flown.

He read the letter slowly, then bolted upright. There could only be one thing deduced from this letter. Jaimis had found the missing girl and was enacting the final touches to his plans. He needed the princes, or it would all be in vain.

No wonder Rastin had announced his betrayal. The time had come for Rastin to fully utilise his new power.

Imren stood swiftly and called out to the apprentice in the hallway. The young man with the white skullcap opened the door, his hand not yet marked with the tattoo of the Asher. "Gather the Council of the Five to the Chamber of Prayers. Hurry."

The young man's brows rose, eyes sparkling, as he realised the implications of Imren's words. There would be rituals of magic tonight.

Imren put the dagger-shaped opener back in the drawer and snapped the stiff drawer shut. With letter in hand, he departed the room and sped to the Chamber of Prayers, praying silently to the Almighty that they were not too late. They would have to stop Rastin's next step, if, Almighty willing, he had not already taken it. They must stop Rastin putting wards around the castle to prevent their entry. For if they could not enter the castle to stop Rastin and his prince, then the two would have won – and the consequences of that were too heavy to contemplate, even for Imren's mind.

When Emme finally opened her eyes two days later, Kye was watching her, and she wondered how she could end up back in his company. Desperate hunger and thirst rapidly overcame curiosity. She licked dry lips, tasted traces of something bitter on them.

"Welcome back," Kye said, eyes smiling at her.

Emme attempted to sit up, but Kye's hand on her shoulder pressed her back down. She surveyed the small, cluttered room. Holly-green walls, split by a dark timber skirting and topped with beige, suggested a lavishness that bewildered Emme. Where was she? She had only once seen such wealth from the inside – right after the owner deceived her into coming to this world in the first place.

A large coat of arms, highlighted with the colours of the walls, hung above a wide dresser. She knew the precise black strokes underneath the image on the plaque were letters of words, but the words themselves were mostly alien to her. Trust. She could sound out the word 'trust' in the middle of the sentence.

A floral washbasin and jug sat upon the dresser, a plush beige towel folded beside it. A grand rug, woven with intricate designs in unnecessary colours, spread across the already carpeted floor. A second picture hung on the wall beside her double bed – a painting of a proud, grey-haired man with thick sideburns and pallid cheeks. The same coat of arms was embossed in miniature onto impractical black robes.

A gilded mirror, carved in heavy sweeps and curls, hung above a wide mantel. She could see the edge of flames in the black-marble fireplace beyond Kye's form. The scent of garlic, old lavender and something stale, stifled the hot air.

"Where am I?"

"You're at one of the major Endorian schools."

"How did I –" She realised in that moment, she felt terribly weak, terribly empty inside. "How did I get to the school?"

"I found you in the snow, and I brought you here. You had a terrible fever but you've survived."

"I think I'm hungry." Emme saw Kye's smile deepen.

"I have some leftover bread here if you want it." He reached down to a painted timber tray beside him.

"Can I sit up?" Without waiting for a response, Emme began to shift in the bed. Her arms felt so feeble, like they might splinter under her weight.

"Here." Kye discarded the bread on the dresser. He leant over, hooked hands under her shoulders and lifted her to a sitting position. He kept her forward, propped the green pillow behind her, and helped her lie back onto it. He rescued the freshly baked bread from the dresser and handed it to her. "Eat slowly. You haven't eaten anything for two days."

"Two days? Really? I remember a tavern. The woman there called me a drunk, then – this." Again she gazed around the tiny room to the sombre oil painting on the wall, the flickering gold of the mirror, the flamboyant coat of arms above the dresser. She ripped off a chunk of bread and put it in her mouth. Her mouth felt parched. "Have you got any water?"

Kye handed her a glass of water from the tray, and she drank it thirstily. "Any more?" She held the glass out to him.

He topped up the glass from a jug of iced water and she sipped it slowly whilst she nibbled on her bread. Emme thought she could feel her body revive as she ate. The rumbles in her stomach began to abate.

"What were you doing out in the snow?" Emme asked after a while.

"Looking for you."

Emme stared at her bread, suddenly very interested in the grains and seeds in it. She felt her cheeks heat. "I didn't want to be found. I left."

"It's just as well you *were* found. You would have died out there."

Emme nodded and briefly met Kye's eyes. "Thank you for saving my life."

"You're welcome," he said gently. "And you're worth it."

"I don't think so. The others don't think so either."

Kye exhaled slowly, leant back into his chair. "Emme, in this country, we don't treat children of unmarried parents like your villagers do. We really don't think the same way about it. No one back home despises you. In fact, they were all really worried about you. Many people went out looking for you, you know."

270

"Really?" Emme put the bread in her lap, her stomach smaller and fuller than she remembered. She took another sip of water, then placed the glass on the dresser beside her; scowled briefly at how unsteady her hands were.

"Yes, really. And the boys would have fought you even if you were the king's daughter. They just get like that at times."

"That's what Halder said, although he didn't put it as well as you did."

Kye smiled his gentle, closed-lip smile, then the smile faded. "I'm sorry people found out your secret. Dusty is very sorry about it too. If he had known what it meant in your world to have a history like that, he wouldn't have spread it around. You see, we just don't have the same concern for the matter that your villagers do. And the only ones in this country who regularly beat anyone about anything are thieves trying to steal your money."

Emme sighed wearily, leant her head back to stare up at the ceiling. "I don't know," she said to the air.

"What don't you know, Emme?"

"I'd like to believe you, but you're . . ." She hesitated, looked back down at her lap. "You're the one who couldn't stand to be near me after that dance we had. I know you realised you shouldn't be dancing with me. I saw it in your face. One minute you looked at me like . . ." She knew she blushed slightly. "And the next you went all cold and walked off."

Kye's brows dipped into a slight frown. "Is that what you think? That I suddenly despised you and walked off?"

"Yes."

Kye nodded slowly, deliberately, his eyes clearly thinking through something. "I'm sorry that it looked like that, and there is a very good reason for my behaviour. Part of it I can tell you, the rest is probably better left for another time."

"Then at least tell me what you can, because when you walked out you . . ." *Hurt me.*

271

Kye nodded again. "Something happened during that dance. Something occurred to me about what you might be here for, and I suddenly wanted to find out if it was true." He swiftly held up his hand to silence her objection. "Yes, I know that's not the way it looked on my face, and I promise you that one day I will tell you exactly what was going through my mind, but right now, all I can do is assure you that it was not even close to a loathing of you." He hesitated briefly. "It was actually . . . entirely the opposite."

"I don't understand."

"Emme, I think I've worked out what you're here for. That night when I left, I came here to this school. This is where one of my contacts lives, and I came to look through some old documents that might prove what I suspected about you."

"And?"

Kye saw the eagerness on her face and briefly had pity on his. "I'm so sorry, but I can't tell you here. Not where it's unsafe. But I would like to take you somewhere safe when you're well and tell you everything."

"Where? Back home?"

"No – not there. Somewhere even safer than that. If I'm *right*, it will be somewhere even safer, but if I'm wrong about you, then it will be a great risk. But I will know by the time we get there whether I am right or wrong."

"How?"

"Just let me work on that, and you concentrate on getting well."

Emme scowled at him playfully. "I was perfectly content to not know why I was brought here, and now you've gone and made me even more curious and confused than the day I arrived."

Kye smiled at her again. "I'm sure I have, but you've trusted me this far. Will you trust me just a little longer to take you somewhere safe and then show you what has been denied you?"

Emme frowned slightly, then nodded, the frown still on her face.

"Good. Now eat, get well. Then when you're feeling strong, and not a moment before, we will leave." Kye stood, put hands behind his head and stretched.

Emme noticed for the first time the dark stubble on his face, the uncharacteristic creases in his shirt and trousers, the discarded travel sack of clothes in the corner, and wondered how long he had been sitting there. He didn't look like he lacked sleep, but he had certainly lived in the chair for many hours.

Kye reached for the uneaten crust, brushed the crumbs from her blanket, and put the portion on the tray near his foot. "You should probably lie back down now." He helped her slide back into the warm sheets. He stared down at her for a moment, almost a father peering down at child he loved. He said at last, "Well, I'm going to go and take a wash and change, then I'll come back and see how you are."

Kye took his rumpled bag from the floor, pulled back the door, and paused beneath the sandstone doorframe. "Get some sleep."

Emme nodded, watched him leave. The door clicked in the frame. She stared at the door until the crackle of the fire drew her attention. Too weak to rise up to look and take comfort from it, she stared up at the ceiling, questions burning her mind until weary sleep claimed her for itself.

◉

"I need that book, Russen," Kye argued in the quiet of Russen's office late one night. He put his half-empty wine glass down on the polished desk in front of him. The spicy maroon wine swirled around the inside of the fine crystal. "You've got to figure out a way to get it out of the library to take with me."

"It's worth more than my wages could ever pay for," Russen said. "If it gets damaged . . . You saw how fragile it is."

"If it's true, she's going to need to see it, or she won't believe it."

"Yes she will. You'll have to make her see it. I'm sure deep down she'll have some idea that it's true."

"You're guessing, Russen. No one knows how this really works. And you've met her. Did you see any sign of any idea of what's going on?"

"No, but –"

"Then telling her is not going to make her suddenly see the truth. She's going to need to see the book. It's going to be hard enough for her to hear it as it is, and she's going to want to deny it with every part of her. Trust me on this – I know Emme. It's going to undo a lot of things she's come to base her life on, and she's going to react very strongly against it if I don't have that book."

Russen sighed angrily. "You are too persuasive, Kye. You're going to get me into trouble one day."

Kye picked up his wine glass again, rested his elbow on the chair arm. "My friend, if we are right about Emme, she will get us *out* of trouble. And then your book will be as valuable as dust to you."

"Yes, I suppose you're right." Russen thought carefully, took a long sip of wine, then said, "I thought that the girl couldn't read."

"She knows some words, but she'll see the picture. That's enough, don't you think?" Kye swished the wine around as he stared into it.

"Well, let's hope so, but she could think it a weak link."

"Not by the time I'm through. There are many other factors in this that I can't discuss here, but she'll understand them."

"Of course – the . . ." His voice trailed off before voicing the dangerous words. "Have you seen any of it?"

"No, but I'm convinced it's there. I just need to prove it. By the time we get to our destination, I hope to have the proof I need." Kye took a sip of his wine, then retracted the glass, stared down into it again.

"I wish you would tell me where you're going. The others will want to know."

Kye's head snapped up and eyes locked with Russen. "No – and you mustn't tell the others about any of this either. It's far too dangerous for you and I to be thinking about these things. The more people who know, the more chance he'll pick up our thoughts."

"But this is the most significant thing to happen since . . . This is the miracle we've been waiting for."

"This *might* be what we've been waiting for. We don't know yet, and until I get Emme somewhere safe, no one is to know. Is that clear?"

"Of course."

"Good."

They let silence replace conversation for a while, then Kye asked, "Did that letter to Halder get posted?"

"Yes, although the message made no sense."

"Not to anyone who might intercept it, but it will make sense to him. It was really just to tell him I had found Emme and that everything was all right. I know Halder – he'd keep looking for Emme like I would." Kye watched Russen for a moment. "What is it?"

Russen looked up from deep thoughts, slightly dazed. "What's what?"

"I know that look. You want to tell me something."

"Yes." Russen paused awkwardly. "Do you realise that if we're right about Emme, then we have to deal with Halder?"

Kye nodded gravely. "I know."

"Do you ever talk about it?"

"Not anymore, but I don't think a day goes by that he doesn't think about it."

"Has he ever changed his mind?"

"No, but I wouldn't stop him if he did."

Russen's brows shot up. "You wouldn't make him honour his promise?"

"No. It's always been Halder's decision. It never even crossed my mind to ask him to make the promise in the first place."

Russen shook his head slowly. "I think sometimes your rigid principles are a weakness."

"How so?"

"Did it occur to you that everything stands and falls on Halder? That so many people stand to lose from his decision?"

"Yes, and did it occur to you that it is literally impossible to make Halder go through with it?" Kye let the words make a mark before he added, "We *have* to trust in Halder. There are no alternatives."

"Yes, I guess you're right."

Russen shifted restlessly in his chair, and the two sat in dark thoughts for a moment. Russen drained the last of his wine, then stood, turned to a decanter behind him and refilled his glass. "So when are you leaving?"

"Tomorrow morning, first thing. Emme says she's feeling better. She has her appetite back, and she's almost clawing at the bedroom door to get out."

Russen replaced the glass stopper, his back to Kye. "Yes, well, if she insists on wearing those boys' clothes and ruining our cover story, then she has to stay in that room." He picked up his wine glass and took it back to the desk. He folded down into the large comfortable chair, slid the chair forward a little. "If you're right about her, will you come and get me?"

"Of course I will. If I'm right, I have no idea what I'm going to do, and I'm really going to need you. This is beyond anything I'm prepared for."

"Yes, me too." Russen frowned deeply. "But I know someone who *is* prepared for it, and right now, I'm willing to bet he's ten steps ahead of us."

"Yes." Kye nodded once as he stared into his wine. "I'm sure of it."

After four days of bed rest, Emme had assured Kye she was well enough to travel, but as she stepped beyond the enormous ancient entrance, she wondered if she had been a little too eager.

Cold air hit, and her lungs fought the chill. Finally she inhaled and stepped out from the portico into the frosty air, the wind tugging at her cloak and skin.

She left behind an opulence of high stone arches; rows and rows of oil-painted portraits lining walls; ornate stone doorframes, cornices and stairwells; and an abundance of arched stained-glass windows. Every wall had been neatly painted in deep greens and maroons, sometimes bordered by mahogany timber panels to the middle of the wall. Clean rugs, intimately matching the walls, seemed to soften every floor but the great vaulted echoing halls. Black iron and gilded candelabras, hanging from ceilings or curving out from walls, held an abundance of candles that burned unceasingly in the darkest rooms.

Now, as she pushed outside against the wind, she could see that the splendour did not confine itself to the inside. Wintry trees lined a wide sandstone staircase, laid out for both function and beauty, that went down and down to the city. On either side, terraced gardens, covered by snow, held the promise of magnificent spring growth.

She gazed behind at the enormous spired mansion. Tiny boys with baby faces and little wings peered down at her from the arched stone portico. They preceded a honeycomb pattern carved into the expanse of the jutting entrance. Each honeycomb held an image of something – a shield, a spear, a face, a coat of arms. Each image, so tiny, had been worked to the finest details. Such artwork would have taken lifetimes to complete.

Fierce stone creatures with powerful hunched legs, sharp teeth and bat wings, perched on two pillars rising from the flagstone entry. They seemed to be guarding something or someone. She wondered what the creatures were, but the bitter, wailing wind swept all conversation away.

She gazed one last time at the building, fixed it in her mind, then descended the stairs. She wondered if she would ever go back there, ever have a chance to roam the vastness that begged to be explored. The school held more elegance and pleasing symmetry than the castle did with its thick unadorned slabs of stone, the immense fortress wall, and the functional, defensive buildings and passageways.

It interested her that the school would get such attention from artists whilst the castle reflected a rough brutality. But then, the castle was for protection, not beauty. Perhaps princes surrounded themselves with interior splendour like the room that Jai – She shook her head. She did wish she would stop thinking that name or remembering that room.

It still puzzled her why any prince would need a gift like that – to be able to hear conspiracies – when the gift was so easily thwarted by changing a name in one's thoughts.

She felt Kye's hand on her back as she descended stone steps, recently cleared of snow by busy grounds staff. "Are you all right, Emme?"

She peered at him from beneath her hood and realised her legs had been a little too unsteady on the stairs. "If I tell you something, will you promise not to make me do anything about it?"

Kye seemed faintly amused. "I find it difficult to make promises about things I don't know about, but I guess I could make an exception."

Emme nodded, satisfied. She was slowly learning that whatever Kye promised, he kept. She wondered what had shaped a man to be so trustworthy. Indeed, he did seem unlike everything her mother had taught her about men, but then her mother had never known this world. Still, Kye had a secret past, and that secret past could well prove her mother right after all. But the more Emme thought about it, which, annoyingly, she so often did, the more it didn't seem right that Kye could have a secret and dark past. Whatever sins Kye atoned for – perhaps murders if he was once a Black Band – it seemed highly unlikely a man like Kye could ever do anything so bad that he had to make up for it every day of his life. "I'm still feeling a little unwell, but I didn't want to tell you because I was so tired of being locked in that tiny, windowless room."

Kye nodded once. "I suspected as much. Don't worry, I won't make you go back there."

"Good." She reached the second-last landing and straightened, resolved not to let her legs betray her again. Even as she thought it, she felt weakness in her muscles from the fever that had raged through her body.

"But I will let you rest whenever you need it," Kye said. "And please don't be too proud to ask for help." His hand pressed her back as he assisted her down the remaining stairs, but Emme did not protest for fear he would march her straight back to the room.

No – Kye would not do that. He had given his word.

They passed a groundskeeper bearing a snow shovel over his shoulder. Without stopping, he tipped his grey, woollen cap to them and said a cheery 'hello'. Emme's cloak did not entirely conceal her boyish clothes, but the groundskeeper did not seem to care as he whistled his way up the stairs without looking back.

They reached the bottom of the stairs. It met with a wide brick and wrought-iron wall spanning the entire perimeter of the school. Two square pillars of bricks towered on both sides of the gate, a large burning lantern on each top. The path briefly continued beyond the gateway until it met with the main road. It had been freshly shovelled, and large piles of snow sat on either side like a white, bordering wall for the broad, cobbled path.

The wind rushed at them through the gate, sucked them back a little, then settled. It carried no city scents; it just smelled cold.

"It gets slippery here," Kye warned her.

She followed him along the last of the path before they stepped up onto the street's compacted snow. A horse and carriage rattled past, the shutters of the windows drawn to hide wealthy travellers inside. The coachman flicked his whip onto the horse's brown back, and the horse picked up its pace. The wheels glided along the icy surface, and the horse's hooves barely dented the white.

With the gusts abating, Emme could smell the scent of freshly baked bread and guessed that a large bakeshop sat nearby. She could see the stir of people begin to surge onto the streets. She glanced up; the clouds were broken today. Eventually short patches of sun would stream through, and the town would bustle with people trying to get things done before severe weather returned.

Kye chose their path with practised ease as he took them down the thoroughfare. He knew when to cross to a less slippery side, when to utilise overhanging gutters, when to take thinner, emptier backstreets only to end up on the main road further down.

Emme could not remember a moment when Kye didn't have confidence with his surroundings. Even in the dark of the Black Band headquarters, Kye knew the corridors, and the exact exit he needed. She observed Kye as he strolled beside her against the main flow of the workday crowd; dwelt heavily on his secrets until an idea formed in her mind – perhaps her subtle tactic with Halder, whilst failing on the perceptive man, might work with Kye. "Kye?"

"Yes?"

"Do you remember that eerie grey-eyed man – the leader of the . . ." She curled her finger at him, beckoned him closer. "I want to whisper something. Come here."

He leant his ear close to her lips.

She whispered, "The leader of the Black Bands."

Kye paused briefly, straightened. "Yes – what about him?"

"Was he considered a gentleman?"

"Yes – most of ones higher up are." Quietly he added, "They need to be to work their way into areas of high society." He watched her briefly as they walked. "Why do ask?"

So Kye *must* have been a Black Band. Everyone, even strangers, said he was a gentleman, and if the ones higher up were the gentlemen, then her suspicions were confirmed. That's how Kye knew exactly where the Black Band headquarters were, how to get the leader's son and how to get to Emme. But then, the pale-eyed Black Band leader didn't know Kye. One would think the leader would, although perhaps the leader came along after Kye left. And it did seem a little odd that Kye could rescue self-professed Black Band members and yet refuse to admit it himself. Unless it endangered somebody to do so. Emme resisted a sigh. How frustrating the mystery was.

Emme deflected. "You know, I don't know how you can all tell just by looking at each other what class you are."

"It's everything – it's speech, it's mannerisms, it's tone of voice, facial expressions, how neat the appearance is, how they stand or walk, even how much eye contact they have with you."

"Everything but money, you mean."

"Yes – that's a good observation. Even those brought up in a wealthy class can fall from grace and become poor."

"Like Illina."

"Yes, and just like Illina, the mannerisms don't leave them. And sometimes poor people who inherit money are never accepted into high society because their upbringing alienates them."

"Everyone says you're a gentleman."

"Do they?" He shrugged lightly. "They could be right."

"So where did you learn it? Were your parents from high society?"

"Yes and no."

"What's the yes, and what's the no?"

"It's complicated."

"Which means 'mind your own business, Emme'." To her surprise, Kye laughed. She blinked up at him.

"No, it means, 'not here, Emme'."

"I see."

Kye led her down streets that both angered and fascinated her. The four-storey sandstone apartments were striking with elaborate stone decorations and flamboyant detailing etched into chunky stone doorframes. Crisp white architraves framed arched windows on upper levels. Large bay windows on the ground floors revealed luxurious interiors.

Smokey-grey winter trees and evergreen conifers lined the spacious streets. Sets of worn stairs, divided from the street by neat stone walls, led down to servants' apartments below ground level.

So much wealth existed in this area, and she felt a stab of anger at the unfair distribution of money.

"It's not right," she said more to herself as they passed an enormous church with large spires, a bell-tower and a myriad of stained-glass windows set into intricately carved walls.

"What isn't?" he asked, following her gaze to the magnificent cathedral.

"How can people live like this when so many die on the streets every night from hunger?"

Kye nodded once, a significant gesture that told Emme he knew and understood how she felt. "It's best if you don't voice those opinions in places like this." His voice was low, his eyes trained for any sign of nearby listeners. "The wealthy don't like to be reminded of their greed, and some have very powerful connections who could frame you for things you'd never think of."

"I see." Emme nodded but the scowl of distaste did not leave her face. More than ever she despised the blood of corruption flowing through the veins of the city.

They drifted on until Emme began to feel too weary, too hungry to go on. "Could we please stop somewhere? I'm feeling really tired."

"Of course. Tell me – what do you really feel like for lunch? What would make you happy?"

"Anything."

"But if you had to choose?"

"Potato. I like potato."

"Well, let's see if we can get you some." He looked down at her, his face blank, but something dark moved behind his eyes. Emme wondered what it was, then he tugged her out of the way as a plush carriage dashed past where she had been standing.

"Watch where you're going," she called after it in vain. She looked up at Kye, noted the expression on his face and shrugged. "Well at least I didn't call them names."

A smile touched Kye's lips, but he kept thoughts to himself.

Kye led her to a large tavern and politely opened the door for her. She stepped inside the warm room with its heavy scent of bread and wine.

Several people looked up at her entrance, noted her curiously, then seemed even more perplexed about the gentleman who travelled with such poor company. Emme felt a swell of pity for Kye. He would take the brunt of the stares whilst she was around.

Kye directed her to an empty table against the right wall and pulled out a chair for her. Telling herself it was because she was unwell, she accepted the chair and let Kye slide it under her as she sat down.

He took the chair opposite her just as a short man in a half-apron approached them. "We're serving hot cheese rolls and baskets of roasted chestnuts," he informed them.

Kye seemed to be thinking over something deeper than the food. Emme tapped his ankle under the table with her foot. He broke from his thoughts and looked up at the serving man. "Two lunches and two glasses of water please."

The man acknowledged the order with a single nod and left the room.

Emme leant across the table and whispered, "How are we

going to pay for this?"

Kye locked eyes with her briefly. "Russen lent me some money, but I'm hoping we have enough."

"We'd better have enough or we'll be doing dishes for a month."

"How much do we need?" Kye reached into his bag for his money pouch. Preoccupied with rummaging through the sack, he asked, "Can you tell me what that sign up there says?" He glanced once at the wall behind Emme. "The middle section is the fee for lunch."

Emme turned around partially in her chair. She scanned the board, then turned back to Kye. "We need two half-rounds. And there'd better be two more half-rounds in there for dinner because I'll be starving by then."

Kye pushed a garment aside, plunged his hand deep down into the bag and seemed to be tugging on something. "How many did you say?"

"We need four half-rounds. Well, two for now at least."

Finally Kye extracted the money pouch, unclipped the brass button, and peered inside, a faint frown, almost like concentration, on his face.

"Don't tell me – Russen didn't give us anything."

"Oh no, he did. There's plenty in here for lunch, and it looks like Russen has given us enough for some dinner too."

"Good." Emme sat back in the chair with a satisfied smile. "Because I was sure you were going to make me be the one to tell the innkeeper that we couldn't pay him."

Kye laughed, and Emme's smile brightened. She rarely heard laughter from him.

Kye stood. "If you'll excuse me, I think I'll go and use the restroom." He handed her the leather pouch. "Don't let this out of your sight." He drifted across the room to the kitchens, knocked once, and the door swung open. She saw him ask something of a person hidden within the kitchen, then Kye was admitted.

Emme peered into the pouch, saw four small imprinted coins inside, shiny and silver and engraved with 'half-round'. She slammed the stiff lid of the pouch down over the dark opening. She hated coins for the arrogant head imprinted on their backs. Her only pleasure was in using the coins to feed hungry children who ironically worked against the image on those coins. That and seeing the slender 'prince's crown' circling his forehead, not the elaborate higher-placed crown of a king.

When Kye returned, the lunch had been delivered to the table, and Emme was already eating it.

Kye picked up a roll and took a bite.

"What's in the other bag?" Emme asked, a flick of her head gesturing to the second sack Kye carried.

Kye chewed and swallowed. "A book."

"That school back there – is that where you borrow all the books for the kids?"

"Yes – I go there a lot. I'm often borrowing and swapping books."

"What's this one about?" Emme reached for a handful of warm, roasted nuts from the cloth-lined basket.

Kye thought about the question briefly. "History, I guess."

"More stories?"

"Not exactly." He took another bite of the roll.

"That's a pity. I like the history stories. So what is it, then?" She popped some nuts into her mouth.

"It's a bit hard to explain. It's sort of a book about traditions."

"Why would you need a book like that? You know all the traditions."

"Well, maybe not traditions. Maybe more old ceremonies and

other matters."

"That doesn't sound too interesting. Is it for the kids?"

"No – for me. And I thought you might want to have a look at it too."

Emme frowned with faint annoyance. "Must I?"

"I think you'll want to see it when the time comes for that discussion." He put his roll down and picked up his glass of water. His eyes stayed fixed on Emme's face as he sipped it.

Emme shrugged. "If you insist. I'm still not very good with the reading you know."

"You'll get there, Emme. You're learning to read a lot faster than you think. I know you don't think so, but you're at a reading level it took most of the others a year to get to."

"That's good to hear. I do prefer the mathematics though."

Kye smiled at her. "So we've all noticed."

They finished their lunch, paid for it and left the whispering tavern guests behind as they stepped out into pale sunshine.

For several hours, they trudged along high traffic streets, then drifted through quieter backstreets.

"So when will we get there?" Emme asked as late afternoon sun peeped through the clouds. She felt the faint warmth drift across her face despite the steam that issued from her mouth. Her feet had long before succumbed to numbness. Overwhelmingly weary, she had been sullen until the sun slipped from behind clouds and filled her with the briefest moment of joy.

"We should be there by this evening. I might stop at a tavern for a meal first, then we'll head on or we won't have anywhere to sleep but those squashy rooms you and I know so well."

Emme shivered despite her numbness to the cold. She responded flatly, "Anywhere but those rooms."

That evening, they stopped at a tavern bordering on the less wealthy part of town. The immaculate, brightly lit tavern had attracted a typical mixture of wealthy, middle-class and poor – normal for a tavern on a social class border.

The poor wallowed in alcohol, the wealthy, obviously travellers, slouched over a meal, whilst the middle-class mingled with friends for a night of social revelry and drinking.

A minstrel, sitting in the corner beside the large, cheery fire, plucked a tune on his lute. Although he sang beautiful songs to the crowd, the hat outstretched on a nearby table remained empty but for one meagre coin.

Uncommonly, the tables were polished, elegant, spread with white linen, each holding its own candle display. A sweet aroma – Emme guessed lavender oil simmering in a tiny pot within the fireplace – replaced sweat, rank alcohol and stale food odours.

Hooded and unnoticed, Emme walked to the nearest corner table and selected the very corner chair, preferring not to have her back exposed to the drinkers behind her. Before the night's carousing would end, many of those casual drinkers would turn into unpredictable drunks.

Kye flipped back his cloak hood, removed the garment. He shook off moisture left by an earlier drift of snow, and hung the cloak over the back of the chair. "They can play all night for very little money," he said, noting the direction of Emme's hooded gaze.

"Why do they bother?"

"They get free accommodation and a meal at taverns. It draws in crowds for the taverns and lets the minstrels have an audience. I've never met a minstrel who did not want to be one, even with the inadequate pay."

"Are most of them from wealthy families?"

"Yes. What made you guess that?"

"Dusty said something once about the expense of musical instruments and music lessons. He told me how some of the kids taught themselves to play. Although, I never did ask how you got the instruments."

"Halder exchanged services for them several years ago. He knew we needed a little bit of joy and something to look forward to."

The conversation ceased when Kye ordered two meals and two glasses of water from a young tavern worker. The ginger-haired man wrote the order into his memory, acknowledged it with a nod, then began to turn away. Emme flipped back her damp hood, and the young man stopped mid-turn. His eyes lit up. "Emme! Good to see you. You haven't been around to our kitchens for a while."

"The weather hasn't been too good lately, so I've been going to the closer taverns."

"Well, you make sure you come and visit us soon. We've all been wondering about you." He smiled warmly at Emme, seemed not to be able to take his eyes from her, then discovered Kye staring at him. The young man blushed and scurried away.

"Well – you have made quite an impression in the city," Kye said with a faint arch of a brow.

Emme shrugged. "I get the feeling no one ever treats kitchen staff with much respect. I guess I just offered it to them."

"Is that what it is," Kye said, a trace of pleasant mockery in his voice.

The kitchen doors burst open, and an enormous man with a red face and tight apron bustled into the room. "Emme," he roared cheerily. "Good to see you." Curious, the crowds looked up at him, but he ignored them entirely. He bustled over to Emme's table and slapped her back. "Tavis told me you were here, but I had to see it for myself. I never thought I'd see the day you'd be a paying customer." He noted Kye for the first time and bowed slightly, his enormous belly barely folding. "Pardon me, sir, I did not see you there. And how is it a gentleman like you knows our Emme?"

"It's a long story," Kye said, voice polite, eyes faintly amused.

"Well, you just let me know if there is anything I can get you." He grinned down at Emme.

"Thank you." Warmly, Emme smiled up at the big man.

"Well, I must go. Lots to do. We've a minstrel tonight, and that always pulls in the big crowds. Do promise you'll come and see us again soon, Emme." He leant down close to her, whispered, "And be sure to use the special back door." He winked.

"I will."

"Excellent." The man turned and waddled from the room. He thumped back the swinging kitchen door. "Get Emme and her gentleman friend a tea each on the house," he roared to the staff, then the squeaky door swung back into position and muffled the kitchen noises.

"I don't see what's so humorous," Emme said after a moment of silence.

"I'm just quite amused by how much they're taken with you."

"Is it so hard to believe that someone could like me?"

Kye raised hands, palms to Emme. "No, no. That's not what I meant. I just don't think you realise how much kitchen staff despise people who beg for food."

"I never begged; I placed orders."

"I would have thought that would be even worse."

Emme shrugged. "Well it wasn't."

The meals were delivered and hot mugs put on the table. "The tea is on the house," ginger-haired Tavis said, then moved to another table to take fresh orders and clear away plates.

Emme scanned the venison and potato stew. "I am so hungry."

She tucked into the food.

When all that remained on their plates were swirls of leftover gravy, they sipped their tea and listened to the music. The lively tunes filled the air and blended with the conversations of the crowds now swollen to the numbers the innkeeper predicted. The minstrel's bland but steady voice did not seem to matter against the captivating songs.

"You must be taking me home," Emme said after a while. "I know where this tavern is. It's not that far from home."

"Do you still think of it as home?" Kye asked over his tea.

"I guess so – if it's true that no one hates me. But I will feel a bit uncomfortable turning up at first."

"I think once you did, you would see how anxious everyone is about you. But you don't need to worry; we're not going there."

"Can't you give me some idea of where we're heading?"

"No – not yet."

Kye darted back in his chair as a drunk slapped hands down on the table and leered at Emme.

"Such a pretty boy," the drunk slurred. "My friends were all betting you were a girl. I told them you were a boy. But you're too pretty to be a boy."

"Get back from me, you vile pig," Emme said in a low voice. "And remove your hands from the table."

The drunk shrugged and rejoined his hysterical friends. Coins changed hands over some vulgar bet.

"Can we go?" Emme asked, face stony.

"Of course."

Kye stood, paid the nearest staff member, then went back for the bags. They donned sacks and cloaks, then stepped out onto eerie moonlit snow.

Loud laughter spilled from the drunks in the room, but Emme did not turn to see who made the sounds. Kye shut the door behind her. Grateful that the laughter barely pushed through the closed timber door, she followed Kye down the street.

Kye looked down at her with a wistful smile. "I'm proud of you, Emme."

"Why?"

"When you first came to us, you probably would have floored a man for doing that."

Emme shrugged. "I'm trying to learn when to pick a fight and when not to. Or maybe I'm just too tired tonight to react." After a while she added, "But if he'd laid a hand on you or me, especially you, he would have come to regret it."

Kye laughed quietly. "You know, I hope you never lose that fiery passion you have."

"I thought you were just trying to say it was a bad thing."

"No, not at all. Sometimes things we think are faults, are actually strengths that we haven't learned to use in the right way. You're extremely courageous, you're passionate, and you're driven to fight injustice. These are all strengths, but your villagers never gave you a chance to use them for good. But since you have been here, you've done so much for the kids. No matter what happens after tonight, I will always be grateful for it."

A chill wind blew through Emme's insides. "I don't like the sound of that last sentence."

Kye took her down a side street that windowless sides of apartments faced. They turned right, into a sour alleyway that bent at its end. They wandered down the right turn, and Emme's brows lifted as she spied the dead end.

Kye stopped at the wall and scanned the stone formation. He noted a difference only his eyes could see and pushed it. The thick wall swung open, its uneven edge the mortar between bricks, and the two stepped inside. Kye lit a candle on the wall, then shut the door.

"I thought we weren't going to these little rooms," Emme said, disappointment sharp in her face and tone.

"I thought it might be a good place to have a quick talk."

"About?"

Kye looked beyond her for a moment, his mind running through something Emme could only wonder about. At last he met her gaze and said, "Emme, do you trust me?"

"I guess so," she said with a casual shrug.

"I mean do you *really* trust me? Do you believe that I would never harm you? Do you trust me to keep you safe?"

Emme felt her cheeks go a little warm, despite the cold that lingered on her body. "Yes, I guess I do." She did. She knew he was a man of honour. Even after knowing her secrets, he had still risked his life to save hers.

Kye studied her face, searched for some reassurance in it. When he seemed to have found it, he relaxed only a little. "Good – because tonight you're going to hear things that you may not like, and I'm going to take you to a place that is going to make you wonder if I'm the enemy or not. But I'm not, Emme. I promise you. Tonight you're going to find out what no one has wanted you to know, and you might think about me a little differently after that; but I can promise you that I'm not the enemy, and I would *never* deliver you into the hands of anyone who was."

Emme frowned, puzzled. "You're frightening me."

"I'm sorry. I just wanted to make sure that you knew this, because you might doubt me for a while tonight. So I wanted to try and reassure you before we got there."

He seemed to be awaiting her decision. Still frowning, she nodded.

"Good," he said. "Now are you ready to go, or do you want to rest for a while?"

"Not in here." Emme stared at the solid, close walls. "I really don't like these little places."

Kye led her out of the secret room and onto the street. The two walked off through the radiating silver snow to a clandestine destination inside Kye's head.

◉

A shadow lurked in the streets. The pallid silver-grey eyes of the shadow watched two people pass and made mental notes about the faces he recognised all too well. The bizarre woman from the barbarian country, and the aloof stranger who had dared to harm his son. He had waited long days for this moment.

When the prince had delivered the letter to the Black Bands to let the woman go, Trehn had felt robbed of revenge to the point where it kept him awake at night. He would never forget those confident blue-green eyes that he longed to see close in death at his own hands.

That death would have to wait. He and his Black Bands had other jobs to do. Although loyal to the men and women of the Black Bands, his ultimate loyalty lay with the prince, the rightful heir to the Kildes throne, and the one who gave the Black Bands all the power they could possibly want within the corrupt city.

Trehn followed the two, his stealth a gift on quiet moonlit nights like this. By now his Black Bands and the soldiers would have reached the headquarters of those troublesome street rats, and would be entering to take them all prisoner. He still wondered how the prince knew of the whereabouts of this headquarters when the Black Bands had been unable to find it. Trehn *had* heard a rumour that the prince now had an Ashrone on side, and that could well explain a lot.

Trehn had never before wished he could be in two places at once. He longed to see the look on the street rats' faces when the soldiers raided them. But he was just as keen to be the one who sealed the fate of that brash leader and the perplexing woman.

The prince had promised him an explanation tonight, and Trehn so deserved it. He had nearly lost his son for this new grand scheme of the prince's.

Trehn followed the two to the end of their destination and his brows arched with surprise. What would they be doing here? The two asked for certain defeat if they entered that place. Were the two so driven to destroy the prince that they would resort to this – their own deaths?

Of course not. Trehn wanted to laugh. It was all too clear now. The aloof gentleman, for all his claims of nobleness, had clearly struck a deal and was going to collect. The woman's life in exchange for what? Money? Reinstatement into society? A promise of power?

Trehn's eyes narrowed. The prince wanted the woman alive and totally unharmed at all costs. Trehn would have to hurry or all could be lost. He turned and sped silently through the snow-covered streets to the nearby castle, where he knew the prince anxiously awaited the Black Band leader's report.

11

"This is odd," Emme said as she looked up at the building towering in the darkness beyond expansive iron gates. "It's almost identical to the school."

"The two were built at the same time, although this one is smaller."

Kye jiggled back the black latch and pushed apart the double gates. They creaked on rusted, idle hinges. Heavy cobwebs, weighted with moisture, hung between the bars.

"Are we allowed to just go in?"

"Yes, although most wouldn't."

"That doesn't sound too good." Emme stepped through the gates and watched as Kye swung them shut.

"You're right – I shouldn't have said that." He worked the latch back into position, then started up the grand staircase with its many snow-covered landings. A sudden thrust of iced air rushed from the dark sides of the mansion, stung their faces, then wailed its way into the city to wreak havoc there. An owl, ruffled by the sudden gust, hooted from a row of unkempt maples that stretched out beyond the bulky stone wall, to the city. A shabby rat scuttled across the stairs in front of them, its long tail dragging, as though disused, within the fold of the stairs.

Only three of the mansion's windows emanated choked light. The rest were empty sockets watching over broken retaining walls, thistle stalks, mounds of snow, and brambles. A single oak pushed up through pavestone edgings and extended its gnarled fingers to seize the pale stars.

Emme scanned the disarray, a forgotten splendour left to crumble.

They reached halfway, and Emme dragged large amounts of cold air into her aching, hungry lungs. "I'm too tired for this."

"Not much further, Emme, then you can rest inside." He lightly pressed his palm to her back, an encouragement to go on.

Her breathing beginning to settle, Emme sighed with resignation and moved up the staircase again. "Is this the home of one of your contacts?"

"Actually, no. I haven't come here since I was a little boy."

"Then how do you know you can trust this person?"

"I just know."

"You're not going to tell me, are you?"

"Not until we're inside."

They reached the final landing, and Emme bent, hands stretched to knees. She inhaled more deep mouthfuls of air, tried to catch her breath.

"Are you okay?"

"I feel really unwell – really weak. I just need to warm up and go to sleep."

"Soon, Emme. I promise."

Kye pressed his forefinger to the rusted doorbell beside the enormous arched oak doors. The same baby-faced winged boys from the school looked down at Emme, and she wondered who would have thought them special enough to be carved in rock.

Moments passed. Kye rang the doorbell again, and the door swung open, snapping cobwebs in its wake.

Two blue eyes, wide-set on a young, pallid face, peered out beneath pale lantern light. "Can I help you?"

Emme warily noted the stranger's surprise at visitors.

"Yes," Kye said. "May I have a word with you inside?"

The young man nodded and stepped back into shadows of a wide hallway.

"Stay here, Emme," Kye said. "I won't be long."

Kye partially closed the heavy door. She heard muffled voices, heard a gasp of alarm, then quiet murmuring again. Emme sat down onto the brick edge that supported a bat-winged stone creature she remembered from the school. She tucked her cloak about herself tightly, frowned at the cold seeping through her thighs.

More murmurings beyond the door. How long did it take to ask someone if they could go inside? She began to fidget.

"Could you hurry it up?" she called out, hoping someone could hear her. "I'm very tired."

Seconds after, the door swung open and Kye gazed out. "It's all right; you can come in now. Once we're inside, you should be safe."

"Good." Emme nodded and walked past Kye into the vast hallway; faced right. A panelled mahogany wall lined the left, the cold sandstone of the front of the building, the right. It stretched in front of her and behind, sealed at both ends by a heavy timber door. Carved mahogany doors, built into the panelled wall, concealed rooms. Heavy. The dark timbers and stained stone corridor felt heavy within the shadows. The various unlit lanterns exuded the scent of lamp oil, and recently stirred dust hovered like insects around the only spilling lantern light in the boy's hand. Did anyone even live in this relic?

The black-haired, lofty young man took them down the corridor, past each door on their left. He held his rattling lantern high to light their steps. He swung the door at the far end, stepped back politely to let them pass. Kye and Emme moved past him into a vast chamber with velvet-padded benches lining the four walls. The light from the lantern wavered briefly as the young man lowered it to close the door.

Emme stared up at the high vaulted ceiling and remembered a similar room at the school, although that assembly hall had been filled with rows of chairs. She noted dust, cobwebs and worn, red fabrics on the chairs.

Their boots tapped on the hollow timber floor, echoing loudly around the cavernous space as the young man led them onward. Once inside the connecting hallway, pavestones and a lower ceiling muted the sound of their footsteps. The musty odour of old fabrics and dust dissipated.

The young man stopped at the first panelled door and ushered them into a small library area. His shifting lantern light touched the heavy shadows of the unlit space. Elevated on platforms on three walls and accessed by two staircases, rows and rows of colourful, thick-spined books hugged the walls. Emme noted the vaulted ceiling and the elaborate timber cornices.

Squat storage cupboards, with simple double doors, had been built into the base of the platforms. Three rectangular tables, each partnered with six chairs, filled the centre. A plump wine-red and forest-green rug covered most of the lifeless stone floor. Behind her, a simple row of bookshelves decorated the final wall. This room suggested frequent use, and the odour of alcoholic cleaning solutions replaced dust and unused lamp oil.

The young man took a flintbox from a gap on a bookshelf near the door, lit the four-pronged candelabras on each table, then left without a word.

"What now?" Emme asked.

"We wait."

The two unloaded cloaks and bags at the entrance. Kye leant, arms folded, against the nearest shelf whilst Emme drifted around the room along the raised platform, stared at lacklustre spines, and touched fingertips to stiff dustless covers.

299

Emme wandered, uninterested, past a sealed door and stopped to peer at a supply cupboard with diamond-pattern glass doors. She noted large quantities of inkwells and feathers. Kye used those. He had a small store of inkwells and feathers in his drawer. He had offered to teach her the use of a pen after she mastered her letters on the slate.

The bottom shelf was neatly stacked with clean papers and envelopes. Kye had some of those too, but not nearly of the quality of these papers.

She moved further around the platform, hand on the cold round railing, then shrugged and descended the nearest stairs.

It did not escape Emme that Kye had been watching her the whole time – watching her with an intensity she had not seen before. He seemed troubled by something, as though she were the cause of some indecision within him. Whilst his body relaxed against the bookshelf, his eyes, unmoving from her, remained uneasy.

Disturbed by that new expression, by the unfamiliar emotions on his face, Emme pretended to examine the elegant black candelabra on the nearest table, stared down into the flames of the fat yellow candles.

Kye turned swiftly at the sound of the door opening.

Emme looked over at the door expectantly – jolted. A chill of a winter's wind iced through her stomach. She saw the sickeningly familiar skullcaps, the heavy tattoos on the backs of two right hands. Two men, framed in the doorway by ghostly lamplight, watched her with an anticipation that alarmed her.

Fear squeezed at her chest, made her heart flutter. *Run, Kye.* Why wasn't he running? Kye nodded to the gentlemen, and she heard them exchange words.

"Kye?" Panic edged Emme's voice. He hastily turned to her. "What are you doing?"

"These men are going to help you." Kye gestured calmly to the newcomers.

"What have you done?" Emme's eyes darted from Kye to the strangers. Good Creator! Kye had given her over to the Ashrones. Kye – she had trusted him. Emme spun on her heels and fled up the narrow stairs for the only other door in the room. Three more steps and she would be at the landing. Slowed by the surreal, each step took years.

Her feet thudded on timber of the landing. She heard sinister monotone chanting behind her but did not stop. She dashed across the platform; smacked painfully into an invisible force that cracked across her body like shattering glass. Books and roof pitched upward as she thumped to her back, dazed. A tingling sting, like a healing burn, rippled across her body.

"Stop!" Kye said sharply. "She's just frightened." She heard steps. "Emme – it's all right." The steps were running towards her. She defied the smarting in her body and levered to a sitting position, could barely make out her hands and feet through the haze of her thoughts.

Moments later she was peering up at the blurry face of Kye. "Are you all right?" He knelt above her, stared down at her.

Emme whisked the dagger from her trousers, but her hands shook violently from fatigue, from fear. "What have you done?" Emme asked, anguish in her voice. "These men are the enemy."

Kye shook his head. "No, Emme. I was wrong. They're not the enemy. Please, let them explain." She blinked once to clear her vision, then saw his raw look of concern. The emotion made her squirm. "Trust me," he said gently. "I told you I wouldn't deliver you into the hands of the enemy, and I meant it."

Emme watched him, scrutinised him. He seemed so genuine. She glanced behind her. The Ashrones stood just beyond the open doorway, calmly watching the two up on the platform.

Kye spoke in a low voice to her. "Just listen to them, and I promise you, if they try anything to hurt you, then I'll be the one to throw the dagger."

Emme frowned deeply, could not seem to make up her mind – doubted even that there was a choice. Again she glanced at the two men behind her. One of them, the older one with downy white hair, attempted a placating smile. She turned back to Kye, no longer finding reassurance in his face. What if Kye was now the enemy too – had been all along?

The pain in her body ebbed, and full vision returned. Adrenalin leaked away leaving only fatigue. Emme sighed. She couldn't remember when she felt this weary. She really just wanted to be asleep somewhere. The dagger in one hand, she pushed herself from the ground with the other. Kye stood with her. She replaced the dagger back into the top of her pants, allowed the silver handle to show prominently, and guardedly followed Kye down the stairs.

The men finally closed the door to the room and stepped the gap between the door and the edge of the closest table. Emme glanced regretfully at the panelled flat of the hardwood door. Somewhere beyond it was a bed, was *her* bed at the street kids' headquarters. If only Kye had taken her there. Even the fear of rejection, rejection from the street kids, did not match the dread she felt inside at being locked in a room with these two Ashrones.

"Emme, we are so glad to meet you," the white-haired man said. "I'm Imren, and you might remember Anderson, the other man you met in your forest." He gestured a hand blotted with pale brown age-spots to the dark-haired man beside him.

Emme's eyes narrowed. Yes, she remembered the sinister man. She remembered both of them.

"Please, have a seat." Imren motioned to the nearest six-seat table.

Hesitantly Emme shifted out the seat furthest away from the two men. She waited until the two men sat, then slowly lowered herself to the chair. Kye took the seat beside her, although right now his presence confused her. He was both a threat and a comfort.

"I'm sorry we frightened you back in your homeland," Anderson said. His indigo eyes, still youthful on a middle-aged face, seemed genuine enough, but Kye had instilled a fear of them into her. How could Kye now be sitting here calmly in their presence when they had brutally slaughtered that poor girl? "We were in a hurry to get to you before Prince Jaimis did."

Emme sucked in her breath, exhaled, "Don't say his name."

"It's all right," Imren said. "He cannot hear us in here. We have wards against that sort of thing."

"Wards?" Her eyes narrowed slightly. "What's a ward?"

"They mean a spell of protection," Kye said to her.

"Well, you must be very confused and frustrated by all of this." Imren's gentle face and tone alarmed Emme with its inappropriateness. He should have been cold, evil-looking with a harsh, chilling voice.

"I am," she said warily. "And being here doesn't help."

The door handle clicked, turned. The panels swung towards the wall, and Emme snapped to her feet, dagger in hand. A gaunt, young man entered, clutching a tray of hot drinks with bony fingers. The young man paused, startled, as light flicked off the dagger blade.

She felt Kye's hand, a gentle pressure on her arm. "It's all right, Emme," he said quietly. Slowly she sat down and replaced the dagger, but her hand remained on the cold iron of the comforting hilt until the relieved boy left the room.

Imren slid glazed pottery mugs and chunky woven coasters around to them. "I hope you like tea."

"Not poisoned tea," Emme muttered, and to her surprise, Imren laughed.

"My dear, we have been waiting for you for over twenty years. We are not going to kill you now."

She looked to Kye who did not express any of the open confusion pulling at her own face.

Not soothed by Imren's words, Emme did not touch the tea in front of her, despite her longing for it. The rest of the room slowly sipped theirs, and Emme began to feel angry at the deceptively casual atmosphere when she herself was feeling as nervous as a criminal before a whipping.

"Can someone just tell me what's happening?" she asked sharply.

Imren set his mug onto the coaster and nodded. "Yes, but this is not going to be easy to tell you. You probably won't like what we have to say."

"If it means I can get out of here and go and sleep in a nice bed somewhere, you can tell me anything you like and I won't mind." Emme meant it. Right now she was too weary to care about anything they said, except that perhaps she was going to die some barbaric death like that Hunston girl.

"Does she know her history?" Imren asked Kye.

"Yes – very well. Well, she knows the incorrect version."

"Very good. It will save us the complication." Imren spoke as if Emme were not in the room.

Emme began to get the feeling all the men knew each other somehow. After all, Imren had not introduced himself to Kye.

"Where shall I begin, then?" Imren muttered to himself, eyes roaming the table as if the answers lay in the polish. He seemed to reach some decision and met Emme's expectant gaze. "Perhaps I should start with this. You remember about the Hunston girl?" Emme nodded. "Well, the Hunston girl did not die. But she did not live either."

304

Emme's brow arched neatly. "Now, that did not make sense at all."

Kye held up his hand to silence Imren's reply. "Let me tell her."

"Very well."

Kye shifted in his chair to face Emme. Emme saw in his face a glimpse of awkwardness she had never seen before. "I thought that the Ashrones were bad, Emme, because I really believed they killed the Hunston daughter so they could have power. But they did what they did to stop the prince because the prince was not worthy of the power the Hunston girl had, and not worthy to be king. I couldn't see it before now, because I too believed that the Hunston daughter had died; but she didn't die – she was removed for a while."

"Removed for a while? Where too?" Emme watched Kye keenly.

"She was removed for a while to a place where the prince would never find her, to a place where she would not have her power, and to a place where she would have no memory of who she was so the prince could never track down her thoughts."

"Right – so where was that place, and what does it have to do with me?"

Anguish passed briefly over Kye's face, and she wondered that he felt that for a woman eleven years his senior, supposedly dead for over twenty years.

"Emme – the Hunston girl was involved in a very complicated ritual to remove her soul, her essence from her body and cause her to be reborn in another form, in another country, in a forest very far away to a woman who thought that a man had assaulted her one night."

Emme coughed once, violently. She stiffened and stared at Kye. Her heart beat fiercely in her chest, clawed to get out. She could feel it ripping at her flesh. She felt hot and cold all at once, and her whole body went sweaty. "No – you can't be saying . . ."

"You are the Hunston girl, Emme."

"What a ridiculous story." Emme glared at the faces around the room. Why were they lying to her? Why was Kye of all people, lying to her?

"Your mother believed she was assaulted, Emme," Imren said. Emme looked at him sharply. "But the truth is, we planted your spirit in her womb, then created you as flesh in the hope that you would grow and come back to us one day."

"My mother wasn't – wasn't violated?"

Kye shook his head, and Emme swung back to him. "Not violated, Emme. Blessed."

"I – I don't believe you." Her voice shook.

Kye looked to the tabletop in thought. At last he got up, walked to his bag and pulled out the heavy antique manuscript. He moved back to the table, flicked through the pages until he found one he wanted. "This book," he pointed to the pages, "is a book of ancient rituals and spells that the Ashrones have used in the past three-thousand years. This particular ritual is the ritual for removing a person's soul to be reborn in another person's body. It can only be used with the person's permission, and only after direct permission from the Almighty to the Ashrones to use the ritual. The person is to be imprinted with a tattoo, a symbol on their wrist, so that they can be identified in their new form. Look at the picture, Emme." He pointed to the illuminated letter of the alphabet. His finger went to the tiny books little scribes touched with their ink-tipped feathers. The feathers drew the symbol that adorned her wrist, the exact complicated shape but for the slightly distorted lines on her flesh.

"But I can't be her. I can't be. I'm Emme. I don't remember being anybody but Emme."

"That was part of the deception," Imren said. "Unfortunately, you could not retain any memory of your former life, or the prince would use his power to track you down. Even with sending you far away, we could not take the risk. We also needed to send you far from this country where your power would not manifest itself. And we needed to send you to a new life for a purpose – to bring you back when the time was right, for a very special reason." His eyes flickered with some hidden thought, and right at that moment, Emme felt sick.

"I can't be her. I'm not. I really would know if I . . ."

"I know it's hard to accept, but it's true," Kye said. "But you're still Emme. You're just Emme with Kara's power."

Emme snapped upright. "Kara?"

"That was her name," Kye said. "That's why Jaimis used that name. I'm assuming he originally called you Kara and had to cover up for it with a story about his sister."

"But I don't have any power. I'm very ordinary." She so desperately wanted it to be true. She wanted to block her ears and storm out of the room, not have to listen to these lies. These terrible, cruel lies.

Kye placed a hand on her arm, a hand meant to comfort her. But it chilled her. Still, she could not bring herself to snatch her arm away. She felt frozen in shock, grounded to her chair. He said quietly, "There weren't any coins in my pouch today."

Emme stared at him, eyes wide. Cold chills shot through her body. "What are you saying?"

Kye looked to Imren to explain.

Imren shifted in his chair, cleared his throat. "The Gift of the Asher is that the owner can create objects whenever he or she needs them. The idea is that kings can use the power to help with poverty, to create weapons when he needs them for times of invasion, to give countries what they need for survival, fairness and justice. When put in the wrong hands, it is utterly dangerous. The king with the gift need only think very clearly about what he needs, and the object is there. He can only control objects, and only ever objects of certain sizes. A limited yet very powerful gift."

Emme's body started shaking. She knew Kye felt it. His hand tightened on her arm, and when she looked back into his eyes, there were depths of concern.

"Tell me about the coins," she said in the calmest voice she could muster.

"I needed to prove to myself that you had the gift. As soon as I suspected who you were, things started to fall into place – the way you always found the exact food you asked for, the way you described how you escaped the castle, the name Kara, that time you once said to me that you always feel older than what you really are. So I tested it. At first I asked you what you wanted for lunch, and was puzzled when it didn't come. Then I realised it had to be more specific, more of a command. So I got you to read the price board and tell me exactly what we needed to pay for lunch, knowing I didn't have any money. When I opened the pouch, the exact amount of coins you asked for were there."

Emme was visibly trembling. "Is it true?"

Kye nodded. "Yes, it is."

"How –" She stopped to gather herself, to hide the shaking in her voice. "How did you plan to pay for the food if – if I didn't ..."

"Produce the money? The master of the kitchens is one of my contacts. He always gives me a free meal. I went to talk to him when I used the restrooms."

Emme started to put the pieces together in her mind, to play with them to see if they fit. Her mother had always said she didn't remember what happened – had always sworn she had only had one drink. *Of course* she couldn't remember what happened. She had gone to bed as per normal, and woken up pregnant with a child from another country.

No. It wasn't right. There were still pieces missing. "If my mother was a virgin, surely *someone* would have known. I mean, you can't hide it from the midwives who –" Emme stiffened as realisation sliced through her. Kye met her shocked expression with deep pity.

The villagers knew. They *knew*. They did not hate her for illegitimacy; they hated her for her ominous conception. *Devil Child*, they had called her. They knew; every single one of them knew that no one had touched her mother. The village gossips would have quickly spread the midwives' discovery. And they all hated Emme for the fear she created in them. Wendaya, all Emme's life, tried to convince herself that Emme was born of abuse, but even Wendaya knew the truth – hated Emme for the supernatural way she had been conceived. Wendaya was not an outcast for her infidelity – she was an outcast because they believed the devil had chosen her to conceive his child. And they feared Wendaya too. And Wendaya believed it. That was why she hated Emme so much – Emme was the devil child Wendaya was forced to raise.

Was there even a law from the Creator that illegitimate children were to be treated badly, or was that a cover-up for why they hated her – an excuse to beat her without reminding themselves of the devilry that conceived the strange child? She had sensed it all her life: they hated her and yet feared her. She thought it was her fighting abilities, her hard-won independence that they feared. But no – it had gone on long before that. That's why they didn't want her at their village dances, why they had nearly killed her one night in a frenzy of fear. They were afraid she was the devil's child and would curse their religious celebrations – would bring evil on future harvests and hunts. Damn them all – they *knew*.

Anger swelled inside at what she had endured for nothing – for *nothing*. "How could you send me there?" She glared at Imren, at Anderson. "Do you know what I went through in that forest? How much people hated me?"

"We're sorry, child." A genuine fatherly expression touched Imren's features. "We did not know what we were sending you to at the time. We only hoped to send you somewhere simple; somewhere totally different from ours without politics and complications so that you would be somewhat empty of knowledge and easy to teach about our ways when it came time to bring you back. And perhaps somewhere that would teach you survival skills – to be strong and courageous like Kara used to be."

"Well you sent me to hell," she half-shouted.

"I'm so sorry, child – I really am," Imren said. "We did not know until we sent a Kildarian to teach you. He was to move into your village to guide you and help to raise you, to make you ready to bring back. But your villagers turned him away when he befriended you. Only then did we realise how much you were suffering, but we could not bring you back. Firstly, you had to will it, and secondly, we could not risk bringing you back here before it was time, lest Jaimis get his hands on you."

"Well he did anyway." Emme still glared at the white-haired man.

"Yes." Imren's face clouded over with a deep sorrow that quenched some of the anger inside Emme. She knew intuitively the sorrow was not for her and wondered at the depth of pain. "There was a traitor in our midst. A man who offered his soul to the dark powers, and joined Jaimis."

Silence tightened the space. Imren seemed to be dwelling on a private anguish as though for the first time.

Anderson jumped into the silence, tactfully deflected attention.

"You see, we get our powers from the Almighty. He is the giver of it, and He alone decides when we can use our powers and how. Our powers are very limited, but they are strong. Rastin, the traitor, gave his allegiance to Althator –" Anderson jolted as though cuffed, and flushed. "I mean, the devil – and earned for himself a much wider power than any of us have seen before."

"Why did you just call the devil that name?" Kye asked. "And apparently mistakenly?"

Anderson nodded as the flush spread to his ears. "An error on my behalf. It is his true name, the power-carrying name. The name carries both access to the devil's power and a way to undermine it. We have been using it for so long in these halls, we forget that it is not to be heard or used by ordinary man."

"And what is this power that Rastin has accessed?" Kye asked Anderson.

"Yes – a very dangerous power, much, much wider. He does not need immediate and direct permission anymore to use his power, and he can do things many of us never imagined."

"Why did he turn?" Kye asked.

"He grew weary of the deadlock," Imren said, discipline pushing grief aside. "And he always did have an affiliation with Jaimis before the murders." He looked at Emme again. "Only four of us knew of your location. Only four had the secret. Rastin waited very patiently for many years, not hinting at his powers, for if he had used his powers, we would surely have detected the evil source and hunted out the traitor. When Rastin discovered your location, he sent for you and began the nightmare that you have been living until now. I suspect that Jaimis moved too early, or you would not have been so fortunate as to escape."

"So, what is Jaimis going to do with me?" Emme asked.

"Well, for a start, my child, Jaimis is not going to do anything with you, now that we have you here safely. But if you leave our protection, Jaimis could find you, and then he will take the power from you and be the rightful king. We believe he has already been setting up procedures to claim your power. He has been using many portals of late which means the Kildes princes must have arrived – essential witnesses to the ritual of taking the power."

Emme felt her body start to shake again. "The power is passed when a man . . ."

"Takes a woman sexually, yes," Imren said bluntly.

Emme's eyes flashed as she stared at Imren. "Filthy pig. He had better not lay a hand on me." Emme felt a whirl of confusion as she realised everything she had thought about men was a lie. Men were not all evil; all men did not want to violate women. Emme was not living proof of men's persistent lust and power over women. She glanced at Kye, felt her cheeks burn as she looked at him. She had been so wrong all that time and yet ironically, the moment she realised it, she also learned that one man did seek to violate her – to *rape* her.

"So now that I'm here, what are you going to do with me? I don't understand why you brought me back? You're only back to where you started from. I'm here, supposedly Kara, with my power, and Jaimis has the opportunity to come and get me. How have you achieved anything by doing all of this and then bringing me back? You should have banished me forever so Jaimis could never get the power."

The three men looked at each other, sent questioning glances.

"Should we tell her?" Anderson asked Imren.

Imren nodded. "Yes, I suppose we should."

"Suppose?" Emme stared openly at the three of them. Her voice was quiet, a little fragile as she said, "Don't you think you owe me an explanation?"

The door flung open, whacked against the nearest wall, and a flushed young man entered, puffing heavily. He wore the white skullcap the others wore, but his hand sat unadorned of a tattoo. "Forgive the intrusion, Master Imren, but there's been trouble." The young man stooped, dragged in lungfuls of air, gestured spread fingers as if calming a frantic crowd. Finally he gathered himself, straightened. "Large groups of children, and a few adults, are being led in chains to the castle. We think they are the street kids people talk of, which means that the prince is ready for his plans."

Kye shot to his feet. "My kids. Were any of them hurt?"

"Many did not look too good, sir," the young man said.

Her street kids. Emme felt sickness swell in her stomach. Her precious street kids.

Imren turned wide eyes beneath high arched brows to Kye. "*You're* the leader of the street rats?"

"I am." Kye's hand clutched the hilt of his rapier, fingers white and tight.

"My – you have surprised me," Imren said. "I had wondered who led those wonderful children – they have been a real blessing to Kildes."

"What does the prince hope to do with them?" Kye demanded of the two men.

"Eliminate some of his opposition and send a warning to the rest. He believes the street rats have no scruples and will rise up against his claim to the throne. He believes your spread to be very wide, judging by the shipments of weapons and the information you manage to gather."

Kye's jaw tightened. "We've got to get those children back before we find out the hard way if he intends to kill them."

Imren stood swiftly. "Let's see what powers the Almighty will lend us tonight. Eston –" He turned to the messenger. "Gather the Council of the Five to the Chamber of Prayers."

The young man nodded, chest still heaving, and scurried away, a hand pinning his white skullcap to his head.

"Follow me," Imren said. He turned and paced to the doorway.

Kye followed swiftly after; long, strong strides indicating controlled haste. Emme scraped the chair back across the rug, stood.

Emme felt a stinging breeze begin to stir all around her, and gasped.

Kye swung sharply to her, eyes keen. "What's wrong?"

"I – I feel like something's . . ." The room began to blur. Distinct books melded into a mass of tawny. The roof swirled like a spinning top. As though the hub of a whirlpool, Emme felt dragged and pulled in all directions at once. An aftershock of the invisible barrier she had smacked into?

"Emme, what is it?" she heard Kye ask. Was she swaying? She slapped a hand onto the table to steady herself, leant forward. She heard the dull thud of the solid chair behind her toppling onto the rug.

Kye did not move, seemed torn between her and the door. His face remained blurred, a smudged painting against the whirlpool.

An abrupt hissing whirr, like air rushing into a tube, made her turn. A large void, a gaping black mouth, yawned into the room, opened larger and larger to swallow her. It swirled and tumbled, a gate into terrifying darkness. She felt pulled towards it, a part of air being sucked backwards. She clutched at the thick edge of the table, but fingers soon slipped across the polish, drawn back by the void. She used strength to pull herself forward with fingers, felt the cold of the table through her torso. The pull of the inhaling mouth strengthened. Fingers groped at anything. She felt knuckles crack against something hard. The pottery mug upturned scalding liquid over her hand and across the table. She yelped, involuntarily withdrew the hand. She had let go. The void had her. Helplessly, she watched the table withdraw beyond reach.

She heard Kye yell, saw him jolt as his body painfully struck an invisible wall. The Ashrones were shouting, faces pale. Their lips moved whilst hands traced patterns, trying to vanquish the void.

"Hang on, Emme," Anderson called, arms outstretched.

Her calves scraped painfully across jutting chair-legs as she hovered over the upturned chair toward the giant mouth.

"Help me." The chair legs no longer scraped Emme's calves. She saw it join the blurred backdrop of room and frantic men trying to get to her. She blinked once, cleared the haze for the briefest moment. She beseeched Kye's anguished, frustrated face as he attempted to fight against the buzzing barrier. Each push against the rippling barricade clearly hurt him. She reached out a hand for anyone, anything that might grab it, but the last thing felt of the room was air around her hand sucking it into the void.

Emme knew the gate, knew the tunnel, knew she would end up somewhere she did not want to be. This time the gate terrified her for what she knew about it, not for what she did not.

Pale light flickered at the other end, and she fought against the current, petrified of what she would see when she reached the light. She prayed that the Ashrones had found a way to turn the gate around, to rescue her.

The light swelled to a round wall, and she felt herself fling from the portal. Her feet touched carpeted floor, and she whisked her dagger from her belt. Too many men lunged for her. Fingers, hands, arms, solid red-breasted torsos, all meshed around her, pressed her flesh to close her in. She felt the terror of confinement, felt her breath begin to quicken. Robbed of strength by sickness and a journey, Emme watched them swiftly overcome her resistance. She tried to stab at out something, felt her dagger tip scrape flesh and saw a redcoat guard step back, hand on a bleeding arm.

Thrust by the impact of strong men, she smacked back against the carpet, dazed. Instantly men were on top of her. She felt the dagger being pried from her clenched fingers and slammed back into her trouser top. The keen edge of it sliced a shallow line down her stomach. She kicked and screamed in rage. "Get off me," she yelled over and over, but strong hands and toned muscles held her tight before she could get in a position to fight back.

"Bring her over," a chillingly familiar voice commanded, and she felt herself being lifted by her arms and legs and carried as though a battering ram. She writhed, tried to free her limbs, but too many hands held her, pinched her flesh. She stared up through a tunnel of redcoat torsos and unrecognisable faces. Feathers plumed from wide-brim hats. Beyond the feathers, she could just see a portion of a beamed roof. The beamed roof became red canvas of a bed canopy. She felt herself being lowered to the bed, then more men jumped over to pin her down. She cried out in rage, in terror. "Get your hands off me, you filthy pigs."

"Gag her," the voice of Jaimis said, "and tie her to the bed."

A rough rag was thrust into her mouth. She choked on it. "Careful," a vaguely familiar voice snapped, "don't hurt her."

A hand, forcefully gripping hair, yanked her head up. More brutal hands tied a cloth tightly around her mouth to hold the gag in place. Her hands were pulled roughly and tied via abrasive ropes to each bedpost.

She glared at the faces around the room. Beyond the redcoats, many unrecognisable men, each in different, distinct combinations of colours, stood around the room, faces sullen. She looked left and saw a harsh face stare at her keenly. She inhaled sharply. The man from the tavern who had given her the weather shock. Not a weather shock, she realised in a blink. The bastard Rastin – the evil Ashrone the other Ashrones had warned her about.

Jaimis was there, sickeningly well dressed with neat hair and a trimmed beard. She could smell the stench of his cologne even from the bed. His cool green eyes regarded her with an intensity of a man about to win everything. The soldiers finished their task, stepped back.

"Now leave us," Jaimis ordered, and the room cleared of all redcoats.

Emme kicked, struggled against the ropes. The room was stuffy, hot. It reeked of Jaimis' cologne. The strong scent of lemon sheets and old rag assailed her nostrils.

"Is this really her?" one of the strangers in the room asked.

"Silence," Rastin said, and the man dissolved to quiet. Rastin rose up, tall and formidable. "Princes of Kildes, you are all here to witness the dawning of a new era. You are here to witness the union of the Daughter of the Hunstons with the Heir of Endoria. Here, in this room, will be the coronation of our new and glorious king. Long may he live."

"Long may he live," the men returned in dreary monotone.

Rastin approached Emme. He touched his dry, hot palm to her brow, and Emme felt a terrible and dark power pass from his hand to her whole body. The power burrowed into her very essence; strapped her up inside until her spirit felt trussed like an animal for slaughter. Without being told, she knew the invisible ropes tethered Kara's gift, to stop Emme striking the prince with her thoughts.

The invisible viscous tar, having bound its victim, poured from her as though burning tar gushing from her skin. It began to fill the room until it encompassed the whole bed. Then it engorged the entire room, making the room feel dark, thick, like she swam in hot mud.

"Watch now. You are here to witness that this is a true and untainted union."

Half the room began to burn red; the other throbbed with green.

"See," Rastin continued, a tone of cold formality. "See how the room glows with the colours of the two families. Red for the powerful and noble Endorian family. Green for the honourable and just Hunston family. Watch, for the two will unite if this is a true union." Gradually the two colours fused like a violent mating ritual until the room pulsed with churning red and green. The luminous lights made Emme squint, made her ill inside.

"Do you acknowledge that this is a true union of the two houses?" Rastin demanded.

"We do," the men said in joyless tones.

"Then pay homage to your new king and queen." One by one the princes filed past Jaimis. They kissed his chunky emblem ring, then pressed lips to Emme's bound hand. She struggled to flick off their kisses with what little movement she had, but it only made friction from the ropes blister her wrists. Pity smouldered behind every pair of eyes that passed her. She silently pleaded with them to do something, to stop this crime. Not one did anything. Not one, under Kildes Law, had the power to stop a union stitched into the very fabric of their society.

Every pair of eyes acknowledged it was rape. Every pair of eyes suffered defeat. Finally the prince they despised would become the king they would fear and hate until their dying day.

Only one man said anything. An elderly gentleman with a full grey-flecked beard turned to Jaimis. "Give her some dignity, and turn down the lights."

The last to leave, Rastin bowed to the prince. "She will give you the power – and you will be king. Serve well, My King."

He closed the door, and the colours disappeared, leaving dim choking light in the room.

Jaimis' eyes danced with lust – lust for victory, lust for her. He approached her, revelled in the terror, the sickness in her eyes.

She struggled, tried to kick him. Tried to knee or elbow him anywhere that might do damage. *Kye!* she screamed. *Kye – you promised. You promised you would always protect me. You promised you would never let this happen again.*

He removed her dagger first, held it up to the light, inspected it. He noted the thin line of blood on its edge, touched his fingers to the stinging cut on her stomach. His selfish concern dissipated swiftly with the realisation the cut was minor, then he flung the dagger across the room. It landed tip down in a cushion on one of the chairs.

He laughed, and Emme knew it was not the dagger he found funny. He laughed at his victory, laughed at the promise of power. Laughed that he had won. He had won.

Kye, she screamed again. *Please help me. Please.* The rag muffled her tearless sobs as he unbuttoned his shirt and threw it to the floor.

He seemed to be eager yet patient, sickeningly patient – a cat with a mouse it longed to devour, after playing with it a while.

Kye! She wanted to stab her dagger through Jaimis' heart. She would kill him. When this was over, she would kill him. She struggled again, managed to loosen the rope on her left leg and snapped her knee into his groin.

He grimaced, doubled over, gasped for air. His face twisted for long moments, then it smoothed. He straightened. His green eyes flickered with something worse than before – more excitement. And in that moment, Emme could see just what kind of a man could murder his own kin. He raised his hand, struck her hard across the face with the back of it.

The pain cracked through her skull, jerked her head to the opposite side. She shut her eyes briefly, squeezed out the throbbing, then opened her eyes and glared up at him defiantly. He laughed at her a little as though she were merely a child having a tantrum. Then he went to the four corners of the bed, yanked each roped tight until she could no longer move even fractionally. She felt the burning pain in every joint stretched to the edge of endurance.

He had won. After all she had gone through, Jaimis the vile pig had won.

He came back, sat beside her on the bed, then noticed the pleading in her eyes. He went to the candles, lit all of them, turned up every lantern, flaring the room into a blaze of light.

He carefully sat back down on the mattress, stared down at her. His hand stroked her bruised, burning face with a gentleness that reviled her. Instinctively she knew it would be the last gentle thing he did. She was determined, in that moment, to hate him with her very being – to defy him at every moment with her mind, if not her body.

He glanced once into a luminous corner, then turned all merciless attention to Emme. "No dignity," he said quietly, and the brutal ritual began.

12

Emme lay in total darkness, alone, frightened. The erosive ropes had long since been removed, and a coarse blanket unceremoniously thrown over her naked body, but she felt too shocked, too vulnerable to move.

Revulsion. Fear. Anger. Despair. The dark emotions scorched through her sickened, burning body whilst her mind involuntarily went over and over what had happened. Her stomach spasmed. Hot and cold rushed across her skin. She rolled to the edge of the bed and vomited over the side.

She used the scratchy blanket edge to clean her mouth, then lurched forward and vomited again onto the shadowed rug.

More hours passed in darkness. She no longer knew how much time had gone by. Three thoughts began to war for supremacy. Jaimis had won, and she felt revulsion for it. Kye had not come for her. Deep distress replaced the revulsion. The Ashrones had not protected her as they promised. Rage rose up to burn distress and revulsion away. The emotions cycled again – each one vied for space. Revulsion. Distress. Rage.

She found strength to set feet to the floor. She rested her head in hands, wiped her face with palms, then stiffly stood. Her whole body ached in ways she had never felt before. How could anyone – *anyone* – willingly go through a depraved act like that?

She dressed cautiously, tested the limit of each ache with slow, difficult movements. The masculine clothes mocked her as they covered over her blemished flesh. They had not saved her.

Had not protected her from the one thing she had always worn them for. She saw no need for them now. No man would ever claim her again, for she was Jaimis' wife, and he had taken what he needed. Now he would return to his lover's bed, leaving Emme free to live in loneliness all her days, free to live with the revulsion she knew she would always feel for herself. She felt nausea swell again, and she sat on the edge of the bed to steady herself. She rubbed at the stale sweat on her face with hands that still shook.

She wanted so desperately to talk to Kye, but knew she could not look at him. She had allowed Jaimis to win – allowed him to rape her. She was spoiled, ruined. She was just a vulnerable, weak woman after all. She had deceived herself so readily all these years – taught herself to think it would never happen to her, when she should have just been preparing for the inevitable. Perhaps then it would not have felt so horrifying as it did now.

Emme stood, lit a candle and walked over to the gilded mirror above a washstand. Deeply sad acorn-brown eyes above a bruised cheek stared back.

"Is this what you imagined, Kara?" she asked the reflection. Her breath appeared on the glass, a frosty haze over her likeness. She smudged it with her sleeve and stepped back. "Is this what you imagined would happen when you sacrificed your life to stop the prince?" The face stared back at her with deep sorrow in its eyes. It pitied her. "I'm sorry I let you down, Kara. You should have been sent to someone else – to someone who could have stood up to Jaimis. But you became me." Still the eyes pitied her.

She wondered who Kara had been in her former life. Beautiful. Kye had called her beautiful. Well, there wasn't much beauty left in her now – just a battered, sad face.

Emme gazed at the pitying acorn-brown eyes; felt suddenly

so alone, so frightened, like a little girl again. She turned away from the eyes, buried face in hands and cried. Streaks of salty water, restrained for sixteen years, poured down her face. She fell to her knees, sobbed brokenly, arms wrapped around herself as though a child seeking protection. She so wanted to be a child in that moment; a child with loving parents to hold her, soothe her, tell her everything would be all right.

When Emme felt empty of all tears and all emotion, she gathered up the tattered threads of her pride, stood and washed her face with the soapy water in the washbasin. Using the folded towel, she patted the water away, soothed red lids with the edge of it. She was queen now, and she had rights, she tried to tell herself over and over to reclaim some vestige of dignity so swiftly lost.

She knew instinctively that Jaimis had not just claimed her last night, he had tried to break her. The brutality, the bruises, the aching – it had been to cripple her spirit, to stop her creating problems for him as a queen with rights and aspirations. Somehow he had known her weakness and had exploited it fully, cruelly. The violence had been nothing short of premeditated.

She *felt* broken. He had crushed something inside her just as he intended. What rights could she possibly exercise to undo the damage of what he had done to her, to Kildes? What was there left to do but to – *The street kids!*

The thought jolted her alive. The streets kids were here, and they were going to die if she did not do something. Jaimis had won her power, but he would not win the deaths of those innocent children.

She hurried to the door, found it locked. She jerked it violently, kicked it, yelled at it, but the lock would not budge.

The window! She ran to the window, flung up the rattly glass pane and peered outside. The bricks she had descended on her first day in the city no longer protruded. She realised with a shiver that Kara's power had created the escape. The ladder! She remembered that now too. The ladder in the snow that the chimneysweep kid had questioned her over had also been Kara's power. *Her* power, she corrected. She *was* Kara. And Emme. A concept she would have to get used to.

"Help me, Kara. How do I get out of here?"

She spotted a servant in plain workman's clothes strolling through the dark courtyard, a shovel over his shoulder, and realised the dawn was coming. He hummed merrily as he walked.

"Hey you," Emme yelled down at him. The servant stopped, stared up, scratched his capped head. "Get me out of here. By – by order of the queen."

He blinked, eyes wide.

"The door to Prince Jaimis' bedroom is locked. Come and get me out of here."

Had the servants been forewarned of the queen's arrival? "Of – of course, Your Majesty." It seemed so. "I'll be right up. I'll just – just go see the Master of Keys." He dropped the shovel into the snow and disappeared into a doorway's darkness.

Emme paced the room with sharp, deliberate turns as light slowly rose over the castle grounds. At last she heard a key scratching in the door's lock.

The door swung open and a shy, weathered face peered around it. "Are you all right, Your Majesty?"

"I'm fine. I'll have that key to the door, thank you."

"Of course, ma'am." The man stepped into the room, handed her the knobbly key. He shifted weight from foot to foot, waited for instructions, then seemed to remember himself. He swept the cap from his head and, clutching it to his chest, bowed clumsily. "I'm one of us groundskeepers, ma'am. Max. If I can ever be of service to you."

"You can start by telling me where the street kids are."

The man scratched thinning grey hair, stared at the ground. "Well, now, I don't know anything about any street kids."

"Then can you take me to someone who does?"

"Well, let's see. Are they – I mean, would they be somewhere in the castle, Your Majesty?"

"Yes, they're prisoners, I suspect."

"Well, now, then the captain of the guards probably knows all about it. If you'll follow me."

He led her through the enormous and elaborate interior of the castle. Tapestries, mirrors, paintings and panelled timber covered the vast stretches of sandstone walls. Unadorned rooms and corridors were painted in dark hues or stark white. Long, faintly lit corridors led to places she could only imagine. Hideous gilded chandeliers, dripping with tear-shaped crystals, hung in even commonplace rooms.

Very few servants hurried through the halls at this early hour. Those who did, carried baskets of linen, trays of baked breads, or cleaning tools on their way to some scarcely dusty sector of the spotless castle.

Max took her to one of the feathered-hat guards on duty. The broad, flaxen-haired guard's keen eyes watched them approach.

"Begging your pardon, sir." The gardener's hands wrung the woollen cap. "But Her Majesty, the Queen, would like a word." The request spent, the gardener stepped back into shadows.

The guard saluted and bowed to her. His feather dipped and bobbed, then he straightened. "How can I help you, My Queen?"

Emme felt anger choke her throat briefly, wondered if the guard was one of several to restrain her on that vile bed. "Are you the captain of the guards?"

"No, Your Majesty. Would you like to speak to him?"

"I would. Take me to see him at once." It amazed her she could muster such a stern, haughty tone. Anger made her feel invincible.

The soldier bowed again, then led her with powerful strides through a maze of corridors to a double door. "I believe he is watching over the king's breakfast this morning."

Emme felt a chill blow through her at the title. A shock of sickness gripped her stomach, but she stiffened proudly. Her precious street kids depended on her to be strong. Resolve washed away nausea.

The soldier gestured to the panelled doors. No handles adorned them, only a two-way hinge to allow easy access. "The door to the king's dining room." He raised a hand to knock.

"Don't bother." She pushed past the guard, flung open the right-hand door.

She stepped into a lavish room complete with large vases of flowers, heavily carved dressers, big latticed windows overlooking a sheltered winter garden, padded stools, and a buffet of plates, bowls and delicate goblets. A large excessively polished dining table stretched through the middle beneath a heavy, ridiculous chandelier of gold and crystal. The table was set with fine crockery, delicate lace placemats and gleaming silver implements. Jugs of fruit juices and platters of sugary pastries, enough for ten, sat before two people.

Jaimis looked up from his intimate conversation with the blonde-haired Ennika, his supposed sister. In the corner, the captain of the guard whisked out his rapier at her sudden entry.

Jaimis' eyes widened. "How did you get out?" He glared at the guard behind Emme who shrugged before hastily disappearing down the hallway.

Ennika's face grew chalky. Long elegant fingers clutched at

Jaimis' arm for support, her eyes watching Emme's every move.

Emme felt a sense of satisfaction; she held the upper hand in this room. She moved straight to the captain of the guard who slowly replaced his rapier. Now *that* face she remembered. The dark, almost black eyes, the soil-brown beard and hair, the thin scar on his left cheek. Those hands, the eerily well-kept hands, had sealed her silence with a dry rag. "Take me to where the street kids are."

The captain hesitated, sent a questioning glance to Jaimis.

"Do you dare deny your queen?" Emme demanded.

"No – no of course not, Your Majesty. I'll take you to them at once." He stepped out from his corner to walk across the room.

Jaimis stood swiftly. His white embroidered napkin fell from his lap to the floor. "I must object," he said, and the captain stopped. The captain looked from one to the other, clearly deciding who to obey. "I have ordered you to stand guard over me whilst I enjoy a leisurely breakfast, and that is what you must do."

Emme felt sick at the sound of Jaimis' voice. Memories of the brutal night rocked her. She glared at him defiantly whilst her mind worked quickly. Clearly the king's commands were greater than the queen's, but only, it seemed, orders preceding hers.

Emme smiled mockingly at the captain, said with sugar and acid tone, "Then tell me where I might find them, and I will go myself."

"They're in the main dungeons," he replied nervously. "I'll have one of my men take you there."

Jaimis hastily moved from behind his chair, paced cautiously closer to Emme, still within the safety of the table's bounds. "My love." His voice dripped fake affection. "What do you want to see the street rats for?"

Emme's head turned slowly, dangerously to Jaimis. She walked over to him, confidently close, eyes flashing. She grabbed

327

his used fork and without warning, stabbed it into his leg. He cried out, grabbed the handle of the protruding fork.

She heard Lady Ennika shriek, saw her rise to her feet, alarmed as blood flowed from the wound. The woman's ashen cheeks drained to sickly white.

The captain of the guard rocketed over.

"Touch me or call me that again," Emme said in a low voice, "and I will kill you. I am willing to die at the hands of your Kildes Law for that."

The captain reached strong arms to restrain Emme, but she shot back a few paces and turned her sugary smile to him. "Just a lovers' quarrel. I'm sure you cannot send your queen to prison for that."

The captain hesitated, silently questioned the king. Jaimis slowly reefed the fork from his leg. It dropped to the stone floor with a clang.

He grabbed a napkin and sopped up blood that spurted like meat juices from a roast.

Emme turned on heels and strode to the door. At the double doors, she spun to face Jaimis, stared coldly at his wincing green eyes. "You got everything you wanted at the expense of everyone else, but you never counted on me. I'm queen now, Jaimis, and you're going to have to kill me like you did your brothers, or I'm going to make your life a living hell."

She turned and marched confidently from the room. Fresh anger bubbled inside and with it, pride. She was Kara-Emme, Queen of Kildes, and she would not let anything defeat her.

Emme hastened through the corridors until she spotted guards. The four stood to attention at her approach, and she noted with a faint rise of brows how quickly the description of their new queen had been circulated.

"One of you: take me immediately to the main dungeons.

Bring some keys. The rest of you: go and bring the Ashrones – all of them – to the castle. No one is to stop their arrival, by order of the Queen of Kildes."

"At once, Your Majesty," the senior of them said. His lion-embroidered, red pinafore flapped out as he spun on knee-high boots. "You heard her. Move at once to the Ashrones." He turned back to Emme whilst the other guards jogged away down the hall. Their suede boots clacked on the timber as they ran, and the rapiers at their side jiggled in time to bobbing feathers on their wide-brimmed hats.

"Follow me, Your Majesty." The man set off at a solid pace down the corridors. Emme followed him down flights of stairs, through dawn-flecked courtyards and to a freestanding building in a state of disrepair near the highest point of the castle fortress. Early morning sun, unhindered by clouds, emphasised every crack, every white speck of peeling paint, the rotting timber of an off-centre doorway. He pushed open the groaning door and entered behind Emme.

Emme smelled the foul stench of aged blood, urine and rotting food that wafted from a distant source. Cobwebs garnished the landing of a staircase that spiralled down to darkness. A windowless, torch-lit corridor stretched the length of six mouldy, lumpy beds. Guards sat upon them engaged in bawdy conversations and a dice game. They snapped to attention, smoothed uniforms as they attempted to stand.

The guard at her side drew a primitive blazing torch from a socket. He took a large keychain from a hook on the wall near the door. The heavy keys jangled as her escort raised a hand to settle the guards. They hesitantly sat back down on their beds.

The closest guard remained standing. "No one but the king is to go down there, sir."

Emme's escort gestured his head nervously towards Emme. "This is your queen." Instantly the guards stood, saluted, bowed. "She has asked to see the prisoners."

"Of course, Your Majesty," the outspoken guard said, head still bowed. "Forgive me."

Her guide took her down the stone staircase that seemed to spiral forever. Emme felt the cold envelope her with each step. The stench grew stronger, and she momentarily covered her face with the edge of her shirtsleeve. Gradually she could hear coughing echoing in the darkness, then murmuring voices. A few more steps down delivered sounds of crying. Distress twisted her stomach, and her pace quickened on the slippery, narrow steps.

The stairs opened to a corridor lined on either side with numerous barred cells. The cold, flat slab floor flickered eerily in the guard's yellow torchlight. Small hands clutched at bars as the light illuminated the closest cells. Faces peered impatiently through the bars, cheeks dimpling where vertical iron pushed against them. Emme noted that the stairs wound down to an even lower, sunless level.

"Emme," a voice said. A freckled hand reached out through the bars.

"Dusty." Emme's voice held raw pity as she ran to the hand. "You there," she barked to the guard. "Light all the torches. Let these children have some light, for goodness sake."

The guard nodded and numbly obeyed.

"Dusty," Emme said as she turned back to the swollen face. Blood crusted his cheek and nose, and she reached in, touched the face gently. "What did they do to you? What have they done to all of you?" She scanned pallid, frightened faces, saw tear-stained eyes, bruises, blood, soiled skin, and heavily soiled clothes.

330

Rotting straw provided their only beds, buckets of fetid water their only drink. Excrement and decaying food from past prisoners had long since rotted to form a floor of compost beneath their feet.

"What are you doing here, Emme?" Dusty asked. "How did you find us?"

"It's a long story. Right now, I just want to get you out of here." She ordered the guard, "Get these children out of this cell at once."

The guard hesitated. "I cannot do that, Your Majesty."

She heard numerous young voices gasp, murmur at the title. She kept her eyes fixed on the guard. "Do you dare defy me?"

"They are scheduled to be tried and executed for crimes against the king on the morrow. I cannot let them out. It is the law."

Executed? Her stomach constricted. "At least take them up for some fresh air and a decent meal," she snapped.

"Your Majesty . . ."

"I take full responsibility for them. They won't escape." She returned to Dusty's face. "Make sure no one tries to escape. Not yet. I'll think of a way to get you out of here."

Dusty nodded.

The guard hesitated still. "Take them, guard," she shouted, "before I have you thrown in here too."

Dusty's eyes widened with questions. "'Your Majesty?' How is that possible?"

"I'll explain it to you, but not here. Up there."

One by one the cells' rusty locks turned under the guard's keys, and the children and adults ran from the prison, cheering and hugging each other. They flooded up the stairs, an unstoppable tide of people longing for daylight.

Emme noted every face, counted them. "Where's Halder?" she asked Dusty.

"He got out. He went looking for Kye, to warn him. He promised he'd come back for us – that he would get us out of here."

Illina gripped Emme in a hug, and Ada whispered a choked 'thank you' before the two ran to the men waiting at the stairwell. Ada kissed Red firmly, then selflessly helped children up the stairs.

Dusty waited until Lydia caught up from her cell. The two hugged each other for long moments. Emme felt pity, regret, burn her. How could everything have gone so wrong, so quickly?

Dusty turned to Emme. "I don't know how you did it, but thank you. And Emme?"

"Yes?"

"I'm so sorry about what happened back home. About what I did to you."

"Never mind, Dusty. It doesn't matter anymore. It really doesn't." She tried to reassure him with a smile. "Go, both of you. The sun is actually shining upstairs."

Dusty's eyes brightened. "Really?" He and Lydia walked arm in arm to the stairwell.

Emme followed after them, stopped when light coughing from a lower level met her ears. "You two go ahead. I'll be up in a minute." She watched them disappear around a bend, then turned to the guard. "Give me those keys and the torch, and you go up and make sure your guards don't haul the street kids back down here until I say so."

The keys jangled as the guard hesitantly handed them over. He passed the blazing torch to her. She waited until he was gone, then headed downstairs, deep into the cold earth. The shock of the invasive cold hit her thin shirt, and she felt a pang of pity for the unknown figure downstairs.

At the base of the stairwell, another row of cells stretched out upon a cheerless stone slab. Relieved, Emme noted the stairs did not continue to even lower levels in this sinister place.

Emme held the torch out and peered into one of the cells. Empty. These cells had not been used for a long time. No straw or excrement lined the floors, just worn stone, freezing underfoot. Manacles dangled from walls, abandoned. Beds, flat boards with no mattresses, hung from chains hooked into the low ceiling. She placed the torch into a socket on the wall at the base of the stairs. It illuminated several cells down before total darkness closed in. The torch behind her made her shadow stretch long across the burnished corridor floor.

Again she heard coughing and took jingling keys down the passageway. She could hear her boots scrape on stone, loud and eerie in the penetrating isolation of the prison block. She tiptoed to muffle the sounds. Her eyes were large and round as she tried to peer into the darkness. Who would be down here? The cough was too light to be Halder's.

She came to the third cell along and to her left heard the grating high-pitched creak of chains supporting the cell bed. She turned swiftly, then felt a torrent of emotions. Fear. Self-loathing. Fury at the injustice.

Kye. He sat on the bed's edge, stared at the ground, seemed not to have heard her over deep thoughts. She lifted the keys, the jiggle making him look up sharply. Instantly he rose to his feet in the gloom.

Her hands fumbled with a key in the lock. "How did you get here?" Her voice sounded choked.

His untucked shirt was tattered, striped with dirt, ripped at the shoulder. A patch of dirt marred his black trousers at each knee. Despite his dishevelled appearance, he stood straight, composed.

He was watching her, so many raw emotions on his face. Uncertainty. Feeble hope. Fear. Longing.

Her shaking hands finally fitted the right key to the lock. She heard the click as the lock turned. The swinging door groaned loudly in the stillness. She took two steps into the cell, then stopped, suddenly afraid he might loathe her for what had happened.

He swiftly closed the gap between them, looked down at her, searched her face. He wanted to know, she realised – wanted to know if what he suspected, what he feared, had come about. She knew he saw pain in her face, a depth of anguish never seen in it before.

"I came for you," he said quietly. "And they caught me. I tried to stop them, but I couldn't get to you in time."

Emme's stomach wrenched. She looked up into those deeply sad eyes and wanted to tell him everything was all right, but it wasn't. Jaimis had won.

"Jaimis –" She choked on the name. "He –" She couldn't finish the words, but didn't have to. He knew. He could see it in her face what had happened. Tears stung her eyes, and she felt foolish for them.

She knew Kye could not think of a single thing to say to her, not a single word to make it better. He wrapped an arm around her, pulled her to his chest, held her head to his shoulder with his hand. He rested his head on hers and just held her.

Her cheek on his chest, she sobbed, freely, openly, while he held her. She could hear his heart beating fast, felt the strong arms around her, and cried that those arms had not been there for her the night before, to save her and take her home.

"Can you forgive me?" Emme asked, tears still running from her eyes, her face still against him.

"Why?" she heard him say. "What could you possibly have done?"

"I couldn't stop him. There were too many men and I

couldn't stop him. I tried."

His arms tightened around her, and she felt him shake his head against her hair. "No, Emme, we've all let you down. We were supposed to protect you, to keep you safe. But we didn't."

Kye drew back a little, looked at her face. He put his palm on her damaged cheek, brushed her red, angry bruise with his thumb. Softly he said, "I hope he was gentle."

Emme shook her head slowly. Fresh tears fell.

Kye's hand stayed on her cheek. "I'm so sorry, Emme. I would have killed him before I let him hurt you."

"It's all right." Tears washed over Kye's hand. "It's not your fault."

"Emme, there's something I want to tell you; something I need to tell you." He steered her to the suspended bed, made her sit. His back against the ragged wall, he invited her to stay close, to lean against him. "I need to tell you about my past."

"It's all right. Whatever you've done, it doesn't matter now."

"No, it does." He watched her in the shadowed cell. "You see – I'm the reason you're here. I'm the reason the Ashrones were preparing to bring you back. They knew about me all along, even though I didn't know about them."

"I don't understand."

"When I was a boy, I met with the Ashrones and they gave me a prediction. That I would . . . That I would one day fall in love with the Daughter of the Hunstons. When the Daughter of the Hunstons died at their hands, I didn't know who to believe. I was crushed. I thought the Ashrones were the enemy, the great deceivers. But they're the ones who saved me."

"Saved you from what?"

"From murder at the hands of my brother."

Emme inhaled sharply.

"My name is Kael Yosiah Endoria, and I am the youngest son of the late king, the only surviving son of the brutal murders at the hands of my second oldest brother."

"Good Creator!" She had seen Jaimis' tattoo, had been too terrified to connect it to Kye's. Had not realised the tattoo meant the two men were flesh and blood. "You're a prince. The tattoo on your back . . ."

"Is the royal symbol, given to me at my royal naming ceremony at five, the year the Ashrones gave me the prediction which is customary for all princes. When I danced with you that night, Emme, I knew I was in love with you, and at first I thought I was throwing away everything I was working for. But as I lay in the darkness that night, I began to wonder if the prediction had been true after all, and it started to all fall into place who you were. I ran all night to the school and looked up a book on rituals the Ashrones have used in the past and realised that there was a violent ritual for relocating a person's essence, only to be used in the direst circumstances. Then I realised that the Ashrones were not the enemy, and all this time they had known about me, about my existence, or they would not have made moves to bring you back. They were waiting for the right time. For Kara's age to catch up to mine."

He sighed wearily. "There's so much I want to tell you. So much you should know. My brother thought I was dead. He sent Halder, his best personal assassin, to kill me, but Halder couldn't do the job."

Emme inhaled quickly. "Halder?"

"He's never been able to explain it, but something inside him broke – the Ashrones had cast their magic. When he looked at me, just a little boy, he couldn't kill me and knew all the gold in the world wasn't worth the task, but he knew that if he didn't kill me, someone else would, so he made plans to fake my death and help me to escape, then he would supposedly retire."

"Kye – take a breath."

Kye sighed, inhaled deeply. "My nurse helped me flee. We ran into the city and lived on the streets for a while. My nurse, she prostituted herself just to make money so I would survive. She became pregnant through her prostitution and died a few days after childbirth. She gave the boy to me to look after."

"Dusty," Emme realised. "Dusty is your nurse's son."

"I named him Dusty to give him a story to his name that would stop him questioning who he was, but I long to tell him that his life has given me life – that he is so much like a brother to me, for his mother was a true mother to me as well. If Dusty's mother had not sold herself for money, I would have died on the streets or been taken by the Black Bands." He paused wistfully. "Then I discovered Russen was still alive. He was once senior advisor to my father but fled the carnage when he realised anyone loyal to the dead king was being murdered. He helped me to survive, showed me many loyal people around the city who were in hiding from the massacre. Russen helped me to grow up as a gentleman. I was educated at the school, and he gave me training for my title on long nights when everyone else was asleep. Dusty was a young boy then and didn't remember anything about his life at the school. I realised he was getting older and at an age when he *would* start to remember things, so I moved to the underground home. We lived there a while, then when I was older, I vowed to do something about the terrible poverty of others. It started when I saved a young girl heading for prostitution. She then saved her friend and that friend's brother, and I knew what I had to do. Save as many kids, orphans, from the fate of the woman who had given her life to help me live."

"Why didn't you come here and claim the throne?"

"Jaimis is the older brother – he was the heir. I have no power to rule anything whilst he lives, and Jaimis would have only killed me before I could produce heirs."

"But you could have killed Jaimis."

His jaw tightened briefly. "I wish now that I had." Lost in his anger, empty silence, so vast in this space, rushed in to fill the absence of words. At last he said, "But I had to wait until I had worked out what to do about the Ashrones. I thought they were evil, that they would try to stop me with their arcane arts. But I was wrong about them, and I know now that they had me think that, so I would not claim my title before they brought you back."

"Then kill Jaimis now. *Please* kill him."

It clearly pained him to hear the pleading in her voice. "What good would that do? If I kill him, I die anyway for killing my king for no good reason, and then we have no Endorians left. The country will be in chaos."

"But he killed your brothers. Avenge their deaths."

"I have no legal basis to kill him. I'm the only one who had proof that Jaimis murdered my other brothers and my father, but it wouldn't stand under the law, for a king cannot be tried for crimes committed before his coronation. If I kill Jaimis, I'll be swiftly executed for murdering the king."

"Then do it subtly. I can put poison in his drink one night."

Kye shook his head. "No, Emme. I refuse to kill Jaimis in the underhanded way he killed my brothers. If I do, I'll be no better than him and not fit to rule. It has to be done by the law and only the law; and if I kill him any other way, I run the risk of being caught for murder and being executed for the crime under Kildes Law." He sighed. "Emme, I've thought about this. I've done nothing but think about this all night when I couldn't bear to think anymore about what he was – what he was doing to you. There is no other way. Jaimis is king now, and everything changes because of that."

"This isn't right. You'd be the better king. You deserve that throne and I – I want *you* to be my husband, not Jaimis." She saw anguish sweep across Kye's face at the title she gave his hated enemy. "But I'm queen now, and I need to make this right. For a start, you should go up and get some fresh air. I've commanded the guards to let the street kids out for a decent meal and air. I have no power to free them though. They're sentenced for execution."

Kye's muscles tensed. "He makes an example of them to the whole city for anyone out there who is thinking of working against him."

"Does Jaimis know about you?"

Kye shook his head. "The guards hauled me in here last night. I told them I was the leader of the street rats."

"You can't let him kill you, Kye. You have to tell him who you are."

"If he executes the street kids, he has to execute their leader – prince or no prince. Either way, Emme, I am dead, and my street kids need my courage right now. I won't let them die alone. Not when I'm responsible for their capture."

"Kye, you can't be responsible for everybody all the time." She stopped; stared at him as she realised he *was* responsible for everybody. He was an Endorian prince, and those street kids were some of his many subjects. *My people,* he had called them. That's where his feeling of responsibility came from. He was their prince.

"I wanted so much to tell the kids," he said more to himself. "But if they knew, knew who I was, Jaimis would eventually hear their thoughts. I had to have my own room or they would see the tattoo and notice that I rarely slept."

Emme looked at him with a puzzled frown.

"Endorian sons need very little sleep. It's why only Endorians are heirs to the Kildes throne. They can rule the country almost every hour of the day when they need to. An hour or two a week of sleep is all I need." He exhaled slowly as he leant his head against the wall. "But they couldn't know. Even now I can't tell them or Jaimis will know, and you mustn't think it outside of this cell either. You must ask the Ashrones to put protection around you to stop Jaimis hearing your thoughts or you will never be safe. He will always know what you're doing whenever he wants to."

"Are you able to hear when people talk about you?"

He shook his head. "The eldest living son has the gift."

Emme ransacked through memories, tried to fit it all together. Yes, it all made sense now. All but one thing. "What was the money for?"

"The King's Gold? Payment for my murder."

"I don't understand."

"Payment *of sorts* to Halder for my murder. Princes use King's Gold – money that can't be used as currency, as a message for their assassins. Two black bags of one hundred and seventy gold pieces for each victim, the name of the victim inscribed on paper and put at the bottom of one of the pair. After the murder, the prince supplies the paperwork for the assassin to have his outdated coins remade at the mint into a far more logical sum of fifty gold pieces. So it's a part payment."

"A part payment? But it goes from three hundred and fourty *down* to fifty."

"Three hundred and fourty coins are enough physical gold to melt down and make something decent. If the prince betrays the assassin by refusing the paperwork, the assassin can use blackmarket means to melt the gold into something valuable to sell. But it won't give him the same freedom and anonymity as a bag of coins. And the prince misses his chance to have most of his gold returned to the mint. It's a forced trust between them."

"I see. Two bags of King's Gold – actual gold." Then Emme frowned in the darkness. "But you had six bags. Didn't – Oh good Creator!" Her lips parted in shock.

Kye nodded slowly, confirmed what she realised. "Halder killed my two brothers, but he has amended for it. There is no hatred between us. I kept the bags as proof of the order to have me killed – of the murder of my brothers. Halder would have testified to the assassinations –"

"But his word would mean nothing," Emme cut in. "Anyone could make up a story like that to get rid of Jaimis."

"If Halder testified, he and Jaimis would have been executed for the crimes against my brothers, even though Jaimis ordered the murders. No man would give up his life for a lie."

Emme could not respond. All words paled against the magnitude of what Halder would sacrifice for Kye.

"And the handwriting on the death labels would have perfectly matched Jaimis' writing." Kye smiled sourly. "Halder's testimony and mine, and the gold, would have ensured Jaimis' execution. But I couldn't use it until I had worked out what to do about the Ashrones, because I thought they would try to destroy me to retain their supremacy." He added after a pause, "And I was in no hurry to end Halder's life."

Emme shook her head slowly. So convoluted, so complicated a path that led to such a simple brutal ending – Jaimis' victory.

"I don't know how to fix this, Kye," Emme said into the silence.

Kye stood slowly, reached down for her. She took his hand and let him pull her to her feet. He stared down at her, his eyes gentle and sad. "You'll make a good queen, Emme. Once people get past your clothes, they learn to love you. I've seen it happen. And you're courageous and proud. Like Kara was."

"Tell me about her. Who am I supposed to be?"

"You're supposed to be you. You're Kara, and you're Emme. Just be you. You're exactly what you need to be, to be queen – strong, defiant and a courageous leader. And you have a burning hatred of injustice like I do."

Tears swelled in Emme's eyes again. "You can't die on me. You can't leave me here alone, with *him*." She waved to the cell door as if Jaimis were there. "You've got to be here for me. You promised you would."

Her words stabbed at him. She saw the anguish in his eyes. He pulled her to him again, pressed her head to his shoulder and clutched her tightly. "I'm sorry, Emme. There is nothing left for me to do."

"There is," she sobbed onto his tattered shirt. "You can be with me, and you can tell me what to do."

"No, I can't. You belong to Jaimis now, and even if I'm caught doing this here with you," he strengthened his hold of her briefly, "I could die for treason. I can't stop him now. He has your power, and he is king. He will stop at nothing to destroy me if he finds out who I am."

Emme cried, shook, wanted to double over against the twisting of her stomach. Her whole being was crying. Her arms flew around Kye's waist and squeezed him, afraid to ever let go. She loved him, she realised. Loved him so much she would die inside if he were executed. For the first time she knew, *knew* why women gave their hearts to men, why they formed bonds of marriage and unity. She would rather die with Kye on the execution block than live a lifetime without him as queen of this cursed world. How cruel to know this now – to finally know love when it was about to be savagely taken away.

Long minutes went by, then Kye tilted her head back. He pressed his lips to her forehead, kissed it, then stepped back from her, unravelled her arms from around his waist. "Let's go join the street kids. They need us right now. Need us to be strong." He held his hand out to her, and she took it. With her free sleeve, she brushed back salty tears from her face. Forced a thin smile.

They left the cell. She took the torch from the socket, and Kye led her from the darkened dungeons.

Together they walked slowly, quietly, up the spiralling stairs to mocking sunshine. There, Emme knew, Kye would let go of her hand and never touch her again.

13

"What's this I hear about you moving the prisoners to one of the guest towers?" Jaimis demanded coolly, anger cleverly contained.

Emme noted with a vindictive smile that he had four guards with him. He was afraid of her. Then she saw his eyes and felt nausea sweep away the brief triumph. Momentarily she could not meet those eyes, those cold green reminders of the previous night. "I thought their last day would be a lot nicer in the tower where they can have baths and eat good food. Don't worry – I have guards positioned at the bottom of the tower. They're not going anywhere."

Jaimis paced the small library Emme had discovered for herself after leaving the street kids to their tower that morning. She had not wanted to leave, had wanted to stay with them, drink in their faces and memories. But she had been told the Ashrones were arriving and had asked to see them in the quiet library area.

A servant appeared from behind the four guards, a thatched tray of food in his hands. He stared, bewildered, at the scene.

"It's all right," Emme said. "Bring the food in, and put it on the table."

Chunky, green-velvet couches framed the edges of a square rug that copied the lines of the windowless room. Each wall, bar the one with the door, had a bookshelf against it. Heat from a central fire somewhere below, pumped from a floor vent into the snug room.

The servant placed the tray on the squat tea table in the middle of the room and hurriedly left.

Emme busied herself with setting out the fine white teacups and pot. She lifted the metal lid of the biscuit canister and set it aside, well aware that Jaimis was still in the room watching her. She pretended not to know he was there, then straightened, hands on hips. "What are you still doing in here?" she asked with mocking pleasantness.

Jaimis' cool green eyes regarded her, and a chill shot down her spine. She inhaled slowly, each second returning her resolve. She hoped he would sentence her to death with the other street kids, but she knew he would not. He could not risk angering the other princes with the death of their queen.

Kye had assured her she would be safe for quite some time. Jaimis needed the queen alive to validate his position as king. But she would need to rely on the Ashrones for protection, for as the years wore on, if she antagonised Jaimis, he would devise subtle ways to kill her.

So, her first order of ruling was to ensure the Ashrones had complete control of the castle with as much freedom to roam it as she could ensure them. She would declare them her personal counsel, and, according to Kye, by law it would give them the right to go everywhere the queen could go. The Ashrones had not visited the castle in a long time – not with the rampant tension between them and Jaimis. Instead, they had ruled Kildes from their Halls of the Asher. Well, that was about to change, for Emme could not live in the Halls of the Asher, and she desperately needed the Ashrones' protection and knowledge.

Jaimis flapped his cloak out behind him as he spun on heels and left. She watched him walk away and noted with another chill, how calm and controlled he was. So much like Kye, she realised in that moment, yet also so unlike Kye, for a darkness, a lust for power, raged in Jaimis' heart.

Jaimis was no fool, and certainly not quick to anger. His calm, cruel control of her the night before had shown her that. She would have to be very careful of him, although she knew he would not touch her again for a long while. The way he limped down the hall reminded her of that. She shuddered as she realised he was not done with her yet. For now, maybe, but not forever. He needed heirs.

"My Lady?" A voice made her focus on an unfamiliar face at the door. "The Ashrones have arrived."

"I want to see the ones they call Anderson and Imren," she said calmly, but felt her heart pound in her chest.

The two Ashrones entered behind a servant who waited until they were in the room before turning to shut the door behind him.

Imren put a finger to his lips, and Emme nodded once in acknowledgement. Imren traced a pattern in the air, concentrated for a brief moment, then flung his hand out. He seemed to be seeing something in the room Emme could not. "It is safe to talk now," he said, then turned to Emme, sadness so apparent on his fatherly face. "Emme, my child. We've heard what happened."

Emme stiffened with resolve not to cry. "Sit down." She gestured to the couch opposite her, and they took their seat. Without asking, she poured them all tea, took a biscuit and pushed the biscuit canister to them. She sat back.

"We're truly sorry," Anderson said. "We didn't know Rastin was able to do that, to get past our wards. He must have connected with you somehow."

"He did. I met him in a tavern one night. He shook my hand, and I felt the connection then."

"We tried to find you," Anderson said, "but Rastin had set up very powerful wards around the castle."

"What happened to Kye?" Imren asked. "He raced to the

346

castle to get you."

Emme's face hardened. "They've imprisoned him. They're going to kill all the street kids in a public execution tomorrow. They say they'll be tried, but it just means read out their crimes."

"Oh dear." Remorse clouded Imren's face.

"Oh dear, what?" Emme said, eyes sharpening. "Oh dear, we now have to work harder to stop him? Oh dear, they must be going through a terrible time in that prison until we get them out of there? What?"

Imren's hands played restlessly in his lap. "I'm afraid we can't stop it."

"Excuse me?"

"Child, the king may execute anyone, other than an Ashrone, who has worked against his ascension to the throne," Imren said. "It's the law."

"But the street kids were trying to stop evil," Emme protested. "Jaimis, the bastard, was working for evil, and the street kids were trying to stop it. Surely that means something."

Imren shook his head. "Not now that he is king. A king's past crimes cannot be held against him under Kildes Law. The time to protest his validity for the throne is before he becomes king, but no one had any evidence that he murdered his brothers."

"Kye did. Kye had the proof."

"Kye was not able to offer the proof in time," Anderson said. "And Jaimis is king now. And under Kildes Law, anyone who works against a prince's ascension to the throne for no good provable reason, as the street kids did, can be tried and executed if the king demands it."

"Damn your Kildes Law." Emme threw the biscuit down onto the table. It shattered into little pieces. "Damn it to hell."

"My child, we must work with what we have now," Imren said, "and always within the law. We cannot change that Jaimis is king, but we can at least find a way to undo any damage his leadership might make on this nation. The queen does have rights and some authority – not as much as the king, but she does have a say. And it is through that, that we must work."

"I don't care about any of that," Emme half-shouted. "Right now I only care that they're going to execute sixty-one innocent people who also happen to be the only friends I've ever had in my life. You find a way to undo that, and maybe then I will think about your precious Kildes."

Awkward silence hovered between them. Anderson coughed slightly. The two men stared at their laps, then Anderson reached for his tea. She saw the cup shake a little as he lifted it to his mouth.

"You're seriously telling me there is no way to stop it?" Emme asked, eyes flitting from face to face. "Please don't tell me that." She could not stop the anguish in her voice. "Maybe I could talk to Jaimis, make some bargain with him. No, damn it." She slammed her fist into her open palm. "I have no bargaining power with that man. Right now, he's not going to do a single thing I ask. He has my power, he has another lover, he doesn't need an heir for a while, and he has four holes in his leg from the fork I stabbed into it this morning." She saw their brows lift high at the statement, but ignored their surprise. "He is going to do this just to get his revenge."

They looked at one another, exchanged knowing glances.

"What?" She stared from one to the other. "What is it?"

Imren leant forward a little. "Jaimis has openly declared before the city that the street kids are outlaws. He cannot let them go now. Under Kildes Law, if the king declares them outlaws, he cannot go back on it unless someone offers irrefutable proof in the street kids' favour."

Emme stood and paced the room, her body tight, eyes

seething. "Damn him. I want to kill him. I really do."

"You mustn't do that, Emme," Imren said quickly. "You will die for it, and we need you as queen."

Emme stamped back to the padded couch and sagged down onto it. "This is terrible." She leant forward over her knees and placed head in hands. "This is just terrible. How could this have happened?" She snapped straight and gestured at the two men. "How could *you* have let this happen?" A pang of guilt clenched her insides. It was all her own fault, not theirs. If she hadn't run away from the Ashrones in the forest that day, none of this would have happened. None of it.

"We're sorry, child. We let you down," Imren said. "But you must trust us over the coming years to try and guide you as best we can."

"Yes, I need you to do that. I'm declaring you my personal advisers, all of you. And I'm going to declare you regents in my absence. And according to Kye, that gives you the right to roam the castle as you wish and put up as many wards and spells as you want to, and it means that if I'm ever not around, you get my rights and authority."

"Indeed it does," Imren said. "A very wise move."

"So go and get your things, and tell the servants I said you could take any room you want to that isn't used. Make sure you scatter yourselves throughout the castle so you can hear everything that goes on and be everywhere when I need you."

"Again, very wise." Imren inclined his head in respect.

"Right now, I'm going to go and enjoy the last moments I have with my friends." She watched the two men nod, stand and leave the room. Then she stared into the untouched teacup in front of her.

She had lied very well, she thought. If she publicly announced the new position of the Ashrones that afternoon, and had someone write it down for her to sign tomorrow, none could attest the Ashrones' authority in her absence.

She felt sorrow well up as she dwelt on the impending deaths of the street kids and Kye. A sorrow touched by the faintest consolation that the evening of their execution, she would be taking her own life with a swift dagger through the heart.

◉

The day dawned cold and miserable. The usual grey clouds hung motionless across the sky, and mist curled around the distant hills Emme could see from her vantage point. Snow coated the castle square where clusters of city-dwellers, poor and wealthy, lingered to watch the beheadings. The execution platform, a portable structure stored on castle grounds for such occasions, had been rolled in front of the main prison where the street kids had been transferred to just an hour ago. Grounds staff swept away the last of the snow from the rickety boards.

Jaimis sat beside her in the royal stands, frowning slightly that Emme had refused to wear the dress and crown ordered to the tower where she had spent the night with her friends. She had sent the expensive dress back to him in tatters along with the empty gold crown her dagger had levered the diamonds from. She had mingled with the first of the crowds earlier that morning in search of the poorest people she could find. Awestruck, they had stared at her stony face as she tucked the diamonds into their tattered-glove hands. Then she had taken her place by the king's side with the dagger concealed in her trouser top.

She had contemplated killing Jaimis before she killed herself, but Kildes needed an heir – even if it were through the womb of that sickly sweet and notably absent Ennika. And with the Ashrones as regents in Emme's place, Jaimis would hopefully not get away with too many more crimes such as the one displayed before her.

The five guillotines loomed, monuments of pure evil, and symbols of how harsh life could be. Why had she expected happiness? Why had she expected happiness for her street kids? Any joy found in life was short-lived, crushed by the strong and the cruel like Jaimis.

Emme scanned the thick crowds with their bags of rotting vegetables. Halder was down there. Thank the Creator he was alive. He stared up at Jaimis beside her with the anger she too felt. She could tell Halder wanted to smash him with one of his blacksmith hammers.

The man Russen was there too, she noted; and wondered how many of Kye's supporters would witness his callous death.

Despite the frown, Jaimis seemed edged with excitement knowing he would finally have retribution. From the royal stands, he gazed at the guillotines, seemed to be imagining sixty-one gory deaths. Kye's would be first. The leader always went first.

Emme felt Imren pat her comfortingly on the shoulder from the row behind. She did not turn to look at him. She knew he sat beside the traitorous Rastin who had not stopped scowling since the Ashrones arrived. Anderson sat on the other side of Imren, the only two she had been allowed to invite.

She felt her stomach churn painfully. She knew she would have to watch each murder. The street kids had made her promise to give them her face, to be there looking down at them so they could believe there was hope after their death. She would give them that, then she would end her own anguish – end the painful memory of those sad, scared young faces, by taking her own life.

The drums rolled, and guards dragged out the line of prisoners, as many as would reach from the dungeons to the platform. The crowds started to boo, and a few rotting cabbages struck some of the young children, made one little girl cry. Lydia stood, dishevelled and bruised, next to the child and despite the terror in her own eyes, tried to comfort the little girl with words and a shaky smile.

Even from that distance, Emme could see Illina's tear-streaked face yet unwavering regal composure. Thick ropes bound her scarred hands in front of her. The other adults were still in darkness, waiting to be brought out when beheadings moved the queue along.

The booing, the shouting, rose to mob intensity. Kye, hands bound, was dragged up first. He stared at the crowds with such calm, such confidence, that it quietened all jeers. The drummers glanced about insecurely and the drum roll scattered to eerie silence. Even in his tattered clothes, the crowds knew him to be a gentleman. Not one rotten vegetable flew at him. The audience looked to Jaimis expectantly.

"This is our cue," Jaimis said and tugged Emme to rise.

She refused to stand and heard the crowds murmur amongst themselves at her open defiance. Slight smiles overlaid sorrow on the older street kids' faces. Even Illina's gentle red lips curled in a sad smile. Hope. She was giving them hope that there would be somebody left to stop the spreading evil of the new king.

Halder nodded to her once, an encouragement to hold her ground. She acknowledged his support with her own discreet nod.

Jaimis' cool eyes regarded Emme briefly, then he conceded the small defeat. "Ladies and gentlemen," he said to the crowd, "I have called you here to ask you to be witnesses to this execution. Here stands before you the leader of the notorious street rats – criminals, thieves, murderers, who have been tirelessly working against me and my ascension to the throne."

Now Emme stood. "Rubbish!" All heads swung to her.

"Now is not the time," Jaimis said with restrained warning tones.

Emme looked to Kye, saw the way he watched her, bittersweet pride in his eyes. She straightened. "If you're going to execute these people, do it for the right reasons. I won't have their memories tarnished by your filthy lies."

The crowd broke into a flurry of conversations, then rapidly silenced when Emme continued to shout over the top of them. "They have not murdered anybody, they have not stolen, and they are not criminals. Yes, they have worked tirelessly against your ascension to the throne, but that's only because you're a repulsive pig and you don't deserve the crown you wear."

The crowd exploded into lively dialogue. They turned to one another, eyes wide with excitement as their mouths moved rapidly and hands gestured animatedly. This had indeed turned out to be an entertaining event for them.

Jaimis grabbed Emme's arm, squeezed painfully, but she did not cry out. Eyes sharp, he said quietly, "Have you finished?"

She matched his dangerously quiet voice. "Yes. Go ahead, *my love*." As if he needed her permission, Emme gestured for the king to go on. She sat back down again.

She saw Kye smiling at her, and his pride in her made her want to openly weep, but she blinked back tears and stiffened. She would join him soon, in the afterlife, then they would be free.

Jaimis seemed momentarily stuck for words. He searched the air just in front of him, then gathered himself. "For the crime of working against my ascension to the throne, I pronounce them enemies of the realm and sentence them to be executed by beheading. If anyone has any evidence to the contrary, let him speak now."

No one moved. All looked expectantly at Emme. She saw Jaimis' nearest hand flex, ready to snap her back to her seat if she tried to rise, but she had no evidence that would free them. Jaimis was king. He was as large as the Kildes Law now, and no one could stop him.

"Then let it be known before all these witnesses here today," the prince continued, "that these sixty-one street rats are guilty as charged. Let the executions begin." He slowly sat down, smoothed his trousers and waited with an eager anticipation that angered and sickened Emme.

Bone sticks rattled eerily on drums as they dragged Kye to the nearest guillotine. He would go first, alone – the punishment for being the leader.

The crowd whipped into a frenzy of shouts and gestures, bloodlust apparent.

Beneath the podium, a large basket waited to catch heads. A group of men stood around a train of wagons that would cart the bodies away to a large unmarked grave. Not even their burial would be dignified.

An elderly priest in jewelled robes stepped up to Kye, book in hand, and muttered something only Kye could hear. The priest scanned Kye's face as he talked, then the priest's eyes widened in shock. Only Emme and Kye knew the significance of the expression; the priest had recognised Kye. Kye swiftly shook his head to silence the priest, and the crowds, mistaking the gesture for denying the last rites, booed and bellowed at him. The priest seemed momentarily torn by indecision. Emme shifted forward in her seat. Would he say something? At last the priest stepped back to the podium corner, head bowed as if in prayer.

The crowd hollered even louder at the priest's exit.

Guards began to raise the central guillotine, and a pinch-faced girl hurriedly positioned the huge basket beneath it.

A gruesome image of the basket filled with her friends' heads, of Kye crumpling decapitated to the blood-soaked platform, speared into Emme's mind. This was real. This was about to happen. It had seemed surreal until now. Violent nausea swept through her stomach. She flung her hand over her mouth to stop herself throwing up but could not prevent it. Her belly pressed her thighs as she doubled over, vomited all over Jaimis' boots. He swore and glared at her.

She felt a strong, comforting hand press her shoulder. She looked about for a handkerchief, felt in her pockets. The drum roll continued above the shouting crowd, and she knew they were still raising the guillotine for Kye. She snatched Jaimis' hand, vindictively wiped her mouth with his sleeve, then without warning threw up again on the ground at her feet.

"Good Almighty," Jaimis snapped. "Get the queen a tonic or something." A servant standing in attendance at end of the row spun on heels and dashed away for the kitchens.

Emme clutched at her stomach. "Damn it, I need a handkerchief, not a tonic. It's because of these executions that I'm sick, you idiot."

The sharp, angled guillotine was raised now. The lewd faces of the possessed crowd reflected off the cold of the blade. She saw them drag Kye to the headrest. He knelt, stared up at her one last time with a look of sadness, of admiration. She clamped her hand over her mouth to stop more nausea.

"Good Almighty." Jaimis shot to his feet. "Get the queen out of here. She's not well."

"I just need a bucket," she snapped.

Attendants scurried away to fetch one. She noted that the executioners had paused in their grisly duty to wonder at the commotion in the royal stand. The crowds were looking from the guillotine to the royal stand and back again, clearly unsure of where the best action might be.

Emme swung feet back under the chair and reeled over her knees, sure she was going to be sick again. Her heels clanged against metal.

She felt into her pockets again, lifted out a cloth. She stared at it with brief confusion, then wiped her mouth.

"Carry on, damn it," Jaimis said to the guards. He looked back at the Ashrones. "Get the queen out of here, she's unwell." He sat down against the farthest edge of his plush chair.

"No, I'm staying," Emme said, and wiped her mouth again with the soiled cloth. "The street kids need me."

She saw Kye being lowered face down to the headrest. He could no longer look at her. She winced, glanced away. Eyes snagged on the cloth in her hand, then sharp thoughts began to stab into her mind, to demand attention.

Her heart began to pound with a new beat, not a beat of fear, a beat of hope. She swung down over her knees.

"Oh no, she's going to do it again." Jaimis leapt up from his chair. The executioners stopped their movements again to watch.

Emme peered between her knees under the seat, then bolted upright. She leapt to her feet. "Stop!" she yelled. "Stop this at once." And the drumroll ceased. The crowds hushed and stared at her. She called out, "I have a very good reason why these people should not be executed." She pointed to Jaimis. "This man is not yet king."

"Sit down," Jaimis hissed at her. "Don't make a fool of yourself. I *am* king."

"No, you're not king, Jaimis. You're a pig, and I can prove it." She looked down at Kye who could only hear her, could not see her. "Stand that man up," she ordered sharply, and the guards rushed to obey. They pulled Kye to his feet. He steadied himself, then stared up at her, confusion apparent to her where all else would see quiet calm.

"What are you doing, child?" Imren asked in a quiet, stern voice.

Emme ignored him. "I think that the crowd needs to be paid for watching this. Yes, I think that there needs to be a big pile of gold on the platform for everyone who came here today to watch. I want ten thousand gold coins on the platform."

The crowds turned to the platform. Mouths gaped as a generous pile of glistening gold appeared on the execution stage. Instantly the tide of the crowds broke and washed towards the gold. The guards fled in the power of their greedy wake.

"Good Almighty!" Jaimis launched out of his chair. "But how . . ."

The princes stood one by one and glared at Jaimis.

"You are not king," one of the princes said to Jaimis. "You clearly do not have the gift yet."

Jaimis, eyes seething, spun to Emme. "That's easily fixed." He whisked out a dagger from his pocket, snapped Emme around and held the dagger to her throat.

"Halder," she shouted, her head pressed painfully to Jaimis' chest. "Get Kye. Now is your chance to tell everyone the truth." She only hoped he could hear her above the enormous resonance of the crowd.

"Guards!" Jaimis yelled. "Get over here."

Emme elbowed Jaimis in the stomach and grabbed the dagger from him but the guards pounded on top of her from behind. It took many of them to restrain her. She noted in the commotion that the mob had subdued the guards on the podium, and the priest had released Kye. He was running, Halder with him, through the multitude.

She heard chanting behind her, two different chants. She realised Rastin had risen up to work some magic and the Ashrones attempted to stop him.

She saw the crowds blur then fade. Blackness descended, enveloped her for the longest time. *Good Creator, not again.* When vision returned, she was in the vast echoing throne room, her feet on colourful mosaic tiles where timber of the grandstand had been just moments before. Near the thorne, Jaimis stood with five guards. Rastin paced hotly about the room, his grey cloak snapping about with each powerful stride. Emme tried to take a step forward, but a shimmering force jolted her body. She winced as the sting, like the throb of smacking against water from a great height, shot across her belly and chest. She tested each boundary and with every painful jolt, realised the tight shimmering cube was impenetrable.

"What are we going to do?" Jaimis demanded fiercely of Rastin. "How could this have happened?"

Rastin continued to pace aggressively. "Nothing should have gone wrong."

"You didn't do it right," Jaimis accused violently. "You should have done something else."

"Idiot!" Rastin roared. "The passing of the gift is beyond any Ashrone. It is as natural as conception and totally out of our hands. The moment you took her, you should have been given the gift."

Jaimis gestured with jerky movements. "Well something went wrong."

"Something did go wrong." Imren's voice in the room made the three of them spin to face him. He stood with Anderson at his side. A portal closed behind him, and the two men regarded Rastin with cold speculation. "Something rather profound seems to have escaped us all. Something so obvious that it is pathetic. We could not send Kara to her new life without her permission, we could not bring Emme to this world without her permission, and we could not take Emme's gift without her permission. The moment

358

you forced her against her will, you lost your chance at it."

"I don't think so." Jaimis marched towards Emme.

Rastin flicked his wrist, and three sides of the cube disappeared. Believing the entire cube to be gone, Emme tried to run to the Ashrones, but the shimmering wall stunned her into brief stillness. She spun right, raced a few steps ahead to where the cube should have ended, then tried to run to Imren. The wall shocked her to a standstill. The gleaming barrier began to spread across the entire room, from wall to wall. Soon it would seal her entirely from her allies.

Terrified, she tried to outrun the growing barrier. Jaimis followed her. She saw her last chance to cross the barrier before the barrier joined the wall. She leapt but too late. The impenetrable barrier moved faster and struck her like a stinging slap over her entire body. She froze again, stunned by pain. Enough time for Jaimis to reach her, grab her wrist. He yanked Emme violently towards him. Face repellently close to hers, he said with unnerving deliberation, "Will it to me, and I will spare your friends."

"My friends are not going to die at your hands." Emme snapped her wrist away from him, took a step back. The wall behind her imprisoned her within Jaimis' reach. "My friends are going to expose you for the murderer you are."

"Then you will suffer. I will take you every night, *all* night – and you know I can stay up all night – until you will the power to me. I'll break you – believe me I will. Starting right now." He gripped her arm. His crushing, angry fingers bruised her.

Emme whisked the dagger from her belt and slashed it down through the tight flesh of the arm that held her. He shouted with rage and let her go. Blood swelled from a long shallow gash.

She tried to run past him but Jaimis kicked out his foot, propelled her forward into the force field. The shot of pain jarred her. The smarting escalated as she involuntarily leant against the barrier, unable to get her balance to stand. She felt her legs buckle, felt herself crash backwards onto the bone-cracking floor. Her shoulder blades hit first, then her skull. She felt darts of pain through her feet tipping the barrier. Pain surged up her legs. Dazed, she stared up at gawking portraits on the dome ceiling. She blinked back water, tried to remember where she was, why her legs stung and throbbed with regular intensity.

Guards dragged her backwards, then pounded down on top of her, pinned her to the tiles. She cried out with rage, with renewed terror as memory returned. A guard kicked the knife from her restrained hand. It skittered across the tiles, out of reach.

She heard chanting, knew Imren and Anderson tried to break through to her. Rastin chanted back, his voice droning on and on in patterns of dark and sinister magic.

Bruises formed as guards knelt on her legs, on her arms, to keep her to the floor. Something buzzed along the force field; she heard Rastin mutter a curse and knew that someone had broken through.

"Get back from her or I will kill you." *Kye!* Kye was in the room. She heard rapiers whisk from scabbards, and she tilted her head up, peered between the knees of two guards. Kye and Jaimis circled each other, intent on killing.

Jagged blue lightning shot across the room, cracked through the air like thunder, and struck a shield around Rastin. He uttered stronger, louder words and shot a crackling bolt of lightning back to the Ashrones. Emme winced at the volume. The two Ashrones faltered briefly, tense against the effort to restrain the fatal blue light. Rastin seized the gap in action, slowly lowered his hands to aim at the two circling men.

Imren cleared away the pulsating light, dashed closer, fast

for a man his age, and blocked the lightning before it struck Kye. Imren returned lightning at Rastin. Emme realised the lightning that flowed from Imren was stronger, faster, thicker. Rastin sweated and cursed under the force of it whilst Imren remained calm with concentration. Anderson had gone, and Emme had brief seconds to wonder where he was.

Jaimis struck first. He swung out his rapier, and Kye deflected the blow. Then the two were locked in a swirl of thrusts and parries as they moved around the room. No matter where Jaimis struck, Kye seemed ready for it. Jaimis stumbled back; hit the ground. Nimbly he dodged Kye's blow and rolled to his feet. Then the two duelled around the room again.

The clang of their weapons, the strike of their boots on the tiles, the hiss and crack of the lightning bolts, echoed over and over through the vaulted chamber. More boots – heavy boots, ran across the tiles.

Emme heard a deep-voiced roar, then heard a guard cry out as hands clutched his shoulders and ripped him away from Emme. The guard was flung across the room like a red toy. The unconscious body slid all the way to a wall, then lay crumpled like old rags.

Relief washed over Emme. "Halder." She watched as Halder easily peeled the guards from her. The rest stood, ready to defend themselves, and Emme scrambled to her feet; felt the ache in her shoulder blades from the tumble onto tiles.

She watched guards and rapiers lunge for Halder. With his bare hands and body he defended against them. "Run, Emme," he shouted as he fractured the leg of the nearest guard with a well-planted thrust of his foot. The nauseating snap of bone made Emme cringe, briefly distracted from her flight.

She saw a glistening dagger across the floor – *her* dagger. She dashed for it. Blue lightning shot at her and she dodged. It burst across her shoulder, the explosion terrifyingly loud as it flung her into a wall. She gasped, winded. Her fragile rib had cracked; she could feel it. The throb of snapped bone paled against unimaginable torture in her shoulder.

"Emme!" she heard Kye cry out.

Dazed, she glanced ahead as Kye tried to move to her. "Behind you," she shrieked, and Kye turned just in time to block a downward stab of a rapier blade. The sickening clang of metal resounded throughout the room again.

Emme lightly touched her severely burned shoulder. The flesh was charred, bleeding. Ragged cotton edges had melted to it. Skin flaked off in black, sooty chunks. The agony shot through her whole body. Steam plumed from the wound. Tears of shock stung into her eyes. She heaved up bile, and the movement punched her cracked rib.

The room, blurred by tears, began to spin. Through the haze she saw white light come for her, heard it crackle and hiss through the air. It struck her shoulder and she instantly felt cooling relief. The flesh began to mend and pain began to subside. The room steadied, and she blinked back tears to see Anderson nod at her from across the room. Her eyes widened. Ashrones, hundreds of them, stood before a backdrop of slowly closing portals. Hands united, they chanted. White, brilliant light burst from their chests towards Rastin. Rastin cried out in terror, tried to block the light with a shield of blue lightning but could not. The light seared him, began to char his flesh. Features twisted and distorted into an unrecognisable mess. He screamed and screamed. Boiling blood spurted from the arching creature. Rastin shrivelled into a blackened, fleshless form that toppled to the tiles, spasmed once, then lay very still. Smoke plumed from the black carcass.

Emme glanced around, saw Halder struggle with two more

guards. A large gash marred his arm, and a thin, red line stretched across part of his stomach exposed through a rip. He cracked the two heads together, then the thundering of many feet echoed through the chamber.

Guards swarmed in, rapiers raised, and circled the room. "Cease this at once," the captain of the guards ordered the infidels. Halder held up hands in defeat and stepped back from the unconscious bodies on the floor.

Emme looked to the Ashrones, but they shrugged, unable by law to touch the guards.

Jaimis was grinning maliciously now as he circled Kye. He knew he had won, again. Kye stopped his circling, stepped back. He dropped his rapier but only a pace away, and Emme noted that his muscles were ready, his eyes watching, waiting for an opportunity to strike. Kye was going to kill Jaimis in front of all these witnesses. Then Kye would be executed.

"Do you remember me?" Kye asked as he watched Jaimis with hunter's eyes.

"Of course I do." Jaimis' eyes still flickered with dark delight. "You're the leader of the street rats."

"Wrong," Kye said. "Look again and see the young brother you ordered to be murdered."

Jaimis faltered. "Kael? But you're dead."

"Don't you recognise this man?" Kye gestured to Halder. "The man you paid to kill me?"

Jaimis' eyes narrowed slightly. "This is a fancy lie," he taunted.

Kye pulled up his tattered shirt, and the room gasped, stared at the brilliant tattoo on his lower back, the tattoo of the Royal Lion of the House of Endoria. Guards' rapiers faltered as they stared from one brother to another. They would not kill Kye now, could only wait to see which brother triumphed under Kildes Law.

Kye knew he had the upper hand. He let the shirt drop back. "This man can testify that you paid him three hundred and forty gold pieces to have me killed." Everyone in the room knew the significance of that sum. "That makes you a murderer of the royal family and under Kildes Law you must be sentenced to death. Your family's blood cries out for vengeance."

"You have no proof of this. It is the word of a man with the reputation for corruption. Prince or no prince, you are the leader of the street rats, and I am heir to the Kildes throne."

Jaimis moved quickly towards Emme as if to claim her. Kye flicked up his rapier with his foot, caught it and swung at Jaimis. Jaimis heard the swish, skilfully turned and deflected the blow.

The two fought again, thrust and parried. Emme tried to stand but the pain in her ribs made her groan. She felt bile rise to her mouth and she swallowed it back down quickly. The splintered bone lit a fire down her side every time she breathed.

The ring of metal on metal made her ill. Someone had to stop this. Holding her broken rib, she stood, staggered for the blade on the floor and reached for it. A sting ripped through her upper arm, and she felt a thin metal blade slide back out from it. Blood gushed onto her white shirt. She looked up to see Jaimis stepping away from her, her blood on his rapier tip, and heard the clang as Kye angrily pounded his rapier onto Jaimis' ready weapon. The heavy blow crushed Jaimis' rapier to his chest. The two pushed against each other, locked into a battle of strength.

"If you hurt her again," Kye said icily, inches from Jaimis' face, "I'll meet out her injuries to you, one by one."

"Ahh." Jaimis stared into Kye's determined eyes. "So she means more to you than just your chance at the throne. It seems we are both fools, for I loved her as Kara and hated that Lian was betrothed to her. Hated that he would be the one to have her. I wish it was him who had lost her, but you will do."

Angry memories filled Jaimis' face. The stronger of the two, Jaimis pushed Kye from him. Kye staggered back a little, locked his leg muscles, arms out to regain balance. His muscles tensed and he readied himself. The two circled each other again.

"So then, perhaps I should remind you that regardless of the gift, that woman is my wife. I took her, and she is mine."

Kye's eyes sharpened but his face remained calm, his concentration unwavering. They circled with strong, agile steps, ready to re-engage in the graceful, deadly sport.

Jaimis' eyes taunted Kye. "And she was a good lay too. Although she doesn't seem to like it violent."

Only Emme and Jaimis saw Kye flinch, but he did not strike out as Jaimis hoped. Instead Kye waited, circling patiently for a chance to move in.

Jaimis laughed cruelly. "You cannot win, Brother. If you kill me before you have proven me the perpetrator of our brothers' murders, you will be executed for treason against the heir to the Endorian throne and the husband of the Gifted Daughter of the Hunstons." He continued to circle Kye, to pace with intentional, wary steps. "And if you leave me alive, I will swiftly sentence you and your street rats to death before you can prove the crimes against me. Then I will take my wife to my bed again and again until she wills me my right. Either way, you cannot have Emme, for I have already taken her."

Emme realised with a sickening wave of terror, that Jaimis was right. Whatever Jaimis' fate, Kye would die. She watched Kye, saw the determination in his movements, the steely resolve on face. He was going to kill Jaimis that very day and would be executed for it. He was willing to sacrifice his love of Kildes and Kildes' need for an Endorian heir, for Emme's honour.

No, this wasn't right. There had to be another way.

Kye lunged at Jaimis and the two, evenly matched in skill, spun and fought their way around the room again. The weapons clanged. The ringing echoed over and over, each shrill chime the bell of inevitable death. No matter who survived, Kye would die.

Kara – advise me. What should I do? She winced as the last of her skin folded back with a sting to the shoulder and the burn disappeared. *Forget Kara. You are not Kara; you are Emme. And you alone have to find a way to stop this.*

Yes, she was not Kara. Kara had died the day she sacrificed her essence, her soul, to Emme. Kara did not exist. Emme did.

Now Emme knew what she had to do. She gathered the dagger in hand and stood. "Kye, Jaimis, enough," she snapped. "I have made my decision."

The two men broke from fierce concentration and pulled back from each other. Only then did Emme notice the back of the room had filled with the street kids. Dusty stood in front, boyish blue eyes closely watching Emme.

"Stand back, both of you," Emme said and watched as the two men obeyed. She winced, clutched her side, then stiffened again with resolve. "Only I can end this." She saw a look of sadistic delight on Jaimis' face, matched by disappointment, loss, on Kye's.

She moved closer to Jaimis, a significant gesture. She could see Jaimis knew he had won, that she had chosen him to save her beloved. She kept a distance from him, two human lengths away, lest he grab her.

Kye held a hand up to slow Emme down. "Emme, think carefully about this." He was pleading with her, but only Emme knew it. He was willing to kill Jaimis and be executed to spare Emme the trauma of a life with his malicious brother.

Emme turned to him, smiled sadly. "I won't have you executed for killing your brother." Jaimis' smile of cruel delight widened. "Jaimis is right. If you kill him today, you will be sentenced to death."

Kye's eyes were shadowed with sorrow. She realised in that moment that he did not care about his lost crown, or of Kildes' defeat. He cared that he was losing her.

Emme surveyed the room. Every face watched her expectantly. Fear darkened the eyes of the street kids. Their life lay in her hands, and she felt the responsibility keenly. The Ashrones watched her, expressions grave, wondering what she would do.

Emme turned back to Jaimis. "Announce to this room the innocence of the street kids and all involved," she demanded.

Jaimis hesitated.

"You are not king, Jaimis, and you have no right to accuse them. Withdraw your accusations before these witnesses."

Jaimis could smell victory. "Very well, I withdraw it."

"And take back your sentencing on your brother."

Jaimis shrugged. "All right, I take back my sentencing on him." Emme knew Jaimis would think up other ways to dispose of Kye.

"And say you don't know this man here." Emme gestured to Halder. "That you've never seen him before."

"Emme," Kye pleaded quietly. "Please."

"Say it!" Emme snapped at Jaimis.

"Emme, no," she heard Halder say. She did not turn to look at him, kept her eyes fixed on Jaimis.

Jaimis' eyes sparkled, well aware that it was entirely to his advantage to deny knowing Halder. He smiled slyly as he uttered the words that would seal his triumph. "I've never seen that man before."

Emme exhaled slowly with relief. "Good – now let me tell you something, Jaimis." She rose up straight and proud, stared her rapist straight in his cold green eyes. Her smooth voice resounded clearly throughout the room. "I am not Kara of Kildes, Daughter of the Hunstons. I am Emme, spelt E double-M E, of Underoak Village. And for breaking the irrefutable law of Underoak Village that any outsider shall not attack or rape any woman of Underoak Village, I sentence you to death." Swiftly she raised her dagger, pitched it straight at him. She heard the nauseating crunch as it hit the exact mark – stabbed into Jaimis' ribs and sliced the edges of his heart.

Jaimis' rapier clattered to the tiled floor. Shaking fingers clutched the hilt of the dagger. Eyes wide, his cheeks bled to white. Blood fountained from the wound and dribbled from parted lips onto his shirt as he gaped down at the protruding handle. A moment when denial burned colour to his face, then he toppled to the tiled floor with a resounding thud.

Complete silence fell. Stunned minutes dragged by.

All faces watched the body on the floor as though disbelieving what they saw. Gradually eyes turned to the Ashrones, to Imren. Imren seemed to be thinking, and for the longest time no one moved, awaiting a verdict. At last Imren's relaxed shrug of shoulders publicly vindicated Emme's actions.

An enormous cheer shot up from the street kids. They clapped and whistled, hugged each other joyfully. The sound of it swelled and tumbled throughout the room until it seemed the entire room rumbled. Above it all, Emme heard Halder roar with an intensity of triumph she had not heard before. A smile touched her tight lips. Halder had been liberated.

The soldiers turned to one another, talked animatedly, and Emme marvelled at their open enthusiasm despite the death of their prince.

Emme stared at the body. Thick blood soaked the pristine white shirt scarlet. An image of the violent night two days before flashed into her mind. She held onto it, superimposed it with this – this image of him shocked, dead, and totally unmissed by everyone in the room. She nodded, knowing she was free of him, of the memory that could have tarnished her forever.

Adrenalin gone, exhaustion overcame Emme. She flopped to her bottom on the floor, folded arms around bent legs and rested her head on her knees. Briefly she closed eyes, listened to the sounds of the cheering, the laughter that warmed her heart. When she opened her eyes, Kye was there, kneeling beside her.

"Are you all right?" he asked, concern unmistakable in his eyes.

"I'm fine." Emme held up hands. "Help me up?"

Kye stood and tugged her hands. She cried out, snatched back a hand and held ribs. "That hurts."

Kye dropped her other hand and came around behind her. He tucked arms under her shoulders and using strength, got Emme up with little effort from her. On her feet again, she groaned as the broken rib protested.

Kye pulled out a stained handkerchief from his pocket, placed it over the blood-flow on her arm. "My poor Emme."

"I'm fine. I'm used to bruises and broken ribs. I was beginning to miss being in pain." She coughed, gasped as pain stabbed through her chest. Blood dribbled down her hand from her arm, and she mopped it with her grubby sleeve.

Kye frowned. "We should get you out of here, get you help."

Emme nodded and submitted to Kye's assistance. The guards fell silent as Kye helped Emme shuffle across the room. The guards removed hats and held them, right hand to left breast. The soldiers knelt, created a red corridor for the two.

"What are they doing?" Emme asked.

"Honouring the new heir to the Kildes throne and their future queen."

A bubble of joy rose inside Emme. Jaimis was dead; she was no longer his wife. She was Kye's, and Kye could now claim the role he had proven himself more than worthy for. The role he had patiently waited for, trained for, his whole life. Kye would be king.

Emme saw the jubilant faces of the street kids watching her. She grew frustrated at her slow, painful steps when she just wanted to be on the other side of the room touching those precious little faces that would never have to hide from the world again. Alive, she realised with a swell of relief. And free. Her true little friends, her *family*, were finally free.

14

Emme turned her head to the door as it opened, shifted a little in the bed. Kye entered, a bunch of winter flowers in one hand, the neck of a floral vase in the other. He kicked the door closed behind him.

"Now, I know you think this is a very feminine thing to have flowers in your room," he said as he put the crimson and olive vase on the bedside table, "but it's traditional to have flowers in your room when you're getting well."

Kye positioned the vivid red camellias in the vase, fanned them out a little. "I forgot the water." His eyes searched the room. He wandered over to the leaf-patterned wash jug beneath a gilded mirror and picked it up, peered into it. He took it back over to the flower display, tipped half the jug's water into the vase, then returned the wash jug to its basin.

"Forget the flowers," Emme said. "Just come and sit with me. I'm terribly bored."

He strolled over and sat down on the jade bedspread, watched her with a silent question.

"Yes, I'm feeling much better," she said. "But that stupid doctor insists that I stay here until the rib heals."

"He's not that stupid. You don't want to make it worse."

Emme rolled her eyes. "Not you too. I've had beatings worse than this and survived."

Kye frowned slightly.

"It's all right," Emme said. "It's not uncomfortable to talk about."

"It's uncomfortable to hear. I don't like to think anyone treated you like that."

Emme shrugged. "It's over now. No one is going to beat their future queen."

His lips curled into his gentle, closed-lip smile. "I can't imagine anyone in this country being courageous enough to even come near you with a fist, after hearing how many boys you managed to defeat in the streetkid headquarters."

Emme let a drift of laughter escape her lips.

Hesitantly, Kye raised his hand, touched her cheek with his fingertips. "The bruise is nearly gone," he said. "You look much better without it."

Emme felt her cheeks burn, and he quickly retracted his hand.

"So how is the maths problem going?" Kye glanced at the tossed-aside slate. He spied the chalk at the base of the far wall, shattered into small pieces. Above it, a distinct chalk mark stained the hanging tapestry. He turned a mock reprimanding expression back at Emme.

"Well?" Emme smiled sheepishly. "It was too hard."

"It just takes a bit of patience."

"I had plenty of patience – for the first two days."

He smiled fondly. "Do you want to know the answer?"

"Of course."

He walked to the slate, picked it up and dusted it off. He selected the largest fragment of chalk, then moved back to his spot on the bed. He scrawled out a few numbers and symbols, his hand working away with ease, then turned the board around, held it up for her.

Emme studied the symbols and numbers, then threw up her hands. "So easy. Why didn't I think of that?"

"Sometimes the solutions to complicated problems are

simpler than we think."

"Is this one of those life lessons you told me I'm going to have to learn a lot of?"

Lips still closed, he laughed softly. "Yes, I guess so."

"Do I really have to learn all you say I have to?" Her eyes pleaded with him playfully. "Can't I just be Emme?"

"No one would ever want to make you anyone other than Emme, but you'll find our world a whole lot less frustrating if you learn a few of our ways. No one can make you follow them, but you'll at least understand us better." With the faintest trace of awkwardness, he added quickly, "Understand me better."

"I think I understand you just fine." She sat back against the mound of pillows. "But don't worry, I'll learn." The two watched each other for a moment, then Emme grew fidgety at the look on Kye's face. She sensed he had something difficult he wanted to say or ask. "So tell me about the others," she said quickly. "How are they?"

"They're having a wonderful time. You'd love to watch the way they explore the castle every day. They've just about sorted out who gets what room, although many of them keep swapping. I'm surprised that after so long underground, they're not spending more time outside."

"Are you going to give them roles soon?"

"Yes. I'll let most of them work here until their lessons are over, and then I'll get some of them jobs in the city. The ones who want to stay, can. Maybe later, you and I could talk about who would be good at what around here."

"Well, anything that involves physical labour, don't bother giving it to Dusty. He's just going to get out of it."

Kye laughed at the thought. "Yes, he's never been good at chores. But he'd make a great history teacher for one of the free schools I'm going to start up for underprivileged people."

"A teacher? He'd never stop talking."

Again the closed-lip smile. "No, but he's very good with stories. You and I both know how much he loves spreading stories."

"Yes, I suppose he would make a good teacher. Does he know yet?"

"About his past?"

Emme nodded.

"I told him, yes."

"And?"

"And he was very excited to hear it. He understood entirely why I couldn't tell him. They all understand why I couldn't say anything."

"I bet he's bragging about it a bit. I can imagine that."

Kye nodded, mirth in his eyes. "Yes, he is bragging about it. But we have to forgive him for it. He's very proud of what his mother did, and he thinks he's practically a part of the royal family."

Emme laughed, shook her head dotingly.

"You don't laugh that much," he said. "I like it when you do."

"You don't either." Emme fidgeted again. "Do you have that – that mind gift Jaimis had?"

"Yes, and it's all taking a bit to get used to. It's like a blur of a million distant voices in my head, and if I concentrate, I can sometimes hear my name, or a name of someone I know. It would take a great deal of practise and determination to be able to tune into conspiracies like my brother did. But that's never what it was meant for."

"What is it for then?"

"For communication. For reporting information to the king. For example, you know from our history that there have been times of great invasions. To be able to tell the king, who rarely sleeps, immediately of the invasion on our shores, is a valuable thing. Then the king can muster the Ashrones to use the portals to gather the country together for war. And that's just one of the many ways the gift can be used."

"But how do people know how to contact you? I wouldn't know how to send you a message."

"Princes of the States, among others, are trained in how to use it properly. We'll all have to relearn a few things, though. We've all spent so long guarding our thoughts from my brother, rather than using the gift to Kildes' advantage, that we've diminished it. I might need to address that, right after I've learned to use it properly myself. Of course, it shouldn't be overused, and I'll make sure people don't just contact me all through the day over anything trivial like finances. We do have paper and pens and couriers for that sort of thing."

"But you should be able to listen out for conspiracies against you."

"I have ears and eyes for that, and the most important thing is to not be the sort of king anyone wants to conspire against."

Emme nodded. "That's very true."

"I'm glad you agree," he teased.

After a moment of silence, she asked, "So what are you going to do about the Black Bands?"

"They're very easily dealt with. I already know everything about them, including where they hide and where their black market trade routes are. I'll simply take steps to infiltrate their networks, then break any power they have over the city."

"And send them to jail?"

"Some of them. Most of them are young children with nowhere else to go. They just need re-educating and given jobs."

Emme nodded. "A great idea. Teach them like you taught the street kids, at this school you're going to start up."

"Exactly." Kye stared down at the chalk slate briefly, then put the slate aside.

"Will you do me a favour?"

"I can think about it. What do you want?"

"Put the Black Bands in a better jail than the one the street kids were put in. It's cruel to put a human being in a place like that – even for the Black Bands."

He nodded. "I did have ideas to make the jails a little less inhumane, but I'm glad you mentioned it. I told you you would make a good queen."

Emme fidgeted with the edge of the soft blanket again. After a while she said, "I meant to ask you, have the Ashrones gone back to their home?"

"Most of them. But they'll visit regularly, especially after . . ."

"After what?"

He frowned slightly, ran his hand across the green bedspread. "You don't have to . . . "

"To what?" Emme had never seen him find words so difficult.

Indecision warred in his face. At last he said, "To pass me the Gift of the Asher if you don't want to. I'm happy to stay prince."

"I know."

"I really am. I don't want to hurt you like my brother did."

Emme put a firm hand on Kye's shoulder, confidently met his eyes. "If you think, for one second, I'm going to let you go and marry another woman and have lots of Endorian heirs with her, you've got another thing coming. And so does she."

He laughed, and she dropped her hand to her lap, blushed a little.

"That's my Emme."

Her cheeks felt even warmer.

He smiled; steadily gazed at her for such a long time that Emme began to fiddle with the blanket again, her eyes a little restless on his face. As he gazed at her, he slowly brought his face to hers. His warm breath brushed her mouth as his soft lips touched hers. Emme inhaled slowly and wondered that so pleasant a thing could have been denied her so long by her mother's lies. Gently his lips pulled from hers and he sat back, watched her quietly with a look she longed to interpret.

"Well, I should let you get some rest." He made moves to rise.

Emme enclosed Kye's arm with her fingers and tugged him back to the bed. "Damn the rest." Her hand cupped the back of his head and drew him close. "This is much better," she said, and kissed him again.

◉

The room fell unnaturally quiet. The banquet hall sat still of all movement but a fork clanging on a plate and a few nervous coughs. Lavish platters of food and large tumblers of wine went briefly unnoticed.

"What?" Emme demanded into the stillness, staring at every face. She stood in the wide doorway, hands on hips and glared at the room.

Kye rose to his feet from his high-backed chair and strode over to her. "You're late," he said quietly and held out his hand to her.

"Well, it took me forever to get into this damned dress." Emme tugged at the tight dark-green velvet bodice and kicked out the full skirt with its myriad of annoying petticoats. She touched the thin emerald necklace given to her as a gift from the state princes. It tried to choke her, and she longed to remove it, but it would only insult the givers.

"You look beautiful," Kye said. "If I may say that without offending you."

"It seems everyone else has other thoughts about the matter," Emme said as they walked down the rows of tables to their chairs. "Or they wouldn't stare."

"They've never seen you in a dress before. They're just a little stunned. And I doubt the thought on their mind is that you don't look good in it."

Emme scowled sightly and kicked the heavy skirt out again in order to take a step. She saw familiar faces watching her as she passed – Russen, Halder, Dusty, Lydia, Ada, Illina, Jase, Jerris, the other street kids. Some of her friends from the taverns were able to spare the night to come. Roul, the kitchen master, matched even Halder's toothy smile.

She saw the Princes of the States, in their traditional outfits, sitting with their families, and felt a flutter of nervousness at what their presence meant.

The Ashrones were there, and many unknown faces of poor people Emme had insisted on inviting. They were the true heroes of Kildes – the ones who had endured the tyranny of Jaimis' reign and kept the country together with their industry despite their poverty. For their courage, they deserved a night of good food and dancing. She noted how they were neatly washed and brushed, but their clothes still displayed their poverty. That would change, Emme promised, as she and Kye worked tirelessly to balance the wealth that had been so cruelly poured into either weapons or the hands of any nobleman willing to lend power to Jaimis.

Already Emme and Kye had spent long hours going over ideas and plans for righting the wrongs of the last twenty years. With Kye's gifts and Emme's determination, the two would make great changes if it took their whole lives.

"I still don't think I'd make a good queen," Emme had insisted that afternoon in the drawing room.

"It's not too late to change your mind," Kye had replied.

"Isn't there any way I can be your wife and not be queen?"

"Think of it this way. All of these plans that we've been working on," Kye's hand gesture encompassed the scattered papers he had been writing on as the two talked, "can only be carried out if we're king and queen. If you really want to help the poor and the needy, being queen of Kildes is the best role you can possibly be."

Emme nodded. "Then I will be the queen of the poor. And you can be king of the rich."

Kye laughed merrily. "It's not going to get you out of etiquette lessons."

Emme scowled at him cheekily.

"But I promise you, you can toss all the etiquette aside whenever the other princes and officials aren't around. Then you can just be you."

"Good – because it's all a stupid game of pretence, and I don't like it."

"To be honest with you, Emme, when they're not at some official ceremony, I rather think the other princes prefer you to be you too. They need their usual ceremonies and rituals to run the way they like them. It makes them comfortable, and we don't want to make them too uncomfortable – not with all the other changes we want to make. But outside of those important occasions, they like you the way you are."

"You're making it up."

"I've seen you get princes to relax who haven't relaxed in years. They laugh with you, Emme, and they're a little curious and a little charmed by you all at once. Just give them their ceremonies and traditions, and then keep all the rest for yourself."

"Do you think I'm ready for tonight?"

He frowned at the question. "That's up to you. I'm not going to push you before you're ready."

"No, not that bit. I meant the banquet. The dancing and dinner. Do I have enough etiquette and training for it?"

He smiled at her fondly. "You'll be fine."

"Well, at least the dress is ready."

"You don't seem very happy about that."

"Oh, it's pretty enough I suppose. But I mean, what if I trip over it or something. Then all my etiquette training will be for nothing."

He patted her leg. "Emme – you'll be fine."

Well, it was time to test if Kye had been right that afternoon. Emme tried to smooth the frown from her face as she walked to the chair in the banquet hall. The dress was everything she imagined it to be: heavy, hot and difficult. Still, she had promised Kye she would do everything right. Perhaps her rather boisterous entrance and her defiant first word in the room had not been according to plan, but she would make up for it.

She made it to the table and sat down with a loud sigh. Conversations began in the room again and soon noise levels reached a peak that allowed Emme to at least feel she was no longer the centre of attention.

"We started the first course," Kye said, passing the platter of crackers and cheeses to her. "Everyone was getting rather restless and hungry, and I thought you wouldn't like to have everyone anxiously await your entrance."

"Very good move," she said to him and took a single chestnut from the central stack.

Kye raised a brow. "Not hungry? That's not like my Emme."

No, she had bigger things on her mind – matters that made her stomach flutter, like straw brooms in her stomach brushing away the hunger.

Emme moved her mind from the flutters, recalled her lessons of the last four weeks, then turned on all the charm she had been taught. She smiled pleasantly at the princes at the table, engaged in light conversations, and picked up the right fork at the right time when the platters of the main course were brought around. She smiled sweetly when one of the princes made a toast to her beauty, when she really just wanted to kick his shin under the table. She sipped her red wine at the end of the toast, when she wanted to tip the abhorrent drink in the nearest vase of flowers.

"You're doing fine," Kye said quietly in her ear when the rich desert was brought around. "It will be over soon." He kissed her temple, then turned back to face his guests.

Her stomach fluttered again, instantly dissolving all desire for the cakes on the table. No, it was just beginning.

After desert, they danced to a few tunes. Emme managed a smile when she was passed from prince to prince, but sighed with open relief when she made it back to Kye's arms. "No more cutting in," she whispered up to him sternly. Her scowl dissolved. "What is it?"

"This is the song," he said quietly.

"*The* song?" Flutters rose in her stomach again, and she felt her palms go clammy.

He nodded. "Are you ready?"

"Of course," she said. "Sort of. I'm very nervous."

"So am I," he said, and the music stopped.

Imren got up on stage and called everyone's attention. "Ladies and gentlemen, please continue to enjoy the evening's entertainment. It is time now for the Princes of the States to gather for the ceremony."

Emme felt her heart quicken in her chest, and she clutched Kye's hand. He squeezed it once and whispered, "We'll get through this together."

They left the room to the sound of applause. Emme gripped Kye's hand tighter as they followed the officials and Imren down the hallways.

They entered Kye's bedchamber. The princes stood around the room in an order Emme did not care to know about. Imren waited in front of the now closed door.

Kye and Emme sat side by side on the edge of the bed closest to the door. Emme looked at the ornate gold swirls on the dark blue bedspread, drew comfort from knowing it was nothing like Jaimis' bedspread. She scanned the posts. No ropes this time – inside or out. Just her free will. She nodded to herself. Her free will. That was the difference; and her choice was Kye.

Imren looked at Emme, his fatherly face shining at her. "Are you ready, child?"

Ready to get those damned princes out of here. "Yes."

Kye took her hand and held it. She knew he could feel the shaking, but he tactfully did not draw attention to it.

Imren gazed about the room until faces looked back at him. "Princes of Kildes, we are gathered here to witness the dawning of a new era." Emme inhaled sharply at the familiar words. She had known they would be the same yet it managed to kick her heart into a faster pace. "You are here to witness the union between the Heir of Endoria with the Daughter of the Hunstons. In this room, there will be the coronation of our new, our noble, our right king. Long may he live."

"Long may he live," the Princes of the States chanted.

Imren walked to Emme and Kye, placed his hand on their brows. Emme felt a rush through her whole body. Not the darkness she expected, but a brilliant light that touched her inside with an emotion the light felt – joy. This was right, Emme realised. This was the true destiny of Kildes, and she would be a part of it. Imren removed his hands, stepped back.

She felt the familiar growing of the power, but it did not drag at her. Instead the joy rose higher and higher until it filled the entire room. It was weightless; not the thickness she remembered.

It floated and tumbled like elm leaves on a breeze. The other princes felt it too, she realised. Their wondering eyes roamed the room as if the joy would manifest itself into reality before them.

"Watch and you will see the colours," Imren said. "You will witness the colours of a true and pure marriage."

The air became colours, as though luminous coloured mist rolled through the room. One half glowed with the beauty of rubies, the other, bright emeralds. It dazzled Emme's eyes, and she could feel the light glowing right through to her inner being. So different – so different from the last time.

"The room reflects the colours of the two households. Green is for the honourable and faithful Hunston house-hold. Red is for the powerful and noble Endorian family. May the two colours be united if this is a true joining of two households."

The two colours touched lightly, then began to fuse. The colours reminded Emme of dancing partners swirling and spinning to delightful tunes.

"Princes of the States, do you acknowledge, as witnesses here, the joining of the two colours and of the two houses?"

"We do," the men said.

"Then you may honour your new king and queen."

One by one the princes walked past Kye, kissed his royal black ring, then kissed Emme's hand, a hand she offered to them freely this time. Gone were the dark expressions and pity she vividly recalled from the last time. Faces were pleased, two winked at her, some grinned openly, others carried their humour with them in silence from the room.

Imren, the last to kiss the ring and hand, paused before he left. "May the Almighty richly bless you both on this night and forever more, for all you have done for Him and for your country." Imren nodded, face crinkled in a warm smile, then he left the room. The colours instantly disappeared as the ancient oregon door clicked behind him.

The two sat quietly on the edge of the bed, neither courageous enough to move or speak. Emme heard Kye's feet shift slightly on the floor. The low fire babbled and rolled over in its bed. She heard Kye exhale slowly. Both stared uncomfortably at the door as if expecting someone to come through it.

Kye broke the long stillness first. "I hope that wasn't too embarrassing for you."

"I'm just glad they're gone."

More silence. Emme fidgeted with the dark-green silk of the skirt. Kye exhaled slowly again.

"Would you like a drink?" he asked after more silence. "I had hot drinks brought in earlier."

Emme shook her head. "No, I don't think I could eat or drink anything if I tried."

Every tiny sound in the room sharpened against more awkward silence. The sound of a glowing log crumbling to red powder in the hearth. The shift of feet on the floor. The swish of Emme's silk skirt as she fidgeted with it. The rustle of Kye's crisp-white linen shirt as he shifted his arms slightly. The misty droplets of rain that began to patter on the window, obscuring the previously visible full moon the Ashrones had predicted with accuracy.

"Are you okay?" Kye asked. He glanced over at her for brief seconds, then stared at the air in front of him.

Emme smoothed the fabric of her dark green dress, then her hand froze. She scowled. "No, I'm not okay. This is all rather silly." She unclasped the emerald necklace and tossed it to the end of the bed, then snapped to her feet and reefed at the front laces of her dress. "I know exactly why I'm nervous." With very little care and much haste, she peeled apart the stiff bodice and yanked the dress from her torso. She shuffled the narrow waistband past hips to the floor, stepped from the puffy ring of fabric and kicked the pile to the wall. She stood there in her singlet and deerskin trousers hidden beneath the dress the whole night. Surprised laughter escaped Kye's lips, and she sighed with satisfaction, said more to herself, "Good – now I can be Emme again."

Kye was still laughing as she bent over, unlaced the men's boots she had concealed beneath the petticoats, and kicked them off. They thudded against the wall, then landed on top of the mangled mass of expensive green fabric. That was Kara's world, not Emme's, and it was Emme who loved Kye.

"I should have known," Kye said. "You're too irrepressible, too exceptional, to give in entirely to Endorian tradition."

Emme laughed warmly as she stood, hands on hips and looked from the pile of clothes to Kye's smiling face. "You didn't think I would be here tonight as anybody but Emme did you?"

Kye shook his head and smiled fondly. "No, and I wouldn't have you any other way. I really wouldn't." He reached out his hand to her. She took the comforting hand, and he guided her back to the bed.

She sat down beside Kye on the smooth bedspread, felt the warmth from his body, saw the affection in his eyes as he gazed at her, all awkwardness gone. She wrapped arms around his neck, and smiled at him with soft brown eyes. "Come, Kael Yosiah Endoria." She drew him towards her. "Let's make you a king."

The story continues…

REDEMPTION

L.R. Saul

A year has passed without any hope of peace.

Emme tries desperately to adjust to her new home and new role, yet Kildes rages against the barbarian in its midst. Riots and protests have broken out across the country. They smash everything Emme tries to do to help the country to heal. Halder, bearing a load of secrets he will not share, has vanished into the city without word. Dusty and Lydia are often seen whispering fearfully in dim corners. Kye has become strangely aloof, unwilling to give an explanation to Emme for his coldness. And the leaders of Kildes search for a reason for Emme to go into exile, a reason they have just found.

The shadow of Jaimis still stretches out across the land. Dark secrets of Jaimis' treachery are slowly being uncovered, the full extent of the plot only just being realised.

And amidst all the upheaval, even darker clouds are gathering over the future of all, for within Emme's courage, sacrifice and loss, lies the dividing line between destruction and redemption, and an opening for the most evil act man has ever known.

www.lrsaul.com